THE TIES THAT BIND

Also by Lyn Andrews

Maggie May
The Leaving of Liverpool
Liverpool Lou
The Sisters O'Donnell
The White Empress
Ellan Vannin
Mist over the Mersey
Mersey Blues
Liverpool Songbird
Liverpool Lamplight
Where the Mersey Flows
From This Day Forth
When Tomorrow Dawns
Angels of Mercy

THE TIES THAT BIND

Lyn Andrews

HEADLINE

First published in 1999 by
HEADLINE BOOK PUBLISHING

10 9 8 7 6 5 4 3 2 1

British Library Cataloguing in Publication Data

Andrews, Lynda M. (Lynda Marie), 1943-
The ties that bind
I. Title
823.9'14[F]

ISBN 0 7472 2037 9

Typeset by Avon Dataset Ltd, Bidford-on-Avon, Warks

Printed and bound in Great Britain by
Mackays of Chatham PLC, Chatham, Kent

HEADLINE BOOK PUBLISHING
A division of Hodder Headline PLC
338 Euston Road
London NW1 3BH

For Gordon Crabb, my extremely talented illustrator, who brings my characters to life, visually, in almost the exact images I have of them in my mind. My grateful thanks, Gordon.

And for my hairdresser Roy Searle, who not only makes sure I'm perfectly 'coiffed' each week, but listens to my moans and complaints with patience and good humour and has proved invaluable for advice and information.

PART I

Chapter One

1937

'Mam says they've done a moonlight flit from the Holy Land.'

Nessie Harrison, aged ten years and two months, imparted this piece of news with immense satisfaction. But the three figures sitting on the low wall that ran around the tannery didn't receive it in the manner she'd expected. The tannery, owned by J. Smush Ltd, wasn't an obvious venue for their gatherings. It stank atrociously in summer and wasn't much better in winter; the residents of Naylor Street never really got used to the smell.

But, despite its drawbacks, it had always been a sort of meeting place. *Their* meeting place. They'd congregated there winter and summer when they'd had time to spare, although during that awkward stage of their development, the transition between childhood and youth, meetings had become fewer. There had been awkwardness, on all their parts, as they realised that they weren't just kids any more. Somehow, almost overnight it seemed, they'd grown up and street games and other such pastimes were no longer shared with the same enthusiasm. But still they would meet sporadically, and now, as before, the wall of Mr Smush's premises was a place that Nessie, the bane of her elder sister Elizabeth's life, was strenuously excluded from.

Elizabeth and Nessie's parents, Delia and Jack Harrison, owned the corner shop situated at the junction of Naylor Street and Gladstone Street. They were open all hours and sold everything from bread to coal. It provided them with a comfortable but far from luxurious living, but Delia Harrison had the good fortune to have a very well-off sister in America who had no children of her own and who was very generous where her two nieces were concerned. All the money she sent to her sister Delia was earmarked for the girls' education. Delia wanted something far, far better for her daughters than a shop or factory job. So Elizabeth was being taught by the nuns at the Convent of Notre Dame in Everton Valley, and Nessie would follow her when she was eleven.

At fourteen Elizabeth was quite tall although she constantly bemoaned the fact that she had inherited her mother Delia's 'bonny' figure. Her eyes were Elizabeth's most attractive feature, large and deep blue in colour, but in Delia's view her daughter's hair was her 'crowning glory', a thick deep chestnut mass that reached her shoulders in natural waves. Delia was sure her striking daughter ought to be able to make something of herself.

'How does your mam know they've done a flit?' Mike Flynn asked.

He was a tall, well-built lad of almost fifteen, with dark brown hair and brown eyes. One of the noisy, boisterous, obstreperous Flynn family who lived in number ten, Naylor Street, he was very interested in the family who were moving in next door. The house had been empty for a few weeks which was unusual but then the Piercesons themselves had been unusual. No one in the street had been sorry when they'd left. Mr Pierceson and his sons spent more time in Walton Jail than they did at home and Mrs Pierceson and her elder daughter hardly left the snug in the Unicorn. The younger ones had been left to run wild. He was quite amazed that his own mam hadn't already found out about the new family. She usually did. There wasn't much that went on in Naylor Street that Eileen Flynn didn't know about. She spent most of her day standing on the doorstep, jangling, leaving, as Delia Harrison often remarked, her house like a junk shop and an untidy one at that.

'She knows 'cos someone told her.' Nessie's voice was full of defiance.

'Like who, exactly?' Ginny Greely demanded. Like her widowed mother, Ginny always liked a bit of gossip. Her hazel eyes had already taken in everything Nessie was wearing and she was envious. She herself had no knitted hat to cover her lank, dark ash-coloured hair, no woollen mitts for her chapped hands and no warm scarf. She pulled her thin brown coat closer to her body, crossed her arms and tucked her fingers beneath her armpits. Her hands were so cold they were numb. Frost was already beginning to glisten on window-panes, doorsteps and cobbles, as well as on the roofs. If the houses were warm then in the morning the lacy patterns of ice on the window-panes were pretty, but Ginny's house was never that warm. Often there was ice on the inside of the glass too. Still, in a few days it would be Christmas and they were all looking forward to the holiday.

Earlier that day Ginny, Mike and their friend Johnny Doyle had left school for good, all of them fortunate enough to have jobs to go to. They'd arranged to meet by the factory wall to talk about their futures and their plans, and Elizabeth, the only one of them staying on at school, had also joined them.

Ginny was going to work in Birrel's Fishmonger's, two doors down from the Harrisons' shop, but she wasn't very happy about it.

'Mam, I *hate* fish! You know I *hate* fish! They're so slimy.' She'd shivered. 'It will be a cold, wet, horrible job.' Then she'd thought about having to cut off the heads with their glassy, staring dead eyes, and the tails and fins. And she'd have to learn how to gut them. It made her feel sick to think about it. She'd have to wear a white coat and a turban over her hair. The coat wouldn't stay clean for very long. She'd seen the state of Mr Birrel's at the end of the day.

'You'll go and you'll be grateful for it. I had to stand Jerry Birrel at least a dozen pints of best bitter before he agreed to take you on, milady,' had been the firm reply from Mabel, her mother.

For Mike Flynn it would be up at the crack of dawn and down to the Salthouse Dock to shovel coal into sacks for Dawson's Coal Merchant's who, along with all the others, had their allocated stock dumped in mountainous piles on to the dockside from the cargo holds. It was a dirty, back-breaking job, but the only one he could find. He had no rich relatives in America nor a barmaid mother who had a little influence with certain customers.

For Johnny Doyle, for whom the three were still waiting, it was the Merchant Navy. He'd signed on as a bellboy on Cunard's *Ascania*. He would make his first trip in the New Year.

'Well, has the cat got your tongue, Nessie?' Elizabeth probed. 'Who told Mam they'd done a flit from the Holy Land? You're sure you're not telling us stories again?'

'She *did* say it!' Nessie shot back at her sister. 'She *did*! Honest to God!'

' "Honest to God" and "the Holy Land". She's a real scream, isn't she?' Ginny said drily.

Elizabeth and Mike both laughed. The Holy Land was the name given to an area in the Dingle in the south end of the city, where the streets were all named after biblical characters: David, Isaac, Jacob and Moses Streets. Like Scotland Road

5

and its immediate neighbourhood, the area depended heavily on the docks, the shipping and all the service industries for employment and, also like Scotland Road, the housing was substandard: old, inadequate and in some cases a very real danger to life and limb. Like their counterparts in Scotland Road, the women in the Dingle fought a daily battle against dirt, disease and poverty.

'Oh, get home, Nessie, and leave me in peace,' Elizabeth dismissed her sister scornfully. 'You made it up. Mrs Flynn would have known, she always does. Get home, you're a bloody pain, always trailing after me.'

Nessie glared at her sister. 'It's true and I'll tell Mam you swore, Lizzie Harrison.'

'And you'll get belted when I tell Mam you called me "Lizzie",' Elizabeth retorted, 'and Ginny and Mike will back me up.'

Delia Harrison had always insisted that her elder daughter be addressed by her full Christian name at all times. Elizabeth was Elizabeth. Not Liz or Lizzie, Bess or Bessie or even Beth. Elizabeth herself wouldn't have minded being called Beth at all but her mam was adamant. They had 'standards' to keep up, she always maintained firmly in her 'Sunday voice', as Elizabeth called it. Elizabeth had never understood why her younger sister was addressed by a derivative of her full Christian name. When she'd protested that it wasn't fair, her mam would reply, 'You're the eldest, you have more sense and I expect more from you.' Just what 'more' was, exactly, she didn't know.

Nessie stuck out her tongue, knowing her moment of glory had passed. Only Mike Flynn had shown any real interest in the new family who had moved into number twelve that day.

'If you don't get home now you'll not get over the doorstep for the rest of the week,' Elizabeth reminded Nessie. Delia insisted her younger daughter be in by half past seven at the very latest.

As if on cue the door of the Harrisons' shop opened and Delia's strident voice was heard along the length of the street.

'Nessie! Nessie, it's turned half past and I want you in this house in one minute flat!'

'See!' Elizabeth said smugly, pushing a strand of hair that had escaped from her beret out of her eyes.

Nessie pursed her lips and glared at them all.

'Vanessa Harrison, get in here this minute or your da will come and get you, and then God help you, milady!'

Nessie turned away, annoyance and apprehension in her eyes. When her mam used her full and, in her own opinion, far too fancy Christian name, she knew she was in trouble. Although she didn't know it, Nessie's opinion of her name was shared by most of the neighbours. As Eileen Flynn always said, it was just Delia Harrison's way of showing off.

As Nessie trailed reluctantly down Naylor Street, Elizabeth looked after her in despair. 'She's a little horror! If I *had* to have a sister why couldn't I have got a decent one, not one like her?' she complained bitterly.

'I've got two of them, so stop moaning,' Mike Flynn muttered gloomily.

Ginny decided it was time to change the subject.

'Where's Johnny? He's late!'

'Oh, you know what his da's like. Even though he has the pub he's all holier than thou. He doesn't think Johnny should mix with the likes of us, especially now he's got the best job of us all,' Mike replied.

'At least he's being *allowed* to get a job. *I've* got to go back to flaming school. But I'm not going to stay there for another four flaming years followed by God knows how long at teacher-training college. I don't care how much she carries on! I *hate* that place! I *hate* flaming kids and I can't think of anything worse than having to teach them. Look at our Nessie! Imagine having a classful like *her*!' Elizabeth kicked her heels against the wall in frustration. 'I wish Aunty Margaret would stop sending money. I don't mind the clothes she sends, they're usually great, it's just the money. It only encourages Mam to get more airs and graces and we have enough rules and regulations already. We live over and at the back of a shop off Scottie Road, for God's sake, and they want me to be a *teacher*! And when our Nessie starts at the convent I'll still be there! Oh, I'll die of mortification, I'll just die!'

Elizabeth's litany of complaints stopped as Johnny Doyle arrived, panting. He was a wiry lad, the 'greyhound breed' was how his father described him. It didn't matter how much he ate, he never seemed to gain any weight. His hair was fine, blond and unruly and was always falling in his eyes. Pushing it back had become a habit. He sat down on the wall next to Mike.

'I thought I'd never get out. He's had me moving crates from the cellar to the yard ever since I got home from school! Thank God he's safely in the bar now and your mam is in the saloon, Ginny, laughing and joking as usual.'

Ginny shrugged. Her mother was a barmaid for both Eddie Doyle in the Globe and in another local pub, the Unicorn. It was hard to make ends meet but somehow her mam did it – just. Thankfully she was easy-going and hadn't become bitter and sour about being a widow with a child to bring up. In fact sometimes she was too easy-going. She liked a drink herself, did Mabel Greely, or May as she was always called. On occasions people made cutting remarks but they rolled off May like water off a duck's back.

'What did your Nessie want?' asked Johnny. 'I saw her legging it off home and your mam was standing on the shop step with a face like thunder.'

'Oh, some nonsense about the family moving into number twelve.'

'What?' Johnny didn't want to miss anything interesting about them.

'She said they'd done a moonlight from the Holy Land.'

'They must really be in a mess,' Ginny interrupted. 'I wonder how they can afford the rent here if they're so skint that they had to move across the city?'

'How do I know? How do I know our Nessie was even telling the truth? She's a nasty little cat. She loves causing trouble.' Elizabeth stared glumly at the ground. 'Things at home wouldn't be so bad if there were more of us. If I had brothers.'

'You're dead lucky that there *aren't* more of you. Our house is like a lunatic asylum most of the time,' Mike retorted.

With only Jack and Delia, Elizabeth and Nessie to share three bedrooms, a big kitchen that doubled as a sitting room, a scullery, and a privy and wash house in the yard, the Harrisons lived in luxury compared to Mike's family. The Flynns were crowded into a two-up, two-down terrace house you could hardly swing a cat in.

Sick of Nessie, Elizabeth changed the subject. 'When exactly do you sail, Johnny?'

'On New Year's Eve, would you believe! I'll miss all the "do's",' he stated morosely.

'You'll get a good send-off though. You'll be half deafened by the noise from all the other ships in the river and the docks. It always sounds great, and with all the church bells ringing too.'

'I know. It won't be the same though, will it? I'll be running around, dressed up in that daft uniform, all buttons and gold braid and that flaming hat! It looks like a biscuit tin stuck on my head.'

'Have you got all your gear then?' Mike asked.

'Yeah. Mam took me down to Greenberg's in Park Lane and got me kitted out *and* she had to pay for it all. They don't provide uniforms for the likes of us. God! I'll feel such a flaming fool.'

'Look on the bright side. No one will know you – the passengers anyway. And you'll get tips as well as wages.'

'Half the crew will know me, though. I'll be skitted soft.'

'Well, I wouldn't mind being skitted soft to see big places like New York, be given three good meals a day, be paid *and* get tips,' said Mike. 'It's better than shovelling coal all day, out in all flaming weathers.' Like Ginny he wasn't looking forward to starting work. Still, he'd have money of his own, even after he'd turned up his keep to his mam, and money of his own was something he'd never had very much of before. If he'd wanted to go to the pictures he'd had to collect empty jam jars for Mrs Harrison and run errands and the like. Once, when as a lad he'd had the money for the pictures but no boots or even a pair of cut-down trousers, he'd stood in the yard and cried until Brenda, his eldest sister, had found a big safety pin and had pinned the back tails of his shirt to the front ones so he could go. When he remembered such hard and humiliating times, filling coal sacks and having a wage of his own began to look good.

'Will you be seasick?' Ginny asked Johnny, although it was more of a deliberation than a question.

'God, I hope not. I'd have half the neighbourhood splitting their sides.'

'I bet half the neighbourhood were sick to start with,' Ginny sniffed. 'Mary Malloy from William Henry Street said their Norman is sick every single trip and he's been going to sea for nearly nine years. It's nothing to be ashamed of.'

'You're not sick on the ferry, so why should you be sick on a ship of that size?' Elizabeth said flatly. She was bored and you could see your breath it was so cold. The lads had their hands in their jacket pockets, the collars of their jackets turned up and their caps pulled down over their ears.

Ginny's coat was almost threadbare. She had no stockings, just a pair of old, broken-down shoes. She was shivering uncontrollably.

Elizabeth took off her scarf and gloves. 'Here, put them on, you're perished.'

Ginny wrapped the knitted scarf over her head and around her neck. 'Thanks.'

'You'd better keep them.'

'I can't. What'll your mam say?'

Elizabeth shrugged. 'I'll say I lost them. Left them in the cloakroom at school. She didn't see me when I came out and I've got more, Ginny.'

'If you're sure . . .'

'I am. Now, shall we go and see if our Nessie was right about the new neighbours?'

'Well, we've got to walk home, so there's no harm in having a look. Are you two coming?' Ginny asked.

Mike and Johnny exchanged glances. There was nothing else interesting on offer, so they nodded and followed the girls.

Number twelve, Naylor Street had the dubious benefit of having a lamppost outside. True, its light brightened the front rooms of the house so there was no need to use the gas light, but it was also frequently used as a meeting place as well as for cricket stumps in summer and one half of a football goalpost in winter, its twin being on the other side of the road. If someone managed to get an old tyre and some rope then it was used as a swing but that usually didn't last long. Some spoilsport adult always took it down. There was no money to spare for toys and games so the local kids had to devise them and utilise what they could find.

The lads considered themselves very lucky that Johnny Doyle had a proper football – a casey – and so were the envy of all the other boys in the surrounding streets. Until then they, like everyone else, had had to use a ball made up of rags.

Number twelve was the same as all the other houses in the street: old, decrepit, soot-blackened, its windows like sightless eyes. The steps were worn and crumbling, but unlike all the other houses, the windows were dirty, their sills and the doorsteps untouched by scrubbing brush or donkey stone.

'It doesn't look as though there's anyone in there at all,' Ginny speculated in a loud whisper.

'There is. Look.' Elizabeth pointed to a bundle of what looked like rags that had been left on the top step. The door was ajar.

'Well, go on then, knock,' Mike urged.

'There's no sign of life *anywhere*,' Johnny pointed out. 'And that could just be a bundle left by . . . anyone.'

'Oh, you two are the living end,' Elizabeth said impatiently as she quickly went up the steps and rapped hard with the dull, pitted knocker. The door itself was sagging on its hinges and most of the dark brown paint had peeled off long ago. Once she'd knocked, however, she did retreat to her place on the pavement beside her friends.

They all heard the whispering, then the sound of footsteps coming down the lobby and finally a shape appeared in the doorway. The streetlight illuminated the figure and they could see that it was a girl. One about their own age too, Elizabeth surmised.

She was first to speak. 'We . . . we've only come to see if we can . . . help, like? We heard you've just moved in today.'

The girl came down the steps and they could see her more clearly. She was small and slightly built. Her black hair was cut short, her eyebrows slanted outwards and upwards like a bird's wing and, with her blue eyes, fringed with dark lashes, her pert button of a nose and pale skin, she had an almost elfin look about her, Elizabeth thought. She also looked afraid.

'There's no reason to be frightened, honestly. I meant it. We just came to help. What's your name?'

The girl hesitated, her glance sweeping over the little group. 'Theresa, but everyone calls me Tessa. Tessa O'Leary.'

'I'm Elizabeth Harrison. Mam and Dad have the corner shop. This is Ginny Greely. She and her mam live in number fifteen. Mike Flynn lives next door in number ten. They're a noisy lot, always rowing and fighting.' Elizabeth's words were tempered by her smile.

Mike grinned. 'Only when me da has spent most of the housekeeping in the pub.'

'And this is Johnny Doyle. His da has the pub, the Globe. Have you got any brothers and sisters?' Elizabeth's tone was friendly. 'I've got a nasty little cat of a sister and Mike's got two older sisters and—'

'Our Harold who's nine and is a holy terror,' Mike finished for her.

Tessa seemed to relax a little. 'I've got two brothers. Our Colin, he's sixteen, and our Jimmy, he's nine too, like your Harold. I had two sisters but they died when they were just babies. There's Mam and Da, of course.'

Elizabeth was bursting to ask if they had really done a moon-light and why, but she curbed her curiosity.

'Have you got a job? I mean, we . . . well, those three have just left school. Today, in fact. As for me, I'm stuck in flaming school. I'll tell you about it sometime.'

Tessa shook her head. 'No. I've no job . . . yet.'

'What about your brother and your da?' Johnny asked.

'Well, Da works on the docks, when he can, and . . . and . . . our Colin is sort of . . . looking.' What she didn't say was that Colin had just been released from Borstal for stealing. It wasn't the first time and it was one of the reasons why they'd moved. But it wasn't the most important reason.

'Oh, he'll get something, Tessa,' Elizabeth said brightly. She liked Tessa O'Leary, she decided, there was just something about the girl that made her warm to her.

'I know you don't really need them, what with the lamppost an' all, but why aren't there any lights on?' Ginny asked.

Tessa became hesitant. 'We . . . we don't—'

'Have any money for the gas meter?' Mike interrupted. 'It's the same in our house. Sometimes we have to sit in the dark or Mam lights some candles while we go and cadge a few coppers.'

Tessa smiled. A genuine smile, full of relief. She seemed thankful they weren't the only ones in the street to be so hard up.

'I'll go and see what I can get out of my old feller,' Johnny offered, thinking he'd have to endure a lecture about lending money to strangers. But they had no light, for God's sake. Even his da, who claimed to be so religious, so Christian, couldn't refuse such a request.

'Do you want me to bring this in for you?' Mike pointed to the bundle.

'No, I don't want you to bring anything in! I want you to mind your own flaming business! Tessa, get in here!'

They all took a step backwards as Mary O'Leary appeared in the doorway and glared down at them.

'We . . . we . . . was only trying to help,' Mike said.

'Well, we don't need your help, so clear off the lot of you,' she snapped.

Tessa bit her lip.

'We *were* only trying to help, Mrs O'Leary. Everyone around here helps one another,' Elizabeth said in a firm but polite tone.

Mary O'Leary eyed her with open hostility. 'A right hardfaced little madam, aren't you?'

'No, I'm not, and if you want credit from my mam you'd better not speak to her in the same tone of voice!'

Tessa gazed pleadingly at Elizabeth.

12

Any more of this and her mam's temper, which was very short these days, would be vented on her for not getting rid of them as she'd been told to do, never mind standing holding a conversation with them.

'Oh, you must be from the shop then.' Mary hated having to be polite to the girl, but she'd already sent Richie, her idle, useless wastrel of a husband, down to see what he could scrounge out of the shopkeeper. She was too tired, too worried, too heartsore to go herself. It would be bad enough having to face the neighbours and their questioning in the days to come.

'Yes, I am,' Elizabeth said quietly.

'And I suppose the rest of you came sneaking around just to get a look at us too.' Mary couldn't hold back her mounting irritation.

'I told you, Mrs O'Leary, we just came to offer our help.'

She'd had enough. 'Clear off! I don't need you all cluttering up my doorstep at this time of night. Haven't you got homes to go to? Tessa, gerrin!'

She turned away and Tessa picked up the bundle.

Elizabeth laid a hand on her arm. 'We're sorry, really we are.'

'I know, but, well . . . she's had a hard time lately and she always has a temper at the best of times.'

'It goes with the name, I suppose,' Elizabeth smiled. 'You know, Irish.'

'Oh, aye, half of Liverpool has got Irish blood in them. My mam and da included,' Johnny said. He felt sorry for the girl.

Tessa smiled. 'I know.'

'Well, if you do need anything . . .' Elizabeth offered.

'Thanks. I'd better go in or she'll kill me.'

When the door had closed they all looked at one another.

'God, isn't she just a bitch!' Ginny exclaimed.

'I know mine's got a temper, but I wouldn't fancy having *that* one for a mam. Oh, I can see some fireworks ahead. My mam won't put up with *that*, especially as they'll be living next door,' Mike said.

'And we didn't find out much at all, except that she's got two brothers,' said Elizabeth. 'But I liked her. Maybe if she comes into the shop or I see her on the street I'll find out more.'

'Your mam will get more out of her than you will,' Mike said sagely, nodding his head.

Elizabeth grinned in agreement. 'Probably. And she'll show her the door if she carries on like that in future!'

The four of them continued down the street, strangely cheered by the prospect of the excitement to come.

Chapter Two

Tessa leaned her back against the door, the bundle clutched in her arms, tears not far away. They had been nice, really nice. Especially Elizabeth from the shop. She hoped Elizabeth's mother would be just as understanding. She had had nothing to eat since last night and she felt faint with hunger and cold.

It was the cold that had affected her the most. Hunger was always with her lately. She was so cold even her bones were aching and she knew she must look awful. She had no coat or hat, not even a shawl. The other girl – Ginny – had had a coat on. It was old and thin, but it was a coat. The navy blue skirt and grey jumper were all she had in the way of protection from the icy weather. But at least they had a roof of sorts over their heads. It had taken Mam a full week to find this house. For seven long days she'd walked the streets in this area, traipsing all the way over here so that they could be well away from the Dingle.

These days she could do nothing right, as far as her mam was concerned. Things had never been easy in Isaac Street, but everyone there had been more or less in the same boat. She thought back over her childhood. It hadn't been unhappy. Mam had been strict with them over clothes and boots. She'd never had a single piece of clothing that was new, but she'd never complained. What use was there in doing that? Da worked on the docks, like most of the men in the street, but not often enough, so her mam had always said. Still, what furniture and pots and pans and crockery they did have was treated with great care. Mam had been strict about that too. The last few weeks had been terrible, really terrible, but today had been the worst day of her life. The tears began to roll slowly down her cheeks.

'Tessa, bring that thing in here!' Mary's voice echoed through the dark, empty house.

Tessa didn't want to go into the kitchen where Colin had lit and placed a single candle on the shelf over the range. Half of all their troubles had come about because of him. Oh, there were times when she wished him to the other end of the earth or even dead. She knew that was sinful but she couldn't help it.

He just wasn't the same as everyone else in the family. Where he got his badness from she didn't know. Even her Mam's lectures and belts had had no effect. Da didn't seem to be too bothered about any of them and left Mam to deal with their escapades, but Colin's behaviour was worse than that.

'Tessa, did you hear me?' Mary called.

'Yes, Mam. I'm coming.'

The kitchen seemed cavernous. The corners were very dark and the flickering flame threw feeble shadows, but as her eyes became accustomed to the gloom she could see her mother sitting on an orange box, her shoulders humped and her head in her hands as if to protect herself from the harsh reality of her life. Colin sat on an empty upturned paint tin. Of young Jimmy, there was no sign.

'Where's our Jimmy?' Tessa put the bundle on the dirty, scuffed lino floor.

Mary raised her head. 'God knows! And God knows I don't care either. I . . . I . . . never thought I'd see the day when we'd be forced to live like this.' Worry and exhaustion made her look haggard. Deep lines showed on her forehead and around her eyes and mouth. She looked sixty, not forty-six. In her eyes there was utter despair. Tessa went over to her.

'Da will get *something*, Mam.' She turned to her brother. 'And *he* can get himself out, find our Jimmy, and the pair of them can go and pick up rubbish. Anything at all that will burn.'

Her brother scowled at her but she ignored him. There was always *someone* nagging him. Making him do things he didn't want to do. He'd had nothing all his life and as he'd got older the unfairness of it all had made him angry and hard. His da had been no example – he was weak and had no ambition whatsoever. His mam ignored him most of the time; she looked on him as a failure but she'd never given him any help or encouragement. All she was interested in was keeping the flaming house clean and worrying what the neighbours were thinking. What the hell! 'Give a dog a bad name' so that saying went, he didn't care. So what if he pinched anything he could get his hands on? Those he stole from could more than afford it. And in Borstal he'd learned that petty thieving was a waste of time. If you were going to steal, then pinch something that would fetch pounds rather than pennies, or take money in the first place. He was biding his time. He'd find out more about the people in this area of Liverpool, then he'd work out the best way to steal enough to get out of this dump.

'One of those lads has gone to try to get us a few coppers for

16

the gas. It'll be all right, Mam, we can use the gas ring then and I'll make us all a cup of tea.'

'Oh, this is a nice start, isn't it? Forced to take charity from strangers.'

'They won't mind, Mam. The one who lives next door said they're always running around to beg for pennies for the gas.'

'A nice lot they must be then!' Mary snapped. Oh, she could kill Richie and Colin. She had nothing, not a single thing to show for twenty-four years of marriage. She had no money to make a home in this house, nor any interest in doing so. It was too shabby, far worse than the one she'd had in Isaac Street.

She'd been so proud of that little house. At first they'd had only the essentials but she'd scrubbed the bare boards in all the rooms and down the stairs every single Wednesday. A scrubbing brush, a bar of carbolic soap and a bucket of hot water were all you needed, she'd often joked with her neighbours. Poverty was no excuse for dirt, that had been her motto.

Gradually, she'd acquired things. All bought second-hand, but washed down and polished. She'd had lino and rag rugs in all the rooms. Her windows had always shone; her curtains were always clean.

'I see Mary's step-dashing again' was an often-heard remark and she'd taken it as a great compliment.

Now she had nothing. Nothing at all. Not even a chair to sit on, let alone a bed to rest her aching head. Suddenly the kitchen door burst open and Jimmy arrived, scruffy and dirty as usual. A few months ago he wouldn't have dared to get into that state.

'There's some lad waiting at the front door. He said he had come to see our Tessa.'

'Look at the state of you, you little hooligan!' Tessa snapped. She sincerely hoped her mam wasn't going to tell her to go and shut the door in the face of whoever it was on the doorstep. 'You and your useless brother can go out and look for rubbish or there'll be no fire! Get out the back way, there should be plenty of stuff in the jigger and people won't see you doing it.' Even now she was considerate of her mam's pride. 'I'll go and see who . . . who it is at the front.'

Before her mother could reply she left the room and walked down the lobby.

It was Johnny Doyle who stood on the step.

'Here, I managed to get sixpence out of my da and that's no easy thing I'll tell you! He's not called "Moneybags" around here

Lyn Andrews

for nothing, although "Scrooge" would suit him better.'

'Oh thanks, that's great. I mean it. I'll pay you back when . . .'

'You don't need to. It's a gift, a pressie, like.'

Tessa nodded with gratitude.

'Well, don't forget, Tessa, if any of us can help you've only got to shout.'

'Thanks. Thanks again, Johnny,' she replied, shyly. He seemed very kind.

As he turned to go she caught sight of her father wandering slowly down the road. She prayed he had been to the shop and not the pub. All the money they had left after the rent had been paid was ten shillings, and that to keep a family on for God alone knew how long. There were so many things they needed, but food and a fire were priorities. They'd all have to get jobs and quickly. Mam had sold her wedding ring and the one her own mother – Tessa's grandmother – had left. Oh, they'd been in the pawnshop more often than on her mam's finger, but she knew it had broken her mam's heart to have to sell them. If Da had spent the money Mam had given him for food on drink, much as she loved him, she herself would kill him. He was never violent or abusive when drunk. Just the opposite: laughing and joking and falling over things. He'd give you the world, except he'd just spent his wages.

'What did you get, Da?' she asked as he came within earshot.

'Bread, dripping, tea, some spuds an' a bundle of chips for the fire,' Richie answered, handing half his purchases to a relieved Tessa. The woman in the shop hadn't been very co-operative until her husband had come out and urged her to put it on the slate. He looked a decent feller but you could see who wore the trousers in that house. Richie had managed to evade the woman's questions as to why they'd moved across the city by asking about work, and her husband had given him the name of one of the blockermen at this end of the eight miles of docks. He was very grateful. It wasn't that he didn't like work; he did, and he worked hard. He was just good-natured and liked a few pints with the lads. It was a habit that had grown steadily over the years as he had realised how shrewish, bad-tempered and nagging his wife had become. She started the minute he set foot in the door. He knew he would never get out again to go for a drink, so he didn't go home. Why, after a hard day's work, a man had to put up with continual complaints and unfair criticism of his character he didn't know. It was better to have a laugh and a joke and maybe even a bit of a

18

gamble in pleasant company than to endure Mary on top note.

'Well, I've got sixpence for the gas meter so we can have some tea with bread an' dripping. Then I'll boil the potatoes. I've told those two to get out and see what they can find to start a fire.'

Tessa forced herself to smile as she entered the kitchen.

'I told you things would be all right, Mam. Look, I've sixpence for the gas and Da's managed to get a few bits. We can have a drink, a butty and some spuds each.'

Mary looked up and glared at her husband. 'We haven't got a kettle. We haven't got a teapot or cups and plates, not any more.'

'Oh, Jesus, Mary and Joseph! I've said I'm sorry. For God's sake don't start again!'

The light of battle filled Mary's eyes. 'Again! I've hardly started on you, Richie O'Leary! We had a decent home, one it took me years to get together. You could have got regular work if you'd tried, but no. Now look at us, it's all gone, every last bit of it!'

Tessa went into the lobby and put the sixpence in the meter under the stairs. Oh, they were going to start again. Would it never end? The yelling, the accusations, the never-ending bitterness that had made her mam old before her time. She went back into the kitchen and, with a match dug out of her da's pocket, lit the gas jet. It had no glass mantle but it did light the place up. The sight of the room in all its dingy, dirty dampness made her bite her lip and fight down the despair that rose up in her.

Colin came back through the scullery with a handful of sticks, pieces of paper, and some orange peel.

'Where's our Jimmy?' Tessa asked him.

'I told him to keep looking. I'd had enough. It's freezing out there. It's not much better in here!' he added.

Tessa rounded on him. 'You idle, useless—'

'Tessa, that's enough, girl. It's been a bad day for everyone.' Richie stopped the tirade of insults and sat down on the paint tin.

'There's not even a decent chair to sit on, is there?' Mary said waspishly. 'Never mind beds or even mattresses.'

Richie looked down at his scuffed and battered boots. When had things gone so very wrong? A year ago, maybe two. He'd just let things slide. He'd let himself get deeper and deeper in debt. And he'd never worried about it until last summer. Oh, he could murder a pint but there'd be no ale for him tonight, or any other night as far as he could see.

'Get back to your brother,' Mary demanded of her eldest son. 'Go on, or there'll be nothing to eat for you, meladdo.'

Sulkily Colin went out, slamming the back door, the sound of which made Mary jump.

'That lad will be the death of me. If he starts again, I'll swing for him. It's your fault, Richie. You've been too soft with him. You were *always* too soft with him!'

'God, Mary, give it a rest!'

Tessa stood in the doorway, an old pan in her hand. She'd found it under the sink. It was so old that the previous occupants had obviously thought it not worth taking with them, wherever it was they'd gone. But it was all she could find. She bent her head and began to cry quietly. The only kind of drinking vessel was one empty and rather dirty jam jar.

Mary looked across at her daughter and then her husband. 'I'll never forgive you, Richie O'Leary, until my dying day!'

Her husband refused to meet her furious gaze. 'Well, that's no surprise, is it?' he shrugged. 'God knows why I ever married you. Why come home from work to be greeted by a list of complaints? I'd sooner stay in the pub.'

Mary's eyes flashed with anger. 'Why I ever married *you*, I don't know. You've always been a drunken waster! Sneaking like thieves in the darkness away from Isaac Street, to get away from people you owed money to! When I think of all the years of hard work that went into making that house into some sort of decent home and then to have both the bailiffs and Mogsey Doran on the doorstep at once to clear the house and leave us nothing. Thrown out in the road we'd have been if we hadn't come here to this . . . this midden!'

She paused, overcome by tears, then, compelled by her rage, went on, 'You still owe money to Mogsey Doran and God help you if he and his cronies find us! And as for *him*, your precious son who was thieving from everyone! Oh God, the shame. Mother of God, the shame of it!' Mary began to cry again. It had all been too much to cope with. Colin's first sojourn in Borstal had brought her the sympathy of her friends and neighbours. 'Easy led, Mary. No real badness in him, luv. He'll learn a hard lesson in there, girl.' The second time they weren't as charitable and then . . . then everything had been taken from her.

Instantly Tessa went to her side. 'Mam! Mam, don't get all upset again, please! Things will be fine now. Da, me and our Colin will get work. Jimmy can get some sort of job before or after school and Saturday. We'll soon have things back to . . . normal.' Things would never, ever be 'normal' again, she thought, but she had to try to cheer her mam up. 'We'll all go out in the morning early and see what we can get. There's lots of factories at this end of the city.'

'And the feller in the shop said to try and see Albert Brown down at number two Husskinson Dock,' Richie added half-heartedly, wondering if the men were decent blokes to work with.

'You can take my useless brother with you, Da,' Tessa said cuttingly.

Mary's sobs diminished. Her anger was spent; without the energy it had generated she felt weak. Oh, if only she could crawl into a warm bed like the one the bailiffs had taken yesterday, with a stone waterbottle or a brick or oven-shelf wrapped in a piece of cloth, but there were no beds, no waterbottles, no comforts at all. However, she tried to smile and look interested in Tessa's words. Her only surviving daughter was a good girl. She always tried to help as much as she could. She'd even gone up to the Riverside Station at the Pier Head with a tray of little silver-coloured brooches she'd bought for tuppence a dozen and had tried to sell them for sixpence each to the passengers arriving and departing on the boat trains. She'd managed to earn a bit of money before the policeman had stopped her for not having a trader's licence. Mary was always sorry after she'd vented her anger and frustration on Tessa's head. Tessa was the only one in the family who tried to help.

If her other baby daughters had survived, the workload would have been more than halved. Fresh tears stung her eyes. Even after all these years she missed them. She could remember their smiles, their first tottering steps. It was a pain that would never go away.

And the present was just as painful as the past. It'd be the bare boards they'd have to sleep on tonight and they'd all be fully dressed or they'd freeze. She felt as though she were standing on the edge of a deep abyss and that if she stepped forward she would fall. Fall into oblivion. She wanted to fall. With all her heart she really wanted to let go and fall, but she knew she couldn't even do that. If nothing else there were Tessa and Jimmy to think of. She couldn't care less about the other two, her elder son and her husband. For better or worse, she'd vowed all those long years ago. Well, she'd certainly not had the 'better'. She dropped her head hopelessly into her hands once more as Tessa put the pan on the gas ring.

21

Chapter Three

The lads and their father all slept badly but neither Tessa nor her mother closed their eyes all night.

She had to get work soon. She just *had* to. Tessa told herself so over and over again. But what kind of work? She'd just left school and she wasn't trained to do anything, not even to be a kitchenmaid or maid of all work. All that was on offer was shop work, if she was lucky enough to get it – or factory work, which was more likely. But would *anyone* employ her looking the way she did?

The bit of fire, which hadn't given much heat in the first place, had died. They hadn't kept the gas light lit for long. The gas supply had to be saved for heating water on the single ring.

She was so cold she wondered if she would wake up in the morning if she went to sleep. That fear was added to all the others and she had cried quietly for most of the night.

Mary wondered bitterly just how Richie and Colin could sleep. Jimmy was excluded by his age from worrying about all the troubles that beset them. She just prayed that they would get jobs. Anything, anything at all. Even if just Richie got work it would be something. She tried to get comfortable on the hard floor but she was cold, so very, very cold. It was the worst night she'd had to endure in her entire life.

She was sorry she had spoken the way she had to the little group that had come to help, but what could they *do*? And they would have told their parents. She had already unwittingly made enemies when she needed friendship desperately. She had her pride, she told herself, but pride wouldn't fill empty stomachs or keep a fire in the range.

She knew Tessa was awake; every now and then she'd hear a half-stifled sob and the sound tore at Mary's heart.

When the fingers of cold grey daylight slipped in through the fly-speckled window-pane Mary gave up the battle for sleep, and with a groan got to her knees.

Tessa was instantly on her feet and placed her hands gently on her mother's shoulders. 'Lie back, Mam, I'll make us a cup of tea.'

'What with, girl?'

Mary's face was grey and her hair was tangled with strands sticking out like straw in a haystack.

'We'll use the old tea leaves, unless someone has thrown them out,' Tessa whispered.

'No one would be as stupid as that, not even your da. What will you use for heat?'

'The gas ring. We must have some gas left.'

Mary nodded and lay down again. 'Just don't wake your da or the other two, not yet.'

There was enough gas left to boil the pan of water. The leaves had lost their flavour but Tessa poured the hot water over them, then added a bit of condensed milk.

She did her best not to let any of it spill as she poured it into the jam jar. It was too precious to waste. She handed the jar to Mary. 'Here, Mam, this'll warm you up.'

'I'll just have half, luv, you have the other. I know you've been awake all night.'

'I'll use the rest of the gas to heat the water to rinse out the jam jar and get a bit of a wash. I want to start off early.'

Mary raised herself on one elbow and then sat up. She pulled her blouse out of her skirt and began to tear at it. Eventually the coarse fabric ripped and she handed the piece to Tessa.

'Use that, Tessa, until we get proper . . . things.'

As she took the piece of what was now a rag Tessa choked on a sob. What had things come to? They were the poorest of the poor. She knew how humiliating it had all been for her mam, but somehow tearing that scrap from her blouse had made Tessa's heart ache more than anything else. Poor Mam. Poor, poor Mam. How she'd suffered these last few days.

Tessa didn't feel much better after rubbing the cloth over her face and hands. Her clothes were creased and wrinkled and her hair was a mess. Thankfully she'd managed to keep her comb and brush by hiding them from the bailiffs under her shapeless jumper, but there was no mirror for her to see the end result. She just had to hope she looked a bit tidy.

When she went back into the kitchen her da and Jimmy were awake.

'Do I look all right, Mam?'

'You do, Tessa.' It was her da that answered, getting stiffly to his feet. Jimmy was rubbing the sleep out of his eyes.

'I'm making an early start, Da.'

'I will myself. Get down there to the stands and see this Albert Brown bloke.'

'Wake that lazy little no-mark,' Mary instructed her husband. 'I'll have to try and do *something* to this place and keep my eye on meladdo here.'

Richie poked Colin with the toe of his boot. 'Get up. It's time to go and look for work, lad. We'll get chucked out of here if we don't pay next week's rent. They don't give you a week free just because it's Christmas.'

Colin reluctantly got to his feet, a look of resentment in his eyes.

As Tessa opened the front door she looked up and down the street. It was not yet fully daylight but lights shone from most upstairs windows, including the ones over the shop. She thought about Elizabeth and wondered how she'd slept. In a warm, clean bed, with sheets, thick fleecy blankets and a heavy quilt, no doubt, she thought enviously.

If Elizabeth was up at all, she'd come down to a warm kitchen and very probably a hot breakfast. 'It looks as though we're not early enough, Tessa,' Richie said as he closed the front door behind them both.

'Oh, don't say that, Da, please! We've *got* to get work today.'

'Well, at least I've got a reference of sorts, but I suppose I'll have to wait on the stands like everyone else.'

Tessa nodded. It was the way the dockers were employed. Picked at random by the bowler-hatted foremen, or blockers as they were called, men fought for half a day's work. It had always been like that for as long as anyone could remember. It wasn't right, but it wasn't about to be changed. There were too many men chasing too few jobs. The employers had the upper hand.

Tessa and Richie both nodded and said, 'Good morning,' to Delia Harrison who was opening her shop. The blinds were already up and she'd turned the sign on the door over to the side that said 'Open'.

Delia nodded back, thinking how pale and scruffy the girl looked. She sighed. There were hundreds of girls like that in this city – and adults too. She hoped they would have a successful day. It was partly a charitable hope but it was a shrewd one too. They would be customers when they had jobs and money.

God alone knew what they had now. No one had seen any furniture arrive, unless they'd brought it with them in the early hours of yesterday morning. All the man had asked for were a few bits, not enough to feed five people – Elizabeth had told her how big the family was when she'd come in – *and* he'd asked her to put it on the slate, something she certainly hadn't been prepared to do until Jack had intervened. She just hoped she wouldn't regret it.

There was no money for tram or bus fares so Tessa and Richie walked along Scotland Road together for a short time, before Tessa bade her father goodbye and good luck.

She intended to start with the shops. The morning was cold but it looked as though it would stay fine; she was thankful that there was no wind or rain. All she had on for warmth was the old grey jumper and navy skirt and she'd be soaked to the skin if it rained. If her clothes got wet she had no way of drying them.

Two hours later she'd worked her way down to the junction of Scotland Road and Boundary Street. She'd had no success at all in any of the shops.

'Even if it's only until after Christmas, sir,' or 'madam,' she'd pleaded with all the shopkeepers, but to no avail. Any extra staff had already been engaged. She was just too late. She leaned despondently against a wall, staring at the dock estate and the factories stretching away ahead of her. Beyond them flowed the cold waters of the Mersey. All the buildings were soot-blackened, including the three famous ones that dominated the Pier Head and were known to sailors the world over. She was hungry and so cold her lips were blue.

' 'Ere, girl, cum an' warm yer 'ands,' a kindly gateman called to her from his dockside hut.

'Ta ever so much.' Her fingers were so numb that as the warmth from the brazier penetrated them she could have cried. 'I'm looking for work, you see.'

'You've no coat or hat or stockings.'

'I know. Things are . . . bad. Really bad.'

'Bad all over, luv.'

'Do you know where I should start first? The factories, I mean.'

'You'll have to walk back. Bibby's, Silcock's, Tate's, the match factory, the BA,' he rattled them off.

'What's that?'

He scrutinised her face. 'Where've you come from, girl, that you don't know it's short for the British and American Tobacco factory?'

'The Dingle.' She didn't want to tell him the exact address or the creditors might find them.

He pursed his lips. It was one of the oddities in this city. The north end didn't know what the south end was doing and vice versa.

'I'd better get on my way.'

'Aye, you'd better. Good luck, girl.'

She smiled at him and began to walk as briskly as her tired legs would let her, along Vauxhall Road. Perhaps she would have more luck at the factories.

Colin had lingered in the house for as long as possible until his mam had yelled at him and virtually shoved him out of the door. There'd been no breakfast, just a few swigs of half-cold tea.

He certainly had no intention of tramping the streets looking for work. There were too many doing that already. He stopped in front of Pegram's Grocer's and gazed into the window. There were boxes and tins of just about everything you could think of. It was Christmas and the shops were well stocked. Outside the butcher's hung rows and rows of plucked turkeys and capons. It would be no hardship just to reach up and snatch one, but if he took it home he'd have to explain how he got it and they'd all have to share it. He moved on, stopping outside Skillicorn's bakery. The smell of fresh bread made him feel faint. No perfume in the world could match that of bread still hot from the oven.

He looked around cautiously. There wasn't a copper in sight, nor many shoppers either. Just delivery carts and lorries and their drivers. A tram trundled along, its trolley sparking on the icy cables. A bus rattled over the cobbles behind it. Some shopkeepers were just opening up and he made up his mind. He pulled his cap down over his forehead. No one knew him around here. He went inside.

'What'll it be then?' the plump middle-aged woman asked him pleasantly, glad to have a customer. She didn't seem at all suspicious, not even of the way he was dressed, but then probably most of her customers looked like him, Colin thought. Shabby and down-at-heel.

'Give us a large white tin and half a dozen of them soft rolls, missus, please.'

She bustled about putting the bread and rolls into brown paper bags. He looked around. He was still the only customer.

'That'll be sixpence.'

He took the bags off the counter, shoved them under his jacket and ran out, the woman's shrieks loud in his ears. He didn't stop running until he turned into Kew Street where there was a piece of waste land. He squatted down on his haunches and began with the rolls. Even though there was nothing to put in them they tasted like manna from heaven. The loaf would last him all day. At least *he* wouldn't go hungry tonight. And if he got the chance to nick an overcoat he would. He'd tell Mam someone had taken pity on him when he'd gone asking for work.

He wandered around the area familiarising himself, noting where the food and clothing shops were, and the pawnbrokers and the shops called 'cannies' or 'canteens' which were little more than a piece of wooden board jammed into the doorway of someone's house. They sold ready-cooked food to take home or eat on the street. He noted too the police stations: Rose Hill, Athol Street, St Anne Street. He'd give them a wide berth. He stopped and spoke to a group of men and boys who lingered on the street corner. They were like himself, unemployed, some from choice, others because they had simply despaired of ever getting a job.

'Try the Labour Exchange. Yer just might get lucky,' one man advised. Colin thanked him but had no intention of going down the 'Labour' – they asked all kinds of questions.

He wondered why his mam didn't go on the Parish, but of course you more or less had to beg for Parish Relief and he knew she wouldn't. By mid afternoon he was cold and fed up. He'd managed to snatch a battered purse from an old woman. It contained a thruppenny bit and a penny. Not much, he thought, but enough to get him a couple of pies from Reigler's. He dare not show his face in Skillicorn's again. He cut through the back entries and, at the junction of Titchfield Street and Tatlock Street, he unexpectedly came across a pitch and toss game.

Gambling in any form always interested him; he took after his da in that respect.

'Any chance of gettin' in on it, lad?' he asked a spotty youth dressed in the uniform of the poor: old, greasy jacket, moleskin trousers, broken-down boots and a once-white muffler wrapped around the neck.

'How much 'ave yer got?' one of the older men asked, casting a suspicious glance over him.

'Fourpence.'

'Ever played before?'

'Nope. Never seen it played before either,' Colin lied.

The smirk on the man's face told him what to expect but

inwardly he smiled too. If this lot thought he was a fool they were soon going to find out otherwise.

The rules were explained and he put on a puzzled expression. He'd lose a couple of times, just to lull their suspicions, and then . . .

An hour later he walked away with one shilling and sixpence and the promise that he'd return tomorrow so they could try and win it back. He had no intention of going back and none of going home either. He'd get a hot meal from one of the cannies, then he'd wander along to Champion Whates lodging house and get a decent bed for the night – after he'd got some sort of coat. There were many advantages of not being known in a neighbourhood but he'd have to watch his step. Too much thieving and illegal gambling and his face and name would soon be common knowledge.

For Richie things hadn't been too bad either. He'd asked one of the men on the stand to point out Albert Brown and then he'd gone over and had a word with him.

'So, how come you aren't going down to the south end, the Coburn and the Brunswick and Herculaneum docks?' he'd been asked after saying they'd moved from the Dingle.

'Not much work down there, boss.'

The blockerman looked him up and down then nodded slowly.

'You'll have to go on the stand like everyone else.'

'I know, boss.'

He'd joined the others, they were all blowing on their hands and stamping their feet for, even though the sun was out and the sky a clear blue, it was freezing. Tomorrow was Christmas Eve and everyone wanted work desperately. There must have been between fifty and sixty men and Albert Brown called out the names of only thirty. But Richie's had been amongst them. The other men melted away, shoulders slumped with disappointment, desperation in their eyes. They'd be back at lunchtime to see if they could get half a day at least.

'You get down with that lot to number two Husskinson. There's two freighters in. One with pig iron, the other with fruit – and I don't want any boxes broken "accidentally" either. I'll check.'

' 'E come over on a razor boat, did that feller. There's no 'Arry Freemans with 'im around,' the middle-aged man walking beside Richie muttered.

Richie knew what he meant. There would be nothing free this

morning. Obviously Albert Brown kept a check on the stevedores who were in charge of the cargoes. But it was a docker's prerogative to get *something* and they all knew the ways and means.

The morning had gone quickly as the pig iron was unloaded and stacked on the dockside. Liverpool dockers were the quickest in the world – when they chose to be. At dinnertime he again took his position on the stand and was picked once more.

'It's a cargo of Irish confetti,' the blockerman informed the gang he'd picked and then divided into two groups.

'Bloody stone chippings!' Richie muttered.

His words caught the attention of the man standing next to him. 'Yer a birrof a day-old chick, aren't yer? I 'aven't seen yer around 'ere before,' his companion said.

'Just moved from over the water,' Richie lied. 'Not much work over there.'

'In the one-eyed city?'

'Aye, Birkenhead.'

'Couldn't yer get work at Laird's?'

'No, they'll only take on skilled, semi-skilled and their own for labouring,' Richie answered. It was partly true. Cammell Laird's was the big shipbuilders on the other bank of the Mersey and most of their labourers lived in Birkenhead.

'Bloody typical!

'I . . . I was hopin' to get a bit of 'Arry Freemans, like, what with it being Christmas an' all.' Richie's expression was hopeful.

His fellow docker looked quizzically at him. 'You a minesweeper then?'

'What if I am? Everyone here is on the lookout to pinch some food. What's the *City of Benares* carryin' then?'

'Fruit. You 'eard 'im. Oranges probably, an' maybe bananas.'

'I've never even seen one, let alone 'ad one to eat.'

'Over rated, lad, I 'ad one once. Broke it off a big 'and of them and ate it. Not much to it. Couple of mouthfuls an' it's gone. Not much taste either. Can't understand all the fuss. And yer get some bloody big spiders in them too. Big, black, hairy ones. Give yer the screamin' shits they would. An' they're poisonous.' He shuddered at the recollection.

'I don't like the sound of that but I wouldn't mind a couple of oranges for the kids, like.'

'Well, sling yer hook so it'll break open a crate and we'll all have some. Take no notice of yer blockerman. 'E says that every time the cargo's food or drink. 'E gets 'is share, believe me, an' the

Paddy Kellys, though they'd have their tongues ripped out before they'd admit it. They'd lose their bloody jobs. Aye, an' soft jobs they are too.'

Richie nodded. Some of the dock police were all right, others were not. Too zealous in their jobs by far was the general opinion.

He'd worked hard all day and his back felt as if it was breaking, but he was going home with pockets full of oranges and his wage for the day. They usually didn't get the pay owing to them until Fridays but Christmas week was different. Surely that would keep Mary from her eternal moaning. He'd even go straight home now too, but not tomorrow. It was Christmas Eve tomorrow; everyone finished at dinnertime and there were more than enough ale houses to pick from along the Dock Road. She couldn't complain. A man was entitled to a drink on Christmas Eve, wasn't he?

Chapter Four

The pale winter sunlight that filtered in through the window made things look even worse, Mary thought. She glanced around the kitchen. There was a large patch of damp above the window, a sign of broken guttering. The ceiling was almost as dark and brown as the door. The skirting boards had all been ripped out and probably used as firewood. She couldn't blame the previous tenants for that, last night she would have done the same thing herself. The kitchen door didn't fit properly, and whenever it was opened or closed it made a scraping noise that went straight through her. There were two uncovered gas jets on the wall; she'd get oil lamps, they were far cheaper and were less of a fire hazard than candles.

There wasn't any use at all in even going and looking at the front downstairs room. In fact she was almost certain that the floorboards in there had also been burned as a means of heating. Desperate people did desperate things. She remembered someone commenting about it yesterday. Dear God, was it only yesterday? She'd have to complain and go on complaining to the landlord to get the floorboards replaced and it would be years, if ever, before she got any furniture for the room.

The range was in desperate need of a good clean with a wire brush and then blackleading. The floor needed scrubbing, the windows needed cleaning. All the walls and the ceiling needed a coat of whitewash with lime added to deter the bugs. That was just one room and she had neither the heart nor the energy to do it. The state of the scullery didn't bear thinking about. Furthermore she had no brushes, buckets, Jeyes Fluid nor even a bit of soap. There was no food either.

All she had left in her purse was ten shillings and she knew no one in this neighbourhood at all that she could borrow from until Richie got paid, *if* he got paid.

She'd just have to muster up what was left of her courage and go to the corner shop. Richie had said they were all right and she didn't blame the woman for refusing credit until her husband intervened. She wouldn't give credit to anyone looking like Richie, and a total stranger, if she had the good fortune to own a shop. It was going to be awful. It hurt her pride but she'd have to put her pride in her pocket.

She tidied her hair with Tessa's brush, tucked her blouse into her skirt and pulled on the second-hand black coat she'd had for over six years. Even the colour had faded, she thought, looking at it with distaste. The only brand-new dress she'd ever had in her life had been her wedding dress and she'd quickly sold that along with her veil and headdress to furnish her first home.

There was no need to close the front door behind her, they had nothing, absolutely nothing to steal. She blinked rapidly as she went from the gloom of the lobby into the sunlit street. She looked up and down the street and wrinkled her nose at the smell permeating the air. Obviously it was a tannery. Nothing else smelled like that.

She walked slowly, she was so nervous. She greeted pleasantly those women on their knees scrubbing their steps, something she'd done herself so often. They'd all answered with a smile but she could feel their eyes boring into her back and knew their curiosity was overwhelming.

When she reached Harrison's she could see that there were two other customers beside herself: a big blowsy-looking woman with an old shawl around her shoulders, and a thin one with a mass of dark hair that was obviously curled with tongs or curling pins. There was a hint of humour in her eyes and she was quite well dressed – for the area. They broke off their conversation as she approached the counter.

'Morning. It's Mrs O'Leary, isn't it?' Delia hoped she sounded business-like but friendly and helpful. The woman looked awful – it wasn't just her clothes.

Mary nodded.

'Our Elizabeth told me she called on you with her friends, like, and of course your husband came down for a few bits and pieces.'

Again Mary nodded. Oh, this was so hard. She knew that she and her family would have been discussed by half the street and that speculation was rife.

'I . . . I'll be paying for them when he gets home from work.'

' 'As 'e got a job then?' Eileen Flynn asked companionably, pulling the shawl around her and leaning on the counter. She had some good news but it would keep. All this would provide an interesting topic of conversation for a week.

'He's gone down to see that blockerman Mr Harrison recommended and I . . . we're very grateful for your help.'

May Greely laughed. 'No doubt I'll meet him over the next two days. They all finish up in the pub eventually.'

Mary could have hit her. There was always someone like her ready with the snide remarks.

Delia gave May a warning look.

'No doubt he will. It's Christmas after all,' Mary answered sharply.

'What can I get you, Mrs O'Leary?' Delia asked.

'A large loaf, a pound of dripping, a quarter of tea, tuppence worth of sugar and a couple of bacon rashers . . . oh, and a small bag of coal.' She could have gone on and on with a list of the things she really needed, but this was all she could afford.

In silence her purchases were weighed out, wrapped and then Delia looked questioningly at her.

'I'll pay now for these, Mrs Harrison. I don't like to run up a bill.'

'Very wise, most people put *everything* on the slate and have half a dozen excuses for not paying.' She looked pointedly at Eileen Flynn, who ignored her.

'Well, thank you and it was nice to meet you, Mrs . . . er . . .'

'Flynn,' Eileen supplied. 'You're my next-door neighbour, so pop in any time and don't be afraid to ask for the loan of anything.'

'And I'm Mrs Mabel Greely. May to my friends. I'm a widow.'

'Aye, and a merry one too,' Delia muttered under her breath. 'And it's Mrs Delia Harrison.'

'Mary. Mary O'Leary. That's me. Richie you've met. Our Colin is sixteen and our Tessa is fourteen and me youngest, Jimmy, is nine.'

'Well, luv, I just 'ope he isn't the little tearaway my youngest is. Yer need eyes in the back of yer 'ead to keep up with 'im, 'aven't yer, May?'

'Never a truer word, Eileen, never a truer word. I'm fortunate that I have only our Ginny and I've never had much trouble with her. Her da died when she was only five. I've been on my own since then. She's startin' Birrel's after Christmas an' you should have heard the complaints! You'd think jobs grew on trees.'

'They don't want to work at all, kids these days. I'm sick of tellin' our 'Arold ter get himself something, even if it's only fetchin' and carryin' from Great Homer Street market on Saturdays. Lazy little get he is!'

Mary didn't want to linger, but what else could she do without seeming very rude and stand-offish? She smiled, and quickly said,

33

'I've sent our Jimmy out today with the same instructions. I'll have to see about him going to school after the holiday.' Then she gathered up her purchases, including the coal, which nearly creased her, and nodded her thanks. She made her way slowly to the door and the street beyond.

'Maybe we should help her,' Delia said. 'She was staggering under the weight of that coal.'

Eileen ignored her. 'Well, that's fine, isn't it?' she commented sharply. 'A few bits an' pieces an' then off she goes with her nose in the bloody air.'

Delia sighed. 'Well, she got what she came for. Just what was it you wanted yourself, Eileen?'

'A tin of conny onny, a few carrots, an onion and five pound of spuds.'

'Blind scouse again?' Delia commented.

'Yes, I'll swing for that bloody useless husband of mine yet. I said, "Yes, it's Christmas, but everyone starts celebrating it on Christmas Eve, not two flaming weeks before!" I've not 'ad a full week's wage offen him for best part of a month an' me tryin'—' Eileen halted her tirade. Both Delia and May had heard it all before, many times, and her dissatisfaction with Frank Flynn certainly wasn't what she'd come here to announce, particularly as her audience had increased by two sets of unsympathetic ears: Maisie Keegan and Katie Collins, who had just come into the shop.

Delia, however, thought she was expected to enquire.

'And you trying to what, Eileen?'

Eileen straightened her shoulders and jerked up her many chins. 'Our Brenda's getting wed after New Year an' I'm trying to save up a bit ter give her a good "do".'

'Is it that feller with a face like a wet week from Breck Road?' Katie Collins asked, folding her arms over her grubby print wrapover pinafore.

Eileen glared at her. ' 'Is name is Thomas Kinsella an' 'e's as decent and 'ard-working a feller as you'd wish to meet. 'E's on the trams. A good steady job with a regular wage. Not like some I could mention.' Eileen knew that Katie Collins's husband was fond of a drink too. 'He lives with his mam an' our Brenda says the 'ouse is a little palace.'

'So, she'll be going to live with him and his ma then?' May asked.

Eileen nodded.

'I wouldn't fancy starting out like that. Is the owld one a bit of a tartar then?' Katie Collins asked.

'She is not! Our Brenda's dead lucky. I had to start off with Frank's mam and she still 'ad five kids at 'ome. We couldn't stay with me mam, God rest 'er, she had eight!'

Delia shook her head. No wonder Eileen's house resembled a junk shop: it was all she'd ever known, having grown up in a two-up two-down in Athol Street with eight brothers and sisters and her parents.

'Where'll the wedding be – St Anthony's, I take it?' Delia queried, shovelling the potatoes from one of the large scuttle-shaped metal bins and emptying them into the canvas bag Eileen held out.

'Yes. It's her parish, remember. Mind you, there's holy murder goin' on over the bridesmaids.'

'Why?' May asked. Everyone was now engrossed in the news: time, shopping and other chores forgotten.

'Well, she said she won't 'ave no little ones. They're a flaming nuisance. So that's upset her little cousins. She's just 'aving 'er mates from work. "And what about yer own sister? What's wrong with our Maureen?" I said.' Eileen looked around with satisfaction. Everyone was riveted, even Delia. 'Do you know what she said to me?'

'No, we're not flaming mind-readers,' Katie Collins replied acidly.

'Our Maureen is too wild! She runs the streets with them terrible common girls from Paul Street. 'Ave yer ever 'eard anything like it?'

'So, what did you say then? What did your Maureen say?'

'Our Maureen didn't say anything, because I told 'er I'd wear meself out giving her a good 'iding if she didn't behave.' Eileen drew herself up with importance. '*I* said to our Brenda that if she wasn't going ter 'ave her own sister then she wasn't getting no wedding out of Frank and me. Old Ma Kinsella and her precious Thomas could cough up for the whole "do".'

'How did that go down?' May asked. There were always arguments at weddings and funerals, but this was priceless.

'Like a stone in the canal. So, she's 'aving our Maureen and them two mates. I've got to find the flaming money for our Maureen's dress and I'll 'ave to rig our 'Arold out, let alone meself!'

'Don't get all upset over that yet, Eileen, luv. We'll all help out.

35

You've got that nice cream straw hat, Delia.'

'You're very generous at lending other people's clothes, May Greely.'

'Ah, don't go getting a cob on, Delia. Where in the name of God is she going to find the money for new clothes for herself?' Maisie Keegan intervened.

'She can make her flaming husband work harder, sign the pledge and go to the Temperance Society instead of lining Eddie Doyle's pockets. I know how much he spends,' May said flatly.

'You would!' Eileen retorted.

'All right, don't let's have a bust-up over it, you know we'll all help out, Eileen,' Delia promised.

'Ta. I knew I could count on you. I couldn't 'ave better friends an' neighbours. You've got to give them a bit of a send-off.'

'It's a pity that others don't take the same attitude,' Delia said before trying to get her customers organised: it was nearly dinnertime and her feet were already killing her. At least the wedding would be something to look forward to in the New Year.

Dusk was falling rapidly as Tessa dejectedly headed for home. She was so exhausted she could hardly place one foot in front of the other. Hunger made her light-headed and the tears that had fallen so frequently this last couple of days blurred her vision once more. She'd tried everywhere and everywhere it was the same story. No jobs going at the moment. Try again after Christmas. After Christmas. They'd all be dead of cold by then. They were half starved already. She was even beyond caring whether her da and Colin had got work.

In a daze she stepped into the road and a lorry swerved and narrowly missed her. The driver cursed her loudly, while the driver of a horse and cart shook his fist at her. Scotland Road was always busy, but more so with Christmas approaching. She was pulled back on to the pavement and she looked vaguely and without recognition at her rescuer.

'Tessa! Tessa, you were nearly run over! You were nearly killed!' Elizabeth cried.

Overwhelmed by disappointment and despair, Tessa began to cry in earnest.

Elizabeth put her arm around her shoulder. 'You're frozen! Have you had anything to eat?'

Tessa shook her head. 'I . . . I've been everywhere for a job. I've

36

not had time and I'm so cold, and so tired, and . . .' she sobbed.

'Here, put this on.' Elizabeth shrugged off her navy blue woollen coat and wrapped Tessa in it.

'You're . . . you're in uniform.'

'I know. I've been to school. Every other school finished yesterday. *We* have to stay on.' She shivered as the cold air cut through her navy blue serge dress with its long sleeves and cream Peter Pan collar and cuffs. She wore fawn lisle stockings, brown shoes and her velour hat with its badge emblazoned with a sprig of lily of the valley and the words 'Notre Dame' in gold lettering above it.

'You're coming home with me.'

'I can't, your mam . . . my mam . . .'

'I said, you *are* coming home with me. At least you can have something to eat and get warm before you go home.'

Tessa let herself be guided along Scotland Road and down Naylor Street.

Elizabeth pushed open the shop door, thankful there were no customers. Her mam was brushing the floor. 'I found her wandering along the road, Mam. She's so cold, hungry and tired that she's almost dead on her feet. She stepped out in front of a lorry and nearly got herself killed.'

'Mother of God, girl, you're in a terrible state. Take her into the kitchen, Elizabeth, I'll be in in a minute. How long has she been out?'

'Since this morning, or so I gather. She's not even got a coat or a shawl!'

Jack Harrison looked up in surprise as Elizabeth steered Tessa into the kitchen. He'd just finished his tea.

'I think Mam will want you to go out into the shop, Da.'

Jack folded his newspaper and got to his feet.

Delia came through a second later.

'Right. Elizabeth, go upstairs and bring down the quilt off your bed while I get something hot down her. Nessie, fetch me a pan and put the kettle on and I *don't* want to hear a single word of complaint. Do as you're told.'

Nessie pulled a face behind her mother's back but went to carry out Delia's instructions. In a couple of minutes Tessa was swaddled in the heavy patchwork quilt, sitting by the range sipping hot sweet tea while Delia stirred a pan of soup and Elizabeth cut slices of bread.

'Your mam was in the shop this morning.' Delia fussed around

37

Tessa, folding the quilt back so she could place the tray with the bowl of soup and slices of bread on Tessa's lap. 'She insisted on paying for the few things she bought and said as soon as your dad got home from work she'd pay for the rest.'

'Mam . . . Mam's got her pride.' Tessa's eyes were still full of tears, but now they were tears of pure gratitude. Oh, it was heaven to be warm again and to be having nourishing food.

'So, why have you finished up here in Naylor Street in that filthy old house that should be condemned? Even the Piercesons, and a right gang of hooligans they were too, wouldn't stay put there!'

Tessa didn't want to tell them the reason. Mam would kill her if she did, but they'd been so good to her. She looked up at Elizabeth imploringly.

'Mam, can't that wait?' Elizabeth intervened. 'You can see she's upset now.'

Delia nodded. 'Perhaps I should go and see your mam, let her know where you are. It's dark and she'll be worried.'

'No! Please, no! I . . . she'll . . .'

'Mam?' Elizabeth pleaded again.

Delia sighed. Obviously things were very bad but the girl was afraid to tell her.

'Well then, will you let Elizabeth take you home once you've got that down you?'

'Of course she will,' Elizabeth forestalled Tessa's reply. She was determined to see just how the family were living. She stood a better chance of finding out than her mam did.

A quarter of an hour later, wearing an old coat of Elizabeth's, a pair of knitted mittens on her hands, and a tam-o'-shanter over her hair, Tessa walked the short distance up the road with Elizabeth. 'I feel so much better now. Thanks, thanks, Elizabeth.'

'Oh, that's OK. I couldn't have left you to go and get yourself killed, now could I?'

'I just didn't know where I was or what I was doing.'

'I could see that. Anyway, what are friends for – and we *are* friends, aren't we?'

'Yes, please. I . . . I've never had a real friend before. Not someone like you.'

'I've only had Ginny from this street, but she's not close. It's all because I have to go to that flaming school. I've no real friends around here and I get skitted something awful because of the uniform.'

'What's the matter with it?'

'It's awful! It's really *awful*, especially the hat. I think they picked the worst style possible. I get kids from Major Lester's school next door yelling after me: "Ay, girl, lend us yer hat, we're havin' soup ternight!" I daresn't take it off or there'd be holy flaming murder from the nuns. I swear they stand in the very top rooms and watch us. You can see right down Royal Street and Everton Valley from up there. Our Assembly Hall's up there. We can only go there to the big hall when we're fourteen. I'll go after Christmas.' Tessa finally managed a smile as Elizabeth pulled a mock-unhappy face.

They had reached number twelve and, as on the previous night, everywhere was in darkness.

'Thanks for bringing me home. I'd better get in now, 'cos she *will* be worried.'

'I'm coming with you and don't start an argument. Mam is always calling me a bossy boots so complaining will only be a waste of breath.'

There was nothing Tessa could do.

Elizabeth followed her down the dark lobby. The place was freezing cold. When Tessa opened the kitchen door Elizabeth gasped aloud at the sight that met her eyes. Mrs O'Leary was sitting on an upturned paint tin, her arms wrapped around her body. A young lad was kneeling by her, his head in her lap. Tessa's da was hunched up on the floor by the small fire that was struggling to burn in the range.

As Mary looked up, horrified to see their visitor, Tessa exclaimed, 'I'm sorry, Mam! Oh, what else could I do? They've been so good to me. I was lost and cold and hungry, they took me in . . .' Tessa was once more in tears.

'She was nearly killed, Mrs O'Leary. She stepped out into the main road.' Pity filled Elizabeth's heart. They had nothing. Absolutely *nothing*.

Mary got stiffly to her feet. 'That's all right, Tessa, luv.'

'But I haven't got a job, Mam. All day I've been looking.'

'That's all right too. Your da has. I don't know where our Colin is.' She shot her daughter a warning look.

Tessa nodded.

'We'll be just fine now, girl,' Mary said to Elizabeth. 'Thanks for looking after her. Thank your mam for me. I'm much obliged.'

Elizabeth just stared at her. Tessa's mam looked exhausted. She shrugged. 'I'll do that, Mrs O'Leary. Goodnight then.'

'Goodnight. Can you let yourself out, Elizabeth?' Tessa asked quietly.

'What do you think I am? Not safe to be let loose?' Elizabeth smiled but inwardly she was horrified. Oh, the Flynns, the Greelys, the Keegans, the Collinses and the others were all hard up but at least they had *some* furniture. The O'Learys didn't have a scrap.

Chapter Five

When she heard the front door close Tessa squatted down beside her mother. Tessa's eyes were bright with tears and her bottom lip trembled as her spirits plummeted again. 'Her mam said you'd been in the shop today.'

'I had to go and get some bits, we desperately needed coal.'

'And that's the last of it, isn't it?' Tessa looked hopelessly at the dying embers in the range. They were losing their glow and their heat; the room would soon become cold again. 'Did you carry it all back yourself?'

'Of course I did. There was no one else to do it.'

'I told her to leave things like that to our Colin,' Richie put in.

'Where is he?' Tessa asked.

'I don't know, luv. He went out this morning to look for work. I've not seen him since.'

'Oh, he'll be all right, Mam. He's always looks after himself. I just hope he doesn't start—'

'He won't,' Richie said grimly.

'Jimmy went out too but he couldn't get anything. Not a single thing and he *did* try. But things are bound to look up soon.'

'I know they will, Mam,' Tessa agreed but without much conviction in her voice. Colin and Jimmy and herself had all tried and failed. This was going to be a Christmas she would never forget – but for all the wrong reasons.

Last year had been worse than all the previous years, but at least there had been a good fire to heat the room, they'd all had a decent meal, and some kind of gift, mainly home-made things. This year she knew there would be nothing.

Elizabeth shut the scullery door behind her and went into the kitchen.

'Well, how *are* things up there?' Delia asked.

Elizabeth shook her head. 'Oh, Mam! It's terrible. They've got nothing at all. There's not even a chair, Mrs O'Leary was sitting on an upturned paint tin!'

Delia looked concerned. 'Mother of God! Was there not a single stick of furniture of any kind?'

41

'No, not one. And there were no lights on and the fire was going out.'

'So why have they come here to live?' Nessie butted in.

'Little pigs have big ears! It's nothing to do with you, Nessie, and it's about time you went to bed and be thankful you've a bed to lie on at all!' her mother snapped.

As Nessie flounced from the room Delia turned her attention once more to the plight of the O'Leary family. Of course the fire would be dying by now, Mary had only bought a small bag and that was this morning – hours ago now. 'I would have thought they'd have some furniture.' Delia looked at her husband questioningly.

'It would be the bailiffs, I expect. They take everything, leave you with only the clothes you stand up in. It's not their fault, it's just a job to them. But that family must be up to their eyes in debt. No wonder they did a flit.'

Jack wondered just how much they owed. Some people made a real mess of their lives. Usually it all stemmed from the fact that the man couldn't get regular employment and so, once they'd sold or pawned everything they could, they inevitably got behind with the rent. It was a downward spiral. He didn't condemn them; there but for the grace of God he could have gone.

'Now I can see why the poor woman looks so ill. The worry, shame and despair of it all would kill you.'

Jack looked speculatively at his wife. 'He looked to be a decent sort, but maybe it was drink and gambling.'

'Drink and gambling and you say he's a *decent sort*! To get into such debt that he's reduced his family to the state they're in now? I certainly don't call that "decent", Jack Harrison!'

'Well, Frank Flynn is almost as bad, Delia.'

'God, don't I know it, but Eileen's never let him get so bad that they'll be turned out on to the street. She's stood at the dock gates and waited to relieve him of his wages before today. Oh, and their Brenda is getting married in the New Year,' she added as an afterthought.

'So who's paying for that?'

'They are, if she can keep Frank out of the pub, and I suppose Brenda's ma-in-law will help out. She can't be short, that lad of hers has a good job on the trams. But what are we going to do about the O'Learys, Jack? We can't leave them like that, especially over Christmas.'

Jack Harrison was thinking the same thing. He'd felt sorry for the man when he'd come into the shop last night. He had a hangdog, confused sort of look about him, as though he were out of his depth with nowhere to turn.

'She's very proud, Mam,' Elizabeth said. 'She's trying to put a brave face on everything.'

'That's all well and good, but if she doesn't get some help soon she'll be in her grave, dead from cold, worry and starvation.' Delia looked thoughtful while Elizabeth watched her closely. She knew her Mam was trying to work something out.

'I'm going to buy a half-hundredweight of coal,' Delia said firmly. 'They need to keep warm and have something to cook with. We'll get them some food too. They must have some kind of Christmas dinner. I couldn't sit down to ours with a clear conscience if we don't help. Do you know if they have *any* money at all?'

'Only a few shillings, Mam.'

'Well, that won't buy much in the way of furniture,' Jack stated flatly.

'Well, we can't take up a collection from the neighbours. Most of them are not much better off themselves – and, besides, she'd go mad. I know if it were me, I would, and she said her husband had work. I hope she's right.'

'Mam, what about Hennessy's? They could get stuff from there, pay what they can now and the rest later.'

'A few shillings won't go far with that old miser and he wouldn't give them anything without some kind of reassurance that he'd get the rest of his money.' Delia was scathing in her reference to the local pawnbroker. There were literally hundreds of pawnshops in the area but Hennessy's was closest.

'Da, if I go down now, maybe I can persuade them, or one of them, to go and see what Mr Hennessy will give them. It mightn't be so bad if I go,' Elizabeth suggested.

'She's got a point, Delia.'

'Yes, yes, I think that might just work, Elizabeth, but it's too late now, he'll be closed.'

'I'll go first thing in the morning.' She just hoped Mrs O'Leary could be persuaded.

Next morning she was up at seven a.m. and at eight she rapped gently on the door of number twelve. Her mam and da had been up in the early hours of the morning. For them it would be a long and very busy day that wouldn't be over until eight p.m. when her mam closed the shop door for good. Dad had gone to the market and Mam was stocking up the shelves, the counter and even the floor until there was hardly any room to turn around, let alone to stand and serve in. However, when Nessie had pointed this out she got a clip around the ear plus an order to 'do *something* useful' from her already harassed mother.

Number twelve looked awful: grim and sort of dead. That was something Elizabeth had never really noticed before.

It was Tessa who opened the door to her.

'Tessa, you look almost as bad as you did yesterday.'

'I know. Come in, we've had another terrible night.' Tessa was thinking how clean, neat and well cared for Elizabeth looked. 'Our Colin didn't come home at all and Mam has been worried sick. As if she hasn't enough to worry about. I told her not to get upset. He can look after himself and he's selfish through and through.'

Elizabeth's brow furrowed in a frown. 'Are you *sure* he can look after himself? He's only sixteen.'

'I'm dead sure.' Tessa hesitated. 'If . . . if I tell you something, will you keep it a secret from *everyone*?' she whispered.

'I swear. Cross my heart and hope to die.' Elizabeth crossed herself.

'He . . . he's been in trouble with the scuffers – twice.'

Elizabeth's eyes were wide with astonishment. 'What for?' she hissed.

'Stealing. He's been in Borstal twice. That's why I'm not worried about him. In fact we'd all be better off if he was kept in Borstal for ever.'

'I can see now why your mam won't tell anyone why you've moved here.'

'Oh, it's not only him. Da . . . Da . . . likes a pint and then he starts gambling and—'

'He's not on his own then. Him next door to you is as bad.' Elizabeth jerked her head towards the Flynns' house.

'We . . . we owe everyone, even the moneylender.'

'Oh, God!' That really was bad, Elizabeth knew. If they didn't get their money back moneylenders quite often got violent, and the interest they charged was extortionate.

'Tessa!' Mary's voice echoed in the empty house.

'It's only me, Mrs O'Leary. It's Elizabeth. I came to see how Tessa is.'

Elizabeth followed Tessa into the dismal room.

'And you too, of course,' she finished politely.

'That was good of you. Mr O'Leary has gone to get a half-day on the docks, he'll be in later. Tell your mam I . . . I'm sorry I didn't come in last night to pay what I owe.'

'That's all right. She doesn't mind.'

'She seemed a fair enough woman.'

'She is and so are the rest of us, except our Nessie and you'd have to be a saint to put up with *her*.' Elizabeth paused, planning just how she would bring up the subject of furniture.

'I can't ask you to sit down . . .' Tessa said apologetically.

'It doesn't matter. I've not come for a long visit, but . . . well, perhaps Tessa and me can go down to see Mr Hennessy. He has stuff that's, well, quite cheap.'

Mary looked down at her cold work-roughened hands. The girl must have told her parents everything last night. 'Is he a second-hand dealer or a—?'

'Pawnbroker,' Elizabeth furnished the answer.

Mary shook her head. There still wasn't enough money. Food and warmth were her priorities.

'I don't think what we have will stretch that far,' she answered dejectedly, choosing her words carefully.

'Oh, that's no problem. He'll let you have things on spec and then you can pay later on. When you get on your feet, like. After Christmas. Mr O'Leary's got fairly steady work, hasn't he?'

'Yes. Yes, I suppose he has, thanks to your da, if a job on the docks can be called "steady".'

For the first time in days Tessa saw a glimmer of hope in her mother's eyes. 'Shall we go down, Mam? Elizabeth and me?'

'I'll come with you. I can see things for myself and get what we need.'

Elizabeth exchanged a look full of relief with her new-found friend. Tessa already had on the old coat that Delia had insisted she keep. She'd slept in it.

When they arrived at Mr Hennessy's cluttered and none-too-clean establishment, Elizabeth thought she detected a look of anticipation in the pawnbroker's shrewd grey eyes and wondered whether her da had been down already to see him after coming home from the market. Her mam would have told him the plan.

'This is Mrs O'Leary and Tessa, they've just moved here and they need some things.'

'What sort of "things"?'

Mary thought hard. If she could just get the bare essentials it would be a start.

'A table and chairs or a couple of benches. Three mattresses and some blankets and a couple of pans, a kettle and some dishes. That's it for now.'

'Do you want flock mattresses or donkey's breakfasts?' He was alluding to the ones filled with straw.

'Straw,' Mary answered in a clipped, business-like tone of voice. She pushed the thought of being so destitute they even had to make do with straw to the back of her mind.

'I think we can manage that. How much have you got to put down?'

'Five . . . six shillings. I know it's not much.' That would only leave her with what Richie had brought home, which had to be put aside to save for next week's rent, and she still owed Delia Harrison money for the bits Richie had bought.

Elizabeth was surprised that the man didn't pull a face and start whining that he wasn't a rich man and he had a business to run and a family to look after, even though everyone in the area knew he lived with his ageing mother. It made her certain that her da had got to him first.

'Right. I'll sort it all out and I'll bring it up on the handcart meself, free of charge.'

Elizabeth raised her eyes to the ceiling. Free of charge! You'd wait a long time for something 'free' from him.

Mary handed him the money. 'And when will you need the rest?'

'By the end of January, at the latest.' He was quick enough to answer, Elizabeth thought.

'I can manage that,' Mary said with great relief. By then, with steady work, they would be well on their way to having the basic necessities again.

Elizabeth indicated a thick knitted black shawl. 'Why don't you throw in that out of the goodness of your heart, Mr Hennessy? It is Christmas Eve.' Tessa had to have something other than that old coat.

The man gave her a nasty look but passed the shawl over to Tessa who wrapped it around herself thankfully.

'If looks could kill I'd be dropping dead!' said Elizabeth cheerfully after they had closed the door of the pawnbroker's behind them. 'The old miser, he's as bad as Johnny Doyle's da.'

'He's the one who has the pub? The Globe?'

'Right. But he won't let anyone run up more than half a crown on the slate and he knows who can pay and who can't.'

46

THE TIES THAT BIND

This piece of information cheered Mary up for a few minutes before she remembered that there was a pub on every corner of every road, or so it seemed.

When they got back to the house it was to find young Jimmy staring at an assortment of items placed in the middle of the room.

'Where did they come from?' Mary demanded.

'I don't know, Mam. I was out playin' in the street with Harold Flynn an' some other lads. Someone's got a real casey but he wouldn't lend it to us. Harold Flynn said he just might get one for Christmas though an' wouldn't that be great?'

'And pigs might fly and wouldn't *that* be great?' Elizabeth replied.

'And the yard is full of coal, Mam.'

'Stop telling lies, Jimmy.'

Mary went quickly out through the scullery and stood wide-eyed with surprise at the small mountain of coal that had been dumped beside the ashcan. It was anthracite too, the best-grade coal, and it must have cost a pretty penny.

The mop, brush, bucket, soap, 'Aunt Sally' liquid soap and Jeyes Fluid must have come from the Harrisons' shop, but the pile of old but clean pieces of towels and sheets Delia must have rooted out of her airing cupboard and cut up. The woman must instinctively have known that she was a clean person who would have been horrified at the state of the place she'd moved to. She was deeply touched, so grateful that tears pricked her eyes. People were good in this part of the city too, she thought, even making sure the gifts of coal and cleaning stuff were delivered when she was out of the house and therefore couldn't refuse to accept them. If Colin and Richie stayed on the straight and narrow, surely she could maintain her dignity, even earn respect from these neighbours who had been so very generous and thoughtful?

'I'll give you a hand. I've nothing else to do,' Elizabeth offered.

'Won't your parents need you to help out in the shop?'

'No. They say I'm more of a hindrance than a help and our Nessie's even worse. I'm used to cleaning and Mam is teaching me to cook. We have cookery lessons at school.'

'She goes to the Convent at Everton Valley,' Tessa informed her mam.

Mary just nodded. That cost money and it was money she herself wouldn't have spent on educating a girl. All they did was

47

get married and have a family, so why waste hard-earned money? She just prayed that when Tessa married it would not bring her the same heartache her own marriage had.

The rest of the morning and early afternoon was spent in trying to scrub the grime off the walls and floor. It really needed a coat of paint, Elizabeth thought as she cleaned the kitchen window with soap, water and old newspaper to make them shine. Tessa was hard at work with a pad of wire wool, cleaning the dirt and rust off the iron range.

When Mr Hennessy finally brought the things they'd bought, the lobby and kitchen floors were clean, as were those in the two bedrooms upstairs. All the windows had been cleaned even though there were no curtains for any of them. A good fire was roaring in the grate and a pan of potatoes was boiling on the hob. Every inch of the scullery including its earthenware sink and single cold-water tap had been scrubbed with Jeyes Fluid and the cleaning utensils were now stored neatly under it.

'They must have been a dirty lot, the old tenants,' Mary had commented.

'Oh, they were. The Piercesons. They were really awful. In and out of Walton Jail by the minute. Everyone was glad to see the back of them,' Elizabeth informed her as she went down the lobby struggling with a straw-stuffed mattress.

Mary had gone very pale.

'It's all right, Mam, no one knows,' Tessa hissed. She knew Elizabeth wouldn't break her promise.

'Anyone at home!' a man's voice called from the front step.

'What is it?' Mary demanded. The man was clutching a large cardboard box to his chest.

'Found this on your doorstep, missus. Here, I wouldn't go leaving stuff around for anyone to walk off with. Happy Christmas!' He dumped the box on the floor and had gone before anyone could say a word.

'Who . . . what . . . ?' Mary was confused.

'Mam was going to put together a few things for you,' Elizabeth said quietly.

'But she's already given us so much – I can't—' Mary caught sight of her daughter and younger son's expressions. They had worked so hard. Her pride would have to take second place to their needs this time. 'Let's open it and see what's inside.'

Elizabeth helped Mary to carry the box into the kitchen and

Tessa and Jimmy Oh'd and Ah'd over the ham shank, the pudding, the oranges, the butter, the jam, the tea and the slab of fruit cake. That was something they'd never had before. Mary sat down at the table and covered her face with her hands so the children would not see her tears.

'Mam! Mam, are you feeling poorly?' Tessa shook her mother's shoulder gently.

Mary looked up. 'No. No, Tessa, luv. Someone up there is looking after us. We'll all go to church in the morning and remember the Harrisons in our prayers.' She smiled gratefully at Elizabeth.

They were stacking the groceries on the shelf in the scullery when the kitchen door opened and Colin came in.

'Hello, Mam! The place looks great now! But who in the name of God bought all this bloody food?'

'Don't you use language like that under my roof! Where have you been all night?' Mary demanded.

'Oh, around. It wasn't much use coming home to an empty house with no job.'

Tessa glared at him. *He* wouldn't have walked the streets as she'd done, or slept rough. He'd been somewhere warm and he'd probably had meals too.

'So where did you get the overcoat from then?' Tessa demanded suspiciously.

Colin had anticipated this question. 'From a feller who felt sorry for me at one of the places I went to for a job.' He stared at his sister, defying her to challenge him. She couldn't and neither could his mam, not in front of the girl from the shop.

'Just don't think you're staying here, idling your time away. Get down to the market – any market – and see if there's any fetching and carrying to be done.' Mary held his gaze.

'Where's me da?'

'Where you should be, at work.'

'They don't work after dinner on Christmas Eve an' it's after three.'

Tessa could have hit him. Why did he always have to go and upset Mam?

'I said go and find *something* to do and keep out of . . . mischief,' Mary said in a tone that brooked no argument.

Colin shrugged and left the kitchen. He wasn't old enough to go into a pub but he knew where he could get his hands on a few bottles of beer. 'Mam, me da's home!' he shouted from the lobby.

The sound of a loud, tuneless voice came to their ears, singing a version of 'We Wish You a Merry Christmas'.

Mary looked at Tessa. 'Tessa, will you go and get him . . . inside.' Despair fell like a heavy cloak over her shoulders. Richie hadn't changed. He was drunk – again.

As Johnny Doyle alighted from a tram and began to walk home along a crowded Scotland Road he slowly found himself grinding to a halt. Obviously there must be a fight or some other kind of disturbance that was holding everyone up. It was nothing new on Christmas Eve, he thought. He'd just have to wait. He still hadn't got his mam a present yet but he'd left it late on purpose. Many of the pawnshops reduced their prices on Christmas Eve. When this lot had been sorted out he intended to call into Cookson's. His reverie was broken by a movement of the crowd and he saw a lad fighting his way through, lashing out at everyone in his path. So that's what the hold-up was, a petty thief. He was amazed however to see Colin O'Leary dash past him. Instinctively he'd leant back, out of Colin's way – he hardly knew the lad but he'd not thought of him as being a thief. Those couple of seconds were enough for Colin to break free of the crowd before Johnny could do anything to stop him. Well, there was a policeman in pursuit, Johnny thought, and he shrugged and walked on in the direction of the pawnshop.

When he emerged, delighted that he'd got his mam a nice pair of earrings at a price that hadn't left him penniless, he began to walk home. It was dark now and cold and he turned the collar of his jacket up and bent his head against the wind. He turned into Naylor Street with the intention of calling on Mike but was distracted by the screams and pleadings of a young girl. It was little Patsy Sullivan from number sixteen, an undernourished five-year-old. She was sobbing and trying to reach up to grab something, just what he couldn't see. But he couldn't mistake Patsy's tormentor. It was Colin O'Leary.

Colin had been relieved and delighted to have given the scuffer the slip. The fact that everywhere was crowded and the policeman too was fairly new to the area had worked in his favour. He'd leaned against the wall of the jigger to get his breath back. God, he hated this bloody area, he'd thought. It was worse than the one he'd come from. Then he'd walked around the corner into the street and had heard a child singing. He didn't know who she was but she was dirty, scruffy and as thin as a rake. She was singing to something she'd had wrapped up in a rag. A doll, he'd surmised, but maybe not. The likes of her wouldn't have a doll, she didn't even have a coat. She epitomised the whole neighbourhood, he'd thought savagely.

'Shurrup, you sound like a bloody cat out on the tiles,' he'd snarled.

The child had glared up at him and then he'd seen what she was nursing. It *was* a cat, well, a kitten, and like her it was half starved, dirty and verminous.

'I'll give you something to sing about!' he'd cried and snatched the animal from her. It mewed with pain at being roughly handled and then swung up and down by the scruff of its neck.

'Give it back ter me! Give it back, 'e's me friend, like!' Patsy had yelled at him.

He'd laughed and had started to torment her, ignoring her frantic pleadings and tears. Then, suddenly, a hand closed around his wrist in a vice-like grip. Colin dropped the kitten with a squawk of pain.

'You're not only a thief, you're a bloody coward as well!' Johnny yelled at Colin. 'Kids and helpless animals!' Little Patsy immediately picked up the mewling kitten and fled.

Johnny caught Colin by the lapels of his coat. 'Listen you, I'm only going to say this once! Around here we don't thieve from shops and we don't torment kids or animals. I'll put your eye in a sling if I see or hear you've been at it again and you can be sure that all the lads and fellers in this street will be watching you too. Now clear off!' Johnny released Colin, aiming a swipe to the lad's head just to emphasise his point.

Colin slunk down the street, hating their new home more than ever.

Chapter Six

As her husband slept off the effects of his afternoon celebrations and the loss thereby of his morning's wages, Mary, aided by Tessa, tried not to show their bitter disappointment at his conduct. They had both really thought he'd turned over a new leaf.

After they'd put him to bed they sat down beside the fire in the kitchen. The room was still dingy and sparsely furnished but at least now it was warm. The flickering flames gave an illusion of cheerfulness.

'I wish I had something to give you, Tessa – aye and our Jimmy too. Poor lad, he'll be the only one in the street who'll get nothing.'

'I don't think he will. An apple, an orange and a new penny is all a lot of kids will get. As for me – I understand.'

'I wish I understood your da.'

'Oh, Mam, don't let's think about it. Has he got any money left? A threepenny bit or a silver sixpence?'

'I'll have a look in his pockets, but I doubt it.'

Mary took Richie's jacket from the back of the chair. He'd gone to bed in the rest of his clothes.

'There's nothing. Just bits of loose tobacco and string. Wait . . .' She searched more thoroughly. 'There's something in the lining, I'm sure. It's torn in a few places.' She drew out the coin and placed it in Tessa's hand.

'It's a silver threepenny bit, Mam!'

Mary smiled. 'We'll give it to our Jimmy, with an orange.'

Tessa smiled too. 'He's no sock to hang up so we'll put it on the table and tell him Santa couldn't find his sock. He'll be made up.'

'What about you?'

Tessa got up and put her arms around her mother. 'I've got you, and we've furniture, food and a fire. That's enough for me.'

Mary kissed her on the cheek. 'You're a good girl, Tessa. I don't know what I'd do without you.'

'Come on, Mam, let's go to bed.'

Mary nodded. 'If straw was good enough for Him in that manger, it's good enough for us.'

Tessa was so relieved that there was something soft to sleep on and some blankets and the shawl and Elizabeth's old coat to cover her that she didn't mind sharing the donkey's breakfast with her mother. Colin, Da and Jimmy shared the other bedroom. Jimmy had his own mattress, much to Colin's annoyance. His da was out for the count and took up most of their mattress.

Mary lay with her eyes tightly closed. The room was quite bright owing to the streetlamp and the fact that they had no curtains. She thanked God for all the blessings that had come her way in the last two days, but although physically exhausted, she found it difficult to sleep. She could not get comfortable at all and just when she was starting to doze off a dull, dragging pain would start and waken her. She did not know what it was and it frightened her.

Tessa too was finding it hard to sleep. She'd been so optimistic that morning. Oh, how could Da be so thoughtless after everything they'd been through? He just didn't seem able to pass a pub without going in. Just what was so special about them she didn't know – apart from the beer. Many of them were terrible. Dirty sawdust on the floor, the bar counter awash with spilt beer, the stink of ale, stale tobacco and sweat. At least that was the impression she got when she passed. Da simply ignored the results of his weakness. Well, this would have to stop. She determined that, first thing tomorrow, when the chance arose, she was going to try as she'd never done before to make him see what was plainly under his nose.

Christmas Day dawned bright, clear and very, very frosty. The O'Learys all tidied themselves as best they could and went to church. Tessa saw Elizabeth and her family immediately. Mrs Harrison was wearing a very smart dark green coat and a matching green felt hat; Elizabeth wore her best navy blue coat and a new light blue hat and she had a small fur muff to tuck her hands into. It was suspended around her neck by a length of cord and was obviously a Christmas present.

Tessa noticed that all the Flynns were there too, and from the slightly greenish-grey tinge of his skin and the puffiness around his eyes, Mr Flynn looked as if he had a monumental hangover. Mrs Flynn and Brenda's grim expressions gave credence to her assumption. She and her mam had also heard part of the row that had gone on next door late last night. The walls were so thin you could hear everything. Her mam had raised her eyes to the ceiling but knew just how her neighbour felt.

Ginny Greely was there too, with May, who was wearing a fancy red and black hat which really didn't go very well with her brown coat.

53

Johnny Doyle and his two brothers, all well scrubbed, their hair plastered down, sat beside their sanctimonious-looking father and pale, washed-out, plain little mother. She constantly darted furtive and, Tessa thought, frightened glances at her husband and her sons.

The O'Learys all looked shabby beside their neighbours, but that didn't bother Colin; he was bored. His mind was wandering from the service to ways of making money. All he had to look forward to today was the Christmas dinner, even though it was only ham and not turkey or goose or capon. But if he wanted to get his hands on anything else, he'd have to be dead careful from now on. Even his da was being watchful where once he'd turned a blind eye to Colin's escapades.

But Da was a fool, spending hard-earned money on beer and horses and pitch and toss. *He* wasn't going to make the same mistakes. He wanted more out of life than a few hours' enjoyment, a hangover, then more hard graft. How Da put up with Mam and her eternal nagging and complaining Colin didn't know. And Tessa was getting as bad.

When the service was over and they'd shaken hands with the parish priest and wished the Season's Greetings to all their neighbours they set off for home. The pavements were slippery and Tessa linked her arm through her father's and made sure they gradually fell back until they were out of earshot.

Jimmy had been telling his mam how he was going to spend the money Santa had left him.

'It's going to be a Happy Christmas after all,' Richie said amiably.

'It is but oh, Da, it's only because of the goodness of the neighbours. Why did you go and spend your wages? I thought—'

'Ah, come on, Tessa, luv, don't you start on about that too. I had enough of it from your mam and it's Christmas. Frank Flynn was in a worse state than me. I saw him hanging on to a lamppost.'

Tessa sighed. 'Da, I'm worried about Mam, really worried. She's had the move to cope with, not to mention our Colin. She's still upset. She . . . we both thought that now you'd be, well, more thoughtful. No one minds you having a couple of pints, Da,' she hurried on before he could stop her. 'But what if our Colin or me don't get jobs? I don't think *he's* even tried.'

'That's a bit unfair, Tessa. He promised me he'd turned over a new leaf. And of course you'll get a job, luv. You're bright, clean and tidy, always on time, never poorly—'

'But all I'm fit for is factory work and I tried everywhere!'

'You'll get something soon, Tessa, and so will our Colin. Unless someone finds out he's been to Borstal.'

'Do you believe him?'

Richie shrugged. 'I'll wait and see.'

Tessa took a deep breath. 'Will you promise me something, Da?' she asked, looking earnestly up into his face.

'What?'

'That you'll try harder in the future to just keep it to a pint before you come home and . . . and no gambling, please?'

His expression changed. 'It's not your place to be asking me things like that, girl.'

'I know it's not, but, Da, look at us! We didn't have much before, and we still owe money, but now we're the poorest of the poor.'

Richie felt guilty. He didn't intentionally go out of his way to spend his wages, it just sort of happened.

'Please? Please, Da? It would mean so much to us . . . all of us,' Tessa pleaded. 'Especially me,' she added. She'd always been his favourite.

Richie was silent for a minute then he slowly nodded. 'Just a pint, Tessa.'

'Promise? Really, really promise?'

'I *really* promise.'

She smiled up at him, some of her fears alleviated. She prayed he did mean it. But how many times had his promises been made and broken?

They'd all had their dinner and her mam and da were sitting dozing by the fire. Colin had gone out with a muttered excuse but she really didn't care where he'd gone. Jimmy had gone in to see Harold Flynn and, judging from the noise next door, all the previous night's animosity had been abandoned. There were shrieks of laughter from Eileen and her daughters and bellowing from Frank and Mike. She was wondering just what she could do and was relieved when she heard the doorknocker. She went to open the door to Elizabeth.

'Mam said if you're as bored as me you can come down to our house for an hour or two. She's fed up with me mooching around and our Nessie is being a pain, as usual, even though she got nearly everything she asked for. If I'd had my way she'd have got nothing, she's just greedy and selfish.'

'Just like our Colin.'

'What's he done?'

'Nothing. He's just gone out.'

'Well, are you coming?'

Tessa ran down the lobby into the kitchen, told her sleepy-eyed mother where she was going and snatched up her shawl.

'How's your mam? Did you have a good dinner?' Delia asked. Jack was asleep in his comfy winged armchair.

'She's having a doze and the dinner was really great.'

Delia smiled and looked across at her husband. 'They're all the same, aren't they? It's *us* who do the shopping and the cooking and the serving and *they* all go to sleep. Go on – you can go up to your bedroom, Elizabeth, and maybe I'll have a quick doze before I start on the dishes.'

'Leave them, we'll do them. I did ours so Mam could have a rest.'

'It's a pity my two don't think like you, Tessa.'

'What did you have to go and say that for? There's piles and piles of dishes! I think she's used every pan and dish we own,' Elizabeth said when they were at the top of the stairs and therefore out of earshot.

'Because your mam's been so good to us, and you and your da too.'

Elizabeth shrugged and opened the door to her room.

'You've got a *fire* in your bedroom!' Tessa was incredulous.

'I only have one on special occasions like now, or when I'm sick or when it really is very, very cold.'

'Oh, isn't it all . . . great!' Tessa gasped.

'I suppose it is.' Elizabeth had never given much thought to it before. 'Didn't you have things like this when you lived in Isaac Street?'

'No. I had some things. A bed, of course. A chest of drawers, a stool and curtains and rag rugs, but you've got . . . everything.' Tessa looked in amazement at the neatly made single bed with its bright patchwork quilt. She gazed at the highly polished wardrobe in which she supposed Elizabeth had lots of clothes, and at the dressing table on the top of which there was a set of little glass bowls, a trinket box and a ring stand placed on crocheted mats. A stool covered in pink chintz was pushed into the knee hole of the dressing table. The curtains were made of the same material and there was even wallpaper. It had a white background with little springs of pink and blue flowers all over it. She'd never known anyone who had wallpaper in the downstairs rooms let alone the bedrooms. There were two pictures on the wall and a small silver-framed mirror.

'Do you want to see the awful uniform we have to wear in summer?' Elizabeth asked. 'You've seen the winter thing.'

'You have a different one for summer?' Tessa said, sitting down on the dressing-table stool Elizabeth had pulled out and placed near the fireplace.

'Well, we'd be roasted alive in that thick scratchy serge.'

Elizabeth delved into the wardrobe and threw a blue dress and then a blazer on the bed. Tessa caught a glimpse of several other dresses and blouses. Elizabeth held up the dress. 'It's like a rag!' It was cornflower-blue rayon with short puffed sleeves and a cream Peter Pan collar with, at the centre, a narrow blue bow.

'What's wrong with it?' Tessa wouldn't have minded it.

'I'm *fourteen*, not four! It's like something you'd dress a toddler in. And I once had the bow cut off.'

'Why?' Tessa demanded.

'It undoes.' Elizabeth demonstrated by a sharp tug on the loose ends. 'And I was chewing these ends. Up comes Sister Imelda and fishes out a pair of scissors hanging on a long black ribbon – they have all kinds of things hidden in those long skirts – and cuts the bow off. "Elizabeth Harrison, if you choose to ruin a perfectly good piece of material, you can do without it!" she says, all huffy-like. Mam wasn't half mad. She had to make another one.'

'Don't you get hot in that?' Tessa pointed to the navy blue blazer lying on the bed. The badge on the breast pocket was the same as the hat badge.

'Yes, and we can't take it off either. We have white socks, brown sandals, and white gloves which are always getting dirty and lost. Mam says I must use them as dusters or handkerchiefs, they're so filthy. And then the hat.'

'Another soup dish?' Tessa laughed.

Elizabeth grimaced. 'It's just as bad. Same shape but it's Panama straw. If it gets wet it's ruined – it goes all limp and soggy. So the last time it rained I took it off and pushed it into my satchel. Mam was furious.'

'Why?'

'Because it was ruined just the same. It was all out of shape and she had to buy another one. I didn't get out of the house for a week for that and I'm not allowed to keep it in here. I think it's under lock and key.' Elizabeth laughed.

'Do you really hate it there? It sounds like fun.'

'Fun! It's nothing like fun! I'm a misfit, you see. The rest of them come from really well-off homes. They all speak with posh accents, so I don't fit in even though Mam pays extra for elocution lessons. It's a waste of time. I just *can't* speak like that! It's all so . . . false. I forget and start dropping my aitches. She pays for piano lessons too and we haven't even got a piano! It's all to impress Aunty Margaret in New Jersey.'

'So what do you want to do when you leave there?'

'I don't really know. I think . . . I think . . . I'd like to work in Woolies. Just imagine seeing all the things they sell!'

'Do you think they'll let you?'

'Not a chance. Mam would make me take the veil first. But I know this much, I'm not staying on. I'm leaving when I'm sixteen.'

'At least you'll have had a good education. You can have a pick of jobs. I can't even get one.'

Elizabeth looked at her closely and then bit her lip.

'What's the matter?'

'Nothing. Before we broke up, I heard Sister Julie saying she needed some help. Some domestic help. She's about a hundred but she sees that everywhere is kept clean. You have to kneel in a corner and say a whole decade of the rosary if you so much as drop a tiny bit of paper on the floor!'

'Aren't there younger nuns who could help?'

'Oh, they do. You're nearly always tripping over one of them polishing floors. There's miles and miles of polished wood floors. That's why we have indoor shoes and outdoor shoes. Another daft idea.'

'Not if you're the nun who has to polish them.'

Elizabeth was deliberating. 'There must be *something* they need *someone* to do. I'll ask Mam if she'll come with me to ask Mother Superior if they have some work for you.'

'Me?'

'Yes. You need a job, don't you, and it would be better than working in one of those terrible factories.'

Tessa looked flabbergasted. 'Work in a convent? Me?'

'Why not? You go to church, you're hard-working, you won't be cheeky or "impudent", as they say, you need a job to help your mam get a decent home together, what more deserving case could there be?'

'Will you really do that? Ask your mam too?'

'Of course. If you get something you wouldn't be able to speak to me of course.'

Hope had taken hold of Tessa. Imagine working in a convent. It would be clean, warm, quiet. Everything a factory job wouldn't be. And she'd be able to see Elizabeth, even if she couldn't talk to her. Maybe they could travel to and from home together. Maybe the new year would really be the start of something new. Something better.

Chapter Seven

Tessa would never forget the day she stood before Mother Superior in the parlour of the Convent. True to her word Mrs Harrison, urged on by Elizabeth's pleadings, had written to make enquiries. She had given Tessa's circumstances and a brief character reference. It had to be brief: she hardly knew the girl, but she was moved by her plight. The reply had come back that if Mrs Harrison would bring the young girl for inspection and interview on Monday 10 January her suitability as a 'lay domestic' would be considered.

'You can't go looking like a rag bag. Oh, God! I didn't mean to say something like that.' Elizabeth clapped her hand over her mouth. It was one of her failings. She always went in with both feet, opening her mouth before she thought about what she was going to say.

Tessa looked down at the creased and none-too-clean navy blue skirt and her shapeless grey jumper, which was already thin on the elbows and cuffs.

'I know what you mean. I *do* look like a walking rag bag,' she replied ruefully.

'I'll lend you something,' Elizabeth offered firmly.

'Nothing too good, Elizabeth, please,' Delia called from the scullery where she was washing up, up to her elbows in soap suds and greasy plates. She did feel genuinely sorry for Tessa, for the whole family in fact, although there was something she didn't like about the eldest boy. Just what it was she couldn't put her finger on. But it wouldn't do for Elizabeth to make a bosom friend out of the girl. It was a friendship that would do her daughter no good at all. Elizabeth's future was mapped out, even though when it was mentioned her daughter pressed her lips together tightly and that stubborn look came into her eyes.

Once upstairs Elizabeth delved into her wardrobe and took out a very dark blue skirt and a cream blouse she had always hated. 'Here, this might do.'

'Don't you think this will look too . . . good?' Tessa said, holding the blouse up. It was a warm winceyette material.

'No. Not if you wear the coat I gave you over it. You'll look tidy, but, well . . .'

'As poor as a church mouse.' Tessa smiled ruefully.

'You'll have to wear stockings or socks or something.'

'I think socks would be better.'

Elizabeth rummaged in the top drawer of the chest and brought out a pair of off-white socks that would have been destined for the rag man anyway when the spring clear-out came around and summer uniform day arrived, which was usually in May and usually on the coldest day of the month.

'Oh, Mrs Harrison, I'm terrified!' Tessa said as they arrived outside the Convent.

Delia looked down at her. She was a rather pretty girl: fine-boned and dainty. With some flesh on her bones, the right clothes, and her hair cut decently, she would be very pretty.

'Don't worry, you'll be fine. Just answer truthfully and in a quiet polite voice,' Delia advised, pressing the doorbell, the loud clanging of which echoed around the hall inside.

Tessa stood on the top step, her stomach turning over with nerves, looking up at the beautiful glass fanlight over the imposing door with its knocker, brass plate and handle shining in the pale, frosty early-morning sun.

The door was opened and a small, elderly nun looked at them questioningly.

'I'm Mrs Delia Harrison. My daughter is a pupil here. This is Tessa, Theresa O'Leary. Mother Superior is expecting us.'

Delia herself felt nervous. The interior of the hall was unnerving. It was painted a dark green colour and the walls were adorned with holy pictures. The floor was covered with black and white chequered tiles and there were four wide polished mahogany doors, one of which the little nun guided them to. She knocked quietly, entered and then returned. 'Mother Frances says you are to go in.'

Delia took a deep breath. She had only ever been in this inner sanctum once before. It was daunting to a woman of the working class.

Tessa was shaking. She looked down at the tiled floor. There wasn't a speck of dirt or a single crack on it.

A middle-aged nun looked at them over her glasses. 'Please sit, Mrs Harrison.' Delia's letter was on the desk in front of her.

Delia sat nervously on the edge of an upright chair and Tessa stood at her side. 'Thank you, Mother.'

Mother Superior glanced at the letter, and then at the large painting of their foundress, Blessed Mère Julie, which hung over the elegant fireplace. She folded her hands piously.

'So, this is the young girl?'

'Yes, Mother. This is Theresa O'Leary.'

'Well, Theresa, why do you want to come and work here?'

Tessa looked up. Elizabeth had prepared her for this.

'Look demure, or at the floor, stand still and don't fidget. Just tell her, plainly.'

'We . . . we have just had to move from the Dingle, Mother. We are almost destitute. I would take any kind of a job and before Christmas I really *did* try. I went to every shop and factory.' She didn't miss the slight shudder that shook the woman's shoulders at the word 'factory'. 'But Elizabeth – Miss Harrison – suggested I come to you for . . . help.'

'Just what happened to put your family in a state of destitution?'

The girl looked downtrodden, pale and under-nourished and yet she spoke well. 'Destitute' was a word she had obviously learned for the occasion – she had probably been coached by Elizabeth Harrison: a stubborn and often impudent girl who was just not the right type for a school like this.

'My father. He works very hard when he can, but some days there isn't any work. He is a docker, and he has . . . weaknesses.' That was what Elizabeth had told her to say.

'Weaknesses?'

Tessa took a deep breath. 'He . . . he likes a drink, Mother, and . . . he gambles.'

'Indeed.'

The frosty tone made Tessa look down into the eyes of the seated nun whose plump, rounded features gave no clue to her character. Tessa hoped her own eyes were honest and pleading.

'But now he's turned over a new leaf and we all want to get back to the hard-working, simple and clean life we used to have. That's why I need work. Please, Mother, he really has made a new start.'

The nun turned her glance to Delia, who nodded.

'I believe your younger daughter . . . ?'

'Vanessa,' Delia supplied.

'. . . is also destined for a superior education. She will come to us?'

'Yes. Yes, definitely, Mother. When she's eleven. She's ten at the moment.'

Mother Superior didn't reply for a few seconds. She was weighing up the prospect of another paying pupil against the cost of taking this shabbily dressed girl into the kitchens.

'Very well. You can start in the kitchens when term begins on Monday. You will be assisting Sister Augustine. You'll work from seven a.m. to five-thirty p.m. and we will pay you five shillings and sixpence a week.'

It wasn't much, Tessa thought, but it was better than nothing.

Delia stood up and placed a hand on Tessa's shoulder. They certainly weren't delving into their coffers, she thought, but she smiled. 'Thank you, Mother. That is very generous.'

'Thank you. I'll work hard and never be late,' Tessa added.

The nun nodded her head and stood up. The interview was over.

Elizabeth made her repeat every single word, and couldn't believe that Tessa had taken no notice of her surroundings with the exception of the hall and that there was carpet on the floor in the parlour.

'I was relying on you. I've only been in there myself once and then I was scared even to open my mouth, let alone gaze around the room.'

'You were scared and you expected *me* to have noticed everything! Elizabeth, I was quaking!'

'We're never allowed near *their* rooms. They're not paying you much. When do you start?'

'When you go back. I have to be there for seven o'clock, so I'll have to leave about a quarter past six.'

'Oh, that's a pain. I wanted to walk with you.'

'I finish at half past five.'

'I'll wait for you. I'll dawdle around inside as much as I can, then I'll wait outside the back gate.'

'You'll be frozen, it's an hour and a half.'

'I don't mind,' Elizabeth said cheerfully. 'Just as long as you take notice of *everything*!'

It was with real pleasure for once that Tessa walked down the lobby of number twelve. At last she had some good news. The kitchen door was half open and she could see her mother sitting at the table peeling potatoes. She'd laid a sheet of old newspaper on the table top. It and the peelings would be burned: putting them into the ashcan would be a sheer waste. They would augment the precious coal.

'Mam! Mam! I got it! I got a job working in the kitchens for five and six a week!'

Mary stood up. 'Glory be to God!'

'I know it's not much and it's less than I could get in a factory but it's clean and warm and I won't mind what I do. Elizabeth is going to wait for me when she finishes school and we can come home together.'

Mary looked into her daughter's dancing dark eyes. 'She's a kind-hearted girl, is Elizabeth, even if her mam's got some fancy ideas. It will do you good, Tessa, to have someone of your own age. You never really had many friends in Isaac Street, did you?'

'No, I didn't, Mam, and Elizabeth is sort of special.'

'Well, she would be with all the money that comes from the rich aunt in America,' Colin said cuttingly.

'It wouldn't hurt *you* to shift yourself, meladdo, and get some kind of a job.'

'Mam, I've told you I'm trying.'

'Oh, you're that all right! You're very "trying",' Tessa snapped at him. She didn't know what he did during the day, but he always came home in the evening obviously well fed. Where he got the meals from she didn't know.

'Give me your old jumper and skirt and I'll wash them through. You'll have to have something clean to start with. At least they can't object to that. You won't be dressed up.'

'But these are Elizabeth's clothes, Mam.'

'I don't think she'll mind you keeping them until I can get your own things washed and dried.' Mary smiled. 'With you and your da both in work regular like, we'll soon be able to buy things and have a decent home again. Maybe there'll even be some spare for clothes . . .'

It was a dark wind- and rain-lashed morning as Tessa set out for work. She had been going to wear her one and only coat, but she had nothing to cover her head, so Mary insisted she put on her shawl; it would at least keep her hair dry.

'See you this evening, Mam,' she said, kissing Mary on the cheek. Her mother stood at the door, heedless of the cold and damp, and watched her walk up the street, her head bent against the weather.

If only she felt better, Mary thought. The pains she'd felt the night before Christmas had become more or less continuous. If only she had more energy, she'd go and get some bit of a job too. She could go cleaning offices – a lot of women did that, usually in the early morning or late evening. There was a small army of them and they all had kids who needed feeding and clothing. But she was always so tired these days and she knew the dragging pains were beginning to show in her face.

Colin took up his usual vantage post on the corner of Scotland Road and Chaucer Street. There was a branch of the Liverpool Savings Bank on the opposite corner. It was a large, imposing building, with tall chimneys and a turret like those on castles. It was two storeys high and its name was painted in gold lettering on the side. He'd watched the place for almost a week now: counting the customers in and out; noting what time they were busy and when they were quiet; what time the staff arrived; what time they left; and when they went out for their lunch.

They'd have hundreds of pounds in their tills, maybe even thousands. He'd also made a note of when the money arrived. It was carried in a big black box by a single man, accompanied by one police constable.

He'd make a proper job of this one. He'd considered taking a partner, it would have been useful, but whom did he know? Whom could he trust around here? Besides, he would have to split the money in half. That was what really settled the matter. He'd wait his chance. In a couple of weeks, when he was absolutely certain of the best possible time. Probably after the money had been delivered and before the rush just before they closed their doors at half past three in the afternoon, he thought. Then he'd be away from this dirty, poverty-stricken hole of a city for good. He'd go to New York on one of those big liners that were always either tied up at the Landing Stage or in one of the docks that his da worked on.

Colin never stole from the shops now in case the shopkeepers remembered him when the police came asking about the bank raid. He usually took the overhead railways back to the Dingle and got a morning's or afternoon's work on the docks down there. There were men who knew him, of course, but he didn't worry about the risk. He earned just enough to get by. Sometimes it was more when he got a couple of full days consecutively. But he was sick of both his mam's and Tessa's questions and jibes. At least Da wasn't always nagging him.

Elizabeth hung around the back door to the Convent. She'd idled her time away as best she could but by four-thirty she could delay no longer. It was freezing and she hoped Tessa wouldn't be long.

She walked up and down just to keep a bit warm. She was perplexed about something her mam had said this morning before she left.

'Elizabeth, I know Tessa is a quiet, well-behaved girl, and I don't mind you being friends, but I just don't want you to consider her as your . . . *only* friend.'

'She *is* my only friend. Hardly anyone around here speaks to me because I have to go to that awful school.'

'It is *not* an awful school. You are getting the best education that money can buy. Anyway, you're still friendly with Ginny, aren't you?'

'Yes, but it's sort of . . . different.'

'You know how hard both your da and me work to keep you there. Even with your aunt's help it's not always easy. There's books, uniform, extra lessons—'

'I know, Mam. So why can't I leave and go to St Anthony's or St Sylvester's?'

If she'd gone to a local school like everyone else, she, like them, would have left by now.

'You will *not* be leaving the Convent. We all want much much better things for you. Your life will take a different turn from Tessa's, that's why I'm telling you not to make such a fuss of her. We've helped her family get settled, and we've helped get her a job, now leave it at that.'

Elizabeth had shaken her head and had left for school. There was going to be a terrible row one of these days, she knew it – she just *knew* it – because she was determined not to be forced to do something she would hate. When she set her mind to something so important, she could be immovable.

The Convent's back door opened. Tessa slipped out. 'I'm sorry, have you been here long? I've no real idea of the time. I have to wait to be dismissed.' She wrapped her shawl around her and over her head and linked arms with her friend.

'No, not really. I've been thinking about something. Well?'

'What?'

'You promised to tell me *everything*! Were they horrible? The nuns, I mean. Did they come popping up behind you, and frightening the daylights out of you? They're always doing that to me. You feel guilty and you haven't even *done* anything.'

'You sound as if you hate them.'

'No, I don't *hate* them, but all the things we do there, like elocution, etiquette, embroidery and walking properly, don't seem to be of much use to the likes of me.'

'Are you still determined to leave at sixteen?'

'Yes. Two more years. Eight terms more. God, it doesn't bear thinking about. Oh, I'm such a misery! I know, we'll go and see Ginny or Mike and find out as much as we can about Brenda Flynn's wedding. Come on, let's run. There's a tram coming. You can tell me everything on the way.'

'I haven't got any money.'

'I have, come on.' Elizabeth grabbed Tessa's hand and they ran laughing towards the tram stop, heedless of the cold and damp. Elizabeth was determined to ignore her mam's instructions about getting too friendly with Tessa. The ties that bound them already would be hard to sever.

After telling her mam about her first day over her tea of blind scouse (with dripping butties to follow), Tessa wrapped herself in her shawl and walked down the road towards the tannery.

Elizabeth had told her of this meeting place but she was apprehensive. Perhaps they wouldn't want her to be included in their little group. But as soon as she caught sight of Elizabeth she relaxed.

'You've been ages!' Elizabeth complained.

'I'm sorry but I had things to tell Mam.' Tessa seated herself on the low wall.

'What's it like, working there?' Ginny asked.

'Not bad at all. It's clean and warm and they gave me something to eat.'

'I wish I could have landed a job like that.' Ginny looked pointedly at Elizabeth, who ignored her. 'I'm frozen to the bone when I get home and if I complain all I get is an ear-bashing from Mam. She doesn't have to put up with the cold when she's at work and—'

'We all know you don't like it, Ginny,' Mike Flynn interrupted.

'How can you like stinking of fish all day? I told Mam I never, ever want to eat fish again.'

'What did she say? Doesn't old Birrel give you anything to bring home?' Mike asked.

'Of course he does. Anything that's a day old. But I just can't eat it. It sticks in my throat and I gag. All I can think about is gutting it.' Ginny shivered and looked even paler.

'I'll be glad when it's March. I hate the winter,' Elizabeth said, fully aware that she was the one most protected against it.

'I can't say I'd like to be Johnny. I bet he's seasick. Out there in the middle of the Atlantic, rolling and pitching all day and night. God, it must be awful,' Mike said, pulling a face.

'How about you? What's your job like?' Elizabeth asked.

'I shovel coal all flaming day. My back feels as if it's broken by the end of it, but at least it keeps me from freezing. Half an hour for dinner we get, that's all, and a round of bread and dripping is all Mam gives me. She's saving up.'

'That's why we came down here tonight. How are things going for the Big Day?'

Mike grimaced and shoved his hands deeper into his pockets. 'Down the drain, that's how they're going. Mam and our Brenda do nothing but row and fight. At least me da can get out and go to the pub.'

'You just said they were saving up, so where does he get the money from?' Ginny demanded.

'Mam's always asking the same question, but at the top of her voice. Probably the whole street can hear her.'

'Has your Brenda sorted out the bridesmaids yet?' Elizabeth asked. The outcome of that row was eagerly awaited by every woman in the street.

'Oh, aye, but half the family's not speaking to the other half. I couldn't care less meself. You're all coming, aren't you? Johnny is – he'll be home just in time.'

'Of course we'll all come,' Ginny answered.

'The whole street and half the neighbourhood will come. Any excuse for a knees-up,' Elizabeth laughed.

'Us too?' Tessa said timidly.

'Yeah. Your mam and da, your Colin and Jimmy.'

'It'll be great. There hasn't been a "do" around here for ages,' Ginny said enthusiastically.

'That's because of the last one, Nancy Deegan's,' Mike said.

'What happened then?' Tessa enquired.

'It got a bit out of hand, like. Her da said the fella she'd married wasn't up to much and that she certainly wasn't getting a bargain in him and his entire family. There was murder – everyone pitched in, the women too. The scuffers had to be called. The bridegroom and the bride's father spend the night in Rose Hill nick. It was dead funny seeing the pair of them being hauled up the street and the sergeant telling the rest of them to get home, or he'd nick the lot of them.'

'I bet the bride didn't think it "dead funny".'

'No, neither did her mam or her ma-in-law.'

'There won't be anything like that, will there?' Tessa asked timidly.

'Fat chance. *He's* flaming teetotal. A right miserable sod he is. I don't know what she sees in him.'

'I do. She's got the chance to get away from you lot and when the old girl dies they'll have the house to themselves. A whole house to themselves! It must be like heaven,' Ginny marvelled.

'There's only you and your mam living over there,' Mike stated.

'Don't forget the lot that have upstairs and if we had a cellar there'd be another lot in that. As it is they're up and down the stairs like yo-yos. The kids are always fighting and screaming and she's always yelling at them and him too. It's just what you need when you get home cold and tired. At the weekends you usually have to step over him in the lobby. Out for the count. Paralytic drunk. Me mam just laughs.'

'Well, if he drinks in the Globe or the Unicorn she won't mind how drunk he gets, it pays her wages and therefore the rent,' Elizabeth said philosophically. 'I hope it doesn't rain on the day, or worse, snow,' she added.

'Is she walking to the church?' Ginny asked.

'Well, Mam wants her to have a hackney with a horse and so does she, but me da says it's a waste of money and she can walk like everyone else does. She says she isn't like "everyone else" and she'll thank him to remember that she's getting out of a slum and into a decent area. That caused another row.'

Elizabeth laughed. 'Oh, you're always making a joke of things.' His family were the noisiest in the street but she liked Mike's sense of fun.

Mike rolled his eyes and grinned. 'Well, if you didn't laugh at the carry-on, you'd cry or go completely round the bend.'

'But you make it sound like a circus.'

'It is. Bloody Fred Karno's is what it is!' Mike replied, still grinning broadly.

Chapter Eight

Had she heard her son's remarks Eileen Flynn would have agreed wholeheartedly. She was getting no help from anyone. All Brenda did was moan. All Maureen and young Harold did was torment her and more often than not Frank took refuge in the pub on his way home from work. Lately she'd taken again to going to meet him down at the docks. It was humiliating for both Frank and herself but she didn't care. At least that way she got most of his wages, though there were still shouting matches when he eventually arrived home. He upbraided her for showing him up before his work- and drinking-mates. She'd yell back that it was bad enough feeding and clothing them all, never mind forking out for a wedding.

'The way he's goin' I'll be pawnin' me own wedding ring to pay for the "do",' Eileen complained loudly to Mary and May when she met them in the shop.

They murmured their sympathy, particularly Mary who wondered if she should use the same tactics with Richie – though he had been much more thoughtful about his drinking lately. Quite suddenly a pain, like a red hot knife stabbing her, tore into her abdomen. Mary cried out and gripped the counter.

'Mother of God! She's goin' ter faint, Delia! May, get a stool or something and be quick!' Eileen held Mary's sagging body from falling to the floor.

Delia ran through into her kitchen, grabbed a three-legged stool and a glass of water and informed her startled husband, who was unloading the stock he'd brought earlier that morning from the warehouse, that she might need him in the shop.

'Have yer got any smellin' salts, Delia? She's a terrible colour,' Eileen yelled.

Mary was beginning to come round as May and Eileen lowered her on to the stool. She was confused. What was happening to her? She made an attempt to get to her feet.

'You sit down there, luv, you're not well at all.'

'I'll be fine. Just give me a few minutes.'

Delia shook her head. 'You won't be fine at all. You look like death warmed up. Come on, I'll take you into the kitchen, Jack will see to the shop.'

'No! No, really, I'm great now. I . . . I've been getting these little turns since Christmas.'

'That was not a "little turn". I thought you'd gone unconscious, out like a light.'

'I thought yer were a gonner, meself!' Eileen added.

Delia and May both glared at her.

'God! A mouth like the Mersey tunnel!' May muttered to Delia.

Mary had now struggled to her feet, and insisted she was well enough to get home alone.

'Well, you go and lie down when you get back. Make yourself a cuppa first then get straight off to bed,' Delia advised as Mary left the shop.

'That woman needs a doctor. I've noticed how poorly she's been looking lately,' Delia said.

'That's as may be, but she certainly didn't want to go into your kitchen,' sniffed Eileen.

'What's wrong with my kitchen, may I ask?' Delia demanded.

'Oh, for God's sake, Delia, don't go off the deep end. She didn't mean that there was *anything* wrong with your kitchen. It's cleaner and tidier and a damned sight warmer than mine or bucket-gob's here.'

'And 'aven't you gorra nice way of puttin' things, May Greely!'

Delia sighed. These days Eileen was as quarrelsome out of her house as she was in it.

'I'm not having a repeat performance of Nancy Deegan's wedding,' Brenda Flynn said firmly as she attacked the pile of ironing which for one reason or another her mam never quite got round to doing. These days, Brenda would pick out her own clothes and iron them and Maureen did the same. The ironing board always seemed to be up and the irons left at the foot of the range.

'That was all the family's fault. Shockin' it was. Even Father Walsh couldn't do nothing with them. I'm not having a performance like that either. You can have a good do without all that fighting and arguing.'

'Everyone rows at weddings,' Maureen said as she experimented with a lead pencil to see if she could shape her eyebrows with it. She wanted a real one from Woolies but her mam had gone mad when she'd mentioned it and called her a painted hussy.

'Not at this one,' Brenda replied firmly, attacking the collar of her best blouse with the flat iron. She would be glad to get out of this house. The place was always a tip and meals were always either half cold or burned to a crisp. Her soon-to-be mother-in-law had been horrified to learn that she couldn't even bake; all she'd been able to say by way of an excuse was that her mam had never baked and therefore had never taught her. She'd promised Thomas that she would learn from his mam and that she'd do all the heavy housework. It would be a real pleasure to see good furniture well cared for and floors polished, to have sheets on the bed and a bedspread and eiderdown. All the latter were luxuries she'd never known. She was certainly not going to have a life like her mam had had, she'd vowed to herself.

'I still don't really like that blue colour,' Maureen complained about the dress she would have to wear.

Brenda glared at her.

'Don't start that again, milady,' Eileen warned, wagging her forefinger at her daughter.

'It's February now, why couldn't we have something bright and cheerful, like red or orange or emerald green?'

'Oh, yes, red and orange would be great, wouldn't it?' Brenda answered sarcastically. 'In red you'd all look like tarts, orange you'd all look like something from the Orange Lodge.'

'And green is bad luck,' Eileen finished. 'That blue is very nice, Brenda, take no notice of 'er.'

'I'm not. It's *my* wedding and they'll wear what *I* want and if you don't like it, Maureen, then you know what you can do.'

'Jesus, Mary and Joseph, don't start on that again, Brenda – and you, milady, keep yer lip buttoned up.'

Brenda turned her attention to the other important matter. 'Mam, have you spoken to Da about the carriage?'

'I 'ave. 'E says you can walk. You can show off the frock from Blackler's that cost four weeks' wages. 'E said you've got more money than sense.'

'I'll freeze!' Brenda protested.

'We'll all flaming well freeze. At least your dress has got long sleeves,' Maureen added.

'If I 'ear one more complaint from you, Maureen Flynn, you'll get a go-along with the back of me 'and,' Eileen threatened.

She'd be glad when all this was over. She had a permanent headache and Frank was no help at all. She often thought of saying to hell with the lot of them and going and joining him in the pub.

'At least you'll be warm, Mam. You'll have a coat and that hat of Mrs Harrison's.'

'That's more for decoration than anything else. It won't keep me warm. I 'ope to God it's not blowing a gale.'

'I'll buy a couple of hat pins,' Brenda said firmly. 'And I hope Da stays sober.'

Eileen raised her eyes to the ceiling. That would be asking too much. She'd have a hard enough time keeping him sober before they even got to the church. It wasn't unusual for the father of the bride, the bridegroom, best man and groom's father, plus most of the male guests, to be found propping up the bar, having a quick bevvy to give themselves Dutch courage before the service. But there'd be none of that from the groom and best man, a friend of Thomas's and also teetotal. After the ceremony she just couldn't care less.

Elizabeth, Ginny and Tessa had a meeting in Elizabeth's bedroom to discuss their outfits.

'I've got nothing but the things you gave me,' Tessa said ruefully after Elizabeth had showed them her dress that had been bought specially for the occasion. It was a deep rose-pink Viyella with a white roll collar and long sleeves.

'I haven't got much choice either,' Ginny added.

'All right, just what have you got, Ginny?'

'A navy skirt, a brown one and a grey one. The grey is the smartest.'

'Well, I've got a grey jumper and a really nice bright pink scarf that you could sort of drape around the neck. You could get some pink ribbon and make an Alice band. That would brighten it up. And I'll do your hair.'

Ginny's hair was fine and a sort of mousy-fair colour. It never looked properly clean because all she had to wash it with was soap. Elizabeth made up her mind to get a sachet of Sta Blonde and use that. She'd dry it and then curl the ends with the tongs. She was good at things like that. She hadn't meant it at all when she'd told Tessa she would like to work in Woolworth's; what she really wanted to do was be a hairdresser, but she hadn't a cat in hell's chance with that.

'Now, you, Tessa. You can wear my cream blouse and Ginny's brown skirt. You could get a piece of narrow brown ribbon and I'll make a bow that you can tie under the collar. Brown and cream go really well.'

'Would that be all right, Ginny? About your skirt, I mean?'

Ginny nodded.

'What about my hair?'

Elizabeth looked quizzically at her friend. 'Will you let me cut it?'

'God! I wouldn't let you loose with a pair of scissors on my hair, Elizabeth Harrison!' Ginny cried.

Tessa looked uncertain.

'It's already short, so there's not much that can go wrong.'

Ginny sucked in her breath and shook her head.

Tessa made up her mind. 'Oh, all right. Just promise to be careful.'

'I promise. Stay there while I go and get Mam's scissors.'

Soon Elizabeth reappeared with a pair of scissors in one hand and towel and dustpan and brush in the other. 'Mam says I've got to clean up and if I snatch you bald she'll kill me. She will too.'

Tessa sat on the dressing-table stool with the towel around her shoulders while Elizabeth, with more confidence than she felt, snipped away.

'It does look better,' Ginny said tentatively.

'Of course it does. She's got a natural wave in it.'

'Oh, I won't end up with a head full of waves and curls, will I? I might lose my job if they think I'm . . . sort of flighty.'

'Stop worrying about them. Tell them it's the St Joan of Arc cut. They can't complain about that.'

'Who was she?' Ginny asked.

'Oh, she was French and had her hair cut short so she looked like a boy and fought with the soldiers against us. So the history book says.'

'What happened?' Tessa's mind for the moment had been diverted.

Elizabeth tutted impatiently. 'She was burned at the stake because she said she kept hearing voices in her head. They thought she was a witch or mad or both, something like that.' Elizabeth stood back and ran a critical eye over her handiwork.

'So who won then?' Ginny pressed.

'We did, of course. Right, now you can turn around.'

Tessa swivelled round on the stool to see her reflection in the dressing-table mirror. 'Oh!' she exclaimed.

'Oh, don't tell me you hate it?'

'No! No. I think it's great! What do you think, Ginny?' It looked so much better, Tessa thought. It had shape and style. Elizabeth certainly had a gift.

'It's much better than it was,' Ginny replied.

'So now will you let me cut your fringe, Ginny Greely? It's always in your eyes and makes you look like a shaggy dog.'

So Ginny submitted to Elizabeth's scissors while Tessa watched closely.

'What would we do without her, Ginny?' Tessa asked, patting her own hair.

'Look a mess, I suppose. But she's terrible bossy.'

Elizabeth flicked the towel at Ginny and they all laughed.

Tessa ran home to show off her new hairstyle to her mam, who was as impressed with Elizabeth's skill as Tessa and Ginny had been.

'I wonder if she could do anything with mine?' Mary knew her own hair was badly in need of attention. Suddenly she leaned forward, clutched her stomach and cried out.

Horrified, Tessa was on her feet. 'Oh, Mam! Mam! Let me go and get Mrs Harrison, or even Mrs Flynn from next door!' she pleaded. Her mam looked terrible. Her face was as grey as her hair and she looked old, so old.

'No! No, Tessa! It'll pass. It always does.'

Tessa bit her lip. She couldn't have failed to notice how her mam had been looking ever more exhausted since Christmas, but Mary had refused to talk about it. Delia had told her about Mam's 'little turn' in the shop, but Mary had shrugged that off too. And there was no money for a doctor even if her mam could be persuaded to see one. She resolved to talk to her da about it.

Richie, however, really didn't think Mary was ill enough for a doctor. 'I know she's not well but sometimes, well, sometimes she just uses it to sort of get at me. To make me feel guilty.'

Tessa was horrified. 'Oh, Da! That's a terrible thing to say! I *do* think she should see a doctor and so does Mrs Harrison.'

'She's fine, honestly. And where would we find the money, Tessa, luv?'

She nodded but she was unconvinced. If only he didn't waste so much money, she thought, there would be a possibility to save up.

Johnny Doyle returned from his first trip two days before the wedding. As soon as he could get away from home, he joined his friends who had gathered at the tannery when they heard he was back.

'I bet you were sick.'

'I bloody wasn't, Mike.'

'Oh, the lies some people tell,' Elizabeth jeered.

'I *wasn't*. A born sailor, so the Chief Steward said. They call him a "Three Ringer" because of the three gold bands on his uniform sleeve. *That* feller is as sharp as a razor and knows all the antics that go on. And you wouldn't believe what half of them get up to,' Johnny said with pride. It was true: to his own amazement he hadn't been sick.

'You've only got to see the state of the stokers *before* they sail.' Mike knew a lot of them, they lived locally. They were all members of Cunard's 'Black Gangs'.

'Was the weather really bad? What were the passengers like?' Elizabeth pressed.

'Most of them were sick and stayed in their bunks all day. The weather was terrible, we were thrown all over the place. One waiter had a broken arm, a steward had a broken leg, and I was dead scared, I'll tell you. God! You wouldn't believe it. Enormous waves came crashing down and all the decks were under water. I just prayed the ship would come up again and she did. Time after time. The noise was frightening. It was as if the sea was deliberately trying to . . . to crush us.'

'I wouldn't fancy that much,' Tessa said hesitantly. She still felt shy among the old friends. She hardly knew Johnny, although he'd been so kind their first day in Naylor Street, and he had greeted her warmly today.

Johnny smiled at her. He really did like her. It was hard to believe she had a brother like Colin. They were as different as chalk and cheese. 'You don't have to worry about me, Tessa.'

She became confused. 'I . . . I didn't mean . . . it like that. Well, I did, in a way, I . . .' She fell silent and her cheeks began to burn. Sometimes she was such a fool.

Johnny pretended not to notice. 'There was a lot of damage. Half the lifeboats had gone and the deckchairs had been swept away. The rails were all twisted and so was the monkey island.'

'What's that when it's at home?'

'Don't you know *anything* about ships, Mike? It's part of the bridge. Not the wheelhouse, but the bits that stick out so the Old Man can see the sides of the ship when you dock.'

'Oh, never mind all that! What was New York like?' Elizabeth demanded impatiently.

'Great! Absolutely great! The buildings are so tall and close together but there's a huge park in the middle. That statue they've got – Liberty – is enormous. You can climb up inside it. And the bridges – well, I didn't think we'd get under the Verrazano-Narrows bridge. It's the first one, after that there's two more. But there's people of every colour and religion and it seemed as if all the hustle and bustle went on day and night!'

'Our Brenda's wedding won't seem much fun after all that,' Mike said enviously.

'It will! I'm all in favour of any kind of "do". They won't let me have a bloody drop of *anything*. I'm too young. And they won't let me into the Pig and Whistle either.'

Everyone laughed. It was a term they all knew. The crew bar on all ships was called the 'Pig and Whistle'.

They'd all trooped up to St Anthony's on the Saturday morning early, so as to get there before the bridal party.

None of the girls wore the outfits they would wear that evening, but Ginny's hair had a lovely shine on it, Tessa noticed, and her own hairstyle had drawn compliments from her da and even from Colin.

Brenda had in the end got her own way over the carriage and Eileen was looking very smart in Delia's hat and coat over a blue and cream check dress she'd got second-hand from O'Dwyer's on Great Homer Street.

She was quite proud of her efforts. They were all turned out neatly if not grandly. Frank wore his good suit, returned from the pawnbroker's for the occasion. It would go back there on Monday morning, as would Mike's suit and Harold's Norfolk jacket. They hadn't let her down. Frank had been shadowed all morning by Maureen in all her finery, much to their mutual annoyance.

'Don't you let yer da out of yer sight for a second!' had been Eileen's exact instruction as she'd removed the curling papers she'd lost a lot of sleep over the previous night.

As the first triumphant notes of the organ thundered out the Bridal March from *Lohengrin* everyone turned to look at the bride.

'Doesn't she look gorgeous!' Ginny hissed to Tessa. If and when she got married it was something like this she wanted.

Brenda did look radiant. The dress was of plain white satin with the high neck and long sleeves the church demanded, but it was trimmed around the neck, cuffs and train with lace. She had a wreath of wax orange blossom on her head that held in place the full-length tulle veil.

'Would you look at the gob on their Maureen,' Johnny Doyle whispered to Tessa.

'She hates the dress – well, the colour anyway. She wanted to wear red.'

'She would. She'd be all powder, lipstick and rouge if her mam hadn't stopped her,' Ginny added in a loud whisper.

'What time are you coming round tonight?' Elizabeth asked.

'Dunno really. As soon after seven as possible.'

'Is your mam going?' Ginny asked Johnny.

'No. I think she wanted to but Da's got a cob on.'

'Why?'

'Because they won't all be in the pub putting money in his till. And they weren't in today.'

'I should think not. Who on earth starts drinking at this time of day?' Elizabeth said indignantly.

'I don't know what he's got to moan about. Half the guests will be in there this afternoon. They should have weddings later, it's murder hanging around all afternoon. The fellers either go to the pub or a football match and all the owld women drink port and lemon and pull everyone to bits,' Ginny added.

'I'll call for you both at half past seven,' Elizabeth said firmly.

'Mam might want us all to go together, us being new, like,' Tessa said.

'My mam won't mind me coming with you.'

'Neither will mine,' Ginny added.

'Besides, it will mean I can get away from our Nessie.'

'Are the younger kids going too?' Tessa was surprised.

'Yes. No one dares leave them at home. God knows what they'd get up to. At least if they're at the "do" everyone can see that they're behaving.'

'It's usually the grown-ups who don't behave. The kids are all right.'

'Except for the time Harold Flynn and Bertie Miller ate all the ice cream and were as sick as pigs. Serves them right.'

'I heard their mams battered the pair of them next day after they'd got over their hangovers.' Johnny laughed.

Delia turned around. 'Will you lot kindly remember where you are, jangling away like that! It's a disgrace.'

They all looked very nice, so Mary told them when Elizabeth and Ginny called. She'd never seen Tessa looking so smart. She knew she herself looked dowdy, as did Richie and young Jimmy. Only Colin looked decent, in a shirt, tie, trousers and sports jacket. Where he'd got them she didn't know. She didn't want to know either.

'You behave yourselves, all of you. We're newcomers, remember, and people have been very good to us. I don't want anyone pointing a finger and saying what a disgrace we are,' she'd instructed all of them.

The party was already in full swing and had spilled out into the street, but Elizabeth pushed her way down the Flynns' lobby to the kitchen followed by the others.

'What a crush!' Ginny complained.

'I know. It's murder,' Mike added.

'What's it like in the back yard?' Elizabeth asked.

'Just as bad,' came the despondent reply.

'Well, I don't fancy standing up all night,' Ginny stated.

'Aren't you going to have a bit of a whirl around the floor then?' Colin asked. This looked like a good "do" and there had hardly been many exciting occasions of late.

'Whirl! Around what floor?' Tessa demanded.

'Don't be such a misery. Enjoy yourself,' he answered before pushing his way to where the beer was, followed by his father.

'We could sit on the stairs,' Elizabeth suggested.

'The kids are there,' Johnny pointed out.

'Well, we'll shift them.'

Clutching glasses of beer that Mike had managed to get for them, they cleared the younger children off the stairs.

Nessie, who wore a huge red bow of satin ribbon in her hair, glared at her sister when told to move. The stairs were a good vantage point. She protested vehemently, but the protest wasn't taken up by the others.

'And you look like a chocolate box with that enormous bow in your hair!' was Elizabeth's parting shot, after Nessie said she looked a mess in her frock.

Tessa sipped her drink and then pulled a face. 'It's horrible.'

'I know. Mike, why couldn't you get us some sherry instead of ale?'

'Because me mam and Aunty Hilda and Aunty Madge finished all that off this afternoon. They're all half-cut now but me mam says that after all the arguing and worry she's going to enjoy the bloody party.'

'I thought your mam and Aunty Madge had had a row,' Elizabeth said.

'That's all over now.'

Elizabeth grinned at him. 'How you put up with your family I'll never know. You're so easy-going, you just take everything in your stride, you never seem to get annoyed.'

Mike shrugged. 'What's the point of getting a cob on over things? There are enough rows as it is.'

'Laugh and the world laughs with you, cry and you cry alone.'

'You've always got some saying or other.'

It was Elizabeth's turn to shrug. 'It's having to go to that terrible school. I wish I had your attitude, it would help me cope with trailing up there every day.'

'Where's the happy couple?' Ginny asked, peering around.

'In the parlour with the ma-in-law, and you should see the gobs on all three of them. The sooner they all get to Breck Road the better. Even me da's given up on them.'

'Why?' Tessa asked.

''Cos he's out for the count. Blind paralytic drunk,' Mike laughed.

'Oh, that's great, isn't it,' Elizabeth said scathingly.

'Well, are you going to have a dance, Elizabeth?' Johnny Doyle asked.

'We'll be crushed to death.'

'I'll make some room.'

'It won't matter much because Arnold Roberts plays everything at the same speed.'

Tessa laughed. 'Where did they get the piano?'

'It's on loan from a blockerman. I just hope he gets it back in one piece or me da will be out of favour, not to say a job.'

Colin had returned and sat down on the stair next to Ginny. He'd managed to swig two bottles of stout and was feeling confident. What's more, little Ginny Greely looked very attractive. He didn't know what she'd done to herself – he'd hardly noticed her before.

'You look nice tonight, Ginny.'

'Thanks. You don't look bad yourself.' Ginny sipped the bitter drink again. She really didn't know him very well.

'That's terrible stuff for a girl to drink.'

'I know, but it seems there's nothing else.'

'Well, put it down and come and have a dance. We can get to know each other better, like.'

Ginny felt shy and not like her usual self at all as she followed him.

Tessa watched him. Ginny was far too nice and far too trusting for Colin, but there was nothing she could do.

Elizabeth arrived back with Johnny, her face flushed. 'It's

terrible! I haven't got a single toe that hasn't been trodden on.'

'Mainly by me. Come on, Tessa, will you chance it?'

'If you want swollen feet then go on,' Elizabeth laughed.

Tessa let Johnny lead her into the parlour where Brenda and her new husband, plus a grim-faced elderly woman, sat stiff as ramrods in chairs that were equally upright. They all had faces like thunder, but their presence didn't seem to be dampening the merriment that was going on around them. In the mêlée she caught sight and sound of Eileen Flynn, propped up against the piano singing 'A Nice Cup of Tea' discordantly.

'I don't think my mam will approve of that,' Tessa shouted over the din.

'What?' Johnny asked.

'The state of Mrs Flynn.'

'Then she won't approve of your da, he's in more or less the same state. Of course, *she's* been at it all afternoon!'

Tessa bit her lip. Some of her exuberance had gone as she thought about her mam. Despite Richie's reassurance, she was still afraid there was something seriously wrong.

'It is a wedding, Tessa. Everyone's come to enjoy themselves. Relax!'

Tessa smiled. She did feel at ease with Johnny now. 'I will! But Ginny looks as if she's enjoying it a bit too much. Our Colin's up to something. He's not to be trusted.'

Ginny *was* enjoying herself. She'd never met anyone like Colin O'Leary before. He was so sure of himself. He'd told her *he* wasn't going to be living here hard up all his life. She'd never met a lad with ambition and plans for the future before.

'Will you come out with me, Ginny?'

She was taken aback. 'Out?'

'Yeah, on a date? We could go to the pictures.'

Ginny flushed and felt a little light-headed. She'd never had a date before and she wasn't very sure what her mam would say.

'I'd . . . I'd like to but I'll have to ask Mam.'

'Is she here?'

'Yes. She got off work early.'

'Then let's ask her.' And taking a flustered and blushing Ginny by the hand he went in search of May Greely.

He found her in the kitchen laughing and joking with a group of men.

'Mrs Greely, can we have a word, please?' Colin smiled at her. He could see no objection: her own reputation wasn't unblemished.

'Who are you?' May demanded.

'I'm Colin O'Leary, Tessa's brother, and I've come to ask you if I can take Ginny to the pictures one night in the week?'

May was startled. 'She's only fourteen.' Then, seeing the protest in her daughter's eyes, added, 'Nearly fifteen.'

'I'm sixteen, nearly seventeen, and I'll take good care of her.'

May shrugged and then laughed. 'Oh, go on then. The pair of you are still wet behind the ears.'

'Oh, thanks, Mam! Thanks, I—'

Ginny's words were drowned by a terrible screeching and screaming.

'Holy Mother of God! What's that? What's Delia doing, for God's sake?'

'I'm trying to separate these young hooligans, that's what I'm trying to do, May, and I'd appreciate some help!'

The noise level dropped considerably.

'I can't believe it. Just look at the mess this little madam has made of Harold's face. I think they've been drinking everyone's dregs.'

Nessie and Harold were yelling and kicking and punching like a pair of small furies and both Harold and Jimmy's faces bore the scratches from Nessie's fingernails.

Mary pushed her way through the crowd and took her son by the ear. She was mortified. Not only was her husband barely able to stand, her younger son was fighting like a tearaway. Now what would people think of them? She caught hold of Jimmy by the front of his shirt and slapped him hard across the face.

Harold and Nessie had been dragged apart but Nessie was still screaming until Delia used the same tactic on her daughter.

'Where's your da?' Delia demanded of Harold.

'He's no use, Mrs Harrison,' Ginny informed her.

Delia looked at Mary and saw understanding in the woman's eyes.

'Right. Home, milady, right now. And you can think yourself lucky your da doesn't take off his belt and use it on you all the way back. Elizabeth, get your coat.'

'Ah, Mam, that's not fair! She's the one in trouble, not me.'

Delia was furious. 'I said, get your coat! Do I have to fetch your father to you too?'

Tessa was at her mother's side. 'I'll take him home, Mam,' she offered, looking sympathetically at her friend.

'Thanks, luv, but I'll see to him myself. As for your da . . . he can sleep on the step for all I care.'

'You just can't trust any of them not to make a show of you, can you? Get out of that door the pair of you,' Delia said grimly. Nessie was in for a hiding when she got her home.

Mary nodded her heartfelt agreement. God knows where Colin was or what he was up to, but she didn't care. She had enough on her hands already with Richie drunk and Jimmy now bawling his eyes out.

''Bye, Tessa,' Elizabeth said. After Mam had finished with Nessie, her sister was going to get a belt from her too; she'd ruined the night.

''Bye.' Tessa turned to look for her friends but couldn't see them so they left, leaving Colin slightly subdued and Mike Flynn wondering where he could sleep with the house still crowded out and both his parents now unconscious. He wished he could go home with Elizabeth. It always seemed so peaceful in their house. It was tidy and organised and no one shouted or yelled, except in extreme cases, and it had to be very extreme indeed for Delia to raise her voice. She'd demonstrated that tonight. She'd dealt with all the fuss quickly and calmly. He looked wistfully at the door through which Jack and Delia had led their children. Oh, yes, it would be great to go home with them.

Chapter Nine

By March it was clear, even to Richie O'Leary, that his wife was seriously ill. All through the winter months of January and February, since she had confessed to the pains, she had seemed to get thinner and thinner. Quite often she couldn't stand the pain she was in and would cry out loud or grip the table or sink so tightly that her knuckles would be white. Her face was that of an old, old woman, drawn, haggard, lined; her eyes looked enormous, ringed with dark shadows.

Tessa had easily slipped into the well-ordered routine at the Convent and had even earned praise from Sister Augustine, always a force to be reckoned with. But it was to Sister Bernadette, the other nun with whom she worked in the kitchens, that she confided her worries, one day when they were both sitting at the big scrubbed table, peeling vegetables, surrounded by pans and enamelled bowls.

'I'm watching her fade away before my eyes,' Tessa said with desperation.

'Then you must get a doctor in to see her, Tessa.'

'We haven't got any money for doctors. There's the rent, the gas, the coal and that's before food and clothes, cleaning stuff and bits of furniture. There's only Da's wages and mine. He's being really great. He's keeping his promises. He only has one pint of beer a day, two on Saturdays.'

'Then you must try to find a few pence a week. You can have all the money in the world, but if you haven't got your health, then you have nothing. Apart from your faith in Jesus Christ.' Sister Bernadette reached over and patted Tessa's hand.

'She just wouldn't see a doctor. She'd go mad if I even mentioned it.'

'In this case I think you will find that the end justifies the means. Don't take no for an answer, Tessa. It's for her own good. She does her best for all of you – isn't it better for *you* to risk a little bit of wrath for *her* good?'

'Yes, you're right. I'll start saving and our Jimmy can go collecting empty jam jars and lemonade bottles and we'll add that to the rest.' She wished she'd made the decision sooner.

'She's right,' Tessa said to Elizabeth as they walked to the bottom of Everton Valley, Tessa with the folds of her shawl held tightly to her face, Elizabeth clutching her school hat for the wind was strong and blustery.

'Just don't tell her until the doctor arrives on the front step. She can't tell him to go away then, can she?' Elizabeth suggested.

'I wouldn't put it past her, she's so stubborn. Oh, Elizabeth, she's so pale and thin.'

'I know. Mam's worried too. She was only saying the other day that she looks like two eyes on a stick. Come in with me first, before you go home, and we'll see what my mam can suggest.'

Tessa nodded. She was really very, very worried about her mam. It seemed a huge effort for her to even lift a pan, let alone tackle the washing and ironing. Either Jimmy, Colin or herself brought the coal bucket in, for that was completely beyond her strength.

They didn't get as far as the shop, for young Jimmy came running at full belt down the street, his face ashen, his eyes wide with fright.

'Jimmy! Jimmy, what's the matter?'

'It's Mam . . . Mam . . .' he panted, clutching at Tessa's shawl. His shoulders were heaving with his efforts.

Tessa caught hold of him and steadied him. 'What's the matter with Mam?'

'She . . . she . . . was just putting the kettle on when . . . I . . . got in. I was next door, but she had to keep sitting down . . . and then . . .'

Tessa shook him. 'Then *what*?'

'She . . . she . . . sort of crumpled in a heap and fell on the floor. I . . . I . . . can't wake her up, Tessa.' He burst into tears but they were ignored.

'You go in and see to her, I'm going for Mam!' Elizabeth instructed before breaking into a run.

Tessa ran inside and found Mary, just as Jimmy had said, lying unconscious on the floor.

Instantly she was on her knees beside her mother and gently shook her shoulders. 'Oh, Mam! Mam! Wake up! Tell me what's wrong! Tell me what's the matter, please?' she begged. She heard her younger brother's sobs but she took no notice, her own eyes were full of tears. Oh, why couldn't Mam hear her? Why didn't she open her eyes? She was cradling Mary's head in her lap, the tears streaming down her cheeks, when Delia Harrison and Eileen

Flynn arrived simultaneously, Eileen alerted by Tessa's cries and Jimmy's sobs heard clearly through the wall.

'Oh, Mother of God! What's up with her?' Eileen demanded of Tessa.

'I don't know. Jimmy said she just crumpled up and fell on the floor. I can't make her hear me!'

'Eileen, help me get her on to the sofa,' Delia instructed.

The two women, assisted by Tessa and Elizabeth, who had followed her mother, managed to lift Mary's inert form on to the old leather sofa that was Mary's latest acquisition from Hennessy's.

'Why won't she wake up?' Tessa demanded frantically.

Eileen and Delia exchanged glances.

'God, she's nothing but a bag of bones!' Eileen said worriedly. 'I never realised. I just *never* realised.'

'Elizabeth, go back home, take five shillings out of my purse and go round to Dr Duncan and tell him he's needed urgently, very urgently.'

Elizabeth ran.

'Maybe we should call for an ambulance?'

'No! If she's anything like me, I'd sooner suffer in me own 'ome than go into a hospital. I've never known anyone yet who came out alive. Usually it's feet first from *those* places.' Eileen shivered.

'They're not *that* bad,' Delia said swiftly, noticing Tessa's appalled expression, 'but we'll wait and see what Dr Duncan says.'

Gently Delia examined Mary's head to see if she had struck it on something as she'd fallen but there was nothing to indicate that she had: no cuts or bruising on her temples.

'Have you got a blanket, Tessa?'

'Yes, there's one on our bed.'

'Is it . . . decent?' Delia asked. The poor woman would be mortified if, when the doctor arrived, all she had to cover her was an old coat. Doctors were very respected, not to say revered.

'It's not too bad.'

'Then go on up and get it, child.'

When Tessa had gone Delia shook her head. 'Whatever it is, I don't think she's long for this world. We've both seen enough of disease and death not to recognise the signs.'

Eileen crossed herself. 'Oh, God luv her, the life she's had. Terrible, terrible 'ard. Worse than me even and that's saying something. And she was always tryin' to provide a good 'ome for them all. Every single thing she has in this poor 'ome is cleaned and scrubbed and polished. There's some kind of 'ot meal on the table for them and 'er washin' is a sight for sore eyes. Always step-dashin' an' all. What do you think it is?'

'I know it's not consumption: in the short time I've known her I've never heard her cough and she doesn't have that sort of "look" about her.'

'Do you think it's, you know, women's trouble?' Eileen patted her stomach.

'I don't know, Eileen, but it's serious. As you said, God help her, she's been dragging herself around since Christmas, getting steadily worse. At least she's managed to get a few more things around her.' Delia glanced around the kitchen. 'Not much in the way of comforts, mind, but she was getting there, bit by bit.'

'She'd have got there sooner if *he'd* stayed off the ale completely and that young no-mark had got himself some work. Steady work, I mean.'

'I know. But Richie's not bad. In fact I quite like him. He's easy-going, always pleasant. There's no harm in him. He's just . . . thoughtless. I don't think he really *thinks* about anything.'

'I know, I've got one the same at home.'

'Tessa's the only one who really worries about Mary.'

They both cut short their deliberations as Tessa came back with the blanket, a fairly thick but coarse grey Army one.

Delia tucked it around Mary. Earlier, Eileen had rolled up Tessa's shawl to make a pillow.

'Will Dr Duncan come out?' Tessa asked, gnawing at her bottom lip.

'Of course he will. He's not like some I could name who won't set foot in a house in this neighbourhood. *You* have to go to *them* and they still look down their noses at you,' Delia answered firmly. She had a lot of faith in Dr Duncan.

'I wish she would just open her eyes, even for a second.'

'Well, she's not banged her head or anything like that, we've looked,' Delia answered reassuringly. 'Go and stand at the door, Tessa.'

Glad of *something* to do, Tessa left the room.

The minutes dragged. They were interminable, Tessa thought as she stood peering down the street. Why was he taking so long? It wasn't all *that* far away.

At last she saw the car turn into the street, accompanied by a small group of scruffy young boys, half of them barefoot.

Elizabeth jumped out and yelled at the entourage and they all scuttled away, then stopped and continued to watch from a safe distance.

'Oh, you've been ages,' Tessa said, gripping Elizabeth's arm while Dr Duncan got out of the car.

'I ran as fast as I could. I couldn't even speak when I got there.'

'I'm sorry, it's just that I'm *so* worried.'

'I know. Come on, let's go into the kitchen.'

The two girls went in, followed by the doctor.

'She's unconscious, Doctor, and I don't know for how long,' Delia informed him.

'Right. The first thing we have to do, Mrs Harrison, is to get rid of everyone except yourself and . . .' He looked around at the small group. Elizabeth and Eileen he knew; the young lad he didn't.

'Me! Please, Doctor? Can I stay?' Tessa begged.

'Tessa is her only daughter, and she's been a great help to her mother,' Delia added.

'Very well. But the rest of you must leave.'

Eileen took Jimmy's hand. 'Come on, lad, you an' our 'Arold can 'ave a sugar butty in our 'ouse and wait for your da to get 'ome.'

'Elizabeth, go on home and help your da and see that our Nessie does her homework. I know she does it after tea but I think tea will be late tonight.'

With a sympathetic glance at Tessa, Elizabeth left.

Dr Duncan then took Mary's claw-like hand, checking her pulse. He eased her eyelids up gently to reveal unseeing eyes.

'Mrs Harrison, could you and the young girl take off her jumper and skirt.'

Gently, Tessa did so while Delia supported Mary. Dr Duncan had taken a stethoscope from his black leather Gladstone bag. As his gaze travelled over Mary's form he shook his head and sighed deeply. He knew he had been called for far too late. In fact, even if he'd been called much sooner there would have been nothing he could do for the poor woman, except to ease the pain. It was cancer. It didn't matter exactly where it had struck first, now she was riddled with it.

'What is it . . . please?' Tessa begged.

He looked up at Delia then Tessa. 'I won't tell you a pack of lies, child. Your mother is ill. Very ill.'

'Is there . . . nothing you can do?'

'I'm afraid not. All I can do is give you some medicine to ease the pain. God help us, the poor woman must have been in agony,' he muttered under his breath. Delia put her arm around Tessa's shoulders. It was best to know, she thought.

'How long?' she asked.

'Not very long, I'm afraid. Her condition must have been deteriorating for some time.'

'Days? Weeks? Months?' Delia pressed.

'Weeks, I'd say. You know I'm not a person who believes in euphemisms or false hopes, Mrs Harrison.'

'Will she . . . will she wake up?' Tessa asked timidly.

He nodded and smiled sympathetically at the girl. Death was no stranger in these mean streets. 'She will, though the medicine will make her sleep for most of the time. But you'll be able to talk to her and on her "good" days – and there will be a few – she'll be able to speak.'

'She . . . she . . . she's going to die?'

Delia held Tessa tightly, her own tears not far away. 'I'm afraid so, luv. You've known – you've seen how much pain she was in.'

Tessa couldn't take it in. She'd known Mam was in terrible pain, but she'd thought that once the doctor had seen her, he would know what was wrong and would then be able to cure her. Now . . . now Mam was going to die. She was going to leave them and there was nothing anyone could do.

As Delia showed the doctor to his car, Tessa knelt down beside her mother and took one of Mary's work-roughened hands and held it to her cheek. She couldn't speak. She felt as though a hand had gripped her throat, she could barely swallow and hardly breathe. Her mam . . . her lovely mam who had suffered so much was . . . dying.

She looked up as Delia returned, accompanied by Richie.

'Tessa, luv, go on down to our Elizabeth. I have to talk to your da.'

'No! No! I'm not leaving her.'

'Tessa, luv, go on. Everything will be . . . settled.' She could hardly say 'all right'.

With great reluctance Tessa stood up and turned away. Her da looked stupefied, she thought, as she passed him.

'I . . . I . . . can't believe it, Delia. I knew she was sick, but—'

'Didn't you even *think* she should see a doctor?'

'She's been like this for ages.' Richie looked down at his wife. He was completely dumbfounded.

'All the more reason. What will you do?'

'Me? Do? I . . . I . . . ?' He was floundering. He couldn't even think straight. What would they do without her? What would *he* do without her? She was the one who held them together through good times and bad. She was the strong one, not him. This couldn't be happening.

'Oh, you're a lot of use, Richie, aren't you?' Delia said sharply. He might be pleasant but he must always have been pretty useless, judging from his behaviour since they moved here and Mary's own words about her husband's failings. She knew he was the reason they were here in the first place.

'I don't know what to do,' he pleaded.

Suddenly she felt sorry for him. He genuinely didn't know and she realised that he had never done so.

'We'll work something out, Richie. We'll all take turns in nursing her. Tessa will have to go on working up there at the Convent.'

'Why?'

'Because you need the money,' Delia answered, but it wasn't the main reason. If she stayed at home, Tessa would just become a drudge, a skivvy at their beck and call, and for a girl as young as she was that just wasn't fair. Oh, she knew there were hundreds like her, struggling to bring up children, keeping families together, but how they suffered for it. They lost an education, and therefore any chance of a decent job. There was little opportunity for a social life and they were thereby denied a chance to be courted. She liked Tessa – in her place, of course – although the girl wouldn't amount to much. All Tessa could expect was to continue in the Convent, meet someone decent and get married. It *wasn't* what Delia planned for Elizabeth, but Tessa deserved her chance. Delia wouldn't turn her back on Tessa's plight, not when time was so short and there were enough people to help out.

'Eileen Flynn, myself, May Greely, Tessa, and some of the other neighbours will work out a plan, so that no one really suffers at this . . . difficult time.'

Richie just stared at her blankly.

Delia lost her patience. 'Oh, get up to the pub, for God's sake. You're more of a hindrance than a help. Just give Eileen a knock, she's got your Jimmy. Where is the other one? Your Colin?'

Richie just shook his head. He had no idea, nor did he care.

'God help her, what a shower of useless layabouts she's had to put up with. Your Tessa is the only one of you with any go about her.'

Silently, his shoulders sagging, Richie turned away.

Chapter Ten

Delia had called a meeting of all the neighbours and, once the evening meal was over and the dishes washed and put away, one by one they arrived and all crowded into her kitchen. Those earliest to arrive seated themselves on the sofa, armchairs and straight-backed chairs that Delia had placed around the room. The latecomers had to stand. Both Elizabeth and Nessie had been sent to bed, Elizabeth under protest.

'I'm going on fifteen, I'm not a kid, like she is. Why can't I stay up? There must be *something* I can do.'

'If there is then I'll tell you in the morning. I don't want to hear any complaints or moans or tantrums, I've enough on my mind without you two making things worse. Get up those stairs the pair of you.'

Delia had been very firm and so they both went off in a huff, Elizabeth because in her opinion she had been treated unfairly. This concerned Tessa and Tessa was her friend and would need all the help she could get now. It was awful for poor Tessa; she herself couldn't even begin to imagine what she would do if it had been her own mam who was lying in bed, dying.

Nessie too was feeling very disgruntled. It wasn't as if she would go up and down the street blabbing about it. It was too serious for that. It must be really terrible for some strange doctor to come and tell you your mam was going to die. Still, she took consolation from the fact that Elizabeth had been excluded too.

'Most of you will have heard the bad news about Mrs O'Leary . . . Mary. For those that haven't: the poor woman is dying. She's been ill since Christmas but never admitted it.'

Maisie Keegan was the first to speak after Delia had passed round cups of tea. 'We don't really know 'er very well, do we? She kept 'erself to 'erself.'

'I suppose we don't, but put yourself in her place, Maisie. The poor woman is dying. She must be worried sick about her kids. She can't keep the home going either.'

'What's wrong with their Tessa? She doesn't seem to do very much up there with the nuns,' Katie Collins complained. She still carried a grudge against Tessa for her daughter Alice could have done with a job like that. The money wasn't good, but there were perks and it gave you a bit of status, not to work in a factory or shop.

Delia glared at her. 'Well, this is a nice way of going on, I must say. Very Christian of you, Katie Collins, when we all took turns seeing to *your* mam when you had to go out to work to keep a roof over your head and food on the table.' Delia's tone was scathing and Katie Collins looked uncomfortable.

Then Delia went on, brisk and business-like: 'She'll need someone to see to her throughout the day and later on I think the night as well. Then there's all the other things. Tessa can get herself and the rest of them out to work and school and then when she comes home from work herself she can see to the evening meal.'

'I'll go in in the mornings and maybe later on in the evening and Jimmy can come 'ome from school with our 'Arold and stay until bedtime,' Eileen offered.

'I don't mind doing the washing,' Maisie Keegan added. 'And there will be quite a bit of that.'

'Not *that* much, Maisie, there's no sheets or anything like that, but I suppose that's a blessing in a way. We'd better start now and save the newspapers. She'll need to lie on them – later on, like.'

'I'll take a turn with you, Delia,' Katie Collins offered grudgingly, 'in the afternoons.'

'I'll give Eileen a bit of help in the mornings. I'm at work all evening,' May Greely offered. 'And when it's time, later on, I'll come in for a few hours when I finish at work, say until two in the morning.'

'I'll see to it that there's enough food and heat, it's the least I can do,' Delia stated.

'What about that useless lad of hers? I don't know what he does for a job, but he never seems to be at home much and he never seems to want for much either.'

'God knows what he does, Maisie, she'd never say, but he'll have to pull his weight from now on. I'll deal with him.'

'What about 'er 'usband?' Maisie asked.

Delia sighed. 'He's as much use as a wet echo. He's just . . . lost. Doesn't know what to do or say. I sent him up to the pub in the end.'

'And what use would that be?' Katie Collins demanded, looking pointedly at May.

'He's out from under Tessa's feet,' Delia shot back.

May got up. 'Well, I'd best get back up there myself. The old skinflint said an hour and he'll dock it out of my wages.' She would have liked to stay on and gossip as sometimes she went for days without seeing her neighbours. She was sorry for the poor woman but she knew Delia was right about Richie. He wouldn't be able to cope very well left to his own devices. It would be Tessa who would carry the heavy burden alone if they didn't help out.

They all began to finish their tea and get their things together.

'There's one thing we haven't talked about.'

'And what's that, Katie?' Delia asked sharply. She'd never had much time for the woman. She was a trouble-maker.

'Where the money's going to come from to bury 'er?'

Everyone, except May, sat down again. It was the greatest humiliation of all for the deceased to be buried in a pauper's grave.

'Do we have to talk about it now?' May asked.

'I think we do.' Delia spoke for them all.

May sighed. 'Look, I'll *have* to be going, but whatever you decide include me in it.' She buttoned up her coat and left them to it.

'What are we going ter do? She won't be in no Burial Club, coming 'ere with not a stick of furniture even.'

Delia had been thinking rapidly. The whole cost couldn't be borne by the neighbours. 'I'll go to all the businesses. Birrel's, the pub, Rooney's Greengrocers up on the corner, and see what I can get out of them. After all, where would they be without us?'

'Eddie Doyle should cough up a fair bit, the amount of money Richie O'Leary has spent in that pub. Bevvied as the landlord's cat half the time, 'e used ter be,' Eileen said.

'That feller wouldn't give yer the sniff of the barmaid's apron,' added Katie.

'And then we'll all have to chip in, like. I know most of you are hard up—'

'Hard up! Giz a laugh, Delia!' Maisie interrupted. 'Hardly a penny ter bless yerself with in our 'ouse. My feller's as bad as your Frank, Eileen.'

'Well, give me what you can,' Delia urged.

'Make sure you tell 'er who's gone up ter the alehouse.'

'I will, Katie,' Delia said firmly, getting to her feet. The conflab was over. She'd known they would all help out.

★ ★ ★

Richie had gone into the Globe and straight to the bar, but he was so confused that he couldn't order his usual. In fact he couldn't speak.

'What's up with you?' Eddie Doyle asked. He was a dour man with very little humour. In fact a lot of the time his customers wondered why they went there. The excuse was that it was nearby, close enough for some of them to stagger the few yards home. Eddie Doyle was a man who said 'the towel's on' and meant it.

Richie could only shake his head.

'Yer'd better give 'im a drop of the Pope's phone number,' Frank Flynn said with concern. In the short time he'd known Richie, he'd never seen his next-door neighbour in such a state.

'Tharrell do! I'll thank you not to be making jokes about His Holiness in the alehouse. And I'm not dishing out glasses of the best Vat 69 whisky unless someone's going to pay for it.'

'An' yer call yerself a good Catholic? Near eating the flaming altar rails on a Sunday an' first inter confession on a Saturday,' Frank Flynn remarked cuttingly.

'The feller's in shock, yer can see that. Give 'im a drop of the crater,' Billy Keegan instructed. 'I'll pay!' He slapped down the money on the bar counter and Eddie Doyle measured the whisky into a small glass.

'Get that down yer, lad,' Billy urged. Richie's hand was shaking as he picked up the glass and drained it in one go.

'So, what's up with yer?' Frank asked.

'It's . . . the wife.'

'Jesus, yer not goin' ter start bloody moanin' about 'er. We come 'ere ter get away from them,' Mick Collins objected.

'She's . . . she's . . . dying.'

There was silence and Frank indicated to Eddie Doyle that more whisky was required. This time there was no request for payment. Eddie Doyle was as shocked as the rest of them.

'How? When? What with?' Mick Collins asked. Richie drank the contents of the glass more slowly this time.

'Delia Harrison sent for the doctor. He . . . he took one look at her and said . . . it was only weeks . . . she had left. Some sort of growth . . . some disease, I can't remember its name . . . has been eating away at her. Oh, Jesus Christ Almighty, and I thought she was just moaning, trying to get sympathy. Trying to make me feel guilty! I didn't know! I just didn't know!'

'How could you?' Eddie Doyle asked with more compassion in his voice than any of them had ever heard before.

'I *should* have listened to her. I should have *thought* more. She's lost so much weight, there's not a pick on her! I didn't stop to think about that even.'

'If we all took that attitude, Richie, we'd go round the flaming bend.'

'That's not much bloody comfort, is it?' Billy Keegan retorted.

Richie continued to shake his head in disbelief.

'Don't worry too much about it, lad, the women are dead good when things like this happen. They'll get themselves organised. Look after her, see to the 'ouse, things like that. And if yer 'aven't got the price of a bevvy, we'll all stand yer a pint.' God knows yer going ter need it, Frank Flynn said under his breath.

Elizabeth was sitting with Tessa in the kitchen. When the neighbours had left she'd begged Delia to let her go. 'Mam, please? It must be awful for her. She'll be on her own and terribly upset, I know how much she loves her mam. She's been worried for ages.'

'All right, but don't be too long. I know it's been a shock but she's got work in the morning and you've got school.'

'Do we both *have* to go? I mean, what will people think?'

'They won't *think* anything. In fact it's the best place for both of you. You can offer up your prayers for Mrs O'Leary and the nuns will too. I'll write a note for Mother Superior, you can pass it in.'

Mary had been moved to her bed and Jimmy was staying next door at Eileen's. Mary had come round for a few minutes, long enough for Delia to give her the medicine and for Tessa to tell her things were being looked after.

'I don't want to leave her on her own, and she will be if I go to work.'

'She won't be on her own, Tessa. Mam will organise everything. She's good at organising people,' Elizabeth answered glumly.

'It's all so ... confusing. I can't think straight. So much has happened so soon. What about Da and Jimmy and *him*?'

'I told you, Mam will see to everything.'

'Where will I sleep?' Tessa's eyes were pleading and full of tears.

'With your mam. Look, I'll ask Mam if I can bring my quilt up, make things warmer and more ... cheerful for you both. And some pillows too.'

'Oh, Elizabeth, I'm glad we came here, what would have happened if I didn't have you, your mam and ... everyone?'

'Don't think like that. Do you still have donkey's breakfasts?'

Tessa nodded.

'Not for much longer. I'll tell Mam you need a proper mattress and a proper bed,' she added generously. She knew her mam and da wouldn't mind the expense. You couldn't leave the poor woman on a straw mattress on the hard, cold floor.

They both jumped as the front door slammed and Colin came into the room, looking very pleased with himself. He'd bought a suit and a shirt with the money he'd won in a pitch and toss game and then he'd been tipped off about a horse. The odds were good and he'd given Bert Meadows, who was a bookie's runner, half a crown to win. It was a dead cert and he'd won a couple of pounds. He had actually been into the Liverpool Savings Bank, to get his bearings: how far from the door the counter was; how many people – staff and customers – were inside at the time; how much time he'd need to grab the money; and just how far he would have to run before he would be safe.

He'd asked the teller with a serious look on his face how you went about opening a bank account. Of course his request had been met with a supercilious smile and a dismissive reply but that didn't matter, he'd achieved his object.

'Where have *you* been?' Elizabeth asked coldly. 'It's nine o'clock.'

'What's up with you two? You've got gobs on you that would stop the Liver clock.'

'If you're interested, your mam is very ill. The doctor's been—' Elizabeth answered.

'Mam's . . . Mam's . . . dying. A . . . a few . . . weeks. That's all.' Sobs again choked Tessa.

Colin looked incredulously at them both. Mam! Dying! In a few weeks! He was shocked to the core. Although he was utterly selfish and there had been many a yelling match between them, and hidings too, deep down he did love his mam.

'She . . . she can't be. She's not old . . .'

'You don't have to be old. Your sisters died, didn't they?' Elizabeth snapped.

Tessa wiped her eyes. 'Why should you care anyway? All you ever did was bring her shame and heartache just like Da did.'

'Where is Da?'

'Where he usually is, in the flaming pub,' Elizabeth answered cuttingly. She didn't like Colin O'Leary at all.

'Does he . . . does he know?'

'Of course he does. He was in such a state that Mam lost patience and sent him up there.'

'I'll go and bring him home,' Colin said quietly, ignoring Elizabeth's ill-concealed dislike of him.

'Aren't you even going up to see her?' Tessa asked.

Colin shook his head. 'She . . . she wouldn't want to . . . to see me.'

'At least you got that one right. Anyway, she's asleep now, so you can clear off and do what you like. Just make sure that you bring some money into the house so she won't have to worry about that.'

'I already do.' Colin glared at Elizabeth. Bossy little upstart.

Tessa raised her head from Elizabeth's shoulder. 'You bring it in but you keep most of it.'

'Oh, clear off!' Elizabeth was exasperated. 'Can't you see you're just upsetting everyone? Go and get your da home. If he can stand, that is. God knows why Mam sent him to the pub. The last thing Tessa and your mam need is a drunk on their hands.'

Colin needed no second telling. Mam was the only person in the family he cared a fig about, the rest of them could go to hell for all he cared.

'Mornin', luv, 'ow are yer?' Eileen bustled in through the scullery.

Tessa smiled weakly. The kitchen was in chaos. There were newspapers on the table as well as half a loaf going stale, a bottle of sterilised milk, and last night's cups and mugs. Clothes were draped over the back of the sofa and a pile of ironing occupied the cushions. Mam would go mad if she could see it.

'I'll go on up, Tessa, luv. See if there's anything she needs. You get yourself out, I'll see to yer da and meladdo. Our Maureen is getting the other two ready for school.'

'Our Colin isn't here. I . . . I don't know where he is. He was supposed to go and bring Da home from the pub but Da came home on his own and Colin didn't come back.'

'Well, 'e's no loss. 'Ow's yer Da?'

'He's got a hangover.'

'Tell me something I don't already know, luv. Frank said 'alf the fellers in the pub were buyin 'im beer and even whisky, but Frank said 'e *was* in a terrible state over yer poor mam.'

Tessa just nodded as Eileen took herself off upstairs. She had had a bad night as she'd lain next to her mother on the straw-stuffed mattress. Through the everlasting hours of darkness, listening to her mother's shallow breathing, she'd wondered how she would feel trying to sleep when her mam was no longer here.

It was beyond imagining. Mam had always been there. Oh, she'd scolded and doled out punishment but she'd also calmed and cared for them too.

How much sleep would she ever get in the future? She would have to lie there night after night, in close physical contact, knowing that by the day Mam was getting weaker, until . . . And then what? How could she ever sleep in this room? She'd be alone. She didn't even have a sister she could share with. As the hours had dragged by the tears ran down her cheeks and she'd fought not to break into sobs which would disturb her mother.

When she heard Eileen call out her name her heart lurched and she panicked. She took the stairs two at a time.

'Oh, what's the matter?' she gasped. 'Is she . . .?'

'She's awake. She wants ter speak ter you, luv.'

Tessa knelt, then crouched down beside Mary. She looked even more pale and drawn than ever and she was obviously trying to fight the drug-induced sleep that had engulfed her.

'Mam! Mam, it's me, Tessa. How are you feeling now?'

'Tired. So tired . . .'

'It's the medicine the doctor left, Mam. You have to try and sleep, then you won't have any pain. Everything is being taken care of. You're not . . . not to worry.' Her voice was harsh with raw emotion.

Mary nodded. 'Tessa . . . Tessa . . .' She tried to reach out for her daughter's hand.

Tessa caught it and clasped it between her own. 'What, Mam? What is it?'

'Promise me . . . promise you'll make something out . . . out of yourself.'

Tessa was confused. This wasn't what she had expected and it sounded as though her Mam *knew*. 'Like what, Mam? I'm fine at the Convent, they're good to me.'

Mary managed to continue, 'I . . . know . . . but you . . . you're still only a . . . skivvy.'

What did her mother want? What exactly was she asking of her? Tessa searched her mind for some job, some occupation that would please Mary.

'Would . . . would a job in one of those posh shops in Bold Street do?'

'No. You . . . can . . . do better.' Mary's breathing was irregular.

'What about a stewardess on one of those big ships, would that be good enough?'

Mary managed a brief smile. 'It would, Tessa. Promise.'

'I promise, Mam.'

'Go . . . go . . . to work . . . luv.'

As Tessa stood up slowly, loath to leave her mother, she turned to Eileen and shrugged. 'What else could I say?' she whispered.

'Not much, but you've just promised to aim too high, girl. Hell will freeze over before a slummy like you will be taken on by one of that lot.'

But as Tessa went downstairs she made a decision. She would try. She would do almost anything to keep that promise.

Chapter Eleven

The tender, pale green leaves were opening on the trees in all the city parks the day Mary O'Leary passed away. It was a day Tessa would always remember. Life had been running so smoothly, she thought, and that had lulled her into a sense of false optimism. She hadn't wanted to think very deeply about the day her Mam would die. She had pushed it to the back of her mind. Mam was ill in bed but, thanks to all the neighbours, Tessa was able to go to work. She was out of the house. For a while, at least, she'd been able to occupy herself with something other than her mother's pain.

Prayers were said every day by the nuns and pupils for Mary. Not that she should recover, but to ease her suffering and ensure her place in heaven, the latter being stressed all the time. Tessa *knew* her mam's place in heaven was assured. Mary O'Leary had done nothing bad in all her life. The money that was still owed was her da's responsibility. He'd been the one to waste it, not her mam. As the weeks passed, even all the prayers had become a normal thing.

It was Eileen who found her. Mary was barely breathing and Eileen had sent Kenneth Keegan, one of the younger Keegan boys who was off school with mumps, for the parish priest. Before he'd left the presbytery, Father Walsh had telephoned Mother Superior to send Tessa home. She'd run all the way down Everton Valley and halfway along Scotland Road before she jumped on a tram. For the rest of the way the tram seemed to crawl along, stopping every few minutes, and the same words went round and round her head: 'Don't let her have died before I get home, Lord! Oh, please, please let me be in time.'

As she entered the house there was no sign of anyone. Richie was at work, she presumed Colin was too and Jimmy was at school. But the house wasn't deserted. Eileen and Delia were both with the priest, who had just finished administering the Last Rites.

'Come here to me, Tessa,' Eileen said. She placed an arm around Tessa as the girl sat gingerly on the edge of the bed that Delia had insisted on buying.

'Is she . . . can she . . .'

'She's not dead, child, but we can only assume that she can hear us,' Father Walsh said as he folded his purple stole.

'Mam? Mam, can you hear me? It's Tessa.' Her voice was low but pleading.

There was no movement of Mary's eyelids; no sound, no matter how faint, from her lips. Tessa clasped her mother's hand tightly. 'Mam, if you can hear me, squeeze my hand.' They all waited but there wasn't even the slightest pressure on Tessa's fingers.

'Mam! Mam, I promise I'll make something of myself and I'll look after Da and the other two—' Her voice broke and the tears she had been fighting back now started to flow without restraint.

Mary's eyes half opened for a second.

'Oh, Mam! Say something, please?' Tessa begged.

Mary's eyes closed and from her throat came a strange sound, one Tessa had never heard before, but which the others had heard many times.

'She . . . she's gone, luv,' Delia said quietly, placing a hand on Tessa's shoulder. 'She's out of her pain now. You go on down with Father Walsh, your da will need you and so will your brothers.'

'That no-mark Colin doesn't deserve anything special, he can look after himself,' Eileen muttered, crossing herself. Delia did the same and wondered just how Tessa was going to fulfil her promise to amount to something and look after her father and brothers.

As Tessa walked into the kitchen they all turned to look at her but she couldn't see any of them clearly, tears blinded her.

'Da . . . Mam's . . . gone,' she managed to stutter before pulling Jimmy to her and holding him close. With a cry, Richie got up and stumbled towards the stairs but Colin didn't follow him. He simply hadn't taken it in.

It was a dream world, Tessa thought. Nothing was real, not even Jimmy's sobs or the silent tears of her father, or Colin's almost blank, uncaring expression. Not the neighbours coming in to help out or pay their respects.

Her mam was laid out in the parlour, a room they had never used. Sheets had been hung around the walls and Delia had supplied a pair of curtains that were permanently closed, all of which hid the damp patches and rotten wood. Four candles burned in their brass holders at the top and the foot of the coffin. Delia had told her she was not to worry about paying for a funeral.

She had collected enough to give Mary a decent burial. It was something that Tessa hadn't even thought about.

She slept fitfully, alone in the bed now. At first she hadn't wanted even to go inside the room again but Delia had insisted.

'Would she be happy with you sleeping on a straw mattress on the bare boards? No, she would not. Tessa, you are the only one in the entire family who gave her any support and help and consideration.'

'But Da . . . ?' she'd queried. 'Won't Da want the bed?'

Delia ignored her. He hadn't done much to provide for them. He'd left Mary to see to everything. Why should he be offered preferential treatment in the form of a proper bed now? One she herself had bought?

'It's *his* duty now to see that you all pull together.' She was thinking of Colin.

'But you know what he's like, Mam did everything.'

'I know, but he'll just have to pull himself together and get on with it,' had been Delia's firm reply.

Delia and Eileen had insisted that she go back to work too. Between them, with May, Maisie Keegan and Katie Collins, they would arrange everything and keep up the routine of housework, shopping and cooking until after the funeral.

Masses were said daily in the Convent chapel for her mam, but Tessa felt that Mam, who was undoubtedly in heaven, would have preferred the prayers to be said for those she'd left behind and who were grieving for her. Her work didn't allow her to dwell too much on things and that was another blessing, so Eileen and Delia said.

Jimmy would be all right, once the ordeal of the funeral was over. He'd miss his mam, but less than herself, Da and Colin. He'd spent the last weeks virtually living with Eileen and, as Eileen said, 'Kids get over things quicker than we do and she's been ill for a bit. He got used to that.'

Da, after the first few days, hadn't touched a drop of either beer or spirits and for that she'd been thankful, but he seemed to be totally lost. He couldn't concentrate for very long or make decisions. It was as if he'd been at sea in a ship in rough weather and had now lost his sheet-anchor.

'Da, you *have* to try. I know it's not easy but we *all* miss her. We *all* leaned on her for help and advice. Now you've got to *try*, Da!' she'd implored. Richie had only shaken his head and looked more confused. What did Tessa expect of him? What was she suggesting?

Oh, maybe in time he would understand and get used to Mary not being here.

He was riddled with guilt. He'd taken no notice of her when she'd become ill. He hadn't listened to Tessa. He should have had more sense. He should never have got in the financial mess in the first place. He should have curbed his drinking. She'd struggled along all these years, keeping a clean and decent home, food on the table, clothes on their backs, boots on their feet, and he'd just let her struggle and worry, while he . . . he'd been no help. He was useless.

Apart from her problems with Richie, Tessa now seemed to argue with Colin every day. Nothing would change him.

'You're going to have to take some of the responsibility now.' Tessa confronted him one morning before he disappeared God knew where, as usual. 'You've seen the state of Da. He can't cope.'

'Well, neither can I,' he replied.

'You can *and* you're the oldest.'

He'd become annoyed. 'I . . . I miss her too, Tessa.'

'*You!* You only ever think of yourself. Look at all the worry you caused her. All that could have started . . . things off,' she'd replied cuttingly.

'Don't put the blame for Mam's illness on me, Tessa. Me da was as bad.'

'At least he didn't go thieving and get caught – twice! You never cared for Mam!'

'I did. In my own way.'

'Well, your way was a funny way of showing it.'

'Listen, Tessa, don't go pointing the finger at me.'

'You're going to have to sort yourself out now. Get some decent work and bring some money in to help me keep a home going.'

He'd turned his back on her and stormed down the lobby, furious, for he'd spoken the truth. In his own way he *had* cared for his mam, but he wasn't going to go down to the docks and sweat and strive for a few pounds a week and then have to give most of it to her. No way. He'd have money soon, plenty of money. Enough to buy Ginny Greely fancy clothes so they could go to the smart places in town without her showing him up. He was quite fond of Ginny. She wasn't demanding and she was in awe of him. She didn't make sarcastic remarks when he told her that soon he'd earn a small fortune and they could live the high life, maybe even leave Liverpool and go to America. She didn't ask questions as to where this money was coming from. He knew that Tessa and particularly Elizabeth Harrison disapproved of him taking Ginny out, but her mam didn't seem to mind and she was the one who really counted.

The sun shone brightly and the sky was blue on the day the horse-drawn hearse stood outside number twelve, Naylor Street. The black plumes on the black bridles barely moved. There wasn't even a breath of wind. It should be grey and cold and windy, Tessa thought miserably. It wasn't a day for sunshine at all.

They would follow the hearse on foot along Scotland Road to the church for the funeral mass and then Mary would be buried in the churchyard.

Tessa wore a grey skirt and a black jacket. It was really one of Elizabeth's blazers. Delia had unpicked the badge and had it dyed by Johnson's. Tessa also wore one of Elizabeth's hats – minus the school insignia – trimmed with a band of black grosgrain ribbon. Her da and Colin had no formal mourning clothes but wore a black armband on their jacket sleeve. Jimmy had one too and a new dark grey herringbone tweed cap, purchased by Delia. Those neighbours who could attend did so and all along Scotland Road, as the procession passed, men and boys removed their caps and women crossed themselves or stood with eyes downcast. Although they had never known Mary O'Leary it was the custom. Richie walked alone at the front of the cortège, followed by Colin, Tessa and Jimmy. She had her arm around the bewildered youngster and was having a hard time to keep her own tears back at the sound of his pathetic, gulping sobs.

Once at the church, she was barely aware of the service. Father Walsh's voice seemed faint and far away. The faces of the neighbours blurred into a single mass. It was only when they finally stood outside before the open grave that she realised the finality of it. Mam was dead. Dead!

The soil pressed into her hand by the priest felt cold and damp and she shivered even though the sun was warm on her face. Father Walsh's words were still indistinct, as were the sobs of her brother and father. The only thing that seemed real was the cold earth in her hand: soil she must now throw on top of her mam's coffin. The noise it made was the most awful sound she'd ever heard. Her heart was breaking.

She didn't remember much of the walk back and, once in the house, Delia, Eileen and May Greely took over, passing cups of tea and ham sandwiches to the mourners. To Tessa it seemed as though the house was bursting with them, and there were so many she didn't really know.

'Why the hell don't they all go home? All they've come for is the food,' Colin muttered to Tessa.

Delia heard him. 'That's a nice thing to say, I'm sure. Many people have had the decency to give up a few hours' pay or gone out of their way to show some respect for your mam! If you ask me, apart from Tessa, Mary's well out of it for the rest of you,' she snapped.

Elizabeth, who had been given time off school, glared at Colin. Her heart went out to her best friend. During the mass she'd tried to understand how Tessa must be suffering, but despite her lively imagination she just couldn't conceive how she would feel if it were her mam. She'd sat at Tessa's side once they'd got back to the house.

'Mam's right. Don't take any notice of *him*, Tessa!'

Tessa turned to her. 'What am I going to do now?'

'The same as you've always done. Tomorrow you'll all be back at work and Jimmy will be at school. Don't worry, Tessa, if you need any help, just ask. Ask me. You know I won't let you down. And take no notice of that lot up there when they start going on about God's mercy and Purgatory and things like that. I don't think they really *know* what it's like to be feeling lost and unhappy. They don't live like we do. They don't live in the *real* world.'

Tessa squeezed her hand, but still wondered if in the months ahead she would cope.

She did cope. As the weeks went by the neighbours gradually left her to manage things. It wasn't that they didn't care any more; they would always be there if she needed them. But the time had come for her to take over. Yet she missed her mam so much still. Many were the times when she let herself into the house and shouted, 'Mam, I'm home,' or turned suddenly to address her mother before she realised that Mary was no longer there for her to share her troubles or her moments of happiness.

It was late in the afternoon on a warm day in early July and she and Elizabeth were walking home. School had finished for the summer, but Elizabeth still went to meet Tessa from work and tried to cheer her friend up. Tessa saw him standing looking up and down the road and she grabbed Elizabeth's arm.

'Oh, God!'

'What's the matter?' Elizabeth asked, breaking off from a litany

105

of complaints about Sister Imelda who was the bane of her life and who had given her so much homework for the holidays that she got a headache just *thinking* about it.

'It's him. It's Mogsey Doran.'

'Who's he when he's at home?'

'The moneylender. He . . . he's found us.'

'Oh, Holy Mother of God! Quick, round the back into the jigger.' Elizabeth virtually pushed Tessa into the entry.

'What will I do? If he sees Da, then—'

'We'll just have to make sure that he doesn't see any of you. Run down the jigger to our back yard while I walk down the street and get a good look at him.'

'But what can you do?' Tessa panicked.

'I'll have to wait and see. Is your Jimmy in with the Flynns?'

'Yes, but he'll be playing out with Harold and the rest of the kids.'

'If I see him I'll shove him into Eileen's house and tell him to stay there. Go on, run.'

Tessa needed no further telling.

Elizabeth began to walk slowly down the street. There were kids outside but they were further down by the tannery end. She hoped that was far enough away, because she couldn't draw attention to Jimmy by chasing him up the street to Eileen's house. She herself felt a bit afraid of the big, rough-looking man who was still standing looking up and down the street.

'Are you looking for someone?' she asked, praying her nervousness didn't show.

'Who are you?' he asked suspiciously.

'My mam and da have the shop. Who are you?'

He ignored her question. 'Do you know anyone called O'Leary?'

She made a great show of trying to think before she finally shook her head. 'Not O'Leary. There's a family in the next street called O'Dwyer.'

'No, it's definitely O'Leary. Richie, wife and three kids, two lads and a girl.' He didn't say that it was Colin he'd recognised in the Dingle and whom he had followed until the lad had disappeared down the back jiggers where he'd lost sight of him. But he now knew they were living somewhere around here.

'Well, I don't know anyone called O'Leary around here and nearly *everyone* comes into the shop at some time,' Elizabeth replied, trying to control her startled expression. She'd just seen her mam run from the shop and yank Jimmy away from his friends and back inside. She sighed with relief as they disappeared from sight before he looked back down the street. Tessa must have told Mam.

'Well, I *know* they're around this area, so I'll just wait.'

Elizabeth took a deep breath. 'You'll have to mind that the scuffers don't see you and arrest you for loitering. They're always walking around in pairs round here. A real pain, they are.'

He glared at her and turned away. He was certain the hardfaced little bitch knew *something*. He leaned his back on the lamppost. He could wait.

Elizabeth had to force herself not to break into a run but saunter down the street as she always did. She even pretended to jump from flag to flag to avoid the cracks.

'What in the name of God do you think you're doing?' Delia asked when she got home.

'That feller *is* the moneylender and he looks dead tough. He asked for the O'Learys and I said I'd never heard of anyone of that name living around here but he's going to just hang around. I told him to be careful he didn't get arrested for loitering.'

Delia cast her eyes to heaven. One of these days Elizabeth's tongue would get her into serious trouble. Still, she'd shown some guts.

'What time does your da get in, Tessa? And Colin?'

'Colin never comes in at the same time every day, but Da . . . he's usually home by seven,' Tessa replied. 'Quite often he walks half the way to save on the fare to buy his tobacco for his cigarettes.'

Delia looked perturbed. 'I'll just have a word with your da, Elizabeth. Stay there, all of you.'

When Delia had apprised her husband of the situation, he looked grim. 'I'll go round all the men in the street that are home from work.' He knew the type of moneylender Mogsey Doran was and Richie and his family had had enough to contend with over the last few months.

Those men that were in followed him to the pub, and he left messages with the wives of those who weren't. He'd had a good look at Mogsey Doran and had even exchanged a few words him. The conversation had been more or less the same as the one Mogsey had had with Elizabeth but Mogsey had nevertheless decided to look in the pub himself. Young Kenneth Keegan had been posted at one end of Naylor Street and Harold Flynn at the other. They had strict instructions to tell Richie and Colin to get inside the house fast and stay there until someone went to inform them of what was happening. As more and more of the men slipped into the pub Eddie Doyle realised that something was up and asked the stranger point blank what he was doing in this area.

'I'm lookin' for a feller named O'Leary. He owes me money.'

'Can't help there, mate.' Eddie Doyle looked around. 'Anyone else know anything about this feller O'Leary?'

Heads were shaken and Mogsey scrutinised all their faces. There was something going on here, he thought. You didn't get fellers in such numbers in the pub this early. Most of them were still in their working clothes.

'Well, I think I might just hang around outside and wait and see who passes, like.' And before anyone could stop him he left.

'Christ Almighty! Get after him. If he catches sight of Richie or Colin or even Tessa . . .' Jack Harrison cried and there was a mass exodus of the patrons of the Globe. Jack, who was first out, was horrified to see Richie walking slowly, head bent, up the street. He'd skin Harold Flynn alive for not warning him!

'I've caught up with you at last, O'Leary!' Mogsey Doran bellowed down the street.

Richie looked up and stopped dead in his tracks, the colour draining from his face. Oh, God! What was he going to do now? Mogsey'd found them. He hadn't given much thought to the moneylender lately. He'd felt as though he'd given him the slip entirely. The group of men, now joined by some of the women, instantly surrounded Richie.

'You've no business round here, so sling yer bleedin' hook!' Frank Flynn shouted, elbowing his way towards the moneylender.

'He owes me. He owes me, it's all legal, like,' Mogsey shouted back.

'Legal my flaming arse! Go an' tell that to the scuffers in Athol Street station, you'll see just how bloody "legal" it is!' Jack Harrison said mockingly.

Mogsey glared at him and then at Richie. 'I'm tellin' you, O'Leary, I want me money an' if I don't get it—'

Frank Flynn was a big man. He grabbed Mogsey by the lapels of his jacket, lifting him off his feet. 'Yer'll do what? You so much as put yer nose around the bloody corner or gerr anyone else ter come round 'ere and I'll break yer bleeding neck. I don't care 'ow big yer think yer are, sod off – and don't come back or you'll effing well finish up under the Landin' Stage. It'll be effing months before they find yer an' even then yer own mother wouldn't recognise yer! Bugger off!' Frank's last words were bellowed in Mogsey's face and he shrank back.

Frank released him and, after looking at the grim, unyielding faces of those who surrounded him, Mogsey straightened his jacket and turned and walked away, seething with anger inside. A gang of young lads followed him, shouting abuse, until they were called back by their parents. Harold got a belt from his father for not doing the job he'd been sent to do.

'Jesus! Thanks! He'd have killed me but for you.' Richie meant every word and he was so grateful that he shook all their hands in turn.

'You'll hear no more from that feller. He knows he'll get a good kicking if he bothers you, and the undertow at the Landing Stage is very strong, he'd be gone in seconds,' Jack said grimly.

'Thanks, lads. Thanks again.'

'You don't owe anyone else, do yer, Richie?' Frank asked.

'No. I must have been mad to have got involved with him. Thank God Mary wasn't alive to see him.'

Jack looked puzzled. 'How do you think he found you?'

'I don't know.'

'I do,' May suddenly announced and they all turned towards her.

'I've a mate who's seen your lad, Colin, hanging around the Dingle quite a few times. It wouldn't have been hard to follow him. I don't suppose Tessa or Jimmy ever go down there, and neither do you.'

'I'll bloody kill him!' Richie exploded.

'I'd find out just what that lad of yours is up to if I were you,' Jack suggested.

'Come on, Richie, we'll go back to the pub. You need a drink down you. I'll pay,' May offered and gradually the crowd moved away as Richie followed her back to the Globe.

Chapter Twelve

They saw nothing more of Mogsey Doran and for that they were all grateful.

That night Tessa stayed with Elizabeth.

'Mam, she's terrified that that Mogsey feller will come back in the middle of the night,' Elizabeth had pleaded.

Delia had agreed. The girl had enough to contend with and she'd been coping very well of late. But her estimation of Richie O'Leary had taken a steep dive.

'I'm glad that Mary isn't here. How she ever put up with him, I'll never know. He's useless. He's weak, he's a spendthrift—'

'All right, Delia, luv, we know his failings, but that won't stop us from looking out for him and the kids if that shark comes back.'

'Don't go saying things like that, Jack. Tessa and young Jimmy are scared.' Jimmy as usual had gone to Eileen's to stay.

That night Richie, urged on by May – who always seemed to be in and out of number twelve these days – had a serious talk with Colin.

'What the bloody hell do you think you're playing at? That feller would have broken my neck, and yours too, if it hadn't been for the fellers in the street.'

Colin scowled back at his father and May. 'How come I always get the blame? Nothing is ever our Tessa or Jimmy's fault. No, I'm the one who always gets the blame when things go wrong.'

'You get the blame because you usually deserve it,' May answered. 'I've seen you hanging around in town, particularly around Lime Street Station and the Riverside Station. Looking for easy pickings, were you? For people too busy with seeing to their luggage that they might not notice a handbag or a wallet that was just waiting to be nicked? And you've been back down the Dingle. That's why it's your fault. That Doran feller saw you an' followed you. He'll have seen what you're up to. I'd watch my step if I were you, Colin, he'd shop you to the scuffers without a second thought. He'd think he would be paying you back.'

'What's it all to do with you?' Colin demanded.

'Don't be so bloody hardfaced!' Richie said sharply.

'I'm not. She's got no right to be saying things like that –

accusing me of pinching bags and wallets!'

Richie glared at his son. It sounded as though Colin was up to his old tricks again. 'You are hardfaced. Don't you speak to May like that.'

Colin looked speculatively at his father. So, that was the way the wind blew, he thought. 'It's "May" now, is it?' There was a note of sarcasm in his voice.

'Listen here, you thieving little toe-rag, what yer da and me do is none of yer business. We're friends, that's all,' May said cuttingly.

Colin laughed. 'Oh aye, pull the other one, it's got bells on! Ouch!' he cried as Richie's hand caught him across the side of the head.

'You'll have some respect! *I* pay the rent, so *I'll* have whoever I like in here. And May's been kindness itself over the months. You should be grateful, meladdo!'

'If you don't buck your ideas up soon and show some respect, I'll put a stop to you taking our Ginny out!' May added. 'She's easy led, but I'm not. Her da wasn't a bit like you and if you don't come up to my expectations then I'll put a stop to your gallop where our Ginny is concerned.' May's voice was firm. From now on she'd watch him like a hawk. She'd never really liked him but Ginny did. He was the first lad she'd ever gone out with and he did make a fuss of her, but Ginny was naïve. She'd believe everything he told her. She herself wouldn't believe the daylight out of him from now on.

Colin stormed out, slamming the front door behind him. The bloody cheek of her. She was nothing but a slut. A loud, common barmaid who could drink and swear and laugh at the risqué jokes with all the men in the neighbourhood. Mam would be turning in her grave if she knew someone like May Greely was in and out of the house that she had struggled so hard to make halfway decent and in which she'd died.

He was about to cross over the road, making his way to Ginny's, when he saw her coming up the street.

She looked concerned. 'Colin, what's the matter? You look dead narked. Who's been having a go at you?'

'I am upset, Ginny. I've just had a right ear-bashing from me da and your mam.'

Ginny looked incredulous. As far as she knew Colin hadn't crossed her mam in any way. 'From Mam? What for?'

'Oh, come on, let's have a bit of a walk. I'm that mad I can't stand still and I *hate* this bloody street. You can't do anything without someone making remarks or accusations.'

She'd never known him to be so angry before. Oh, he was impatient sometimes, and he was often moody, but she took no notice of his moods. They usually didn't last long. She tucked her arm through his. 'So, what did Mam say to you, Col?'

'That if I didn't buck my ideas up she'll stop me seeing you.'

Ginny stopped and looked at him quizzically. 'Buck your ideas up? What does she mean by that?'

'How do I know? Get some kind of boring, useless job that pays buttons, I suppose.'

'You don't want to do that, Col. You'd be just like all the other lads around here, except for Johnny Doyle that is.'

She didn't know just *what* Colin did all day but he seemed to get by. She sensed that he didn't want her to ask point blank. She supposed he lived by his wits, for he was sharp and clever, and he was never short of money.

Some of his anger left him. He had her support at least. 'They were both blaming me for that Mogsey Doran coming here looking for me da.'

She looked up at him. 'That wasn't your fault.'

'According to your mam it was. She said he'd seen me around. What am I to do? Stay here all day, not going anywhere?'

'That's not fair! How were you to know *he'd* see you. You're not some kind of mind-reader! And why shouldn't you go into town or anywhere else anyway?'

'It's not *me* who owes that feller money, it's Da.'

'Of course it's not you, you wouldn't be that daft. Maybe I shouldn't say it but I often think your da lives in a world of his own. He seems to be able to just . . . well, ignore things, hoping they'll go away.'

Colin nodded and they walked hand in hand along the main road towards the tram stop. They'd get the tram to Lester Gardens, it was only a few stops.

'Have you noticed that your mam and me da are always in and out of each other's pockets these days?'

Ginny pondered the question, then she nodded. 'They are, now I come to think about it.'

'I said as much and got roared at.'

'Do you think they . . . well . . .?'

'Will get married?'

'Mam likes a drink and a bit of a flirt but that's all. It's years and years since me da died and she's never really bothered with anyone.'

'She's never been livin' over the brush, like?'

'No! She never brings anyone home. I've never had a string of "Uncles", if that's what you mean.'

Colin sniffed, disappointed.

They got off at the bottom of Royal Street outside the Astoria Cinema where sometimes they went to see a film. The little park was set back off the busy road and was nearly always deserted. It was sandwiched between two streets of mainly commercial buildings and always looked a bit neglected. There wasn't much grass; it consisted of gravel pathways with mainly evergreen shrubs interspersed with the smaller summer bedding plants. There were a couple of arbours with wooden benches. Ginny sat down on a bench obscured by a large rose bush that had been left to go back to briar. She liked Colin O'Leary very much. He treated her so well. He was always buying her little things, taking her out to places most of all the other lads she knew wouldn't dream of going. And, again unlike them, he had plans. Plans which seemed to include her too.

She glanced sideways at him. He was a handsome lad and she was well aware that she looked like a mousy little slip of a thing. She would never be pretty, let alone a raving beauty. She felt very honoured that he'd chosen her even though he could have had his pick of the girls. When she encountered the flirtatious and often openly brazen glances cast in his direction by other girls, she felt jealous because nearly all of them were more attractive than herself. Maybe she would look a little bit pretty if she had the right clothes and the right hairstyle. She didn't have Tessa's big dark eyes and waving dark hair, or Elizabeth's mop of really beautiful hair or her education, but Colin seemed to like her the way she was. Maybe that in itself was appealing to him: that no one else seemed to want her. She pushed that thought from her mind as he put his arm around her and drew her close to him.

He did still like her, in fact in some ways she was great, he thought, but he was getting restless. She never made any demands on him. But just because he confided in her, in a vague sort of way, of course, didn't mean he had any intention of becoming seriously involved or of marrying her or anything. He wanted someone with Tessa's looks and Elizabeth's education as a wife, but with the submissiveness of Ginny. When he found that combination, and he was certain he would eventually, then he'd get married and not before. But, he wondered, was his da thinking of marriage? He certainly didn't want to have to put up with

113

calling a floosie of a barmaid 'Mam'. He had loved his mam, in his own way, and wouldn't put up with a replacement yet she had never understood how he felt about the rotten hand fate had dealt him. She'd slaved all her life for what they'd had and was as honest as the day was long. His philosophy, on the other hand, was to take everything that came your way, by fair means or foul. No, Mam had never understood that.

His da was useless. He'd always needed someone to make decisions. He'd always shied away from responsibility. Another thought came to mind. If his da did marry May Greely then Ginny would become his stepsister and that would put paid to any hopes she might have of ever marrying him. He'd be in the clear on that one and without him even having to tell her.

Elizabeth and Tessa were sitting on the steps of number twelve. 'We're going to have to say something to her,' Elizabeth said firmly. They had been discussing Ginny and Colin.

'What? If I tell her what a little rat he is she'll never believe me. I'm his sister, for God's sake,' Tessa replied.

'Exactly. You know him better than anyone, better than your da even.'

Tessa liked Ginny and she didn't want her to get hurt. She was an inoffensive girl and she was obviously smitten by Colin's attentions. 'Do you think I should say something about . . . well, you know?' she asked.

Elizabeth pondered this. 'She'd get a cob on if she found out that I've known all along and she hasn't. And she might go and ask your da or even tell her mam and get her to ask if it's true.'

'That would be worse, in fact it would be terrible. Her mam would go mad. Easy-going or not, *that* would put the fat in the fire and *everyone* would get to know. May Greely isn't known for keeping her mouth shut.'

'Shut up, here comes Ginny,' Tessa whispered.

'You look pleased with yourself, Ginny,' Elizabeth said, drawing her skirt aside so Ginny could sit down on the warm step too.

'Where've you been?' Tessa asked.

'Only to Lester Gardens with your Colin. He's really annoyed with my mam and your da, Tessa.'

Elizabeth and Tessa exchanged wary glances.

'What over?' Elizabeth demanded.

'Oh, the usual stuff, all about him "bucking his ideas up". Mam told him it was his fault that that Mogsey feller had found you here – as if it could have been! – and gave him the length of her tongue.'

'I'm glad she did. Maybe he'll take some notice of her. He just ignores everyone else,' Tessa said crossly.

'Honestly, you're always making him out to be some sort of hooligan,' Ginny replied indignantly.

Again there was a furtive glance between the two friends.

'He is. He always has been. He does exactly what he likes. He never considers anyone else at all and believe me I *know* what I'm talking about.'

Ginny jerked up her chin defiantly. 'You don't know *everything* about him just because he's your brother. He's . . . different when he's with me.'

'How different?' Tessa demanded.

'Well, he never goes on and on about things like work and jobs and money.'

'He always seems to have enough to take you out, Ginny, but where does he get it? We don't know. Mam often said he'd end his days in Walton Jail, and I think she was right.'

Ginny bristled with indignation but Elizabeth managed to head off the torrent of defensive words that she could see were bubbling up on the other girl's lips.

'Ginny, it's because we're your friends that we care about you. We're just pointing out that maybe you shouldn't believe everything he tells you.'

'Why not?' Ginny demanded hotly. In her opinion they weren't acting much like friends.

'Because . . .' Tessa paused. Should she tell Ginny or not? No, she couldn't. She just shrugged.

'You see?' Ginny said triumphantly. 'I *know* he's not a hooligan, far from it. He . . . he's different with me. And he's got plans, big plans for the future.'

'What plans?' Tessa cried. Oh, God, he wasn't going to start again, please, she thought.

'Plans for the future. *He* doesn't want to spend all his life in some dead-end job, always counting the pennies. No, he wants to be *someone*. Have a better life and . . . and he wants me to be part of it.'

Tessa looked helplessly at Elizabeth. This sounded ominously familiar.

Elizabeth shrugged. 'He's not about to do any of that without an education, is he? I mean, businessmen have to have certain standards. It's all talk, just wishful thinking.'

'It's not!' Ginny retorted, her cheeks beginning to grow pinker.

'It is, Ginny. He's always been like that, full of big plans, but they're only in his head. He . . . he'll never amount to much,' Tessa added.

Ginny got up, her hazel eyes cold with anger.

Elizabeth grabbed at her arm. 'Ginny, we don't want you to get hurt. We *do* care about you. We're *not* making all this up. Tessa's his sister, she sees him every day of her life.'

'Well, I'm not listening to *anything* either of you say. You're a nasty spiteful cat, Tessa O'Leary, and you . . . you're just jealous, Elizabeth Harrison.'

Elizabeth let out a whoop of laughter. 'Me! Me, jealous! What in God's name have I got to be jealous about? I can't stand him, the slimy little toe-rag! Sorry, Tessa.'

'There's no need to apologise to me for our Colin. Look, Ginny, we really don't want to fight with you. We just don't want to see you get hurt.'

'I won't because *he* won't hurt *me*!' Ginny said before flouncing across the road to her own house.

At half past two the following day Colin took up his position across the road from the Liverpool Savings Bank. Today was the day. It had all been perfectly planned but he felt as though there was sweat standing out on every pore in his body. He was certain that people were looking at him strangely. Then he pulled himself together. No one was looking at him at all. Why should they? He was no different to many people on the street and they were all absorbed in their own problems. Even the two old shawlies on the next corner were engrossed in their gossiping.

He counted the minutes in his head and dead on time the money arrived. He balled his fists in his pockets. He had to stay calm. That was the secret. Calm, unruffled and unhurried, as though it was a thing he did every day of his life.

The cashier and the attendant police officer departed and once they had gone out of sight he crossed the road, slowly. This was it. Everything depended on the next few minutes. All the things he wanted, everything he'd dreamed about was just minutes away. His chance to make a new life, in a new country where no one knew him, where he was certain he could make even more money. Jesus, it was no use carrying on thinking like that: it was undermining his confidence and his nonchalant appearance.

He pushed open the heavy wooden door. He looked around once, then made his way to the highly polished mahogany counter. The bank was empty, just as he'd reckoned. He had to force himself to walk slowly and not glance around all the time, or look uneasy or furtive. God, but it took some nerve. He was sweating profusely and he was certain that any minute now he'd wet himself with sheer fright.

The teller was shuffling paper and barely glanced up at him until the untidily written note was pushed towards him. Colin grasped the short thick piece of wood that was in his pocket – it was in fact a catapult – and moved it slightly so that in the confines of his jacket it resembled the barrel of a gun.

The eyes that now met his own were wide with terror and the teller began to grab all the notes in the drawer. It seemed to take ages. Now his whole body was shaking, something he fought to control as the seconds dragged by.

'Get a bloody move on!' he hissed at the pale-faced young man.

The contents of the drawer, including some golden guineas, were stuffed into a canvas bag. No one seemed to have noticed what was going on. He snatched it and moved on to the next teller. A woman. He'd only left himself time to get money from two. It would be enough. Any more and the whole place would erupt.

With trembling hands he shoved the note under the woman's nose but wasn't prepared for the outcome. She began to scream at the top of her voice and was joined by the first teller, who shouted, 'Thief! Thief! Thief!'

The door of the bank opened and a rotund man he'd never seen before came in. Colin's nerve broke and, dropping the bag, he turned and ran, shoving aside the bewildered customer.

Their shouts followed him as he ran down Scotland Road towards Byrom Street. He knocked people aside without a thought, terrified that any minute a policeman would confront him.

By the time he reached the Technical College he could go no further. He was exhausted. He was shaking and sweating, gasping for breath, and to make matters worse he had wet himself in sheer terror. He sat down on the steps that led up to the main door of the College and dropped his head in his hands. Jesus Christ! What a bloody useless failure he was! For a few minutes he'd had a couple of hundred pounds in his grasp. If that bloody woman hadn't started yelling he would never have lost his nerve. If he'd picked another cashier, he'd have got clear away with two bags. Now he had nothing, except the determination to try again. He hadn't gone through all the weeks of waiting and watching and planning to waste it as he had just done. So much for his fine plans. But he would wait. He had plenty of time on his hands.

PART II

Chapter Thirteen

1939

The months of January and February of 1939 were bitterly cold. Winter held the city in an icy grip and took its toll of lives; the young, the old, the infirm and the poor suffered particularly. Moreover, dark clouds were hanging over Europe and the first rumblings of war evoked a sense of dread in those who had fought and survived the Great War – the war to end all wars as it had come to be known. Spain was in the throes of civil war, the Royal Air Force were taking delivery of four hundred planes a month and air-raid shelters were being distributed to the residents of houses in London. But all this was of little importance to Richie and his family.

In number twelve, Naylor Street the house was so desperately cold that no matter how high the fire in the range was banked up with slack to keep it going through the night, by morning there would be ice on the inside of the kitchen window.

Upstairs, although now there were proper beds with blankets and quilts, they all slept in old jumpers, cardigans, socks and woollen long johns – even Tessa wore them.

She was always first up and as she raked out the ashes and reset the fire she shivered uncontrollably, although she wore her heavy shawl over her clothes.

It took her only seconds to dress. She kept all their clothes on a rack above the range to save them from becoming frozen stiff. Still, by the time her da and the lads came down it was to a warm room with a dish of hot porridge on the table. She made it the previous night and left it on the hob so it wouldn't be stone cold.

They did have more in the way of comforts than they'd had a year ago, for Richie still kept his daily consumption of ale to two glasses per evening and often it was May Greely who paid for the second one. She felt sorry for Richie. He was still looking to someone else to find solutions to his problems. If she was honest, May realised it wasn't a wife he needed, it was a mother, but maybe that was why she was fond of him.

She had taught Tessa the very basic skills of patching and darning, something that Mary had never found time to do, for she had always insisted on doing such tasks herself.

May also kept an eye on Colin, who, after a few more rows with herself and Richie, seemed to have settled down. He'd got a job as a labourer in a big haulage company in Vauxhall Road. It didn't pay very much and he had to turn a third of it up to Tessa but he was fed up going looking for casual work at the docks, north or south. He wanted a regular sum of money and it would help lull suspicions at home.

He hadn't given up the idea of a second attempt at robbing a bank, but whenever he did think about it, he'd remember the sheer terror of his first try.

He was always complaining to Ginny about the shortage of money. It meant they couldn't go out to the pictures or the music hall as much but she didn't mind. Her feelings for Colin had grown month by month, something her mam did not view with approval or pleasure.

'Mam, I'm nearly sixteen. I've been working in that flaming shop for over a year now and you know how I hate it.'

'I don't see what your job has to do with anything, *and* you're still only a bit of a kid to me, *and* I still don't trust him. I just hope you aren't letting him take liberties with you, because if he is—'

'Mam! He'd never do anything like that! What kind of a girl do you think I am?' Ginny had interrupted, but with guilt as she thought of the times when she had let him take exactly the kind of liberties her Mam was talking about. But she loved him and he loved her so where was the harm in it? She'd never let him make love to her properly, she was too scared of getting pregnant.

'I would hope you're a sensible girl. A lad never marries a girl who lets him have his own way, no matter how much he says he loves you.'

'Well, I *don't* let him "have his own way" so can we please drop the subject.'

Tessa and Elizabeth also kept a watchful eye on their friend.

'Do you think he'll ever get her an engagement ring?' Elizabeth asked as she and Tessa walked down Everton Valley, muffled to the eyes in scarves and hats. Tessa now had a good thick warm coat in a dark grey herringbone tweed. She'd got a cheque from Sturla's department store in Great Homer Street and she paid off the debt at ninepence a week. Delia had given her a scarf, hat and mitts that had been knitted for Elizabeth, who was always losing such things.

'Hardly anyone has an engagement ring. They're lucky to have a wedding ring and often that spends more time in the pawn-broker's than on their finger.'

'Well, has he said anything to her?'

'Like what?'

'Oh, honestly, Tessa O'Leary, you are so aggravating sometimes, you know very well what I mean!'

Tessa laughed. 'If you meant has he said he loves her and that he'll marry her – one day – then Ginny is out of luck. It may look like he's settled down, on the surface, but I know him. He's got something on his mind; he's just biding his time. I wish she'd meet someone else. She's not bad-looking now. You keep her hair nice and she's got some decent clothes but no, she hangs on to him.'

'Well, it's no use us trying to prise her away from him, it always ends up in a fight.' Elizabeth decided to change the subject: 'What did they give you today?'

Tessa was carrying a wicker basket covered with an old but clean piece of material. She used it to carry her bits and pieces around and also to bring home anything Sister Bernadette gave her in the way of food.

'A big jar of thick pea soup. I had some for my dinner and it's great. It's got pieces of ham in it.'

Elizabeth pulled a face. 'I know, we had it too.'

'You're really finicky with your food, do you know that? I'm always amazed your mam lets you get away with it. She never lets your Nessie leave things or refuse to eat something she doesn't like the look of, let alone even taste.'

'And speaking of our Nessie, what's she still doing hanging round the tram stop?'

Tessa followed Elizabeth's gaze and saw Nessie, now in the uniform of the Convent, standing at the tram stop looking decidedly put out and fed up.

'What's up with you? Why aren't you home by now?' Elizabeth demanded.

Nessie had just started her first term and her elder sister avoided her like the plague. 'There's no trams running. I've been here ages and I'm frozen stiff.'

'How do you know the trams have stopped?' Elizabeth demanded.

'Because there haven't been any. Sometimes you're so stupid.'

Elizabeth made a swipe at her but Nessie jumped out of reach.

Tessa intervened. 'Oh, stop it, you two, or you'll both be

reported and then there'll be trouble. Maybe the cold and ice have done something to the wires.'

'I've never known that to happen before. They only stop when it's really foggy.'

Tessa shrugged. 'I suppose we'll have to walk home.'

'It's just a pity *she* didn't think of that ages ago, instead of hanging around for non-existent trams. And you've got a cheek to call me stupid, Nessie Harrison! Mam 'll probably have half the street out looking for you, so you'll catch it when you get home,' she finished with some satisfaction.

Nessie broke away from them and began to walk quickly along Kirkdale Road.

'I've never known anyone like you two. You're always fighting.'

'Brenda and Maureen Flynn were always half killing each other when they were younger. Oh, I meant to tell you, she's going to have a baby. Mrs Flynn came in to tell Mam last night. She's made up she's going to be a grandma, or a nin as she said. Mam hates that word.'

'Why?'

'How do I know? You know Mam – she's got some funny ways. She said it sounds "common". Dad said it comes from the Welsh word for grandmother, *Nine*, but Mam only said she didn't care where it came from—'

Their conversation was interrupted by the unmistakable rattling and rumbling of a tram.

'Honestly, Nessie, you're a real pain *and* you tell lies. What's that behind us? A flaming horse and cart!'

Nessie turned back as Elizabeth started to wave her school scarf wildly and the tram slowed down.

'Mister, will you tell *her* that the trams haven't been running!' Nessie demanded of the driver.

'You're right, girl. There was a dispute at the Spellow Lane depot. It's all over now, storm in a teacup, but there's been no trams for over two hours.'

'See!' Nessie cried triumphantly.

'Oh, get a move on, you're holding everyone up. Pay your fare, sit down and shut up!'

Tessa tugged at her friend's sleeve. 'Elizabeth, leave her alone, everyone's looking at us and the pair of you will be reported for making a show of yourselves and your uniforms. You know what they're like back there. I'm sure they have spies on every tram and bus.'

Elizabeth paid both their fares and they moved down the tram, past Nessie, who just scowled at her sister, and continued to sulk until they all got off at the top of Edgar Street. Then she walked ahead of them, head down and hands in her pockets until she collided with a man.

'Sorry,' she mumbled from the depths of her scarf.

'Are them two behind you your sisters?'

Nessie looked up. She didn't know him and she didn't like the look of him. He was big. Very big.

'One of them is my sister, the one in the uniform.'

'Who's the other one?' he demanded.

'What do you want to know for?'

'That's my business,' he snapped.

'She's just a friend. Her name's Tessa. Tessa O'Leary.'

'Thanks, kid, now push off home,' he replied.

Nessie had walked away but before she reached the corner of Edgar Street and Fontenoy Street, she heard Elizabeth's screams. She turned swiftly but was rooted to the spot with fear. The man she'd just spoken to had hold of Tessa by the shoulders. She was fighting back with all her strength but Nessie could see it was useless. He was dragging her towards the entry between Naylor Street and Oriel Street. Elizabeth was lying on the floor, holding her right arm.

'Nessie! Nessie! Go and tell Da! Find a scuffer! He's taking Tessa away and I think he's broken my arm! Go on, Nessie! Run! Run!'

Nessie took to her heels, her face white with shock.

Despite the terrible pain in her arm, Elizabeth managed to get to her feet. She looked around for help but there was no one. Where was he taking Tessa? Who was he? She got up, wincing in pain, and slowly began to follow them down the entry between the two streets.

She could still hear Tessa's cries but they were much fainter and muffled. The only light there was came from the upstairs windows of the houses. The bottom windows were obscured by the back walls. She peered into the gloom, trying to count the number of houses, hoping to see where Tessa was being taken, but she began to feel dizzy and leaned against the wall. She had to get home! She just *had* to tell someone. He might beat Tessa or assault her or, she shivered, even kill her. What was it he'd shouted at her before he sent her sprawling? Something about someone called 'Doran'.

She could hardly put one foot in front of the other, the pain was making her feel so ill. Her progress was slow but as she turned into Naylor Street she saw someone running towards her and she burst into tears.

'Elizabeth! Elizabeth, are you hurt? Who was it? Where's Tessa?' Jack Harrison was panting.

'Oh, Da! My arm! I think it's broken and I feel . . .'

Her father lifted her gently and carried her the rest of the way to where Delia stood on the shop step waiting anxiously.

'Is she all right, Jack? What's been going on?' Nessie had come tearing into the shop screaming that a man was half killing Tessa and Elizabeth and it had been a few minutes before either herself or Jack had managed to get any sense out of her.

'She says she thinks her arm is broken. She's shocked and sick with the pain.'

Delia whipped off her shop coat. 'I'll get her to Stanley Hospital right now. I'll get a taxi.'

'Mam! Mam, he took Tessa!' Elizabeth cried.

Jack squatted down on his haunches. 'Tell me what happened – slowly, Elizabeth, slowly.'

He listened in silence to his daughter's sobbing explanation, then he got up. 'It's someone connected with Mogsey Doran!'

'Oh, Holy Mother of God! I thought we'd seen the last of him!'

'So did I. If his bloody mate harms a hair of that girl's head I'll kill him myself.'

'Elizabeth, did you see where he took her?'

'The ninth house down Oriel Street. Oh, please, please, Da, go and help Tessa! Go now! Right now, in case anything happens!'

'Delia, can you see to her? Get her to hospital and back?'

'Yes. What are *you* going to do, Jack?'

'Round up everyone in the street and go and get Tessa back,' he replied grimly. Before this night was over Mogsey Doran would be missing one friend and would be on the receiving end of such a beating that if he survived he'd be crippled for life.

Soon Delia's kitchen was crowded with grim-faced men and lads of all ages. They had their own code of morals, their own way of handing out justice. To snatch a young girl like Tessa literally off the street and then drag her to some house and do God alone knew what to her, just because her father owed a few pounds, came high on their list of crimes requiring violent retribution.

'So you reckon it's number nine, Jack?' Frank Flynn asked.

Jack nodded. Richie was sitting white-faced and rigid with fear for his daughter. He'd thought all that was behind them. Nothing had been heard from Mogsey since that last time he'd shown his face in Naylor Street. Now he'd got Tessa, his lovely, caring, hard-working Tessa.

'Right then, you lot come with me, the rest of you go with Frank. You go to the back door, we'll go to the front,' Jack instructed.

'What if the bastard's got a lookout?' Mick Collins asked.

'He's right, Jack. This has all been carefully planned. He'd be a bloody fool not to have someone, a couple of kids maybe, to watch the street and the entry,' Frank Flynn replied.

'Then we'll go first, Frank. I'll take the street, you take the jigger. Then the rest of you follow, in twos or threes if necessary. Does anyone know anyone who lives in Oriel Street?'

'No one really well,' Billy Keegan answered. 'Fred Jessup sometimes comes into the Globe. I only know him to nod to. Do you think Doran might have planted some of his cronies in the street?'

'No. There might be another couple of fellers with him tonight but we'd have heard if half the street had new lodgers. You know what the women are like for jangling.'

'Do you think that Mogsey feller will be with this bloke?' Billy asked.

'I don't know but my guess is that he won't. Too bloody yellow-bellied to come himself after last time. But if he's not, then we'll all have to go down to the Holy Land. Mind, I expect there'll be more than one thug holed up there.'

'We don't want no trouble with the scuffers, Jack,' Mick Collins warned.

'There won't be, but if the worst comes to the worst we'll drag whoever's involved into Rose Hill nick. When they know what's happened they'll turn a blind eye to any "injuries". I think they call it "Resisting Arrest", and they'll add a few of their own "injuries". One way or another they'll get what's coming. I hope Doran paid them well.'

'What about . . . him?' Frank Flynn enquired in a low voice, jerking his head in Richie's direction.

Jack shook his head. 'Leave him here until we get back. Where's that no-mark of a bloody son of his?'

'God knows. Whoever knows when that lad's at home or what he's up to?' Billy answered scathingly.

'What am I supposed to be up to?' Colin asked, pushing his

127

way through the group towards his father. There'd been no one in the house when he'd arrived home and he'd gone to see Eileen, who had told him he'd better get along to the Harrisons' as something had happened to Tessa.

'God, 'e's like the bloody Scarlet Pimpernel, comes an' goes an' yer never see nor 'ear him,' Frank remarked.

'Mogsey Doran's hard case snatched your Tessa on her way home. He's holed up in number nine, Oriel Street. We're just going to get her.'

Even Colin was stunned.

'Look at the gob on him. He's goin' ter be as useful as his bloody da,' Billy said.

'Stay here and see to your da, lad. Delia's gone to the hospital with our Elizabeth. That feller broke her arm when she tried to help Tessa. Nessie! Nessie! Come down here and make some hot sweet tea for Mr O'Leary and his lad,' Jack cried from the bottom of the stairs.

A white-faced and still shaking Nessie crept down in time to see them all leave. Oh, this was terrible! Terrible! They'd never believe her at school. At that thought some of the fear and shock left her and a gleam appeared in her eyes. If, or rather when they got Tessa back she'd have a great tale to tell, particularly to that Patricia Armstrong who was so snooty. And all because she'd stood patiently, if stupidly, waiting for a tram to come along.

At the top of Oriel Street Jack met a police sergeant and constable. The street was almost deserted. As he walked towards them he saw small groups of men appear from the bottom of the street. They either leaned against the corners of the intersecting streets or stopped and stood under the streetlamps, ostensibly discussing something important.

'Evening, Officers,' Jack greeted them both politely.

'Good evening, sir. Anything we can help you with?' the sergeant asked.

'Not really, thanks. You're new, I haven't seen you before.'

'Been here a couple of months. We were called to a disturbance.'

'What kind of "disturbance"?' Jack asked.

'The non-existent kind. The house where it was supposed to be was in darkness – not a sound from inside and not a soul to be seen either.'

Jack shook his head. 'Bad that. Wasting police time.'

'I pointed that out to the neighbour who made the complaint.'

He looked up and down the street. 'Well, don't let us detain you. A bit of business, is it?'

Jack nodded.

'Right then, Constable, let's be on our way.'

They know, Jack thought. They damned well know that we're up to something. They couldn't have helped notice the number of men who had suddenly appeared.

The pair were well out of sight by the time the others joined him.

'Better make it quick. God knows what they're doing to that girl. Someone complained about a disturbance.'

'What did those two say?' Frank asked.

'Nothing much. They know something is going on. Let's get a move on. It must have been Tessa screaming that the neighbour complained about.'

'Fine bloody carry-on! What's up with the fellers in this street that they hear a girl screaming and do nothing except call in the bloody scuffers? I'll bloody break every bone in his body if he's laid a finger on that girl,' Frank confirmed, thinking of his own daughter Maureen.

Tessa was huddled up on the floor in a corner of the dark kitchen, sobbing quietly. She had never been so afraid in her life. When she'd been dragged in and flung across the floor she'd got up and had flown at her captor like a vixen, screaming as loud as she could and using her feet, nails and teeth. Then a pain had exploded in her head as a blow sent her reeling and she'd crawled into the corner. She could feel her lip swelling and taste the saltiness of her blood. The whole side of her face was throbbing but the pain was the least of her worries. What were they going to do with her? Who were they? There was more than one, she'd heard them talking. Then there had come a loud hammering on the front door. She'd tried to get up and shout but a large hand smelling of dirt and tobacco had almost suffocated her. Eventually after the hammering had brought no results the hand was removed and she had been kicked back to the corner. Her only hope was Elizabeth, but as she'd fought and kicked she'd seen her friend sent sprawling and heard her screams of agony. She remembered that Nessie had been walking ahead. Would Nessie have run home? She would certainly tell her Mam and Dad that Elizabeth was hurt. Would Elizabeth be able to tell them where she was? She didn't really know herself. It had all happened so quickly that she couldn't remember how long it had been before she'd been thrown into this house. Oh, Mam! Mam! If you can hear me, help me! Please, Mam! Don't let them hurt me! Let Elizabeth have got home! She repeated the words silently over and over again.

She didn't know how long she'd been there – an hour, two, three? – when she heard the roar and the crash of the back door as it was kicked open. She tried to scream and flatten herself further against the wall. Now what? Oh, Holy Mother, what was going to happen to her now?

'She's in here!' Frank Flynn roared and simultaneously she heard the shouts and the splintering of wood as the front door received the same treatment as the back.

Then she was lifted gently.

'Tessa, luv, are you hurt?'

She broke down helplessly as she recognised Jack Harrison's voice. She was safe. They'd come to find her.

'All right now, luv, it's all over. We've a bit of business to attend to here, then I'll take you home.'

She sat on the floor with her hands over her ears as the whole house erupted into a cacophony of shouts, curses, yells and screams of pain, then she was being lifted gently up in a pair of strong arms.

'Take her home, Frank. Our Delia should be back from the hospital by now and if I meet any scuffers it might be awkward to explain why we're carrying the poor kid home.'

Frank nodded. Their work here was finished. All the men were drifting out through the back door and down the jigger.

Jack closed the front door as best he could and thought how strange it was that there were no other doors open or people out on their steps to see what was going on. It was also rare to find an unoccupied house in this area. Probably the occupants had been paid to 'go on a bit of a trip'. Maybe all the neighbours had been threatened – but that was unlikely to have much effect in this area and someone *had* complained.

He rubbed his right hand ruefully. His knuckles were skinned and his shoulder was aching but it was nothing to the state those three were in. He smiled with grim satisfaction. Doran had been fool enough to come too. He probably intended to send word to Richie, demanding his money for Tessa's safe return. Well, he'd send no one any kind of message now. Frank Flynn had stamped on both his hands as he'd sprawled on the floor. Mick Collins had finished the job with a heavy and well-aimed kick of his booted foot to the spine. Doran might never walk again and he doubted that the other two would either. They hadn't put up much of a fight, realising that the odds were against them. They were both lying sprawled in the lobby.

He saw the two policemen as he reached the top of the street.

'Finished your "bit of business"?' the sergeant asked pleasantly, his gaze taking in the state of Jack's clothing and the beginnings of a black eye.

'Yes, that's right, thanks. All accounted for.'

'Anything we can do?'

'Send for an ambulance. I think there's someone in number nine who might need one.'

The sergeant nodded slowly but the constable looked perturbed. 'An ambulance? Sarge, hadn't we better—'

'No, lad. There's nothing to worry about. When you've been on the job for as long as I have you know about these things. It's just letting yourself in for a mountain of paperwork. Inquiries, statements, interviewing the entire street and getting no co-operation or thanks.' He addressed Jack again. 'I presume the "patient" won't be pressing charges?'

'I can safely say he won't. None of them will.'

'More than one.'

'Right. Well, goodnight again.'

Jack nodded and walked on. On his own the young constable could have made things very awkward for them. Thank God the older man knew the way things were done around here. They looked after their own.

Delia was back with a very subdued Nessie and a worried Elizabeth whose arm was in plaster up to her elbow.

'It's her wrist. It will take time to heal. What happened?'

Both Richie and Colin got to their feet.

'Where is she? What have they done to her?' Richie pleaded. All the time he'd sat there alone, save for a very quiet and subdued Colin, he'd prayed that Tessa would come back unhurt. He was riddled with guilt and fear. It was all his fault and he'd never forgive himself ever. If . . . if anything had happened to her he'd fling himself into the river. He should have done without his beer and his smokes, walked to and from work, in fact anything that would save money to pay off that bloody loan. He felt numb, he couldn't bear to think what was happening to Tessa.

Colin had felt afraid too. More trouble. It was all his da ever seemed to do – cause trouble that he didn't seem to be able to sort out. He'd left it for all the other fellers in the street to attend to. He'd never really had much respect for his father and now his opinion of Richie sank even lower.

'It's all right, Delia, luv, Tessa's fine. She's got a cut lip and a very sore face and she's been through a terrible ordeal, but she'll get over it. I doubt whether those three will.'

'Three!' Delia cried.

'Aye, Doran himself and two hard cases. All on their way to hospital by now I shouldn't wonder.'

'Jack, did anyone see you . . . any of you?'

'No. I think the neighbours knew something and stayed out of sight.' He didn't tell her about the police, that would really have worried her.

Elizabeth got up off the sofa, tears in her eyes as Frank Flynn carried Tessa in.

'Oh, Tessa, luv!' Richie cried.

'She's not too bad, Richie. Shock, a cut lip, a bruised face.'

'I'm going for Dr Duncan,' Delia announced, snatching her coat from the hook on the wall.

'I don't think there's any need for that, luv. There's nothing broken. I'm certain of it.'

'Oh, Tessa, Tessa, I'm sorry. I'm sorry, luv! It's all my fault!' Richie took her in his arms and buried his face in her hair to hide his tears.

Tessa managed a smile as she hugged him. 'It's not your fault, Da . . . It's all over now.'

'It is. None of them can walk. This time we did the job properly. We should have done it the first time.'

'Well, let's not start on that, Jack. Let me see to her, she's staying here tonight. She can share our bed with Elizabeth. I'll double up with Nessie and you can have Elizabeth's bed.'

Delia knew that Tessa and Elizabeth would both draw comfort from each other and she herself would be there on hand should Nessie wake up with nightmares. This was something to give an adult nightmares, let alone an eleven-year-old child.

Chapter Fourteen

It would take some time for Tessa to get over her injuries and her fright. She was so exhausted by her ordeal that as soon as she'd laid her head on the pillow in Delia and Jack's warm and comfortable bed, she was asleep. Both she and Elizabeth had been given hot sweet tea with a drop of whisky in it. It helped dull the aches and pains.

Delia went herself to see Mother Superior to explain why Elizabeth would not be in school for quite a while and why Tessa wouldn't be back at work until the beginning of the following week. She'd had the doctor out to both of them, despite all their protestations, although there wasn't much he could tell her that she didn't already know: that it would take time for both of them to get over it.

To his questions about how the girls had sustained their injuries she'd replied that they had both been fooling around and had slipped on the icy cobbles and had fallen heavily and awkwardly. Knowing that if he suspected any foul play he would report it to the police, she made a great show of being furious that girls of their age had been acting like five-year-olds.

He advised an aspirin from time to time for the pain both in Elizabeth's arm and Tessa's bruised face and cut lip.

'That was five shillings wasted. He only told me what I already knew, that they were shocked and hurt,' she told Eileen later that day.

'I don't know why you put up with that feller, I don't. Five shillings just to come out and see them! 'E's got a nerve.'

'I suppose it's his professional opinion you have to pay for, and his time.'

'Some professional opinion! Doling out aspirins!' Eileen had remarked before getting back to the subject that engrossed the entire street: Tessa's abductors. 'Them moneylenders should all be horsewhipped and flung in Walton Jail. Taking advantage of people's troubles! Do you remember that one from Paul Street – Molly Kirkbride? She was in such a state that she borrowed four pounds off one of them and do you know 'ow much she actually paid back? Nearly twenty and it took 'er years. 'Im out of work, 'er with five kids an' her ma-in-law living with them. I tell you,

Delia, they all need bloody 'orsewhipping!'

'Well, at least that lot got what was coming. Now, what can I get you?'

Mother Superior did not view the situation with sympathy, nor could she understand why a woman like Delia Harrison and her family had got mixed up with the likes of the O'Learys. She was a shrewd woman and not a sight nor sound escaped her. Brief snatches of conversation from both the kitchen and the classroom had enabled her to sum up the situation.

The girl, Tessa, worked diligently, was quiet and biddable, always punctual and grateful for any help. She was also devout – but she was still a common little slummy. And of course the Harrisons, who now had two daughters at the school, were not the usual type of parents who sent their daughters here. They were working class and nearly everyone else's parents were professional people or had a private income.

'You do realise, Mrs Harrison, that this is a crucial time for Elizabeth,' she stressed. 'She will be taking her exams this year and the results are very very important if she's to go into the lower sixth form.'

'Oh, I do realise that, Mother. I'll make sure that the time she is off will not be wasted. She will study. Would it be at all possible for books to be sent home? Vanessa could bring them and take back the completed work.'

The woman was determined at least, the nun thought. 'I think that can be arranged. But how will she be able to cope with the written work?'

Delia thought for a minute. 'Would it be acceptable if she . . . read it out and either myself or my husband were to actually write it down for her?'

'You mean dictation? It's highly irregular.'

'I realise that but as you've just said, Mother, this is an important time for Elizabeth.'

The nun pressed the fingertips of both hands together and pursed her lips. 'You would have to sign to say that it is completely Elizabeth's work. That there has been no assistance with grammar, spelling or input from any other person.'

Delia flushed a little. Just what kind of parents did the nun think her daughter had: cheats?

'Of course. We wouldn't have it any other way,' she replied with a cold edge to her voice.

All the way home it irritated her. There was always the same attitude and it boiled down to the fact that the nun just didn't want the daughters of shopkeepers and the like in her precious school. Well, next time she wrote to Margaret she'd tell her. Her sister had been widowed for fifteen years and Lars Van Holste had been a rich man. She'd met him on the ship carrying her to New York and had been married a month later. Everyone in the family had been utterly surprised. Margaret wasn't a beauty but she had a certain attraction and a lively personality. Over the years, in her letters, Delia had come to realise that her sister was a very shrewd woman. Not calculating and unfeeling, but she kept an eye on her finances and watched her shares carefully. Oh, Margaret would write to Mother Superior, pointing out that her nieces should have the best education and treatment that money could buy, and if Notre Dame couldn't or wouldn't supply that graciously, then there were other establishments that most certainly would.

She was still annoyed when she got home. Jack was in the shop, which was empty.

'Sometimes I don't know how I keep my temper with that woman. I *know* she's taken Holy Orders but she's such a snob! I thought pride came high up on the list of the seven deadly sins.'

'It does. What did she say to upset you?'

'Nothing. Well, not in so many words. It's just her attitude. Come through while I put the kettle on, we'll hear the bell if we have a customer. I'm frozen.'

Both Tessa and Elizabeth were in the kitchen. 'What did the old dragon say?' Elizabeth asked her mother.

'That will do from you, milady! You just remember she's a nun and deserves respect.' Under her breath she asked God to forgive her for her hypocrisy. 'You are to do your schoolwork at home and either your da or me will write out the answers. It's all been arranged. You've got to pass your exams or your aunt will not be very pleased and neither will I. Oh, damn! There's the shop bell. You can make your da and me a cup of tea.'

'How can I?' Elizabeth asked.

'I'll do it,' Tessa offered 'And I'll bring it out to you, Mrs Harrison.'

Delia nodded her thanks as she donned her shop coat and followed her husband through the door. It was the lunchtime rush. There were not many people around here who could shop for a week all at the same time. They shopped from day to day or even meal to meal.

'I thought I was going to get out of doing any work.'

'Don't be daft. You didn't honestly think they'd let you sit around all day reading those love stories you've always got your head in?'

'Well, I didn't think I'd have to do homework. I'll have to know it all really well if one of them is going to write it out for me. I wonder how she managed to get them to agree to that?'

'It doesn't matter how.' Tessa filled the teapot and left the tea to brew. 'You're going to have to tell them soon about not wanting to stay at school.'

'I know, but I'll have to take my exams just the same. I can't leave without *anything*.'

'Well, I don't envy you. Why don't you want to be a teacher? It's a really good job. It's a profession. Just think how terrified everyone is of their teachers.'

'I know but I'm fed up with school! I really *hate* it and I don't like kids at all. I can't help that. I'd make a terrible teacher and ruin God knows how many kids' educations.'

'Well you're going to have to say all that to your mam and da.'

Elizabeth pulled a rueful face and let her breath out slowly. 'I know. Maybe I'd better tell them tonight. Will you stay with me?'

'What good would that do? I can't say anything to help because I think you're mad to pass up a chance like that.'

'I know, but just *be* there. That will help.'

Tessa nodded. 'Oh, all right then. But I'd better pour the tea and then go back home. The fire will be almost out by now and if it is I'll have a terrible time getting it going again.'

All afternoon Elizabeth rehearsed what she was going to say but no matter how she put it, she knew it wouldn't make things any better. She had to steel herself for an almighty row, but one she fully intended to win because she had very different plans for her future.

Nessie came home laden with text books and exercise books.

'It's all written on a piece of paper and I'm to take back the Geography and Maths tomorrow,' she informed her sister with some satisfaction. She'd been the centre of attention all lunchtime and at breaks too. Everyone wanted to hear every detail and for once she felt important and confident.

Of course she didn't tell them about what her da and the others had done, she told them it was the police, guided by Elizabeth's information, who had found Tessa and brought her home. Nessie was far from stupid.

Elizabeth groaned. 'I'd forgotten that flaming Geography test. I can never get the trade winds right and what use is it anyway? I'm never likely to go anywhere near the southern hemisphere or even the Equator.'

'Well, it's got to be done by morning,' Nessie replied firmly.

'Go and get Tessa for me will you, Nessie?'

'What for? She certainly won't know anything about winds of any kind and besides, it's nearly teatime.'

'I'd forgotten that. Just go and ask her to come down straight after tea.'

'What will you give me?' Nessie demanded.

'I'll give you a clout with this plaster on my arm. Go on, Mam won't mind.'

Nessie went off in a huff, slamming the scullery door behind her.

When the meal was served Elizabeth hardly ate anything. Delia didn't press her or complain, thinking she was still in shock. She pushed the food around on her plate, her stomach churning. But she *had* to do it, she just *had* to.

She usually helped her mam to clear away and wash up but now all she could do was clear the table with her left hand. She jumped nervously as she heard Tessa's voice in the shop.

'Is everything all right at home, Tessa?' Delia asked as she folded the tablecloth and put it into one of the drawers of the dresser.

'Yes, thanks. They've all had their tea and I've washed up. Our Jimmy's gone next door, as usual, and our Colin's gone out, as usual. Mrs Greely called on her way to work.'

Delia raised her eyebrows. 'As usual!'

'Is your hand still hurting?' Tessa asked Elizabeth.

'It sort of throbs. Does your mouth hurt?'

'Only when I try to smile.' Tessa sat down on the sofa beside Elizabeth and jabbed her friend in the ribs with her elbow.

Elizabeth took a deep breath. Her whole future would be decided in the next half-hour.

'Mam, sit down. There's something I want to say to you.'

Delia looked at her quizzically. 'What?'

'Sit down, please.'

'Holy Mother of God, is it that bad?'

'I suppose it is, in a way. I . . . after . . . after my exams I'm not going back to school and I don't care how much you rant and rave, Mam, I mean it. I don't want to become a teacher. I'd be terrible. I'd ruin all the kids' lives and that wouldn't be fair. In fact it would be almost a crime and definitely a sin.'

Delia's eyes narrowed. She was taken aback but she should have seen this coming.

'I think this is something your father should hear. I'll be back.'

As she went into the shop Elizabeth looked pleadingly at Tessa.

'There's nothing I can say,' Tessa hissed.

When Delia returned with Jack in tow, Elizabeth's resolve wavered. They both looked very grim.

'So, what's all this your mother's just told me?' Jack demanded.

'Da, I know it's not what you want for me, what anyone wants for me . . .'

'No, it isn't and especially not your Aunty Margaret! Do you realise just how much money has been spent on educating you? It runs into hundreds of pounds and you want to throw it all away.'

'Mam, I don't want to throw it all away! I *will* have qualifications.'

'And just what, may I ask, do you intend to do for a job?'

'I . . . I want to be a hairdresser!'

'A *what*!' Delia could hardly believe her ears.

'A hairdresser. All properly trained with an apprenticeship. You know I'm good at it, Mam.'

'I don't care how good you are at it, you are *not* going to be a hairdresser!' Delia shouted, then thought fleetingly of just what her neighbours and customers would say.

'Well, I'm *not* going back to school either!' Elizabeth yelled back.

Tessa cringed.

'She's got books, Mam,' said Nessie triumphantly. 'I've seen her with *The Art and Craft of Hairdressing*. She hides it in the bottom of her wardrobe. Under that box she's got her Communion dress in.'

'You sly sneaking little tell-tale, Nessie!' Elizabeth yelled.

'Nessie, that will be enough! Take your own homework upstairs and don't come down until we've sorted this out,' Jack said in a voice that brooked no argument.

'Oh, what am I to do with her, Jack? A hairdresser? A *hairdresser* of all things, for God's sake! We had such plans for her. What am I going to tell our Margaret?' Delia clasped her hands as if in supplication.

'Elizabeth, for the last time I'm telling you that you *will* continue your education.'

'I *won't*, Da! I *won't* do it! I'm not going back there. I'll leave home, run away, before I'll go back. And I'll keep running away no matter how many times I'm brought back. I . . . I'll even go to a House of Correction for Girls! I *will*!' Elizabeth was near to tears but she meant what she said.

Jack looked at her and knew she wasn't just bluffing or making idle threats. She could be very very stubborn at times.

Delia sat down at the table, covering her eyes with her hands. What had got into Elizabeth? She knew, she'd always known what was planned for her. Maybe it had something to do with Tessa. She wondered if she should have allowed the friendship to develop. But she'd thought that if Elizabeth went on to Teacher Training College the gulf between them would widen and they would grow apart. She didn't think that Tessa had deliberately tried to manipulate Elizabeth, if anything it would be the opposite way round; she knew her daughter. Oh, things were such a mess. The events of the last few days had been bad enough, and now this!

There was silence in the room, broken only by the ticking of the clock on the dresser. Tessa twisted her hands helplessly and Elizabeth held her breath.

At last her father spoke. 'If you are so determined that you would leave your home and shame us by being placed in an institution for wayward girls, then perhaps some enquiries should be made about an apprenticeship.'

'Jack, are you mad!' Delia cried.

He shook his head and gestured her to remain calm and silent.

Elizabeth seized the opportunity. 'I'd be so grateful, Da, really I would. It's . . . it's my whole life I'm thinking of and I *have* thought about it, hard.'

'She . . . she does have talent . . .' Tessa said quietly and hesitantly.

Jack nodded curtly.

'What am I going to say to our Margaret, just tell me that? After all she's done! After all the money she's sent! Hundreds of pounds! And that ungrateful niece of hers has thrown it all back in her face!'

'Tell her the truth, Delia. You never know. Perhaps, in time, Elizabeth might have her own salon. Nessie might be the one who becomes a teacher, who knows?'

It was Delia's turn to shake her head. He'd taken Elizabeth's side. She didn't understand him or his thinking. Apprenticeships; salons; Nessie being a teacher. Nessie wasn't half as clever as Elizabeth, she had to work so much harder and Elizabeth was throwing everything away!

'Elizabeth,' Jack went on, 'I want your solemn word that you'll work hard for these exams. That you'll matriculate with good marks.'

A great wave of relief and gratitude surged through Elizabeth. 'Oh, Da, I *will*! I promise I'll do really well. Do you . . . do you mean it about an apprenticeship?'

'Well, if it's what you really want I suppose I do. But one slip-up, one set of bad marks and it's back you'll go into the lower sixth.'

Delia groaned and gave up the fight. She was seething inside and she'd give Jack a piece of her mind when the girls were in bed.

Sensing that her presence was adding to the friction between her parents Elizabeth went back to Tessa's house.

'I did it! I really did it!' she cried as she plumped herself down on the sofa. The house was empty; Tessa's da had gone to the pub.

'I never expected you'd be allowed to be a hairdresser. Wasn't your da great?'

'Oh yes, though I bet he's getting the length of Mam's tongue now. He knew I meant it, you see.'

Tessa was incredulous. 'Would you *really* have left home? Run away?'

'Of course I would. Da knew that. And I'd keep on running away until I got my own way. I'd *hate* to have to go to some terrible institution but I'd have gone.'

'You are the most determined, stubborn and often stupid person I've ever met, Elizabeth Harrison.'

'I know but now perhaps I'll get a bit of peace. It looks as though our Nessie's future will be concentrated on from today.'

'You've got what you wanted,' Tessa said wistfully. 'I won't be so lucky.'

'Why not? I'll help you, and you can ask Sister Bernadette too. You're always saying she's a real lady. She'll teach you manners and how to speak to people and things like that.'

'But wouldn't I need some qualifications? I haven't got any.'

Elizabeth turned her attention to Tessa's plight. 'I can't see them wanting much. I mean, all stewardesses do is look after people and you can do that. You've been looking after the family ever since your mam died. Why don't you go and ask at the shipping offices just what you'll need – when you feel better, that is?'

'Will you come with me? I'd be terrified.'

'Of course. You helped me and what are friends for?'

Tessa felt hopeful, really hopeful now. Sister Bernadette would teach her the things she would need to know and what Elizabeth had said about looking after people was true. If she got a good reference from the Convent that would surely be as good as a qualification.

Delia was still tight-lipped and fuming but she had agreed to write to the large hairdressing establishments to see how much an apprenticeship would cost. Two days later Tessa and Elizabeth both got the tram into town.

It was a clear but windy day and Elizabeth held on to her hat with her left hand. Her right arm was in a sling and her coat was buttoned over it. Tessa looked neat and tidy in her grey coat and red scarf, mittens and tam-o'-shanter.

'Which one shall we start with?' Elizabeth had asked.

They'd made a list of the most likely shipping lines who carried passengers and therefore stewardesses: Cunard, Canadian Pacific and Elder Dempster Line. They'd also looked up in the atlas just where the ships of those lines sailed to. Cunard went to New York and sometimes cruised around the West Indies. Canadian Pacific sailed to Canada, Australia and the Far East, and Elder Dempster plyed to and from the west coast of Africa. The latter was also the 'mail' shipping line.

'Elder Dempster. They're not as big as the others. I might stand more of a chance with them.'

They got off the tram outside the Town Hall and walked down Water Street. India Buildings was at the bottom of the road, part of it facing the Pier Head.

The offices of the Elder Dempster Steam Ship Company were on the second floor and they climbed the stairs, shunning the lift. As Tessa said, she was scared enough already and she'd never been in a lift in her life. When they reached their destination Elizabeth pushed open the door that led to the reception area.

'Go on, just ask them plainly. I'll wait here.'

Tessa looked very nervous and bit her lip.

'Stop that! Look confident,' Elizabeth hissed.

Tessa made her way to the polished counter where a middle-aged man was writing in a large, heavy book. 'Yes, miss, can I help?' he asked genially.

'I . . . I . . . hope so, sir.'

'If it's about the next ship bound for Dakar I can give you an itinerary.'

'No, no, it's . . . nothing like that. I . . . I want to be a stewardess

141

and I'd like . . . to . . . know . . .' Her nerves got the better of her and she fell silent.

He smiled at her. 'How old are you?'

'Sixteen, sir. I've worked in a convent for a year so I'm used to hard work and I've looked after my family since my mam died.'

'It's not that. You can't go away to sea until you're at least eighteen. Twenty-one with some companies.'

'Oh.' Tessa was disappointed.

'Come back when you're a couple of years older and I'm sure we can do something.'

She nodded her thanks, turned away and walked to where Elizabeth was waiting.

'Well?'

'I can't go yet.'

'What do you mean – yet?'

'I'm not old enough. I've got to be at least eighteen.'

'That's not fair! They take lads on at fourteen and sixteen – look at Johnny, he's been with Cunard for over a year now.'

'Well, that's what he said.'

'Oh, typical! One rule for them and another for us.'

'Oh, Elizabeth, get off your soap box.' Tessa was disappointed and dejected. It had taken so much courage just to come and ask.

Once outside they walked back down Water Street to the Pier Head.

As usual the river was busy. There were ships tied up at the Landing Stage, the ferries were criss-crossing the choppy grey water, the dredgers moved slowly up and down and there were ships anchored mid-river, waiting to come alongside the Stage.

Tessa sighed as she stood, hands on the railings, looking towards the estuary.

'Don't be disappointed, Tessa, you've got two years to learn all kinds of things. Sister Bernardette and even Sister Augustine would help you. I'm sure when you're eighteen they'll take you on at once.'

'Do you think so, really?'

'I *do*.'

Tessa didn't reply. She looked pensive. I'll do it, Mam. I really will. You'll be proud of me, I swear it. I'll keep my promise, she said to herself. When she at last turned away there were tears in her eyes. Could a girl from the slums really get on in life? Could an ignorant girl like her who had come to Naylor Street in rags rise one day to the position of Chief Stewardess?

Chapter Fifteen

Delia had a shop full; it was late on a typically showery April afternoon and this was the teatime rush. Jack hadn't been feeling too well all day and she'd made him rest as much as possible. There was little Elizabeth could do to help her, with her arm still in plaster, and besides, she had a great deal of reading and learning by rote to do.

'Right, who's next?' she asked briskly, although she felt far from business-like. She'd been on her feet more or less since seven that morning and her back, feet and calves were aching. She also had the beginnings of a headache and wondered if she was sickening for something. Both she and Jack worked very hard. The only day she had off was Sunday and quite often people came to the back door asking for whatever it was they'd run out of. She looked questioningly at those nearest the counter.

'Well, I am but you go before me, Maisie, your feller gets 'ome before mine,' Katie Collins said generously. She'd had a bad week and money was very tight but she didn't want Maisie Keegan to see the few bits she could afford. She didn't mind the other customers knowing, not even Eileen Flynn, but Maisie had a mouth like the Mersey tunnel and it would be all around the parish that Mick Collins had drunk the housekeeping again.

'I'll 'ave a quarter of boiled 'am, Delia, luv, an' 'alf a pound of them tomatoes.'

'Boiled 'am on a Thursday? 'Ave yer come into some money then, Maisie?' Eileen asked.

'No, but I'm goin' ter our Rita's ternight, 'er feller is due 'ome from sea an yer know what she's like at 'ousework. That feller of 'ers is dead fussy. Always goin' on about clutter, an' not puttin' things away, an' beds not made proper, like. Yer can't 'alf tell 'e's a flamin' steward. Do yer know what the latest trick is?' Maisie stopped to make sure everyone was giving their full attention. Delia sighed heavily. It was no use trying to rush Maisie.

'Well, go on then, Maisie, girl, we 'aven't got all night,' Eileen urged.

Maisie straightened her shoulders and patted her hair, well satisfied by the look of avid curiosity on her neighbours' faces. 'He won't 'ave no crusts on the butties!'

'Why not?' Katie demanded.

''As ter 'ave them all cut off. 'E says it ain't "proper" to 'ave them on "sandwiches" – if yer please.'

'It's a flaming sin that! Wasting good food,' Eileen remarked – with some justification, Delia thought.

'I've got to say I agree with you. Working as a first-class steward with Cunard has gone to his head.'

'That's just what I said ter our Rita. "Rita," I said, "tell 'im that iffen 'e wants ter carry on like that yer want more of an allotment left yer." But she won't. 'E 'as 'er demented when 'e's on leave, she's always glad ter see the back of 'im an' I can't say I blame 'er. So I'm goin' ter give 'er an 'and, like. But I can't leave my lot without something ter eat.'

Privately, Delia thought that a quarter of boiled ham and a few tomatoes wasn't much to leave for a man and his two sons when they got in from work and that Maisie should leave her sister to cope with her husband and the odd ways he had.

'Mick was saying that the news isn't too good,' Katie Collins said conversationally.

'What news?' Eileen demanded.

'That feller with the funny name, you know, the Minister for War. 'E was on the wireless.'

'You 'aven't gorra wireless.'

'I'm tellin yer what some feller what's got a wireless set said ter Mick,' Katie said sharply in reply to Maisie's comment.

'Oh, God help us all! Tell me it's not going to start all over again,' Delia said, looking around the shop. There was a momentary lull; all the women present had lost fathers, uncles, brothers and cousins in the last war. Delia herself had lost both her elder brothers in the mass slaughter that had been the battle of the Somme.

'At least that fightin' in Spain is over.' Maisie broke the silence. 'That's *good* news anyway.' She cast a disparaging glance at Katie. Everyone knew that war was drawing closer but no one wanted to think about it.

'Well, the government have said that the Territorial Army is goin' ter be doubled and there are more arms factories to be built an' trainin' camps and 'undreds of thousands of uniforms made, an' the Corporation is givin' out air-raid shelters ter nearly everyone, except us,' said Katie.

'Why not us?' Maisie asked indignantly.

'Because we 'aven't got anywhere ter put them. They won't fit into a yard, you've got to 'ave a birrof a garden.'

'What are we supposed to do then?' Eileen was just as indignant.

'We're to go to municipal shelters, so they say, or cellars, if you've got one.'

'God, them 'ouses that 'ave got cellars 'ave families livin in them! You'd be crushed to bits.'

''E also said they were goin' ter ev-evacuate all the kids.' Katie stumbled with the unfamiliar word.

'If I were you, Katie, I'd be telling Mick not to be taking so much notice of the wireless or wasting his money on flaming newspapers. We don't *want* another war and we don't want to hear about that Hitler or the other one, the Italian feller that's got up like a toy soldier with all that gold braid on his uniform – Mussolini. We've enough on our plates to cope with. Is that it, Maisie, or is there anything else?' Delia finished.

'No, that's all, luv.'

'One and fivepence, then. Do you want it on the slate?'

'If you don't mind, Delia. 'E gets paid termorrer, I'll settle up then.'

Delia reached under the counter and brought out a large book. She opened it at the page that read 'Keegan. Number 16' and added the amount to the one already owing.

'Now, Katie, it's you and we'd better get a move on.'

When things eventually quietened down Delia breathed a sigh of relief and went through into the kitchen where Elizabeth was reading a book. Jack was there too, looking as if he was in for a heavy cold or a dose of bronchitis.

'I'm worn out. Why do they always have to come in together? Can't they stagger it a bit? And Maisie Keegan was full of herself as usual. Some tale about their Rita and her husband. Katie Collins was full of her usual doom and gloom too.'

'Oh, aye, what is it now?'

'Mick has been listening to someone's wireless and reading things out to her from the paper too by the sound of it.' Delia put the kettle on the gas ring.

'What things?'

'Things I don't want to know about. Arms factories, training camps, air-raid shelters.'

Elizabeth looked up. 'Is there going to be a war, Mam?'

'I hope not. Dear God, I hope not. You've never been through one, I have.' Elizabeth followed her mother's gaze to the photographs of her dead uncles on the dresser.

Jack shook his head. It was growing more and more likely. He'd read that eighty thousand air-raid shelters were being distributed each week. If the bombing of innocent civilians was likely, as had happened in Spain, then they'd need them all. And if those two maniac dictators were power mad and determined to get themselves Empires, like Britain had, then who knew where it would end?

'Well, thank God we've no sons and that you're too old, Jack.'

'That's just what a feller wants to hear when he's feeling like death warmed up,' Jack said mournfully.

Delia shook her head as she made the tea but before she could even pour it out the shop bell rang tinnily.

'Oh, blast! Elizabeth, do you think you can see who it is while I get a few sips of tea?'

'Mam, I'm supposed to be learning this.'

'I'll go, Mam. I'll come and tell you who it is and what they want. It can't be *that* hard to weigh out sugar and tea and stuff,' Nessie offered, thinking of the pile of homework she herself had to do and how best to postpone it.

'All right, Nessie. I suppose you can manage. I'll be out in five minutes.'

Nessie found May Greely in the shop.

'It's all right, Nessie, there's nothing I need. I've come to see your mam.'

'Oh,' Nessie replied rather dejectedly. 'You'd better come through.'

Delia was surprised. 'May! What's wrong? Why aren't you on your way to work?'

'I am. I told him I wouldn't be in until five. There's something I want to tell you. Do you think Elizabeth could go to Tessa's? Our Ginny's over there.'

'Of course she can if it's that important.'

'It is.'

Delia looked at her closely, It didn't look like trouble, May didn't seem upset.

'Nessie, will you go back out into the shop, please? Elizabeth, put that away and go to Tessa's.'

Both Elizabeth and Nessie looked startled and very curious.

'You keep as near to the door as you can, Nessie. See what you can hear,' Elizabeth whispered once they were into the shop. 'Mam, what time am I supposed to come back?' she shouted.

'In half an hour,' came the muffled reply.

Nessie could hardly contain her curiosity. 'I wonder what's up?'

'I don't know, just keep listening and hope no one comes in and wants serving,' Elizabeth answered.

For once they were of the same mind and there wasn't an argument.

When Elizabeth walked into Tessa's kitchen she stopped dead. Tessa and Ginny were sitting on the sofa; both were pale and looked dazed.

'What's up with you two?'

'I . . . I just don't believe it,' Ginny said, shaking her head.

'Believe what?' Elizabeth demanded.

'Da . . . Da's going to—'

'Marry my mam,' Ginny interrupted Tessa.

Elizabeth's mouth formed an 'O' of surprise. She was speechless.

'They told us just before Da went out and Mrs Greely went to . . .' Tessa also shook her head in disbelief. It still hadn't really sunk in.

Elizabeth had regained her composure. 'So that's what your mam wanted to talk to my mam about, Ginny. I got chased along here and our Nessie is minding the shop.'

'How could he? How could he, Elizabeth? Mam . . . Mam's only been dead a year!' Tessa cried.

Elizabeth pulled a small stool from its place by the range and sat in front of the two disbelieving girls. 'Didn't you notice anything?' she asked.

'Like what?' Ginny asked.

'Well, I suppose like them . . . going out?'

'She's always in and out of here all day and night. How were we supposed to know?' Ginny answered.

Elizabeth was still trying to take it in herself and she wondered how her mam and da were taking this piece of news. 'You won't have to call her "Mam", will you?'

Tessa couldn't reply to this at all. There was no one who could take her mam's place, least of all May Greely.

'Will I have to call him "Da"?' Ginny asked. She hadn't thought of that aspect of it. It was so long ago since her own da had died that it would be difficult to think of Richie O'Leary as 'Da'.

'Oh, who knows *anything*! Oh, why? Why did he have to do it? It was all right the way . . . things were.' Tessa broke down in tears. She just couldn't comprehend why her father had to marry anyone. Didn't he care about all the years he'd spent with Mam? About all the hard work and sacrifices Mam had made? He'd been lost and heartbroken, just as she'd been, at losing Mam. So how could he change so quickly? How could he forget so quickly?

Elizabeth was trying to think of things to say to cheer both Tessa and Ginny up. 'Well, look at it like this, you'll both be better off. You can share all the housework and shopping and cooking. Your Jimmy is always next door and Colin is always out – somewhere – and there'll be more money coming in, and your mam can bring all your stuff over here. You *are* going to live here, Ginny, aren't you?'

'Yes. That's why they told us together, like.'

'Does Colin know?'

Tessa nodded. 'He didn't say anything. He just slammed out.'

'So, what's new? What about Jimmy?'

Tessa's tears had stopped. 'I don't think he really understood. All he wanted to know was did it mean he'd have to stop going next door to Harold.'

'So, when is it going to be then?'

'They didn't say.'

'It won't be too long, Mam said the sooner the better to give the owld biddies less to talk about.'

Tessa burst into tears again. 'I . . . I don't think I'm going to be able to . . . face people. What will I say?'

'Why do you have to say anything? Let them jangle,' Elizabeth replied firmly.

'You know what they're all like around here,' Ginny wailed, feeling just as upset and confused as Tessa.

'Well, if you don't say anything and just look as if you're not upset at all they'll soon get fed up and start on something else.'

'I don't think I can do that! It . . . it will hurt too much. It will look as though I've forgotten all about my mam already and I *haven't*.'

'No, it won't, Tessa. People *do* know how much you loved your mam and how much you miss her. If anyone asks me or our Nessie, that's what I'll tell them. That you'll never forget your mam but you understand about your da and Mrs Greely.'

'Will I have to change my name?' Ginny asked, wiping her eyes. She was getting used to the situation already. Elizabeth was at least talking sense.

'How should I know? I don't think so anyway. And do the same as Tessa if anyone is hardfaced enough to ask you outright what you think. If you both put on brave faces it will be "much ado about nothing",' Elizabeth finished, remembering her Shakespeare from her English Literature lessons.

Tessa was still dabbing at her eyes but Ginny looked much happier until Colin barged into the kitchen. 'I thought *you'd* be here, Elizabeth Harrison. There's no show without Punch,' he snapped.

Elizabeth glared at him and got to her feet. She was almost as tall as him. 'I was sent here by your future stepmother.'

'With the mouth on her I'll bet we're the talk of the neighbourhood by now.'

'Oh, that's rich coming from you, Colin O'Leary. The whole street has got you taped,' Elizabeth replied sarcastically.

Colin ignored her. 'Ginny, will you come for a walk with me? We're not going to get any peace and privacy here. Da's gone off to the pub to announce the happy event. Everyone will be buying him ale and *she'll* be lapping up all the attention.'

As they left Tessa dissolved into tears again and Elizabeth put her arm around her, scowling at Colin's retreating back, but Tessa knew her brother was just as appalled as she was by the news. He'd never had much time for May; by the look of it, he'd have less from now on. For once in their lives they both felt the same way.

Delia felt quite taken aback herself. It was the last thing she'd expected but she was glad May had come and told her before the street gossips got wind of it – and they would. Nothing got past them; the walls were so thin you could hear almost everything that was going on in your neighbours' homes.

'I'm pleased for you both. When is it to be?'

'The end of the month. We've been to see Father Walsh and it's not going to be anything big or showy. Neither of us are spring chickens by a long chalk. In fact you'd be a long time looking at a chicken before you'd think of me,' May laughed.

They'd decided that their feelings for each other had grown and would continue to grow and so it made sense for them to get married. She'd been a widow for years and Richie had left a decent interval after Mary's death.

'We're just going to have family and a couple of friends. Maybe have a bit of a meal out somewhere. That'll be the best way to keep some of the gossip down. Oh, I know tongues will be wagging but it's all above board, we've nothing to hide.'

Delia nodded. May was good company and she was still a

good-looking woman, attributes that made her popular with the customers of the pubs she worked in.

'Will you be giving up work?'

'I'll have to give up one of them, probably the Globe. I mean, it's not going to look right me serving me own husband. Eddie Doyle's not going to be happy but I earn more working in the Unicorn. You know what a flaming skinflint Eddie is. And talking of him, I'd better be making a move.'

'Well, we both wish you every happiness, May, you've been a widow for a long time and it's not easy for a woman on her own,' Jack said sincerely. He liked May Greely.

'And thanks for coming to let us know personally before it becomes public knowledge. What about the kids?' Delia added.

May shrugged. 'Colin just slammed out and I left our Ginny and Tessa looking as though they'd been hit by a steamroller, but they'll get used to the idea. They'll have to.'

As Delia closed the door behind May she looked at Jack quizzically.

'Well, that's a turn-up for the book. Didn't you suspect anything?' he asked.

'No, I didn't. Well, if I'm really truthful I did suspect that something was going on but it certainly had nothing to do with marriage. God forgive me for such uncharitable thoughts.'

Jack grinned. 'At least she came and told us. In half an hour the street will be up! There'll be women hanging over the yard walls as far down as the tannery. It's the best piece of gossip since Richie moved here.'

Delia looked concerned. 'I wonder how Tessa's taking it? She worshipped her mam and it is only a year since the poor woman was buried.'

'What about Ginny?'

'I think she'll be all right. In fact I think Richie will come off best. More money, more help, and someone to make the decisions. You know how utterly hopeless he is, Jack. Oh, don't get me wrong, I like him, but you've got to admit he's not much use dealing with trouble or making decisions. But I suppose most of the men in this street would be useless if they were widowed. Look at Frank Flynn and Mick Collins – couldn't organise anything to save their lives. No, I think they'll be good for each other. She's easy-going but she can get strict with the kids. She'll stand no nonsense from them. She'll also watch that Richie doesn't drink too much or get into debt again. I'll say this for her, she's always been a good manager. Apart from a couple of port and lemons I've never known her to waste money or get into debt and that's unusual around here, especially for a widow. And she's never . . . well, tried to earn money by "other means".'

'You know, Delia, you really surprise me sometimes. You must have *thought* about May going on the streets to earn a living to mention it at all.'

Delia became flustered. 'Nearly every woman in the street must have *thought* about it, Jack. That's not saying one thinks she *would*. No, give her her due, she's always stayed respectable.'

Nessie, who had hardly been able to hear anything because she'd had two customers in, caught the end of the discussion. If she could, she'd wheedle it all out of Elizabeth because Mam certainly wouldn't tell *her* all the ins and outs, not by the look on her face. She was annoyed about *something* because her cheeks were pink and her lips were pursed up as if she'd been sucking a lemon.

'Well, aren't you going to say anything, Ginny?' Colin asked as they walked to the tram stop. They always went to Lester Gardens these days, weather permitting.

'What do you want me to say, Col?'

'I dunno.' He, like Tessa, was shocked and disgusted. He knew what May Greely wanted, beside the obvious. She'd been fed up managing on her own all these years. She wanted security, more money, a whole house instead of a couple of rooms. He'd never liked her and he knew the feeling was mutual. But when he thought of the two of them occupying that bed, the bed Delia Harrison had bought and in which his mam had died, it turned his stomach. She'd manipulated his da and like a fool his da had fallen for her tricks. There was however a good side to it and one he was thankful for.

'I suppose it will be a bit strange, like, to start with. But as Elizabeth said, we'll share all the housework and the washing, ironing and things like that. There'll be more money coming in so we'll stand a good chance of keeping more of our wages and then we'll be able to go out again, Col, like we used to do and have more things . . . special things, like.'

Although he was working, Colin always said they couldn't afford 'treats', as he called going out to specific places. He was saving up, he'd told her once when she'd got really upset about it. She thought he was saving up for a ring for her, so she'd not complained any further.

'But we won't be able to, Ginny.'

She looked up at him. 'Why? Don't you love me any more?' Tears sprang to her eyes and her bottom lip began to tremble.

'I do, Ginny, but don't you see? We'll be family. We'll be related.'

She was still mystified. 'Yes, but . . .?'

God, but she was thick, he thought, and she was looking at him in that stupid way she had.

'We'll be stepbrother and stepsister. We'll never be able to be together, to get married, like. It's not allowed and not only by the church.'

The realisation hit her as though she'd been punched in the stomach. 'Not . . . not . . . get married?'

'No. *I* don't want them to get married, Ginny, and that's the truth.' It was, he thought. For once he wasn't lying. 'I don't see why they can't keep things as they are.'

Ginny's eyes were now full of tears. 'Did . . . did you say that?' Oh, talk to your da, Col, please. Make him see he's not being . . . fair, and I'll tell Mam I . . . I . . . love you and want to marry you but if she's marrying your da then . . .' She broke down in sobs and he put his arm around her.

'It won't do any good, Ginny. You know your mam, she's determined, and Da . . . well, nothing I could say would change *his* mind. He's not much time for me and neither has your mam. I'm sorry, Ginny, but we'll just have to treat each other as brother and sister, there's nothing else we can do.'

This was terrible! She'd not given that side of it a thought, but Mam was ruining their lives and Colin didn't seem to be bothered. She struggled free of his grip and began to run. She didn't know where she was going to – even if she went to the ends of the earth it wouldn't help. She loved him and now he'd been snatched away from her and it wasn't right! How could they do this to her?

Chapter Sixteen

Ginny was inconsolable. She walked the streets in a daze, barely seeing anything through a mist of tears. When she returned home it was late, very late. May had just come in herself but she had not been worried by her daughter's absence, thinking Ginny was still over with Tessa.

'Ginny! What's the matter with you? You look terrible. I know it was a bit of a shock, luv, but your da's been dead for years. I can understand Tessa being upset, she only lost her mam last year, but there's no need for you to get yourself into this state. We'll all get on like a house on fire, you wait and see.'

'I don't care about anyone being dead! Or about getting on,' Ginny sobbed.

'Oh, come here to me, luv. I'd no idea you'd get so upset.'

As May tried to put an arm around her daughter, Ginny shied away. 'You've ruined my future, Mam! You've ruined it and you don't care.'

May wondered what on earth had got into her daughter. She'd never seen her so upset. And what did she mean by 'ruined'? 'What do you mean by that, Ginny?'

Ginny tried to fight down her sobs. 'Colin and me, that's what I mean. We'll be stepbrother and stepsister.'

May was still mystified. 'So?'

'We'll never be able to get married, that's what I mean! And it's all your fault, Mam!'

'Ginny Greely, you're far too young to be thinking of things like that!' This aspect hadn't even occurred to May.

'I don't mean now! When we were older! I love him and he loves me and you've *ruined* our lives!'

May was perturbed. 'Ginny, luv, pull yourself together. He's the only lad you've been out with and you're far too young even to know what love is.' She doubted that Colin O'Leary was capable of loving anyone other than himself.

'I'm not! I'm not!' Ginny protested. *She* knew how she felt, Mam didn't.

May pushed her gently down on the sofa. 'Ginny, now you just listen to me. You're only sixteen. You've got your whole life ahead of you. You'll have plenty of fellers wanting to take you out and one who will, eventually, love you, *really* love you, and want to marry you. Colin O'Leary isn't the only lad on earth.' She tried to be lighthearted, to lift Ginny's spirits. 'Fellers are like trams, there's always another one coming along. Now, stop that crying and go to bed, you've had a long and upsetting evening.'

Ginny wasn't placated and her Mam's flippant attitude only made her more angry and upset. 'I don't *want* another lad. I just want Colin! Oh, I'll never forgive you for this, Mam! How can I live under the same roof as him and just stop loving him? I'll be seeing him every day of my life and I won't be able to stand it! I *won't!*'

'Oh, Ginny, wipe your eyes. If I'd have known you were going to get this upset I'd have told you on your own, not with Tessa and *him*.' But Ginny refused to be comforted and ran from the room, leaving May staring after her and genuinely concerned.

This was something she hadn't known about: that Ginny hoped one day to marry Colin O'Leary. That was something she certainly didn't want to happen. She'd not even guessed that Ginny was so fond of him. She disliked and distrusted the lad: he was trouble with a capital 'T'. He'd had poor Mary demented, long before they'd moved here, or so she had heard. She didn't know exactly what he'd done but there had been speculation long before she'd seen him lurking around railway stations. Well, she was determined that he wasn't going to have her demented too.

Mary, God rest her, had been so ill that she'd had enough to contend with. Thank God she'd never lived to see all the trouble there had been with Mogsey Doran. But she, May, was fit and well able to cope with Colin and his antics.

Perhaps seeing him every day would open Ginny's eyes to just what he was really like. Maybe the saying 'familiarity breeds contempt' would prove true. She certainly hoped so.

She sighed heavily and took off her shoes. She could hear Ginny sobbing in the other room. She put the kettle on as she always did: that last cup of tea helped her to unwind. Well, both Ginny and Colin would just have to make the best of it because Jack Harrison was right. She'd been on her own for too long, Richie genuinely seemed to love her and she was very fond of him. She didn't love him the way she'd loved Harry, Ginny's da. And she could never block out the memory of that terrible day when they'd come to tell her he'd fallen into the almost empty hold of the cargo ship *Liberty* and was dead. He'd broken his neck and back and died instantaneously, the blockerman had said. But that had been when she'd been a young woman with a five-year-old child.

She'd just have to leave Ginny to get over the forthcoming marriage. She'd be there on hand if Ginny wanted her, but the best thing she could do was let time resolve the situation. 'Time is a great healer', she always said.

Tessa had hardly slept all night, she was so upset. What made it worse was the fact that after *they* were married they would sleep in this very bed. She and Ginny would have to share the front downstairs room, Colin and Jimmy would stay where they were and Da and . . . *she* would have this room where her poor mam had died. She'd never get used to it – ever.

After work she'd gone to see Elizabeth. She'd not wanted to go straight home.

Delia shook her head when she saw the girl's wan face, the dark eyes reddened from weeping. She was obviously taking it hard and Delia could understand why.

'I didn't get much sleep last night,' Tessa admitted in response to Elizabeth's queries when they were alone in the kitchen.

'I don't think Ginny did either. Mam was saying to Da that she's really upset and that it was surprising. Then she said that Ginny had had a row with her mam last night because she won't ever be able to marry your Colin as they'll be related. Just why she wants to marry *him* I don't know. She could get lots of fellers.'

'I know. Maybe living in the same house will put her off. She'll see what he's really like.'

'If she wants to see, that is. Mam's always saying, "There's none so blind as those who don't want to see".'

'Oh, I don't even want to go home now, Elizabeth. I've lost all heart. I don't care whether there's a meal ready for them or not, or if they've got clean clothes, or . . . anything.'

Seeing Tessa so lost and miserable, Elizabeth racked her brains for something to take her mind off things. She lowered her voice: 'Mam's started to write to hairdressing salons.' At last Tessa looked interested, she thought with some relief.

'Which ones?'

'Hill's and Marcel's. They're both in Bold Street. She said seeing as I'd got my own way I might as well do the thing properly and try for an upper-class salon. I'll be the best-educated apprentice they've ever had. She's still not speaking to me. She's furious.

She's tried about six times to write to Aunty Margaret and each time she's finished by tearing up the letter and throwing it in the fire. Da says she'll come round but I don't think she'll ever forgive me.'

'You'll just have to show her, and your aunty, that you were right.'

'I know. I intend to be the best, or at least *one* of the best hairdressers in Liverpool. I'll go to all the competitions and things like that and win prizes. I'll need people to practise on though.'

'Well, there's me and Ginny and maybe Doreen Keegan and Alice Collins.'

'Oh, Alice'll let me. Anything to look smart and fashionable without it costing a penny. She's just like her mam, is that one.'

'When do you think you'll be able to start?'

'Working, you mean?'

'Yes.'

'After I leave in the summer.'

'You can practise on us though long before that.'

'Yes. I can do both yours and Ginny's hair for the . . . wedding! Oh, God! I'm sorry, Tessa! I never think. I just never bloody think!'

'I don't even want to go to that,' Tessa said with the hint of a sob in her voice again.

'I know, but you'll have to.'

'Our Colin won't. He never does anything if it doesn't suit him.'

Elizabeth quickly changed the subject. 'I think Mam is going to make sure that our Nessie does as she's told from now on. I heard her telling Da that she wasn't going to go through all this again with Nessie.'

'Do you think Nessie will be a teacher?'

'It doesn't look as though she's much choice. But she won't mind that – she'd make a good one. She's bossy and full of herself *and* she'd think she was going one better than me. But she's got years yet, anything could happen. She might even end up as a nun! Wouldn't that be a laugh!'

'Would your mam like that?'

'No – it would be wasting all that money again.'

'But nuns do teach.'

'I know. Don't I have to put up with them all day? But you don't need an expensive education to be a nun. All you have to know are the Latin prayers and responses to the mass.' Elizabeth blithely dismissed all the other and more serious aspects of taking Holy Orders.

Delia had written to the two top salons in Liverpool and in due course she received replies. An apprenticeship would cost two guineas and all equipment and overalls were to be purchased by the apprentice.

'More money!' Delia said irately.

'It's not as expensive as school, Mam,' Elizabeth said coaxingly.

Delia ignored her. She still wasn't reconciled to the prospect of jibes and sly comments from customers like Katie Collins and Maisie Keegan.

'You are to present yourself on Thursday evening at six-thirty at Hill's and at Marcel's on Friday at seven p.m.'

'Will you come with me?' Elizabeth could hardly contain her joy, but she didn't want to show it openly. Mam was still upset.

'Well, I can't let you go on your own. You'll put your foot in your manners for certain if I'm not there to watch you.'

'Mam, I wouldn't do anything like that! I'm not stupid!'

'Well, that's debatable. You'd better get out the clothes you want to wear and make sure they're clean and pressed.' Delia folded both letters and put them behind the clock on the mantel.

When her mother had gone back into the shop Elizabeth reached up and took them down and read them for herself. A little shiver of happiness ran though her.

Oh, she'd show them all. She meant what she'd said. She *would* be the best *and* she'd have her own salon one day. Then perhaps Mam would be proud of her. She really wanted her to be. She didn't care if Nessie did become a teacher, but it was very important to her that both her mam and her aunt be proud of her. But as she hugged the letters to her chest she found some of her natural self-confidence and assertiveness had deserted her.

It was a long time since the five of them had all gathered by the tannery wall, but Johnny was home so they'd agreed to meet. These days they didn't see nearly as much of each other as they used to.

'You two don't look very happy. Mike told me the news,' Johnny greeted Tessa and Ginny cheerfully.

'Did you have to start off like that?' Elizabeth said. Her right arm was still in a sling but there were only a couple more weeks to go and then the plaster would come off and she'd have to go back to school.

'Well, it's *news* to me. What's your mam going to do, Ginny?'

'Apart from ruining my life, you mean?'

Johnny patted her arm sympathetically while Mike looked down at his boots. The whole street was divided over this wedding. Some people thought it would be the best thing for both Richie and May, and Mike's own mam was of this group. Others, like Katie Collins for one, thought it was a disgrace, Mary having been dead for only a year. The usual 'decent' interval was two years. They said May was just looking for someone to ease her burdens; she wasn't getting any younger and no one liked a barmaid who was growing old. It wasn't good for business. 'No one loves a fairy when she's forty!' was the way Katie Collins had described it.

'She's going to leave work – well, your da's pub anyway,' Ginny went on, sitting on the wall beside Johnny.

'Oh, that'll please him no end! Your mam's a good barmaid. He won't get another one unless he's willing to cough up more money. I can't say I blame her. The older he grows the more miserable he gets. He drags Mam down to Our Lady of the Angels in Fox Street now. They have a novena every Tuesday night.'

'What's he praying for?' Elizabeth asked.

'I don't know but I think Mam's praying that he'll stop being such a flaming misery and actually treat her better. He uses and speaks to her just like a skivvy. One of these days I'm going to tell him a few home truths. He's not going to like it, but he deserves it and Mam deserves better. She only gets one night out, once a fortnight, and that's to the Union of Catholic Mothers. And only one new outfit a year when he must be minted!'

'Let us know when this row is going to be and we'll all go into hiding,' Mike joked, but he felt sorry for Mrs Doyle. She was so quiet and inoffensive.

'So, will you be home for the wedding?' Elizabeth asked.

'No.'

'I wish I wasn't,' Tessa said miserably and Ginny nodded.

'It's on the last Saturday in the month and it's only going to be quiet, so Mam said.' Elizabeth paused and fiddled with the knot at the back of her neck that held the sling in place. 'Mam's going. They were both invited but they can't close the shop, not on a Saturday morning. I asked could I go instead, to support Tessa and Ginny, like, but they said no.'

'I'm to have a new costume. Well, the first costume I've ever had – the first "new" *anything* I've had.'

'And so am I,' Ginny added. For once she'd look smart and grown-up and it would be such a waste. She didn't know how she was going to stand in church in the same pew as Colin and listen to Father Walsh ask the questions and receive the answers that would separate her from Colin for ever.

She'd even wondered whether, when it came to the part where the priest said, 'If any person here present knows of any consanguinity, affinity or spiritual relationship speak now or forever hold your peace,' she could cry out and say that it wasn't right, it wasn't fair. But she couldn't do that. There was no reason why they shouldn't get married. It was going to be awful.

'You'll look great, both of you. Just like the "bloods" I have to look after.'

'The what?'

'The "bloods". It's slang for passengers, although there don't seem to be many on the next trip.'

'Why?' Elizabeth asked.

'The news, dope! It looks as if there's going to be another war and you can't help people remembering what happened to the *Lusitania*.'

They'd all heard of the tragedy of the Cunarder that had been sunk in May 1915 by a torpedo with the loss of 1,198 lives, mainly those of women and children.

'What will you do if there is a war?' Mike asked.

Johnny shrugged. 'Join the Royal Navy, I suppose. I can't see anyone wanting to cross the Atlantic. It'll be full of U-boats. What about you?'

'Probably Royal Navy too.'

'You're too young, both of you. Your birthday is on the same day,' Elizabeth reminded them.

'We'll be seventeen after Christmas and besides, we can lie about our ages. They did in the last one,' Johnny replied defensively.

'Yes, and look what happened then. Thousands of lads of sixteen and seventeen were killed. I bet they won't let *that* happen again. Anyway, no one wants to think about war,' Elizabeth dismissed the subject.

'Tell that to that Hitler feller,' Johnny said firmly. 'I heard you aren't going back to school after the next holidays.'

'I'm not. How do you know anyway? Mam's told no one.'

Johnny looked at Mike and winked.

'Oh, I should have known,' Elizabeth said resignedly. 'Your Mam, Mike.'

'She heard it from Flo Conway who lives—'

'Next door to us,' Elizabeth finished. So, the news was already

159

out. Her mam would be furious. 'I'm going to be a hairdresser.'

Johnny looked at her with open scepticism. 'You're bloody mad, do you know that, Elizabeth? A cushy job as a teacher, all that time off, bossing all those kids around and good money and security.'

'That's just it. The bit about the kids. I hate them and I'd have no patience with them. You know how our Nessie gets on my nerves and she's grown-up compared to the ones I'd have to teach.'

'She's got to go for an interview at two places in Bold Street,' Tessa informed them.

Mike looked amazed. 'God, we're going up in the world. Bold Street!'

'Mam said if I'm going to do it I might as well do it properly.'

Mike's respect for Elizabeth increased. She'd always been different to the other girls in the street because she came from a well-off family, by his mam's standards anyway. But her independence was part of the reason he liked her. She could be a bit of a 'madcap' at times but she knew her own mind and was certainly determined. 'It must have taken a lot of guts to tell them,' he said admiringly.

'It did. There was murder. She's still giving me the cold-shoulder treatment.'

'But you got your own way in the end. You always do, Elizabeth Harrison,' Mike said with a grin.

'I wish I did,' groaned Ginny. 'No matter how I'd carry on, it wouldn't make any difference. Mam's going to marry Tessa's da and that's that. Everything between Colin and me will be over.'

'I didn't think there was anything much between you,' Johnny commented.

'There is . . . was,' she corrected herself.

'I've told you, Ginny, you're better off without him. You can do better,' Tessa said firmly and was rewarded by a glare of hostility from Ginny.

'Oh, this looks as if it's shaping up for a battle royal,' Mike said.

'It's not. Things will work out.' Elizabeth frowned at him. 'Anyway, Johnny, you ought to talk more to Tessa about the "bloods". She wants to be a stewardess.'

'The best of luck, Tessa, but if there's a war there won't be any passengers to look after,' Johnny pointed out.

'Oh, trust you, Johnny Doyle! You're full of enthusiasm and good news!' Elizabeth said sarcastically. 'That's just what she wanted to know, I'm sure. Anyway, there's nothing definite about any war, it's all talk.'

Tessa slid off the wall. She was going home. Things were bad enough without hearing that her dream might never ever be possible.

Johnny followed her. 'Tessa! Tessa! I'm sorry.'

She smiled sadly at him. 'What for? I know you didn't mean to disappoint me.'

'I didn't, honestly. Do you really want to be a stewardess?'

Tessa nodded.

'They work awfully hard. Everyone thinks they have the time of their lives, off seeing the world, but you have to make a special trip to see *anything*. Docks are the same the world over. In rough weather you have to dance attendance on your "bloods". Most of them are sick. It's really not a lot of fun, Tessa.'

'It doesn't sound it. But I'm not afraid of hard work or cleaning up after people. It's what I've been doing for years.'

Johnny was contrite. 'I *have* put you off. I can tell by your voice. I'm so sorry, Tessa.'

'You haven't. It's . . . it's something I promised Mam I'd do.'

'Well, if . . . when the time comes, if there's anything I can do to help, you will ask?'

'Thanks, Johnny. I'd be glad of any help.'

He smiled and pushed his hair away from his forehead.

It was a habit she liked, it made him seem sort of appealing. But she couldn't tell him that, could she?

On the Thursday evening Elizabeth was ready. She'd dressed with care, helped by Nessie for although the plaster had come off her wrist was still very sore. She finished her outfit off with a small pillbox hat and was thrilled to be wearing her first pair of nylon stockings. She'd spent ages making sure the seams were straight but she felt and looked so 'grown up' she was certain no one would take her for a schoolgirl.

Her mam looked smart too, she thought, in her two-piece costume in brown and cream dogstooth check. She certainly wasn't going to that place looking as though she hadn't two halfpennies to rub together, she'd told Jack firmly. 'You always look so smart when you're dressed up, Delia,' he'd replied encouragingly, knowing how much she was hating the idea of this interview. No matter how well established and well known the salon was she just didn't want Elizabeth to go to work there. She was very, very disappointed in her elder daughter.

All the way into town on the tram Elizabeth was nervous. What if they decided she wasn't hairdresser material? What if they were terribly posh and objected to the way she spoke? All the elocution lessons had helped but she still had an unmistakable scouse accent. She began to wind the strap of her shoulder bag around her wrist.

'Stop that, for heaven's sake. I know you're nervous, and so you should be, but stop fidgeting,' Delia snapped.

Hill's was the kind of place where once you opened the glass door you felt as though you were stepping into another world. The atmosphere was hushed, almost as if you were in church, Elizabeth thought.

The Art Deco-style reception area was carpeted and the desk was behind a frosted glass panel which had, as its centrepiece, the figure of a dancing lady. On either side were glass cabinets containing cosmetics and perfumes in very fancy bottles. Beyond that was a small area where clients could sit and browse through magazines while waiting to be summoned to one of the enclosed cubicles. Two of them had the doors open and a young girl was on her hands and knees washing the marble-effect linoleum. Elizabeth caught sight of a washbasin, a comfortable chair and footstool and mirrors surrounded by lights. Everyone she could see wore pink overalls with the shop's monogram embroidered in gold on the pocket.

A well-groomed young woman was sitting at the reception desk, her blonde hair dressed in a very complicated style of upswept curls and waves. What make-up she wore was lightly applied and her fingernails were painted with pink polish.

'May I help?'

'I . . . we . . . have an appointment to see Miss Mercer.'

The receptionist consulted her appointment book. 'You must be Mrs Harrison and Miss Harrison. Would you care to wait while I inform Miss Mercer of your arrival?'

Delia nodded and looked around her. Who could afford to come to somewhere as utterly luxurious as this, just to have your hair done? She felt almost as nervous as Elizabeth.

The receptionist returned. 'Would you follow me, please?'

They were led to a small cubicle which looked like all the rest except that there was a desk and two chairs and a small index file.

Miss Mercer was small and dark-haired and, again, immaculately turned out. Elizabeth would be like a fish out of water here, Delia thought, hopefully.

'Please sit down, Mrs Harrison.' Miss Mercer indicated a chair.

'Now, Miss Harrison – Elizabeth – would you like to tell me why you wish to become a hairdresser?' the manageress asked in a soft but firm voice.

Elizabeth swallowed hard. She'd prepared herself for this. 'It is something I enjoy and I don't want to sound arrogant, Miss Mercer, but I do seem to have . . . well, a flair for it. I practise on my friends.'

The manageress looked enquiringly at Delia who nodded her head.

'Well, that's important. You realise that you will be indentured for three years as an apprentice, and then two more years as an improver?'

'Yes, Miss Mercer,' Elizabeth replied quietly.

'You will have a thorough grounding in all aspects of hair-dressing but you will have to work very long hours.'

'I don't mind hard work at all and I *will* be learning all the time. I really do want to be a good hairdresser.'

Miss Mercer looked closely at mother and daughter. 'You agree to all this, Mrs Harrison? I can assure you that she will receive the best training.'

Delia again nodded. She just couldn't say the words 'I agree'. They stuck in her throat.

'I see you are still at school. And a very good one too. When would you be able to start, should we offer you an apprenticeship?'

'When I finish in July.'

'*After* she has matriculated and with above-average marks.' Delia was determined to show the woman that she wasn't getting an unqualified, ignorant slip of a girl. There couldn't be many girls who had expensive private educations who were hairdressers.

Miss Mercer smiled. 'Then I will be in touch very shortly and perhaps one Saturday you could come in, just for the morning, so I can see how you shape. Of course you will only observe, but there are other duties apprentices must do.'

Elizabeth lost some of her nervousness. It wasn't absolutely sure but it looked as if she would be offered an apprenticeship.

Miss Mercer rose and accompanied them as far as the reception desk. Once outside, Delia breathed a sigh of relief. She'd felt almost panic-stricken in there. She hoped it hadn't shown.

'Well, at least we will know just what we are facing when we go to Marcel's tomorrow. You'd think they were doing you a great favour by taking you on, when it's the other way around. *We're* the ones who are paying, not them.'

'Do you think after we've been to Marcel's we could go and have a look at the kind of things I'll need to have?' Elizabeth asked. She still felt as though she were walking on a cloud.

'You can. I'm far too busy to be traipsing around hairdressing wholesaler's.'

Some of Elizabeth's euphoria disappeared. She'd got what she wanted but obviously Mam wasn't going to give her her blessing. If she achieved her ambition and got that apprenticeship, would she be losing her close relationship with Mam? She couldn't suppress a tinge of sadness at the thought.

They went through the same ritual at Marcel's the following evening and again Elizabeth got the impression they were willing to take her on. If she was offered an apprenticeship by both Hill's and Marcel's how would she choose? She knew she couldn't ask her mam. Mam wanted nothing to do with it. She had liked Miss Knowles and the decor was very plush, even more so than at Hill's. But Marcel's staff seemed friendlier; two of the younger girls had actually smiled at her, as had the receptionist, and the salon was bigger. She'd have to discuss it with Tessa.

Although May had said it was to be a quiet wedding, there was nothing she could do to stop half the women in the street attending the service in St Anthony's Church on Saturday 29 April. Those who genuinely wished Richie and May good luck and happiness cast supercilious glances at those who did not.

'Hypocrites, the lot of them!' Eileen Flynn had whispered to the woman sitting beside her.

Delia had been invited officially and had even agreed to stand for May, although she wouldn't hear of the title matron of honour being used. Frank Flynn agreed to be best man for Richie and, as he'd said to Eileen, 'Thank God they 'ad the sense not to ask those two girls to be bridesmaids and that Colin to be best man.'

'She's not that stupid, isn't May Greely,' Eileen had replied. In her opinion May really wasn't getting much of a bargain in Richie O'Leary, but still, it was her life.

The bride wore a dress of crêpe de Chine with a cream background covered all over with pale blue flowers. A large picture hat, more fashionable in the early thirties, covered her dark hair in which there wasn't a hint of grey, and she carried a small bouquet of spring flowers.

Elizabeth, who had come despite her mother's instructions, sat in the very back pew. She thought May looked nice – a bit too fussy, perhaps, but all right – and both Tessa and Ginny looked great. She'd already seen their outfits and she'd done both their hair last night. Her wrist was now almost completely healed and she found that the more she used it the less stiff it became.

Alice Collins was sitting next to Elizabeth. 'Ginny Greely looks almost pretty,' she remarked.

'What do you mean, "almost"?' Elizabeth demanded.

'Well, you've got to agree she's never looked as nice before.'

'That's because I washed and set her hair. I did Tessa's too,' she whispered back.

Alice looked interested. 'Do you think you could do something with mine? I couldn't pay you though,' she added quickly.

Elizabeth nodded. 'Of course I could.' The more practice she got the better. 'Doesn't that colour suit Tessa?' she added and Alice craned her neck to get a better view.

Elizabeth had accompanied Tessa and Ginny to buy the outfits. They'd gone to T. J. Hughes's in London Road. Tessa's was a bright pink two-piece with a fitted jacket which showed off her small waist. Ginny had chosen, with her help, a cornflower blue dress and jacket. 'It suits your colouring, Ginny,' Elizabeth had urged as Ginny had shilly-shallied over it. 'You've got shoes and a bag, all you need is a small white hat. We should get one in C & A and it won't be expensive,' she'd advised.

'It does,' Alice said, knowing if there was any more conversation, albeit whispered, they would both be in trouble.

Elizabeth felt so sorry for Tessa and Ginny. She knew Tessa would be thinking of her mam and Ginny would be torturing herself over Colin. At least they hadn't had to share the same pew, something she had pointed out last night to Ginny's relief. He sat with Jimmy on the left-hand side of the church while Ginny and Delia and May's sister-in-law from her first marriage sat on the right side. But the ceremony was still going to be an ordeal for them, and then they would have to get through not only the rest of the day but the rest of their lives as well.

Chapter Seventeen

Elizabeth was weary when she got off the tram. This August had been so hot and humid that she'd welcome some cooler days, which hopefully would come with the start of the new month. Tessa was waiting for her, for although they came home from opposite directions Tessa had insisted on it.

'You used to wait for me for over an hour, winter and summer, so I'm going to wait for you,' she'd replied firmly to Elizabeth's arguments. 'You look worn out.'

'I am. I never expected it to be *such* hard work – and it's so boring.'

'Don't go saying that to your mam.'

'I won't, but honestly, Tessa, I seem to spend more time sweeping up, washing floors and cleaning mirrors than I do watching and learning. All that stuff, which cost Mam a small fortune, and I only get to hold the hairpins, if I'm lucky. At this rate it'll be years before they'll let me cut *anyone's* hair.'

Delia had thought the list was endless when she'd gone with Elizabeth to the wholesaler's Osborne and Garret the week before Elizabeth started at Hill's. She'd been a little disappointed not to be offered a place at Marcel's, but at least it made the decision for her. She had had her results and had indeed matriculated with very good marks. But that fact hadn't made her mam very happy. 'It's the waste, the sheer waste I can't forgive, Jack,' she'd heard her mam say the day after. So she didn't view the list of equipment in a favourable light. Two pairs of scissors were required, never to be used on anything except hair. That had been stressed emphatically. Then there were thinning scissors and an open 'cut throat' razor, also to be used for thinning and tapering, but not for a very long time. In the hands of an apprentice a razor was a lethal weapon, so Miss Mercer had said. The list continued with two steel combs, one 'light', one 'heavy'; a tail comb; clippers; two sets of waving irons, medium size 'B' or 'C'; and – to their surprise – even four coloured hairnets.

'I would have thought they'd have enough of their own,' Delia had remarked caustically. Finally there were her three pink overalls. Why she needed three God alone knew, Delia had commented.

166

'And there's so much to learn. It takes ages to pin curl and wave and the setting lotion they use is like glue, it leaves your fingers all sticky. Then there's all the different perms, and how to wind them: hot, tepid and cold perms, and those Callinan perms which look horrendous. You have to sit there for hours with your hair wound around these curlers attached to a machine that looks like something from another planet. I couldn't *stand* all that. Thank God I don't need a perm. And then there's Marcel waving with the heated irons.'

'I thought that was a kind of perm,' Tessa remarked.

'So did I, but it's not. It's all done with waving irons and like everything else, it takes hours. It's not as . . . glamorous . . . as I'd thought.'

'It'll be worth it though, in the end I mean,' Tessa tried to cheer Elizabeth up.

'I suppose so, but at the end of days like this I really do wonder. Maybe I should have been a manicurist, at least they get to sit down.'

'Oh, stop moaning. Look how well you did Alice's hair. She was made up. Even her mam said she hardly recognised her.'

Elizabeth had cut Alice Collins's shoulder-length brown hair to just the level of her ears and had waved it, fixing the waves with clips until it was dry and then showing Alice how to brush it out and pin curl it so it would hold the style.

'I'm sorry to go on so, Tessa, but I've no one else to tell. Mam doesn't even want to know what I do all day.'

Tessa frowned. 'Is she still that bad?'

'Yes. I just don't talk to her about it now. Da's OK but he doesn't really understand anything I tell him.'

'What about Nessie?'

'Oh, she's interested even though she tries to hide it. Now she and Mam have decided she's to be the teacher in the family, she's so smug I could kill her.'

Tessa shook her head. Nessie wasn't half as bad as Elizabeth painted her. With a bit of effort on both sides the open hostility between them could be avoided. They were sisters after all.

When they arrived back at the shop Delia came through from the kitchen and smiled at Tessa. It was a smile that held little real warmth for she partially blamed Tessa for Elizabeth's change of career. If she'd wanted to, surely Tessa could have persuaded Elizabeth that hairdressing was not a wonderful career. Tessa's opinions carried a lot of weight with Elizabeth.

'I'll have to get straight back. I've things to do and everyone will be wanting their tea.'

Elizabeth nodded. Her friend had to run a house as well as work at the Convent. Tessa made her look spoilt and lazy, so she resolved not to complain about her lot any more.

Ginny was sitting, just staring into space, when Tessa got home – as she seemed to be every evening when Tessa returned. Things had been very strained at number twelve after Ginny and her mam had moved in with Richie, but over the months they all seemed to have settled down, except Colin and, because of his presence, Ginny. She seemed to have become quieter and more withdrawn.

In truth, Ginny was finding life utterly miserable. She hated her job at Birrel's but lacked the energy to look for anything better. Then there was Colin. She saw him every morning and for at least some part of the evening, although he went out quite a lot, and even more so at weekends. At first she wondered if he went out so much because he couldn't stand to be in the same room as her and not be able to hold her or kiss her. But if it was he gave no sign of it. And they were almost never alone so it was impossible to say anything about how *she* felt.

All through the summer on her Wednesday afternoons off, she'd sat at home reading *True Romance* or wandered into town to buy something. She now had quite a few nice outfits but she never went anywhere to wear them. Before her mam's marriage Colin sometimes used to meet her in town. How he'd managed to get the time off she didn't know, and after some coaxing he'd bought her a few little trinkets and sometimes they'd gone for tea in the Kardomah Café in Bold Street. Now life wasn't worth living; it was an effort just to get through every day. She couldn't talk to either her mam or Tessa about it because they didn't like him and were glad to see them lead separate lives.

The following Wednesday evening, Ginny found herself alone in the stifling kitchen. Tessa and Colin were out; Jimmy was next door; her mam was working and Richie (or Uncle Richie as she now had to call him) had gone to the pub. Ginny looked around her at the clutter and mess. She and Tessa and Mam were supposed to split the housework between them, but her mam never seemed to do anything at all. She didn't get up early, saying she worked late. She didn't go shopping, she sent either Ginny or Tessa. She did do a bit of the ironing, but that seemed to consist only of her own and Richie's things which left the bulk of it to Tessa and herself. She cooked, but never washed up. She never baked, Tessa did that. Her mam had shown her how to and Tessa had tried to teach Ginny but she couldn't be bothered to learn. She hated cooking. You spent hours preparing, boiling, roasting, baking, and it was all gone in about five minutes. Ginny rubbed her eyes. If she stayed in here for another night she'd go mad.

She went into the front room that she shared with Tessa and brushed her hair in the way Elizabeth had shown her. She was quite pretty, she thought, looking at her reflection in the mirror. Surely he must see *something* attractive in her? Taking her cardigan from the pile of neatly folded clothes on top of the ottoman, she left the house, closing the front door behind her.

She had no real idea of where she was going or what she would do. Should she go to the Pier Head and go for a sail on the ferry? On her own, with no one to share the trip with? No. Should she go into town to the cinema? Again she'd be on her own. There seemed to be nothing she would feel happy and comfortable doing on her own. Happy! she thought bitterly. She'd never be happy again.

Eventually she caught a tram. She'd go and sit in Lester Gardens. It wouldn't help, in fact it would only make her feel more miserable, but she couldn't help herself. She'd been so happy when she'd sat there with him all those times. But there would be very few people there and no one would notice if she indulged in a few tears: weeping for the love she'd lost through her mam's selfishness. Mam *was* selfish – and thoughtless, telling her that Colin wasn't right for her and comparing him with a tram! Well, so far there hadn't been anyone else and she doubted there ever would be.

When she got off the tram she walked the few yards to the little park. It was a lovely evening, warm but no longer sticky. The flowerbeds were a riot of colour and she could smell the sweet perfume of the roses and night-scented stocks. The evening would have been just perfect, she reflected, if only . . .

She heard a girl's laughter but took no notice until she heard the boy laugh too. The colour drained from her cheeks and she clapped a hand over her mouth to stop herself from crying out. He was *here*! He had brought someone else to *their* park! Oh, why had she come here? If she hadn't she would never have known. But just *who* was with him? She made up her mind to confront him.

Colin was sitting on the bench, his arm around a very attractive but flashily dressed girl who was still laughing. Her thick mass of black curled hair was held back with bright red plastic slides that matched the colour of the dress she wore. Her fingernails were painted red too.

Vera Morley from Blackstock Street! She was known in the entire neighbourhood to be little more than a common tart. Ginny's heart dropped like a stone and she couldn't help herself. She ran forward yelling, 'I hate you, Colin O'Leary! I *hate* you! Taking up with . . . *her*! She's just a slut! And you brought her . . . *here*!'

The smile vanished from his face. He was surprised and annoyed. 'Ginny, what's the matter with you? Have you followed me?' She had no claim on him. The bloody cheek of her. He could take out whoever he liked, he didn't have to ask *her* permission. He and Vera stood up, Vera with a mocking smile in her eyes and her red lips curled with contempt. It just increased Ginny's fury.

'No! I . . . I came here for some peace. How could you like her? She's a common, dirty little tart! She's had more fellers than hot dinners! Everyone knows about *her*!'

Vera, stung by these accusations, flew at Ginny screaming and trying to rake Ginny's face with her fingernails. 'You lying little bitch! You're just jealous because you look a bloody mess! Because it's *me* he likes to take out! *Me* who knows how to give him a good time. You're just a miserable, ugly little kid. He likes proper girls. Girls who don't keep moaning and following him around.'

Her words made Ginny tremble with fury and she grabbed Vera's hair and pulled with all her strength. Vera screamed in agony as a whole handful was wrenched out.

Colin decided it was time he intervened. He caught Ginny by her own hair and dragged her away from Vera.

'Stop it! Stop it! Get home, you bloody nuisance! Vera's right, you're a miserable, plain little kid. Just you wait until I tell your mam about you, although *she's* nothing but a bloody floosie herself. Go on, get home!'

Ginny broke free and started to run towards the gates. Colin made no move to stop her, instead he turned his attention to Vera who was sitting on the bench crying more with anger than pain.

'Take no notice of her! She's a nasty little bitch. I have to live under the same roof and believe me I know what she's—' The rest of his comforting words were interrupted by the screeching of tyres, the high-pitched neighing of a frightened horse, the rumble of wheels on the cobbles and then the shouts of angry men and the shrieks of horrified women.

'Oh my God! What's she done?' Colin covered the few yards to the park gates in seconds and was just in time to see a young policeman hanging on to the bridle of a carthorse for dear life to stop it bolting. The driver was shouting at it and yanking the reins back with all his strength. A lorry was turned broadside on to the on-coming traffic and the driver was jumping down from its cab. On the cobbles between the tram lines he could see a figure lying stretched out and recognised with sickening certainty that it was Ginny. She must have run straight out into the road. He forgot all about Vera Morley. If Ginny was dead then he'd be for it both from her mam and his da and most of the neighbours too. None of them liked him and he knew why. Johnny had told everyone about what he'd done on Christmas Eve. The Doyle boy had been right when he'd said that no one stole either from each other or the shops – they seemed to take a pride in the fact, which Colin found hard to understand. And surely no one could get angry over a bit of fun with a scruffy kid and a mangy kitten, but again it seemed as though they had.

'Ginny! Ginny!' he cried, pushing his way through the small group of people that had already collected. He dropped on to his knees beside her and lifted her head. She was breathing.

'Do you know who she is, the silly little bitch?' the lorry driver asked, bending down.

'Yes, she's my stepsister.'

The policeman and carter had got the horse under control and, wiping his brow with his handkerchief, the constable joined Colin and the lorry driver.

'She ran straight out in front of me, there was nothing I could do! She didn't even bloody look. Right out and hit the bonnet. I swear it, Officer.' The man was very shaken.

'It's all right, I saw what happened and it could have been a lot worse if that flaming animal had bolted.'

'It's his stepsister.' The man inclined his head towards Colin.

'So what happened?' the constable demanded, lifting Ginny's limp hand and feeling for a pulse.

'We had a row. She followed me here, then she just ran off . . . and . . . and before I could stop her she'd gone and then I heard the . . . the noise.'

'Well, she's breathing and she's got a steady pulse but I'll call an ambulance.'

The traffic was now at a standstill and the crowd was getting bigger. Two more policemen arrived. One began to direct the traffic and the other dispersed the crowd, except for the two witnesses, and started to take statements from the shaken carter and lorry driver.

Colin felt numb. Ginny was still unconscious.

'Where's the ambulance? What's the hold-up?' he demanded of the first policeman.

'It's on its way. Don't try to move her at all. She might have a broken arm or leg or shoulder.'

Colin tried again to revive her. 'Ginny! Ginny, it's me, Colin. I'm sorry, Ginny, really I am.' There was still no response and he just knelt there dazed until at last they heard the clanging of the ambulance bell and it was waved through by the officer on point duty.

She was examined gently and her eyelids fluttered open.

'Ginny! Ginny, are you all right?' Colin cried.

'Don't try and sit up, girl, take it easy,' the ambulance driver said quietly. 'Now, luv, can you move your arms and legs?'

Ginny raised them, wondering where she was and what had happened to her.

'Good. Nothing broken. Now, does your head hurt? Do you feel sick?'

'It . . . it hurts here.' Ginny put her hand to the side of her head. 'But I don't feel sick. What happened? I want my mam.'

'It's all right, Ginny, I'm here. I'll help take care of you,' Colin promised. Relief was washing over him. Thank God she wasn't badly hurt.

With his help and that of the driver and constable she got into the ambulance.

'We're going to take you to Stanley Hospital, luv, just to make sure you're all right,' the second ambulance man told her.

Ginny was still dazed and unable to understand why she had to go to hospital and why Colin was with her and looked so worried. She closed her eyes. Her head really did hurt so she'd think about all that later.

'Where do you live, lad?' the ambulance man asked.

'Naylor Street. Are you *sure* she's not badly hurt?'

'There's nothing broken but she might be concussed. She took a nasty fall. She was lucky she didn't end up under the wheels of the lorry or the hooves of that horse. Those damned animals have caused more deaths and injuries than I can count. One sudden noise and they're away like an arrow from a bow, trampling everyone and everything in their path and quite often killing their driver. They should bring in a law that says they should have ear muffs as well as blinkers.'

Colin wasn't paying any attention, his eyes were fixed on Ginny's inert form.

'Listen, son, I think when we arrive at the hospital you'd better go home and tell someone what happened. If she needs any kind of operation they'll have to give their consent and be there.'

Colin nodded, his heart lurching sickeningly. He'd not thought of that.

When he at last arrived home everyone was in and Jimmy was in bed.

'Holy Mother of God! What's up with you?' May cried, thinking she'd never seen him in such a state. He looked terrible.

'It's Ginny. She . . . she's in hospital.'

'In *hospital*! Why? What happened?' May demanded.

'If you've done anything to hurt her I'll kill you, I swear I will!' Tessa cried.

'I didn't do *anything* to her! I had a date and she . . . she followed me. We had a row and she ran off, straight into the middle of the main road.'

May crossed herself and sank down in an armchair.

'Where did they take her?' Tessa demanded.

'Stanley Hospital. It's all right, I went with her. She's not badly hurt. She banged her head. The ambulance feller said you'd better go along there just in case. It wasn't my fault! She . . . she just ran!'

'She would if she saw you with someone else! You know how much she thinks of you. She's stupid where you're concerned,' Tessa yelled at him.

'I can't help that!' Colin cried defensively. 'She knows there's nothing I can do . . . now.'

'You wouldn't have done anything even if she hadn't become your stepsister! You don't love her. What did you say to her to make her run off like that?'

'I didn't say *anything*, Tessa. God's truth!'

'Liar! I know you and I know Ginny. It's *your* fault!'

'It's not!'

'For the love of God stop fighting! I'm going up there.' May picked up her bag.

'I'm coming with you. She's my friend as well as my stepsister,' Tessa stated, snatching up her own shoulder bag. They departed quickly, leaving Colin with Richie. The two men were upset and shaken.

'You'd better make amends, lad, if she's not hurt, otherwise May will have your hide!' Richie said with foreboding. 'Trouble should be your middle name!'

When they arrived at the hospital May and Tessa were shown into a side ward by a sister whose apron crackled with starch as she walked. She hadn't been very co-operative about letting them in to see Ginny at this time of night until May had become angry and said she wasn't leaving the hospital until she'd seen her daughter and that even if they called the police she wouldn't be moved.

'I'm her *mother*, for God's sake! Haven't you got *any* pity in you?'

Ginny was lying in the iron-framed bed with a bandage around her head. Her face was almost as white as the bandage.

May gently patted her hand. 'Ginny, luv, it's me. It's your mam.'

Ginny opened her eyes. 'Oh, Mam! Mam! I'm sorry.'

'There's nothing for you to be sorry for, luv.'

'No, there isn't,' Tessa added, bending and kissing Ginny on the cheek.

'I . . . I remember running out. I couldn't see.'

'Don't upset yourself. You've got to rest, that sister said so and she's a tartar, believe me. You were very lucky, thank God, just a bit of concussion, that's what she said was wrong with you. But, luv, you could have been killed.' May was in a state of shock herself. Ginny looked so pale that she could be mistaken for a corpse.

Tessa took Ginny's hand. 'What did he say to you? Did our Colin upset you?'

'I don't remember. I don't even remember going . . . anywhere.'

'But he was with you in the ambulance!' May urged. She'd kill him if Ginny didn't get better.

Ginny tried to shake her head but winced in pain. 'No. No . . . I don't think he upset me. He was very worried about me.'

Tessa exchanged glances with May.

Ginny began to cry. 'Oh, Mam!'

'Ginny, stop that, luv, it's only going to make you feel worse. You'll be coming home tomorrow, but only if you don't upset yourself. Sleep now and get well.'

Obviously trying to make Ginny remember what had happened before she'd run into the road was something they might never achieve, Tessa thought. But she was determined to find out who her brother's 'date' had been and, by the look on her face, she'd get all the help she needed from May.

Chapter Eighteen

Ginny came home the following afternoon. She was still pale and shaken but at least she hadn't been seriously hurt and for that they all thanked God.

'How is she?' Tessa asked the minute she got in from work.

'She's slept a lot but that won't do her any harm. Will you keep your eye on her while I'm at work, Tessa? I don't want her to get upset or excited.'

May was combing her hair in front of the mirror that was on the mantelshelf, but she looked concerned. 'I've been down to see Jimmy Birrel. She's not going into work tomorrow.'

'Of course I will. Can I go in and see her?'

'Of course, luv, it's your room as well, but if she's asleep, leave her.'

'I will.' May was genuinely worried, Tessa thought as she opened the door of the room that she and Ginny shared. The curtains were drawn and had been all day and the room was stifling; she'd have to have a window open later.

Ginny was awake. 'How are you now?' Tessa asked, taking off her linen jacket and hanging it on the knob of the brass bedstead.

'I don't feel too bad but Mam won't let me get up or have the window open and it's boiling hot.'

'Well, she's right about staying in bed, but we'll have the window open, that's if the noise outside won't bother you?'

'No. There's not much noise anyway.'

Tessa drew back the curtains and pulled the sash window up, then drew one of the curtains halfway over to keep the sun out of Ginny's eyes.

'Don't complain too much, Ginny, about lying in bed all day. Make the most of it.' She smiled, sat down on the edge of the bed and took Ginny's hand. 'Do you remember anything . . . anything more, I mean?'

'No. I've tried to but I just get more confused and then my head aches. I do remember running out of the park and that I was crying, that's why I didn't see the lorry or the horse and cart. The next thing I remember was when I came round I was lying on the cobbles and my head was in Colin's lap and he was holding my hand and looking very worried.'

'Can you remember what he said to you?'

'Not really. He kept saying he was sorry and that I was to lie still. Then I remember an ambulance and a policeman and then the hospital and then you and Mam. That's all, Tessa.'

Tessa squeezed her hand. 'Well, don't try any more to remember, things may come back bit by bit if you don't force them. Ginny, you could have been killed. Your mam was terribly upset; we all were.'

'I know, I'm sorry, Tessa.' Ginny still looked pale.

'Well, you won't be going in to work tomorrow, your mam won't hear of it. She's been to see Mr Birrel.'

Ginny managed a weak smile. 'It's almost worth it to get away from all that stinking fish.'

Tessa smiled back. 'You know how partial your mam is to a nice bit of haddock.'

Ginny squeezed Tessa's hand. 'He really was upset, Tessa. Colin, I mean. So he must still love me.'

Tessa sighed. She was going to get to the bottom of this. 'I suppose he does,' she answered, getting up. 'You lie there and rest, I'll bring you something in to eat.'

Ginny smiled and closed her eyes. She really couldn't remember why she'd dashed out into the road like that. But Colin *had* been there and *must* still love her.

'She still can't remember anything before she ran out,' Tessa informed May.

'I know and I don't want to press her.'

'Well, I'm going to find out. He was at the back of it, I'm sure.'

'I wouldn't argue with you about that, Tessa. Will you see what he has to say for himself? I've got to go to work now.'

'I will,' she answered firmly.

May left and Tessa began to prepare the evening meal.

When he arrived home Colin did look worried, Tessa thought. He also looked guilty. Young Jimmy was next door and wouldn't be back until bedtime and Da wasn't home yet.

'Right. Now you can tell me what really happened. Just what did you do or say to Ginny that made her so upset that she was nearly killed?'

'What has she told you?' Colin asked defensively. All day he'd been worried that she would remember and that he'd be in for it when he got home.

'Never mind that. What did you do? Don't tell me you're not responsible, I know you too well.'

'Like I told you, I had a date and Ginny must have followed me. I told her to go home and leave me in peace. I'm a free man, she's got no claim on me.'

'And that made her run out? Who were you with?'

'Does it matter?'

'If it's part of the reason why Ginny is lying in there now, yes, it does.'

Colin hedged. He went into the scullery ostensibly to wash his hands but Tessa followed him.

'Don't you walk away from me, Colin O'Leary! Who was it?' she demanded.

'God, Tessa, you're like a dog with a bloody bone! If you must know it was Vera Morley from Blackstock Street. I've taken her out a few times, but she had nothing to do with what . . . what Ginny did.'

'Oh, what do you take me for? I didn't come over on the last boat! Vera Morley! She's not much better than the Maggie Mays on Lime Street. In fact she's worse. At least they are open about it and they get paid – or does *she* get paid too?'

Colin's face went scarlet. 'Trust you to think like that!'

'You know, for once I'm glad that Mam's dead. At least she doesn't have to face the fact that you've been carrying on with *that* one. But you haven't answered my question. Did you or she say anything to upset Ginny?'

Colin became irate. 'I've told you, Tessa, no one said anything!'

She didn't believe him. Later she'd go and see Vera Morley and find out the truth.

Colin hadn't made any move to go out after his meal. He just sat reading, or pretending to read, the *Evening Echo*, but he did look up in concern when Tessa announced she was going out.

'Where to?' he demanded.

'To see Elizabeth. Any objections?' she snapped.

He returned to the sports page.

'How is Ginny? I heard about the accident,' Delia asked when Tessa came into her kitchen.

'She's going to be all right. A couple of days in bed and she'll be back at work.'

'What possessed her to do such a thing?'

'I don't know, but I'm going to find out.'

'Isn't that her mother's responsibility?'

177

'She's gone to work.'

Delia raised her eyebrows, but went into the shop without saying anything.

'What happened?' Elizabeth asked. She'd been full of curiosity all day, ever since Eileen had told her the news as she'd walked up the street to the tram stop. Eileen, of course, had heard everything through the walls and had taken up her position on her front step as early as she could to inform anyone who passed by.

'She can't remember, but it's something to do with our Colin and that Vera Morley!'

'Vera Morley! God, she's like the station bike!'

'Hush, your mam will hear you! I *know*! I'm going to see her – will you come with me?'

'Of course, but don't tell Mam or she'll have ten blue fits!'

'Where are you going? You said you'd help me with my Latin,' Nessie asked as she came downstairs.

'I said I *might* help you, and where I go is my business,' Elizabeth answered.

'She won't be long, Nessie, and then she'll help you.' Tessa pushed Elizabeth towards the door. There was no use antagonising Nessie for no justifiable reason. She'd started to grow up and out of some of her less attractive character traits.

'I wonder what she looks like?' Elizabeth mused as they walked along Vauxhall Road to Blackstock Street. It wasn't the quickest way, but it was more direct.

'Haven't you ever seen her?' Tessa looked incredulous.

'No and I've lived here longer than you have.'

'She looks what she is.'

'Oh, this will be great!'

'No, it won't, Elizabeth! I don't want to even speak to her but I'm going to find out the truth for Ginny's sake.'

They walked the rest of the way in silence.

Blackstock Street was similar in character to Naylor Street: the houses were the same, the crowd of scruffy kids playing in the road or the gutter were the same. They asked what number house Vera Morley lived in.

'Number ten and I wish to God she'd clear off out of this street,' was the reply.

The house didn't look all that bad, Tessa thought. The windows and curtains weren't very clean but that wasn't unusual. The front door was closed and that *was* unusual, especially as it was a warm night.

Elizabeth hammered loudly on the knocker and they both waited. They'd wait all night if they had to, Tessa thought determinedly. Eventually the door was opened by a girl of about seven who wore only a pair of grubby, grey-looking knickers and whose dark brown hair was matted and very probably verminous. 'Is your Vera in?' Tessa asked.

'Who wants ter know?'

'You hardfaced little madam, get in there and ask her to come out here,' Elizabeth demanded. The child disappeared and eventually they heard footsteps on the bare boards of the lobby and Vera appeared in the doorway.

Elizabeth was taking in every detail. It was the first time she'd ever seen anyone who was called a tart. The girl was a couple of years older than herself, she judged. Her thick black hair was pinned up with fancy combs. She wore powder and rouge. Her eyebrows were plucked and pencilled and her mouth was a red gash out of which a cigarette protruded. She wore a grubby purple satin dressing gown that had multicoloured flowers embroidered on it and which clashed horribly with her red lips and nails.

'Who the 'ell are you?' she asked.

'I'm Ginny Greely's stepsister, Colin is my brother, and I want to know just what was said to make poor Ginny run into the road,' Tessa demanded angrily.

'Who bloody cares!' Vera blew smoke rings and watched them rise.

Tessa was infuriated and snatched the cigarette from her mouth and threw it into the gutter. '*I* bloody care!'

''Ere, they cost money,' Vera cried belligerently.

Elizabeth weighed in. She felt like smacking the girl hard across the face. 'So? We're not leaving until you've told us.'

Vera crossed her arms over her bosom and leaned against the doorframe and looked bored. 'I was out with yer brother, we were 'avin a laugh an' a joke in Lester Park when she appeared. She must 'ave followed 'im. Then she starts screamin' an' yellin' and callin' me names. Well, I wasn't standin for that, not from the likes of 'er. He told her to sod off an' leave us in peace an' then she went for me. Dragged a whole 'andful of 'air out me 'ead, the little bitch! I told 'er she was an ugly little kid who didn't know what fellers like Colin want and he agreed. He said she was a bloody nuisance! Then off she goes.' Vera shrugged, drew a cigarette packet from her pocket and lit another Woodbine.

Tessa was livid. 'She's *not* an ugly little kid! She's a quiet, pretty,

179

good girl! Too good for the likes of him!'

Vera shrugged. "Er sort are two a penny around 'ere.'

'And your sort are paid in pennies!' Tessa shot back.

This annoyed Vera. 'Bugger off! Go on, clear off! It's nothin' ter do with me!'

Elizabeth, who was very sarcastic when she chose to be, and who was an expert in the art of the studied insult, after all her battles with Nessie, looked Vera up and down slowly and appraisingly. Then she turned to her friend, a serious, speculative expression on her face.

'Would you say she was worth a sixpence, Tessa, or would that be too much? I mean, she's not very clean and possibly not even attractive under all that make-up. She probably doesn't have a bath very often, so she must stink to high heaven. No, on second thoughts you're right. About tuppence is all I'd say she's worth. Of course, you'd have to see a doctor afterwards in case you'd caught anything, that would be more expense.'

'You . . . you toffee-nosed little cow!' Vera screamed at Elizabeth before slamming the door in their faces.

Elizabeth grinned. 'Well, she didn't like *that* much, did she?'

'Sometimes I think you should be on the stage, Elizabeth Harrison. I really do. You certainly knew how to deal with her.'

'It's a gift,' Elizabeth replied airily. 'Now, what are we going to do about your Colin and poor Ginny?'

Tessa looked thoughtful as they walked back up the street. The woman who'd given them the number of the Morleys' house was standing on her doorstep, a toddler asleep in her arms and another clinging to her skirt.

'Whatever it was yer said to 'er, girl, it took 'er down a peg or two. I've never seen 'er with a gob on like that!'

'Just a few home truths,' Elizabeth answered, and they walked on.

'Are we going to tell her what those two said?' Tessa asked.

'We can't. I really don't think we should, unless she remembers herself.'

Tessa nodded her agreement. Elizabeth was making sense. May, when they told her about their visit to Vera, agreed too.

'But what about Da and our Colin?' Tessa asked.

'You leave both of them to me, Tessa, luv! I'll skin that little sod alive! Vera bloody Morley instead of our Ginny!'

'But she can only remember good things about him,' Tessa reminded her stepmother.

'Let her go on thinking that, but I'm going to make sure that *he* stays away from her in future. Oh, I wish to God she'd find someone else, I really do!'

'So do I,' Tessa said with equal passion.

Colin had sat in the kitchen for the whole time that Tessa was out. If she did find out the truth from Vera there'd be murder. May had never liked him and now she'd be livid. He had to get away from here. But where to? He didn't have much money. He'd spent most of it on Vera and he hadn't got his money's worth either.

His thoughts turned again to the Liverpool Savings Bank. Should he try again? He knew where he'd gone wrong last time. He'd have to try a different branch, they'd be certain to remember his face. There was a branch in County Road, he'd go there. He'd go through all the watching and waiting again, but at least he knew which was the right day to go. This time he wouldn't be greedy. He'd just approach one teller. He couldn't take the risk of failing. Then he'd be away from here. A new life, that's what he needed, a new life in a new country. But he'd better make it soon. He was aware, as were all the men he knew, that war was imminent and that if it was declared then travel to America would stop. He'd go tomorrow and give the place the once-over, then by the end of next week, on Friday, he'd make his move.

After she'd left Tessa, Elizabeth bumped into Mike Flynn, quite literally. They were both walking with heads down, lost in thought.

'God, you gave me a fright!'

'And you gave me one too,' she answered. 'Where are you going?'

'To see your da actually. Where have you been?'

'To Blackstock Street with Tessa.'

'What for?'

Elizabeth told him.

'He's a bloody little creep. There's no one around here who likes him.'

'I know. I just hope Ginny sees some sense, but if she can't remember anything she'll go on thinking he was her knight in shining armour, kneeling on the cobbles beside her, all worried and concerned. And that's something no one wants!'

Delia was surprised to see Elizabeth come in with Mike Flynn.

'Elizabeth, how's Ginny?'

'OK, Mam.'

'Is there anything wrong in your house, Mike? You look serious.'

'No, everything's great. I've come to see Mr Harrison, if that's all right with you?'

'Of course it is, go on through. I'm just going to tidy up this place and lock up.'

'Do you want me to stay or shall I go upstairs?' asked Elizabeth.

'No, I don't mind you staying.'

Jack had just made himself a cup of cocoa.

'Now here's a surprise. You've not come on the cadge, have you, Mike?' he half joked.

'No, I've come to ask you for some advice. My da's hopeless. All he's interested in is beer, fags, horses and greyhounds. The thing is, Mr Harrison, I've been working down the Salthouse Dock for Dawson's for nearly two years and I'm sick of it. I'm not qualified for anything else, anything that pays well and that's interesting, that is.'

Jack nodded. The lad's only alternatives were the docks and a dead-end job like the one he had.

'And we all know that there's going to be another war, but I'm too young for the services.'

'Oh, don't say that!' Elizabeth cried.

One look from her father silenced her.

'To have a trade is to have a future, lad, but before you can get a trade you've got to serve an apprenticeship, just like milady here. The pay is buttons and the hours are long.'

'At least he'd get some pay. All I get are "expenses".'

'Don't let's bring that up, Elizabeth, please,' Jack said firmly. 'The only thing I can suggest is that you go to evening classes.'

'But they don't have them for things like, well, engineering.'

'Of course they do, lad. Get yourself along to the Mechanics Institute and have a word with someone there. They'll be able to tell you what's on offer. You'll have to have patience though, you'll have to stick with Dawson's for a few years yet.'

Mike got up. 'I won't mind that so much if I know there is going to be a better job at the end of it. Thanks. Thanks, Mr Harrison, you've been a big help.'

Jack shook his hand. Mike was a good lad and he wished him well. He hadn't had much of a life up to now.

Elizabeth got up and went to the back door with him as her mother came in from the shop.

'What did he want?' Delia asked Jack. Mike Flynn didn't usually come into the shop.

'To ask advice about getting a decent job, eventually.'

Delia raised her eyebrows. 'Well, he's the only one in that family with any nous but I'll be surprised if he gets anywhere with his attitude.'

'What attitude?'

'Always clowning around, making stupid jokes about people. In fact turning everything into a joke. I can't see an employer putting up with that for long.'

Jack shook his head and picked up his newspaper. Sometimes with his Delia it was better just to keep quiet.

'What made you think about doing something else, Mike?' Elizabeth asked, leaning against the doorframe.

'Tessa and her plans to be a stewardess, I suppose. And I do want to get on in life. I don't want to finish up like Da.'

'You mean married with a gang of kids all squashed into a two-up, two-down?'

'Well, I hadn't thought that far ahead. I just mean that I want more than beer and fags and gambling.'

'Good for you.'

Mike looked abashed. Somehow this talk about the future had changed things between them. He didn't know how or why, but it had. 'Elizabeth, if I get on to a class, would you . . . well, would you help me, like?'

She looked interested. 'With homework, you mean? I'll try, but some of the things you'll be doing will be all . . . well, sort of technical and I'm useless at anything like that. I couldn't even master Algebra or Geometry.'

'I can't see it being all that technical to start with.'

'I suppose you're right. Yes, I'll be glad to help you, Mike.'

He shuffled his feet and twisted his cap in his hands. 'Can I ask you something else?'

'Of course.'

He was trying to frame the words.

'Well, what's up with you?'

'I'm trying to think how to say this.'

She was bemused. 'Say what?'

'Will you . . . will you come out with me, Elizabeth? To the pictures?'

She was taken aback and began to blush. She'd never really thought about him like *that*.

'If you don't want to, it doesn't matter.'

'Oh, I do! I mean . . . I'd like that.'

'When? This weekend?

'Could we make it next? Mam's got plans this Sunday, and Saturday is our busiest day and I'm always completely worn out by the time I get home. Half the time I fall asleep in the chair.'

'All right, Sunday week, then. I'll look in the *Echo* at what's on in town. Will it be OK with your Mam and Dad?' he queried.

It wouldn't, she knew that. Well, with her da maybe, but definitely not her mam.

'Maybe we should wait a bit before telling them. Mam still hasn't really forgiven me for leaving school.' She certainly didn't want to make any more trouble.

He nodded. He understood exactly how Delia would feel, that he definitely wasn't good enough for her elder daughter.

'I'll be seeing you down by the tannery next week sometime. We'll fix it up then.'

She nodded. 'I'd better go in now.'

'See you, Elizabeth,' Mike said as he walked down the yard. It had been a really great evening for him. Now he had some hopes of being able to better himself and he'd finally plucked up the courage to ask Elizabeth out and she'd neither laughed at him or refused.

'What were you two talking about out there?' Delia asked. She still didn't like Elizabeth hanging around with one of the Flynns.

'Oh, nothing much. I'm going to help him when he starts at that Mechanics place.'

Delia looked shrewdly at her daughter. 'Just you see that you don't let me down again, Elizabeth.'

'Mam! How long have I known him? Since we were babies! I've known Johnny Doyle for that long too, but I don't intend to marry either of them!'

'I sincerely hope not! Now, isn't it time you saw to your own 'homework'?'

Elizabeth fetched her books but somehow she couldn't concentrate on *Therapeutic Treatments for the Hair and Scalp*. Fancy Mike asking *me* out, she thought. It was really a surprise. They'd been friends for years, as she'd told her mam, but now it seemed as though friendship was being turned into something else, and she didn't feel at all unhappy about it. Quite the reverse.

Chapter Nineteen

By the following Friday Colin knew as much as he needed to know about the routine of the bank. He'd not been to work all week, although he'd gone out and returned at his usual time. Things at home were very strained. No one was speaking to him, except Ginny, and every time she spoke directly to him either Tessa or May would interrupt and change the subject. Besides, he couldn't stand Ginny gazing at him like a moonstruck calf.

He was so confident of success that this time he'd packed a small bag with his few possessions and had hidden it under the bed. Cleaning under the beds was something that only Tessa did and she only ever did it at weekends. Ginny or May never cleaned that thoroughly.

As he stood outside Frost's, a small department store opposite the bank, he felt again all the nervousness and tension he'd suffered the last time. But his whole future depended on the next five minutes and he was determined not to let his nerves get the better of him.

He crossed the road slowly and opened the door. The decor was much the same as the Scotland Road branch and he quickly appraised the two tellers who were entering sums of money in large books. He decided to go for the elder of the two. Just as he'd done before he shoved the note towards the teller and gestured with the catapult in his pocket.

The eyes that met his were full of fear. 'I . . . I'm sorry but . . . but there's not much here.'

Colin began to panic. 'Where the bleeding hell is it, then? It only arrived fifteen minutes ago, I watched the feller bring it!'

'In the safe.'

'Then go and bloody get it and be quick.' He again pointed the stick in his pocket towards the older man. Then he gestured at the younger teller: 'You! Don't you make a move or I'll use this bloody gun!'

The young teller was rooted to the spot. Colin felt the sweat spring out of every pore in his body. He paced up and down, his eyes darting from the young teller to the door and back again. The elderly man returned after what seemed to Colin a lifetime. Every minute he'd expected a customer to come in, just like last time.

'It . . . it's all there.' Two canvas bags were placed on the counter. Colin snatched them up, shoved them inside his jacket and ran out. Once on County Road he walked quickly away. County Road was intersected with narrow streets of red-brick terraced houses. He'd use these streets and the back entries, avoiding the main road, until he reached the junction with Spellow Lane, then he'd get a bus or a tram home. There was always one waiting. It was a sort of terminus, a halfway stop between Aintree and Fazakerley and town.

A number 22 tram was waiting and he paid his fare and went up the narrow stairs to the upper deck. He needed a cigarette to calm his nerves. He fumbled in his pocket and drew out a battered carton of Woodbines. There was only one left and as he lit it he thought from now on he would be able to afford expensive cigarettes, not Woodies, *and* he'd have a proper lighter and not a box of Pilot matches.

He felt elated. His nervousness disappeared and he felt an enormous sense of relief. Two bags! *Two* bags! There was obviously more on Fridays because people wanted money for the weekend and the banks were closed on Saturdays. He must have hundreds of pounds. His fingers itched to count it and he could hardly wait to get home.

When he finally reached his stop he went down the back jigger to Naylor Street and was relieved to find the house was empty. May was out. He went up to the bedroom and emptied the contents of both bags on the bed. The crisp new notes seemed to cover it entirely. He picked up a five-pound note. He'd never even seen one of the large white notes before. He crumpled it up in his hand and the sensation this gave him was something he'd never experienced before either. He stood for a few minutes looking at the money. He was rich! He was rich beyond his wildest dreams! He pulled himself together and stuffed it back into the bags, then, pulling his bag from under the bed, he put both the smaller canvas ones with all the notes inside, except the one he had crumpled. That one he put in his pocket. Now he'd head for the Cunard Building and the first ship out of Liverpool bound for America.

He looked around at the shabby room. He was well out of it, he thought. The place was not much better than a doss house. He left without a second glance, closing the yard door behind him, and walked down the entry with a spring in his step.

On his way to the Pier Head he stopped off in Church Street and bought a suit, three shirts and two ties in Hepworth's. He also went to Lewis's and bought pyjamas, a dressing gown, new underwear, shoes and socks, toilet requisites, a trilby hat and a large suitcase. In the changing room, he took out three more five-pound notes, to pay not only for his purchases but his fare. He couldn't go scrabbling around in his case for money. In the Gentlemen's toilets he put on his new clothes and set the trilby at what he thought to be a rakish angle. He left his old clothes there. Then, full of confidence and elation, he set off for the Cunard Building, the middle one of the famous trio on the waterfront.

When he arrived and the clerk looked at him with respect, he felt like a new person.

'Yes, sir? May I be of assistance?'

'I have to go to New York and I'm in a hurry. Business, you understand,' he added.

'You're in luck, the *Ascania* is due to sail at five o'clock. You'll just have time to embark. I presume you have your official documents?'

Colin panicked but then decided to bluff it out. 'Of course I have. I wouldn't be here otherwise.'

The clerk nodded. 'United States Immigration are very strict. Now, what class will you be travelling?'

'Second class, please.'

'Return?'

'Yes.' There was no use arousing suspicions by asking for a one-way ticket.

'That will be twelve guineas please, sir.'

Colin counted out the notes and coins and waited for his change and the ticket.

'*Bon voyage*, sir!' the clerk said pleasantly.

Once outside he crossed the open cobbled space, his hand shaking as he looked at the piece of printed card. This was his ticket to the future. But something was nagging at him. There was something he'd forgotten, he was certain. Then the realisation struck him like a blow to the stomach. Johnny Doyle sailed on the *Ascania*! He stopped dead. God! What was he going to do now? Think, that's what he'd have to do. He crossed to the tram terminus and sat on a wooden bench. If he waited for another ship he was taking a terrible risk of getting caught. Then he could be looking at ten years in jail. What if he went to London or Southampton? You could quite easily lose yourself in London or catch another ship from Southampton but it would take time and time was one thing he didn't have. No, he couldn't stand that. He'd have to risk it. If Johnny saw him he'd have to make up some story, but if he stayed in his cabin all day, just venturing out for meals, he may never see hide nor hair of Johnny. He worked mainly in the first-class sections of the ship. There wasn't a choice. He'd have to go because he certainly couldn't stay.

As usual the Landing Stage was busy. There were passengers and their families and friends; luggage being loaded; last-minute supplies being taken on board; the tugs already alongside and an official of the Cunard Line waiting at the bottom of the gangway for tickets.

Once on board he found his way to his cabin, guided by a steward. The ship was full and the companionways seemed to be crowded with people. Some were sitting on their luggage.

The steward looked harassed. 'Over-booked again! It always happens, every trip. I don't know what they do in those offices. You'd think they'd have enough sense not to give a cabin to two different sets of passengers! Well, the Purser's Office can sort it out. Here we are, sir.' He fumbled with a key, muttering about 'unnecessary *bon voyage* parties and flaming kids running riot', and opened the door.

Once inside Colin looked around. There was every comfort here, he thought, but it wasn't as grand as first class would be. He could afford first class but that would have drawn attention to himself and he would have needed a trunk full of fancy clothes which he'd never wear again. To him this small carpeted cabin and its bunk, made up with crisp white sheets and heavy white counterpane with the Cunard emblem embossed on it, its porcelain washbasin and thick white fluffy towels was sheer luxury.

He opened his case and unpacked his few belongings into the highly polished wardrobe, thinking he should have bought more shirts and trousers. Still, he could buy them in New York. He sat down on the bunk. New York! He'd only ever heard stories about it. How big it was, how tall the skyscrapers were. How modern everything was. How it teemed with people of all creeds and colours and how you could still make fortunes there if you were lucky. Oh, he'd get on in New York all right.

He took the two canvas bags out of his case and then placed them on the floor and counted the money. He was set up for life. It had been his lucky day. He put most of the notes back into the bags and stuffed them under the mattress. He wished he could go up on deck to join the crowds and watch as they pulled away and sailed downriver towards the estuary, leaving Liverpool and his old life behind, but he couldn't risk it. He did experience a surge of excitement as he heard the three loud blasts of the ship's steam whistle and then the answering ones of the tugs, the ferries and the other ships on the river, and felt the deck beneath his feet begin to move. He climbed up on the bunk and looked out of the porthole: the *Ascania* was being pulled out into the river and he could see almost as far as the lighthouse on Perch Rock. He was on his way.

When there was no sign of him by ten o'clock that night Ginny began to worry. May was at work, Richie had just come back from his nightly visit to the Globe and Tessa was engrossed in a book.

'Something must have happened to him! He's always in from work about six or half past.'

Tessa looked up. 'Don't worry about him, Ginny. He used to stay out all night when Mam was alive, when we first came here. He'll come to no harm, believe me.'

But Ginny wasn't satisfied and by eleven o'clock she had convinced them that something must have happened to him.

'Oh, Ginny, for heaven's sake, go and look and see if his things are in the bedroom, if it will calm you down,' May said impatiently. She was tired and she certainly didn't really care where the lad was.

Ginny went upstairs and returned looking even more worried. 'Well?' May demanded.

'Everything has gone. He's left. He's run off. Come and see.'

Reluctantly Tessa and May followed a tearful Ginny back upstairs and after checking the chest of drawers and the old sea chest they looked at each other.

'So, the bird has flown. I wonder where to?' May said without much interest.

'Well, I'll be honest, I can't say I'm that bothered. He can look after himself and he may be up to his eyes in . . . something. That wouldn't surprise me either,' Tessa said.

May nodded her agreement and then began to try to comfort her daughter, who had dissolved into tears.

'Ginny, he won't be gone long. He'll be back. He's done this before,' Tessa tried to reassure her friend.

'Who knows what gets into fellers' heads, luv? Some just can't settle for long in one place, but they come back, usually when they're broke and hungry. He'll be back, luv, you wait and see.'

Ginny wiped her eyes but didn't reply. She wasn't convinced. She knew she wouldn't get much sleep tonight, she was so worried.

On Saturday morning the *Daily Post* was full of the robbery. It had been an audacious crime, committed by someone who had 'nerves of steel', so the newspaper commented. The police had a good description of the thief who had got away with all the bank's takings and the money that had only arrived fifteen minutes earlier. It was a professional job, well planned and carried out with speed and efficiency. They were looking for a tall, well-built lad of about nineteen to twenty-one, with dark hair.

'Well, that covers most of the lads in the city,' Richie commented dryly.

'I thought you said they had a good description?' May said.

'I did. It says so here.'

'Well, I don't call that good.'

'It says the teller would recognise him again—'

'They've got to catch him first,' May interrupted. 'Do you think your precious son will put in an appearance today?' she asked sarcastically.

'I've no idea. You know what he's like.'

'I do,' May replied. It wouldn't bother her if he never crossed this doorstep again. It would give everyone a bit of peace and quiet, and maybe Ginny would begin to see him in a different light.

By Saturday night the *Ascania* had left Cobh in County Cork behind and was steaming out into the Atlantic. Colin was bored sick. He saw only the steward, there was nothing to do at all except count his money and even that pleasure was waning. He'd tried to make plans but that didn't work either as he had no idea what he really wanted to do, or what was on offer in the huge country he was bound for. When he went for his meals he got glimpses of the public rooms and they looked so interesting and inviting that he began to think of venturing out. If he had to stay in that cabin for another five days he'd go mad. After all, the ship was full. Maybe he'd been over-cautious. If he just went for a quick wander round, not stay out for too long, there wouldn't be much of a risk in that. He'd mingle with the crowds, act casually and do nothing that would single him out for attention. He'd be all right.

He was very cautious at first, continually glancing around to see if anyone was watching him, until he realised he must look very furtive. He leaned on the rail of the Promenade Deck, lit a cigarette and looked down at the grey-green water that slid by, broken only by the white spray of the ship's bow wave. What was the matter with him? He looked like everyone else. Why on earth should he worry?

Next morning after breakfast he wandered along to the Library and Gentlemen's Smoking Room, which was furnished with cane and wicker chairs and tables and potted plants and pictures of oriental scenes. He relished his cigarette; he was a 'Gentleman' now. Then he strolled along the Boat Deck, looking out at the waters of the Atlantic that surrounded them and would do so for the next four days and three nights, breathing the damp salty air and thinking of just what he would do without 'official documents' when they reached their destination. He'd have to devise some form of dodging U. S. Immigration Officials. He had his return ticket, he was 'on business': maybe he'd accuse the steward of stealing his documents. That was a possibility. The problem would keep his mind occupied for most of the journey. He pulled his hat further down to make sure it didn't blow away, stuffed his hands in his pockets and walked on, totally engrossed.

Johnny Doyle had been told by the Chief Steward to make certain that all the chairs and rugs had been put out on the Promenade Deck as the deck steward was 'indisposed'. Johnny had had to hide a grin. 'Indisposed' meant either drunk or hungover: no wonder the Chief Steward had a face like thunder.

He was walking along with an armful of thick tartan rugs, for it was always chilly on the Atlantic, whatever time of year it was: the speed of the ship generated wind. He happened to glance down to the Boat Deck, then he stopped and leaned over the rail. It couldn't be! It couldn't possibly be! It was just someone who looked like him!

At that moment Colin decided to light a cigarette and stopped and fumbled in his pocket for his Senior Service cigarettes and lighter.

Johnny let out his breath slowly. It *was* him. It was Colin O'Leary. What the hell was he doing on board? No good, that was for certain. Just where had he got the money from? He detested Colin O'Leary — he'd never forgotten his wanton cruelty to that poor litte girl – but what about Tessa? If she learned that he had shopped her brother, and in so doing brought more shame on the family, how would she react? He struggled with his conscience for a while until he made up his mind. O'Leary must have committed a serious, possibly violent crime to be running to the other side of the world and he knew that Tessa would almost certainly understand. He deposited the rugs on the nearest chair and walked away, heading for the Purser's Office to study the Passenger Manifest. If it *was* Colin, then he'd find some way of searching his cabin.

It was no hardship to find Colin's name and cabin number. Second class too, he thought. He went to find the steward.

'It'd be more than my job's worth to give you a key to 108. What do you want it for?' Taffy Williams asked.

'I've got some suspicions about the feller who's in there.'

'What sort of suspicions?'

'He's someone I know. He lives in our street and has a job as a labourer, so how come he can afford a second-class cabin?'

Taffy pondered this for a moment. 'OK, boyo, I can't give you the key but I can come with you. He's not on my section, it's Paddy Mahr's bit along here, but he's gone to see what he can scrounge from his pantry lad.'

They both looked around quickly then the Welshman opened the door.

'He hasn't got much in the way of gear, has he?' Taffy said disparagingly as Johnny searched the small wardrobe.

'Where else would he hide something?'

'Under the mattress on the bunk. They all do it, they think it's safe. It's the first place anyone looks if they're out to pinch something.'

Taffy yanked up the mattress while Johnny searched underneath. His fingers closed over something.

'I've got it.'

'What is it?'

'A canvas bag – no, two by the feel of it, and they're full of something.'

The bags were pulled out.

Johnny was stunned. 'Bloody hell! He's robbed a bloody bank! Look at the lettering. *Liverpool Savings Bank*.' Johnny looked inside one bag. 'It's stuffed with money!'

'Then we'd better take it to the Three-Ringer. I'll take it and say I found it while doing the bunk. I'll have to say I was helping Paddy out. Returning a favour, see.'

'God, I knew he was crafty and light-fingered but I'd no idea he was into big stuff like this! Perhaps you should tell his nibs I know him.'

'OK. Wait for the summons then.'

'I'll be up on the Prom Deck, where I'm supposed to be.'

He still couldn't believe it. Colin O'Leary, robbing a bloody bank! He had some guts, he'd say that for him.

Fifteen minutes later the 'indisposed' deck steward appeared to summon Johnny to the Chief Steward's office. He was surprised to see both Taffy and Colin already there, and as soon as Colin clapped eyes on him the colour drained from his face.

'Right, Doyle, do you know this feller?'

'Yes, sir. His name's Colin O'Leary, he lives in the same street as me.'

'And what does he do for a job?'

'He's a labourer for Mathews Haulage in Vauxhall Road, sir.'

'I told you, I *won* the money on a horse,' Colin interrupted, recovering his wits. 'Well, on a couple of horses. I had a good day!'

'It would have to have been a whole herd of bloody horses, and why is it in these bags marked the property of the Liverpool Savings Bank?'

'That's what the bookie gave it me in, I swear to God!'

'Taffy, go to the Purser and ask if *Mr* O'Leary has lodged his passport and visa with him, and then find the Master-at-arms.'

'I . . . I didn't have time to get them. I . . . I decided on the spur of the moment to get away from Liverpool! Start a new life. We live in a slum.' He glared at Johnny, furious with him and with himself. Why, oh why had he gone wandering around the ship?

'Well, you're going back to Liverpool. The Master-at-arms is on his way. You'll be locked in your cabin for the rest of the voyage *and* for the return trip, then you'll be handed over to the Liverpool City Police and you can tell them that fairy tale. I've heard better excuses from a bevvied pantry lad!'

'I knew you'd come a cropper one day, O'Leary,' Johnny said to Colin as the Master-at-arms and the Assistant Purser came to take him away. Then Johnny thought of Tessa. Oh, life wasn't fair at all for some people. She'd had the moonlight flit, her mam's illness and death, her da's marriage to May and now this. He knew she'd cope, just as she'd coped with all the rest – Johnny had great admiration for her resilience – but this time she'd hardly be able to hold her head up with the shame of what her brother had done. He only wished there were something he could do to help.

On Sunday morning Elizabeth dressed with more care than usual for mass and hoped her Mam hadn't noticed. Mike was bound to be there with the rest of his family. They'd arranged their date for tonight and she could hardly wait.

Although it was a beautiful sunny September morning everyone seemed very preoccupied and apprehensive.

'I know that the prayers at mass this morning will be more fervent,' Delia said to Jack as she adjusted her hat to the right angle, but not with the care and attention she usually gave it.

'Bound to be, luv. We'll know before dinnertime the outcome of that Ultimatum but I can't see that little butcher backing down. They were bloody brave, those poor sods in Poland. Cavalry against artillery. There was no way they could win.'

Elizabeth looked at her parents with mounting apprehension. She knew, as did the rest of the entire city and country, that if there was no reply to the Ultimatum by eleven o'clock then there was only one course open to them. War.

Father Walsh's sermon that morning was all about the evil that was spreading over the world and the terror, death and destruction that Satan in the guise of Herr Hitler was responsible for. They prayed hard for the poor brave people of Poland and for those who had died trying to stem the might of the German army. There was no talk of 'praying for peace' now, Elizabeth thought, as there had been every Sunday for months. She closed her eyes tightly and tried to envisage just what the future would bring, but she couldn't.

Eddie Doyle, his timid little wife and two younger sons were waiting after mass and gathered a group of their neighbours and customers together.

'Do you all want to come back with me? We've a wireless set. There'll be no drink served, though. Not at a time like this.'

'I would 'ave thought we'd all *need* a drink at a time like this,' Frank Flynn said.

Eddie ignored him and led the group out on to Scotland Road.

It was a quarter to eleven when they were all finally settled in the saloon bar and the big Bakelite wireless set had been carried in and placed on the bar counter next to the handles of the beer pump, which were covered with a clean teacloth that Eddie obviously had no intention of removing.

Elizabeth had manoeuvred herself through the group until she was near to Mike and they exchanged glances of foreboding.

At five to eleven Eddie Doyle fiddled with the knobs and the wireless crackled into life. There wasn't a sound in the room as the tired, sad voice of Mr Chamberlain, the Prime Minister, told them that 'peace in our time' was over and that 'this country is now at war with Germany. We are ready.'

All the older women were crying silently. Delia hid her face against Jack's shoulder, remembering the terrible day when all those telegrams had been delivered in Liverpool, two of which had informed her that both her brothers were dead. Even now, twenty-two years later, she could still hear her mam's heartrending cries. The older men too looked drawn and worried. They had so many memories, all of them bitter, of brothers, cousins, mates who'd not been so lucky as themselves. Only in the young men and lads was there a total lack of understanding.

'For the love of God, Eddie, take that bloody teacloth off! I never thought I'd live to see it happen all over again.' Jack Harrison spoke for everyone.

'And this time it won't just be the soldiers and sailors,' Frank Flynn added. His words brought back all they had read about the bombing of civilians in Spain.

'All right, but get the kids out of here.'

All the younger element left their parents inside, glad to escape that doom-laden atmosphere.

Ginny, Tessa, Elizabeth and Mike huddled together.

'I'm scared stiff already,' Ginny said timidly.

'We all are. We don't know what to expect. It's not the same just *reading* about it in the newspapers. It . . . Things will happen to *us*,' Elizabeth added quietly.

Alice Collins joined them. 'Have you heard anything about your Colin yet?' she asked Tessa.

'No, and I've more important things on my mind,' Tessa replied, refusing to meet Ginny's gaze.

'Oh, God!' Tessa cried.

'What?' Elizabeth demanded.

'Johnny! Johnny Doyle. He sailed on Friday. What if the Germans start attacking shipping straightaway.'

'They won't have reached America yet, but they'll be safe enough,' Mike tried to reassure her, while wondering just how safe the ship would be on the return trip.

The group began to drift away to their homes and Mike turned to Elizabeth.

'What about tonight? It said in the paper last night that they'd close all the cinemas and theatres, if war was declared.'

She was disappointed. It would have been a distraction.

'We'll just go for a walk, everyone will be so upset they won't notice.'

'I know. Da fought in the last one and he won't say a word about it, not even when he's bevvied, and that's a miracle in itself.'

Elizabeth nodded her understanding. It was going to be an awful day. The King was going to speak on the wireless tonight, so they'd said. Kids had already been evacuated, air-raid shelters had been provided and gas masks – hideous things – must be carried all the time. Her mam had been hoarding food for months, even though they'd been told not to.

'Will we still go to work?'

'I suppose so,' Mike answered.

Elizabeth looked up at him. 'Promise me something, Mike.'

'What?'

'That you won't lie about your age and join up!'

'Don't you want me to go?'

'No, not yet. Not until you're . . . old enough. Please?'

He took her hand. 'I promise.'

'You'd better not let your mam see you holding hands,' Tessa said quietly with a lilt of amusement in her voice. Observant as ever, she had noticed how Elizabeth and Mike's friendly relationship had changed recently.

'You're right.' Reluctantly Elizabeth slid her fingers from his.

The rest of the day was indeed awful, spent in nervous speculation about the future. But they had no inkling of what the war might really mean to them until a couple of days later.

'Now what?' Mike asked, as Kenny Keegan came running towards the tannery wall where the four friends had gathered once again. 'What's up, Kenny?'

'It's just come through an' Mr Doyle's dead worried and Mrs Doyle's crying,' the lad panted.

'What for?' Elizabeth demanded.

'One of them German U-boats sunk the *Athenia* on Monday!'

'Oh my God!' Tessa cried, clasping her hands tightly.

'She was going back to Glasgow an' . . . an' they don't think that anyone is left alive.'

Tessa grabbed hold of Elizabeth's arm. 'Johnny's out there too! If they can sink one ship so soon, what chance do any of them have of making it back?'

'Oh, Tessa, don't think like that!' Elizabeth pleaded.

'No, don't. They'll be all right. The *Ascania*'s bigger and faster and they'll do a quick turnround and run for home. He'll come back, Tessa. He will!' Mike was trying to convince himself as much as Tessa.

Tessa just nodded, and there were tears in her eyes.

'I never thought you cared about him . . . like that,' Elizabeth said as they turned the corner into Naylor Street.

'I . . . I do.'

Elizabeth gave her friend's hand a squeeze. What would happen to them all in the days, months and even years ahead? she wondered. Would the life they knew change beyond all recognition?

Chapter Twenty

The news of the sinking of the *Athenia* reached the *Ascania* by means of wireless telegraphy, and the Captain ordered the rest of the journey to be made at Full Ahead. He just prayed that the weather would hold.

Although sworn to secrecy so as not to worry the passengers, the crew had been told and emergency lifeboat drill ordered each night after midnight. All lights that could possibly be extinguished were put out. There was an air of fear on board now that hadn't been there on Friday when they'd sailed.

As Colin wasn't classed as a passenger any longer, the steward, Paddy Mahr, decided to inform his 'prisoner', who in his opinion was a surly little sod, of the situation.

'And how are you in yourself this morning?' he asked as he brought in the breakfast tray.

Colin just scowled at him.

'Wouldn't you think it was a grand day, looking out there?' He inclined his head in the direction of the porthole. 'But won't we all be glad when we're back home? Even you, me young bucko.'

'What kind of bloody stupid remark is that to make?' Colin said acidly.

'Sure, it's far from stupid. The crew and passengers of the *Athenia* would gladly swap places with us all. Wasn't she sunk by a torpedo on Monday? A hundred and fourteen souls went down with her, God rest them all.' The steward crossed himself.

Colin looked at him in amazement. 'Why?'

'Oh, it's "why", is it now? Because war was declared on Sunday morning and here we are stuck in the middle of the ocean with God alone knows what lurking down there.'

The terrible reality of their position dawned on Colin. They were easy prey. The *Ascania* was a merchant ship, she had no guns or depth charges. Was it better to reach Liverpool and ultimately Walton Jail or sit here never knowing if he'd end up being drowned?

'Now that'll give you something to keep your mind occupied. It's saying some prayers I'd be doing if I were you.'

Johnny was scared too. 'What kind of a chance do you think we'll have?' he asked the Second Steward, who'd called him in to give him a pep talk. The Chief Steward had summoned them all, in groups, and informed them of the situation, but as Johnny was so young – in fact the youngest crew member – he'd asked his second-in-command to reassure the lad.

'Good. The Atlantic's a big ocean and it's the most treacherous. When we reach New York we'll do a fast turnround and the Captain will order Full Ahead for the whole way home. At twenty-nine knots we'll outstrip any U-boat, but we won't be sailing again with passengers. Every merchantman will be commandeered now by the Government for convoy duty.'

Johnny nodded, feeling better now. He didn't really mind not sailing again with passengers and he was too young for the Royal Navy.

'So, it's fingers crossed and pray to God the weather stays good. Get off now, lad, and try not too look so worried. The last thing we want is for the passengers to suspect something's up. Time enough for them to worry when we reach port.'

After a fortnight with no news, everyone in number twelve, Naylor Street was concerned about Colin. Ginny was frantic.

'I know something's happened to him! I just *know* it!'

'Well, I have to admit that he's never stayed away for so long,' Tessa said.

'Do you think we should inform the police?' May asked Richie.

Richie looked serious. 'Give him until tomorrow night. We know he intended going somewhere, he took everything with him. Maybe he's gone to look for work in London.'

'That wouldn't surprise me, him not telling us I mean,' Tessa added.

'You're right, Tessa, he's probably got a job and a room down there.'

'And he wouldn't bother to write to us to stop us worrying,' May added. 'I don't think he's come to any harm, Ginny, luv.'

'But he never said a word to me! He didn't even say goodbye.'

'Maybe he didn't want to upset you, luv,' May said soothingly as she exchanged glances with Tessa.

'He wouldn't have gone and joined the Army, would he?' Ginny asked tearfully.

'I doubt that very much,' May answered. King and Country would be the last things on his mind, she thought.

But Ginny wouldn't be pacified. She *knew* something had happened to him. She was certain he would never have deliberately gone for so long without telling her, even though he'd been distant the week before he'd disappeared. He'd taken her to hospital after her accident though, hadn't he? That must mean something. But she still couldn't remember what had happened before she'd been knocked down.

Richie, urged on by Ginny and Tessa, who was more concerned for Ginny than her brother, finally agreed to go to the police.

'I know he's eighteen but that doesn't alter things,' May said as she gave his jacket a brush-down. 'Go, and let us get a bit of peace from milady in there,' she whispered.

They were all surprised by the loud hammering on the front door.

'Oh, maybe he's back! He's come back!' Ginny cried, making for the door.

Tessa caught her arm. 'Ginny, why would he be knocking on the front door? He'd come in the back way or just open the front door, he's got a key.'

The hopeful light in Ginny's eyes dimmed. Tessa was right. A feeling of dread settled over her again. It was increased as a uniformed police sergeant accompanied by a burly man in a serge suit and bowler hat came into the kitchen, followed by Richie.

'Oh my God!' May cried.

'Am I right in saying that one Colin O'Leary resides here?' the sergeant stated, referring to his notebook while the calm but penetrating gaze of the CID man swept the room and all their faces.

'Yes. What's happened?' Richie replied.

'Oh, what's happened to him?' Ginny begged tearfully. She was certain they'd come to tell them that something terrible had happened to poor Colin.

'We've had a message from the Master-at-arms on the *Ascania*, due into Liverpool tomorrow, that they have a Colin O'Leary on board, under lock and key. He's suspected of robbing a branch of the Liverpool Savings Bank, although he claims' – the CID man pulled a piece of paper from his pocket – 'that he won the money he has in his possession on a couple of horse races and the bookie's runner gave it to him in the bags marked with the bank's name.' He stopped and glanced at the faces of the four people in the kitchen, noting their expressions.

'He claims that he was with a "Ginny Greely" at the time of the raid.'

Ginny sat down slowly at the table. This wasn't happening.

Colin wouldn't do something like rob a bank! But why was he on a ship? Where had he been going? Why hadn't he told her? And why had he said he'd been with her? None of it made any sense to her. Colin just *wouldn't* do something as terrible as that. He *must* be telling the truth about winning it. Oh, she wished he was here so she could ask him.

'Are you Miss Ginny Greely?' the sergeant asked.

May was instantly by her daughter's side. She was as stunned as the rest of them, but Ginny looked as though she were about to faint.

'Yes, she is, and I'm her mam.'

'Well, were you with him on the afternoon of Friday the first of September?'

Ginny broke down in tears. 'I . . . I . . . can't remember! I . . . can't remember *anything*, Mam.'

'Come on now, luv, don't get upset. We all know you were at work, or did you take time off?' May asked.

'I . . . I . . . Oh, Mam!' Ginny became incoherent. Until she saw him, *actually saw* him, she didn't know what to think or say. If he'd been falsely accused she'd stand by him, but was he innocent?

'She's not going to be much help. She had a bad accident not so long ago and it's affected her memory,' May informed them.

'How convenient,' the CID man said with heavy sarcasm.

'Go and check the records in Stanley Hospital if you don't believe it,' May said.

'You know he's been in trouble before? Borstal – twice. Now it looks as if he's graduated to bigger things.'

'Oh, Holy Mother of God!' May cried while Richie looked sheepish and Tessa sat down on the sofa and covered her face with her hands. Oh, this was terrible! She certainly didn't believe Colin's trumped-up explanation and neither would her da.

'Why didn't you tell me?' May demanded.

'I . . . I . . . thought he'd learned his lesson and I didn't want to upset you, May,' Richie replied guiltily. He really should have told her.

'Upset me! Upset me! Do you think I'd have let him take our Ginny out if I'd known that?'

'All right, that's enough. You can sort all that out between yourselves later.'

'When will he be home?' Richie asked them.

'Tomorrow morning. He'll be taken into custody as soon as they dock and probably go to the Main Bridewell in Dale Street.'

'Can we see him?' Richie asked.

'I don't want to see him ever again!' Tessa cried bitterly.

'You can, if he wants to see you. I imagine he will because he won't see you for a long time after that. He'll get eight years in Walton, if he's lucky. A hundred and fifty quid is a lot of money, as well as possessing a gun.'

'A gun!' May shrieked.

'Or what we assume was a gun.' He wasn't going to tell them that no one had actually seen it.

'Well, we'll leave you in peace now to carry on the argument, but we'll see you tomorrow, particularly you, Miss Greely. Be down at the Bridewell by half past eleven.'

No one made a move to escort the two men to the front door, they were all too shocked.

When the front door slammed Tessa broke the silence. 'Oh, I *hate* him! I really *hate* him! How could he do this to us?'

'And why did you never tell me he'd been in Borstal, Richie?' May demanded angrily.

'May, would you have married me . . . taken all of us on, if you'd known that?' Richie pleaded.

'I certainly wouldn't have had *him* under the same roof as the rest of us but I'd have still married you. But we'll talk about that later, when we're on our own.' She nodded towards the two shaken girls.

'How are we going to hold our heads up now?' Tessa exclaimed, her cheeks pink with anger. Then she turned to her stepsister. 'Oh, Ginny, please stop crying. Maybe now you'll see what he's really like. He's lying, he's robbed that bank all right and now he's using you to try to get himself off the hook.'

Ginny couldn't stand any more. She got up. 'I . . . I don't know what to think!'

'You're not going to go on believing him and protecting him! How can you?' Tessa cried passionately.

Ginny rushed from the room in floods of tears. He'd been in trouble before and they'd known but hadn't said a word, and now . . . Oh, she didn't know what to believe any more.

The following morning, as they were getting ready to go to Dale Street, Johnny came to the back door.

'I've just this minute got home, Tessa. Have you—'

'Heard? Yes. The police came yesterday.' She leaned against the sink. 'Oh, Johnny, how am I going to cope with all this? It will be in all the papers, everyone in the whole city will know!'

'I'm sorry, but people *will* understand. At least in this street they will. Everyone had him taped as a bit of a crook. Don't you remember that Christmas fiasco?'

She looked up at him, her eyes bright with unshed tears. 'Yes, of course, we knew he was a petty thief, a chancer – but bank robbery!'

'I know, and I'm the one who caught him.'

'You?'

He nodded and then told her. 'I don't know what he was going to do when he got there. He had no passport or anything.'

'Oh, he'd have lied his way out of that. Jumped ship, anything. Johnny, I feel so ashamed.'

'It's not your fault, Tessa.' He took her hand. 'You know we . . . I'll stand by you.'

'Will you? Truthfully?'

'Yes, truthfully. You're the best . . . the nicest girl I know and other people know that too. The fellers around here like your da, they won't blame him – well, not much. Nearly every family has its black sheep. He's yours.'

'But it will all come out.'

'Maybe it's best if it does. Clear the air, sort of. Then you can all start again.'

'Thanks. I really mean that.'

'How's Ginny?'

'In a terrible state. She's cried all night and the more we all try to reason with her, the worse she gets.'

'Surely to God she doesn't believe his story?'

'I don't know, but I think she does.'

'That fairy tale won't hold water! Won it all on the horses and the runner gave him the bags! God, you'd have to be an idiot to believe that.'

'I know, but where he's concerned she *is* an idiot. *And* he's using her.'

'How?'

'He's saying she was with him that Friday afternoon when everyone knows she was at work.'

'Can't her mam talk some sense into her?'

'She's tried. We all have.'

Johnny shook his head. Colin was worse than anyone he'd ever known. Fancy using someone like poor Ginny to try to clear himself.

'Will you . . . will you come with us?' Tessa asked

'Yes. I've to go down there anyway. They want another statement from me, even though I told them all I knew when they came aboard as soon as we'd tied up. I'm not looking forward to it at all. I was even afraid we weren't going to make it home, not after the *Athenia,* but now we have, the last thing I want to do is this . . . *and* I've no job any more.'

'It couldn't have been a worse day and it's only just started.'

'Don't worry, we'll get through it.'

On the way into town they were all silent and preoccupied, none more so than Ginny. Over and over again the questions had flown round in her head, but at the bottom of her heart she just couldn't believe he'd do such a thing. May had told Tessa to stop trying to get her to see reason, she was in such a state already.

'She's so stupid,' said Tessa sadly.

'I know. She's bloody besotted with him,' May answered grimly.

The large room in Hatton Garden was full of people: police officers of all ranks, CID men, women who were obviously street walkers, and ordinary families like themselves.

Richie approached the counter where two desk sergeants and a constable were dealing with enquiries.

'Excuse me, I'm Mr O'Leary, I've come about my lad, Colin. You took him off the *Ascania* this morning.'

A well-dressed woman who was complaining that she'd lost her dog and no one was doing anything about it looked at him with interest, to the relief of the constable, who quite cheerfully could have strangled her.

'Right, take a seat over there, someone will be with you in a minute.'

May, Tessa and Ginny all found a seat on a long wooden bench that was half occupied by another family. Richie and Johnny stood beside them, leaning against the wall.

It wasn't long before the plainclothes police officer who'd come yesterday arrived.

'Is he . . .?' Richie asked.

'Aye, he is. Downstairs in the cells.'

'Can I see him?'

'No. He won't see anyone, except Miss Greely.' He shrugged. 'It's his right, just as it's his right not to say anything at all, apart from giving an alibi.'

Through all the confusion that filled her mind Ginny looked up. It was her he wanted to see. He didn't even want to see his da.

'He's up to something, Tessa,' Johnny whispered, while Richie and May remonstrated with the police officer.

'I know, and Ginny's in no state to be here at all.'

May sat down again, fuming. There was nothing anyone could do, apparently. The only person he'd see was Ginny.

Ginny didn't notice the dismal surroundings as she was led downstairs to the cells full of miscreants of one kind or another. Colin was in one by himself and as soon as it was opened Ginny threw herself at him, crying and flinging her arms wide.

When Colin caught her and pulled her close the feeling of relief was so intense that he started to shake. Thank God she still seemed not to remember their argument in the park before her accident. He'd been desperately worried she would have done. Then Ginny was prised from his embrace.

'Sit down there, miss, and *you*, sit the other side of the table.'

They did as they were told but Colin looked up at the man. 'Can't I even have a minute with her? You can see how upset she is.'

'No. It's not allowed. I'll stand by the door and there's to be no touching either!'

Ginny tried to pull herself together. 'They say . . . they say . . .'

'I know, Ginny, but it's not true!' he protested in a whisper. 'They wouldn't believe me. That bookie's runner set me up, giving me my winnings in those bags.'

'But you'd left! You'd taken all your things.'

'I know I did. I was going to America to get a better job, so we'd have a better life, both of us, Ginny. I was going to send for you when I got a good job and somewhere nice to live. I swear I was. I didn't tell you because . . . because I couldn't stand to see how upset you'd be. You'd think I was running out on you.' He was lying through his teeth but she was his only hope. 'No one would have known us there, Ginny. No one would have known we were related and it's not by blood anyway. We could have got married there, Ginny, and I'd have treated you like a princess, you know I would.'

Ginny smiled through her tears, forgetting all the days and nights she'd worried and wept for him.

'I didn't do that robbery, Ginny, I swear to God I didn't! I was unlucky and I'm sure that bloody Johnny Doyle had something to do with it. You know he doesn't like me. He's always tried to make me into a villain, just because I got caught up in a shop that was being robbed.'

'I . . . I believe you, Colin. I *knew* it wasn't you.'

'I had to say I was with you, Ginny. You were my only hope, and you still are. If you love me, then help me now, for God's sake.'

'How?' She would do anything, anything to help him. He'd done it all for her. He loved her and wanted to marry her and he knew he couldn't do that in this country. And he'd have given her everything she'd never had in her life before.

He glanced at the CID officer then back at her, dropping his voice to a whisper. 'Say you were with me on that Friday afternoon. Tell them you took time off from work to go out with me. We went to New Brighton, but you couldn't tell them that because they'd all have gone mad – and they *would*. We went on the fair, had fish and chips, walked along to the fort and back, then we went home but not together, of course. You had your overall in a carrier bag. Please, please, Ginny, if you love me, tell them and don't let them scare you. They'll try, they'll *all* try, but if you don't stand firm I'll be in jail for years and years and we won't be able to get married, ever!' He leaned back in the chair. It was as much as he could do, now it was up to her.

When he'd said not to be scared she'd felt her heart turn over, but she'd do it. He was innocent. He wouldn't lie to her. How could she have doubted him? He loved her and she was the only one who could keep him out of jail. She nodded.

Colin let his breath out slowly. He just hoped to God she'd be strong enough to stick to her story because she was in for a right grilling, but at least now he had a chance. He stood up and so did Ginny.

'Miss Greely is ready to make a statement, aren't you, Ginny?'

'Yes.' Ginny jerked up her chin and squared her thin shoulders. She'd fight every step of the way for him.

The CID man returned to Richie and his family. He was fuming inside but he didn't let it show.

'Well, it seems as though *Miss* Greely is prepared to lie for him. She is saying she was with him that afternoon.'

'She can't have been, she was at work all day!' Tessa cried. Oh, she might have known he'd twist Ginny around his little finger.

'She says she went absent for the afternoon, didn't tell you, went off to New Brighton with meladdo down there. Can her employer throw any light on things?'

'No. On Friday afternoons he takes it easy. Most people have already bought the fish for teatime. He has a young delivery lad, but you couldn't believe the daylights out of him. He spends most of his time skiving, so he wouldn't know if she was there or not,' May answered. Jimmy Birrel spent his time in the Globe.

'What about customers? Would anyone have gone in and found the place empty?'

'You'd have to try and find someone and where you'd start I don't know.'

It lay unspoken between them that the police would get little or no information out of anyone in the area.

In the midst of all this, Tessa couldn't help but wish Johnny'd never let on to the police about Colin. If Colin had got to America he'd have been out of all their lives forever. Yet deep down she knew Johnny'd done the right thing. Colin was utterly ruthless. He needed stopping. But look what he was doing to Ginny!

'Oh, Da, do something!' she cried. 'He's going to get Ginny into terrible trouble!'

'I know, but what can I do?' Richie replied.

'Well, if you can't do anything, I bloody well can and will. She's my daughter and she's not going to perjure herself for the likes of him. I want to see her,' May demanded.

'Follow me, missus. Maybe you can talk some sense into her. Tell her that perjury is a crime and she can go to jail as well as her boyfriend.'

'He's *not* her boyfriend! He's her stepbrother!' May snapped. She could *kill* him.

Ginny held out against them all. In vain did May plead and then shout at her and the police did the same. There were times when she broke down and sobbed under the tirade of shouted condemnation and threats heaped on her by the CID but she stuck to her story. At one stage they'd left her all alone in a cell for what seemed like hours and she'd been terrified but she hadn't broken. She hadn't let him down. They would have to cut out her tongue before she did.

When Tessa, Richie, May and Johnny were allowed to go home they were all exhausted. Despite Johnny's statement and the identification by both tellers, plus the fact that all the notes had matching serial numbers, they couldn't actually prove that it was Colin who took them. There was nothing anyone could do while Ginny stuck to her guns, giving Colin an alibi.

When they arrived home May closed the front door firmly. 'I've had enough, Richie, without having half the street in here wanting to know everything. I've a headache that's so bad I can hardly keep my eyes open. In God's name, what's the matter with her?'

'You go and lie down. I'll bring you up a cup of tea and some aspirins,' Tessa offered. If only they had let *her* talk to Ginny; she was sure she could have broken Ginny's resistance. Yelling at and threatening Ginny just didn't work. You got more by reasoning and coaxing.

Her da was soon asleep in the armchair and she wanted to go over and see Johnny, but she couldn't venture out of the house because *someone* was bound to collar her.

She had fallen into a light doze herself when she was awakened by the scullery door being opened. It was Elizabeth, still in her Hill's overall.

Tessa put a warning finger to her lips and gestured that she follow her into the room she shared with Ginny.

'What's up, Tessa? The whole street knows that your Colin's been arrested.'

'Oh, Elizabeth, it's terrible.' Tessa sank down on the bed. 'In fact it couldn't be worse.'

'All Mam could get out of Eileen and Mrs Doyle was that the police had called here last night and that Colin had been arrested on board Johnny's ship.'

'He was. He robbed that bank on County Road and got the first ship out. It was the *Ascania* and Johnny saw him and reported him and when they arrived this morning the police arrested him.'

Elizabeth's mouth formed an 'O'. She was momentarily bereft of speech.

'I told you it was terrible. And that's not all. He said he was with Ginny when the bank was robbed and she's lying for him. God knows what he's promised her or what she'll be going through now.'

Elizabeth gasped. 'Will she be able to stick to her story? Why does she want to lie for him anyway? I mean, robbing a bank is really serious, she must know that.'

'She does. He could get eight years or longer and they'll put her in jail too for perjury.'

'Oh, poor Ginny!'

'Poor Ginny's right. She . . . she's so besotted with him she'll believe anything he tells her. May's in bed with a headache and Da's worn out with it all and so am I. I wish they would throw him in jail and chuck away the key! Ginny would get over it. Oh, Elizabeth, I never thought she could be so stupid!'

'Does she know that she could go to jail as well?'

'She must do. The police must have told her that. We haven't seen her. The last we saw of her was when she went with them to the cells – except her mam, of course.'

They both fell silent, thinking of Ginny's state of mind.

'What am I going to tell Mam?' Elizabeth asked.

Tessa gnawed her lip. Delia would have to be told something but at least she could keep her mouth shut.

'Tell her . . . Oh, you may as well tell her everything. She at least can keep things to herself.'

Elizabeth nodded slowly. 'When do you think she'll be home?'

'I don't know, but I don't think they can keep her all night. She isn't the one who has done something wrong, it's *him*!'

Elizabeth squeezed her hand and left. Tessa's own head was thumping now and she lay down on the bed wearily.

It was half past six when both Ginny and Colin walked arm in arm down Naylor Street. They were fully aware of the curious gazes from behind the net curtains but Colin told Ginny to hold up her head. She had nothing to be ashamed of and neither did he. He grinned to himself as he thought of the expression on the CID man's face. He was livid but there had been nothing he could do. They had Ginny's sworn statement and his own. Put that beside the clerk from the bank's and it was stalemate. They didn't have enough evidence to charge him. The case was dismissed; they couldn't hold him any longer; he was a free man. He patted Ginny's hand, he really was grateful to her. However, he knew the police would be watching his every move from now on. He'd have to get out of Liverpool just the same.

There was only Richie in the kitchen when they arrived. 'Good God! You're out!'

'I told you I was innocent. I told you I didn't rob that bloody bank. No one believed me except Ginny.'

'Your mam's upstairs lying down,' Richie informed Ginny.

'I . . . I won't disturb her.' Ginny herself was exhausted. She felt as though every ounce of strength she had had been spent. It had been a nightmare and she didn't know how she'd held out for so long.

'Ginny's very tired too,' Colin said.

'Why don't you go and have a lie down? Our Tessa is,' Richie advised. Ginny nodded with relief.

Once they were alone in the kitchen Richie turned to his son. 'So? You got her to stick to her story then? Made her commit perjury?'

Colin didn't answer.

'Now what are you going to do?'

'Join the Army.'

Richie laughed. 'Oh, running away from Ginny again?'

'No, I'm not. She'll understand. Don't my King and Country need me? I'm eighteen. I'll go down to the recruiting office tonight. I've seen posters up everywhere.'

'And then you'll be far away from here by the weekend and you'll leave us to cope with all the gossip.'

Colin shrugged. It wouldn't be a bad life in the Army, in fact it would be a bit of excitement. He'd tell Ginny he was doing it for her, for everyone, for King and Country. She certainly couldn't argue with that. And he'd leave the money with her, he knew she'd keep it safe for him. She wouldn't touch a penny. He eased himself down on to the sofa and stretched out. He was bone weary himself – but he was free.

PART III

Chapter Twenty-One

1940

Life hadn't changed that much at all after a year of war, Elizabeth thought as she sat on the tram on her way home from work. She was still at Hill's but had progressed to being allowed to set, which she'd quickly mastered, the pin curls being the worst and the most time-consuming aspect.

The months following the Declaration had been called 'the Phoney War' for everyone had expected an invasion which had not come. There had been bombs. The first one had fallen in August on the other side of the Mersey, almost a year after the Declaration. Since then the sirens had wailed intermittently and in October some of the raids had caused damage and loss of life.

People had even got used to the blackout, but it had been a bit of a fiasco to start with. She'd walked straight into a lamppost that had been there for years and was fortunate not to break her nose. You just had to concentrate more, look where you were going and listen for cars and trams and buses. Bicycles were more of a problem, you didn't really hear them. She'd found a way around that though. As she walked she swung her shoulder bag by its strap backwards and forwards in an arc.

As she alighted from the tram, which had been painted grey and whose headlamps were masked with hoods, windows covered with wire mesh and bumpers painted white, she stopped and listened. She heard the footsteps growing fainter as the passengers dispersed, then she called out. 'Tessa? Tessa?'

'Is that you, Elizabeth?' Tessa called, crossing the road.

Elizabeth waited for her. It wasn't often these days that they met each other coming from work, with Tessa having to travel all the way to and from Kirkby to the munitions factory.

When they were near enough to see each other, Elizabeth peered at her friend closely. 'You look worn out.' Tessa's shoulders sloped with weariness and it was evident in her voice.

'So do you,' Tessa replied.

'I am but at least I don't have to work with all those terrible chemicals and gunpowder. Has anyone else's hair turned green this week?'

'I heard that Maggie Simpson from Athol Street's did.'

'Why in God's name don't they wear their turbans? It would protect their hair and they're not *that* bad. You always wear yours. Honestly, what with the chemicals and the peroxide they use to bleach their hair, and no turbans, it's a wonder they've any hair at all. Look at the state Alice Collins was in. I *told* her not to use full-strength peroxide, but no, she knew better and then who was it she came running to when it started to break off in chunks – me!'

'And she wasn't very pleased when you'd finished either.'

'I *had* to cut it that short or she'd have looked like a dog with a bad case of mange. She wears her turban now though.'

'I suppose I've been lucky really, I mean nothing awful has happened to my hair, my skin hasn't turned orange and I haven't had an accident, thank God. I'll never, ever forget Tilly Barton's screams when that detonator exploded in her hands and she lost two fingers. It was terrible, really terrible.'

Elizabeth shuddered and changed the subject. 'Did you see anything of Johnny today?'

Tessa shook her head. Both Mike and Johnny now worked in munitions. Not filling shells and assembling detonators but handling big bombs and engineering heavy weapons.

'Mike was talking about joining the Navy after Christmas. They'll be eighteen.'

'I know. Johnny said they'll go downtown together.'

'I wish they didn't have to go. I know I'm being selfish but . . .'

Tessa nodded, knowing what her friend meant. Over the last year her feelings for Johnny Doyle had grown and she knew Elizabeth felt the same way about Mike Flynn. Of course Elizabeth and Mike's meetings and outings had to be a closely guarded secret for Delia would be horrified and would most certainly have tried to put a stop to it. And Elizabeth, normally so forthright and defiant, was acutely sensitive about this, her first love. The last thing she wanted to do was announce it to her hostile mother.

'I wanted to talk to you.' Elizabeth said, 'I've made a decision.'

Some of Tessa's weariness disappeared. 'A decision about what?'

'About leaving Hill's and going to work with you.'

'With me? Out in Kirkby?'

'Yes. I've thought about it a lot. I know all the disadvantages. Having to trail all the way out there, having to get up at some ungodly hour and work till I drop with dangerous materials. But

214

messing around with women's hair is too frivolous when I could be doing something really useful. And all my clients are interested in is how their hair should be set or should they have it cut. You wouldn't think there's a war on at all, the conversations out of them.'

Tessa shook her head slowly. 'Your mam's going to go mad! She's still not forgiven you for leaving school and you know how she feels about factory work.'

'Well, there's a big difference between factory work in peacetime and wartime. She can't argue about that. Everyone's got to do their bit.' Elizabeth suddenly grinned. 'And I'll be earning pots of money. Now I only get money for "expenses". I have to rely on Mam for nearly everything and I'm seventeen.'

'Once your mam's finished with you, you won't get to be eighteen,' Tessa answered ominously.

'Oh, I know there'll be murder. I'm expecting it, but this time there won't be any letters full of excuses and apologies to Aunty Margaret. Even *she* can't complain about war work.'

'Why is everyone so terrified of Aunty Margaret? Have you met her?'

'No – well, yes, but I was a baby so I don't remember. It's just that Aunty Margaret's got money and had the guts and foresight to leave Liverpool. I'm not afraid of her and Mam isn't really, they *are* sisters.'

'So are you and Nessie!'

'That's different. I mean, Mam thinks she has to spend Aunty Margaret's money wisely.'

'Yes, I can see that, but surely not if it makes you or Nessie unhappy?'

Elizabeth shrugged. 'Oh, I don't know. She's never nasty or sarcastic in her letters. Will you come home with me?'

'You mean like I did before?'

'Yes.'

Tessa pursed her lips. This was going to be as bad as last time. 'I suppose so, but I can't leave them waiting for their tea. I'll have to go home first.'

'What's wrong with May doing the cooking?'

'She burns everything – and I mean *everything* – and she's always fussing about having to get ready for work.'

After the initial decision to close on the outbreak of war, the pubs, cinemas and theatres had reopened.

'OK, but will you come down straight afterwards?'

215

'I promise. This is getting to be a bit of a habit.' Tessa smiled at her friend as she disappeared inside the shop.

The kitchen was in the usual state of chaos when she arrived home. May had been in all day but the room was untidy and cluttered. There had been no attempt to do any of the ironing. The table was still littered with dishes and papers and bits of lipstick in old plastic tubes and she knew from experience what the scullery would look like. She sighed heavily. If the truth be told, she and Ginny ran this house. May contributed nothing except some of her wages. All she ever seemed to do was read newspapers and women's magazines, fuss over her appearance and drink tea.

'Isn't Ginny home yet?' Tessa asked.

'No, luv, she said she was going into town at the end of her shift to buy Christmas presents.'

Ginny was also in munitions though she worked a different shift to Tessa; like her, Ginny had far more money in her pocket than she'd ever had in her life before. So did Richie. He worked full time on the docks now – it was a Reserved Occupation, crucial to the war effort – and often there was plenty of overtime. Because of that they now had furniture in all the rooms as well as curtains and rugs. They even had a long runner of carpet in the lobby and up the stairs so when Jimmy and Harold Flynn went up or down it didn't sound like a herd of elephants. Her da had nailed it down; brass stair rods were still beyond their means. They had decent bedding though, warm blankets, heavy quilts, sheets and pillowcases and proper towels. They had many more clothes too.

She took off her coat and pulled off the turban. She didn't mind it but it was loathed by many girls and women. She ran her hands through her short dark hair, and wondered just where to begin. Da would be in soon too, wanting a meal, and Jimmy was always hungry. When there wasn't overtime Richie was an ARP Warden, like Jack Harrison, Frank Flynn and Billy Keegan. Mick Collins was a volunteer fireman, something his wife never missed an opportunity to mention to the chagrin of her neighbours, especially Delia Harrison. 'Why him?' she had demanded of Jack. 'You can drive. In fact any fool can drive, what's so special about Mick Collins?'

'Delia, if I wanted to be a fireman I would be. I just think – hope I'll be more use as a warden. I might volunteer for an anti-aircraft gunner, although I hope to God we don't need to use those guns very frequently.'

This had at least pacified her.

Jimmy and young Harold Flynn were messenger boys, not that they'd had any messages to carry yet, but they took great pride in the second-hand bicycles they'd been given. Had it not been wartime the bicycles would have been raced up and down the streets to everyone's peril, their riders included, but they were for 'official' use only and so great care was taken with them. They were washed and polished and oiled and kept under tarpaulins in bad weather.

Tessa decided she'd start with the meal and then when Ginny was home and the ordeal with Elizabeth and Delia was over, she and Ginny would roll up their sleeves and get stuck in. She wasn't seeing Johnny tonight, he and Mike were in the Royal Naval Reserve and went for training. May and the rest of them didn't mind living in a house that resembled a tip, but she did, and her Mam would turn in her grave to see what her family had come to.

It was almost half past seven when Tessa arrived at the shop.

'You look worn out, Tessa,' Delia commented. Elizabeth had said Tessa was going to drop in after tea.

'I am and I've still not finished. Ginny's gone to town for Christmas presents and the place, well . . .'

Delia nodded her understanding. It wasn't a bit fair on the girl, she thought. The others should pull their weight.

'Mam, there's something I want to tell you,' Elizabeth blurted out before Tessa had even taken her coat off.

Delia stared at her. 'Oh, now I see it all. You've dragged Tessa down here for support. I seem to remember that the last bombshell was preceded by the words "Mam, there's something I want to tell you". Now what?' she demanded.

'I'm going to leave Hill's and go to work in munitions. I can't spend all day with stupid, pathetic, wealthy old women who care more about their flaming hair than the state of the country. I've got to do my bit for the war effort—'

'I've heard that it won't be long before all girls and women will be sort of conscripted into munitions, working on the land or in the Army, Navy and Air Force,' Tessa interrupted.

'Then she can wait until they do and go and work for the Navy or Air Force.' Delia was fuming. Just what influence Tessa had on Elizabeth's judgement she didn't know. But Tessa had been a thorn in her side ever since she'd come to Naylor Street. Somehow all the plans she'd had so nicely worked out for Elizabeth, Tessa had managed to thwart. She *had* felt sorry for the girl. She *did* like her – in her place. Both Elizabeth and Tessa knew that. But oh, she really should have put a stop to this friendship long ago. Well, she'd remedy that right now.

She turned to Tessa. 'And you, milady, can keep your nose out of other people's business! You've interfered once too often.'

Tessa shied away, tears instantly springing to her eyes.

Elizabeth was on her feet. 'Mam! How can you say such things to Tessa? She's had nothing to do with it. *I* decided on my own. She's said nothing. In fact when she's described what it's like working down there it's almost put me off.'

'And she's right about that! You are sliding further and further down the ladder, you'll amount to nothing, absolutely nothing in the end! A factory girl. A common little factory girl! Oh, that's very nice, isn't it? Won't everyone in the street be delighted! And how do you think I'll feel? And how will your aunt feel when you go surrounding yourself with girls and women just like Tessa?'

'Mam, don't you talk about my friend that way! I won't have it! I *won't*! When this war is over, if it ever gets started that is, I'll go back and finish my apprenticeship. I want to *do* something for the war effort and it doesn't require me to leave home and work on some farm or get a job where I'd be at the beck and call of some toffee-nosed soldier, sailor or airman who's just wearing a uniform so people will think how great they are when all they're doing is sitting at a desk!'

Delia got to her feet, her face scarlet with rage. 'How dare you speak like that, Elizabeth! How *dare* you! I forbid you to have anything more to do with Tessa O'Leary! You have had all the advantages that money can provide and now you're quite happy to sink to the level of a factory girl, like her. She came here with nothing! Not a coat on her back, running from the creditors, with a brother who had already been to Borstal twice, a useless wastrel of a father and a dying mother. God rest Mary O'Leary's soul. She was the only one in the entire family who had any pride and sense of decency.' She pointed a finger at Tessa. 'I *won't* have her undermining my authority and my plans in that sneaking manner!'

Elizabeth couldn't believe what she was hearing. Oh, she'd expected her mam to be angry, but she'd never expected this vicious attack on Tessa. What had got into Mam?

'I'm going into munitions, Mam, and Tessa will always be my friend, and I don't care what you say about it! Your opinion doesn't matter! You wait until Da hears this. You're a snob, Mam, that's what you are. You think you shouldn't live around here and have to mix with *these* people. Oh, no, you should be off somewhere in Breck Road or Walton where you wouldn't have to speak to them. You could walk around with your nose in the air as much as you liked!'

The sound of Delia's hand as it caught Elizabeth fully across the cheek was like a rifle crack. Just at that moment Jack walked into the kitchen.

'Delia! Delia! What the hell is going on?' he demanded, taking in Nessie's horrified gaze, his wife's almost puce complexion, Elizabeth's obvious fury, the red marks of Delia's fingers on his daughter's face and the tears that streamed unheeded down Tessa's cheeks.

'She's a snob, Da, that's what she is! I told her I'm going to work in munitions and she blamed Tessa. Then she started saying terrible, terrible things about Tessa,' Elizabeth cried.

'Do you hear her, Jack? She wants to be a common factory girl. She wants to work with *her.*'

Before Jack could do or say anything, Tessa jumped up and ran out of the back door, ignoring Elizabeth's cries that she come back. She'd never felt so awful or so humiliated in her life. She'd always thought Delia Harrison liked her. In times of crisis in the past she'd always helped and supported her. Now . . . now . . . she just didn't know what to think.

She collided with Ginny in the back yard.

'Tessa! Tessa, what's the matter?'

Tessa couldn't speak. She could only shake her head.

'Come on in and tell me all about it. Who's upset you now? I've never seen you like this.'

Tessa let herself be led into the kitchen where she sat down at the table. There was a letter on it addressed to Ginny, which immediately made her forget Tessa's problems.

Ginny picked it up and clasped it to her, unable to hold back the renewed flood of joy that filled her. She'd written dozens of letters to Colin but this was the first one he'd sent her. 'It's from Colin! Oh, at last! I haven't opened it yet but I'm so thrilled!'

It was too much for Tessa. She got to her feet and snatched the letter from Ginny's hand. 'For God's sake, Ginny! I don't want to hear about a stupid letter! I *hate* him and you're the biggest fool I've ever met! He's no bloody good, can't you understand that? Because of him and Da we finished up here broke and now . . . now . . .' She couldn't go on. What was the use? She threw the letter back at Ginny and fled into the front room where she collapsed on the bed and sobbed into the pillow.

Nessie had quietly closed her books and gone upstairs. She had no wish to be any part of the row that raged around her. Elizabeth was yelling that just because they had a shop that didn't make them any better than anyone else in the street. Da was shouting back, telling her not to be so hardfaced and how dare she upset her mother. Elizabeth took no notice, saying she would go and move in with Tessa and Ginny if her mam didn't stop being such a snob. Both she and Delia were crying. Nessie had never heard anything like it before – and the neighbours were bound to hear every word.

Elizabeth was ordered to bed but refused to go; Nessie heard the back door slam. Then, after a couple of seconds of complete silence, she heard her father's voice raised again and her mam starting to scream back. In the end Nessie stuffed her fingers in her ears and pulled the pillow over her head.

Ginny, her eyes red from weeping, her cheeks streaked with tears, opened the door of number twelve to Elizabeth.

'What's the matter with you?' Elizabeth demanded.

'Tessa . . . Tessa . . . called me names. It was over Colin. He's written to me—'

'Don't you know how upset Tessa is? Bloody hell, Ginny, don't you care about *anyone* else but *him*? Where is she?'

'In the front room.' Ginny sniffed. Why was everyone being so nasty to her? They'd spoiled her happiness at Colin's letter and she'd wanted to tell them he was coming home on leave after Christmas. But she knew her mam wouldn't be overjoyed.

Tessa was still sobbing quietly and Elizabeth's heart went out to her. Oh, she regretted nothing she'd said to her mam. Tessa was her friend. She put her arm around Tessa's shoulder and drew her to her.

'You take no notice of her, Tess! Da's giving her a right ear-bashing. I just don't know how she could say such things! She *is* a snob! I said I was going to move in here unless she changes her tune.'

Tessa raised a blotched and tear-stained face. 'You . . . you'd do that?'

'You should know me better than that, Tessa O'Leary. Didn't I threaten to face an Institution for Girls the last time there was a row? They both know I meant it.'

Tessa managed a weak smile. 'You always do. You always get your way.'

'No, I don't. Not all the time. But with something like this . . .'

'I can't understand why she . . . she said those things.'

'She's furious that I'm not just doing what she would like me to do. She didn't want me to leave school but I did. She doesn't want me to work in munitions but I *will* – and what's more I'm going to write to Aunty Margaret myself and tell her why. Come on, dry your eyes and go and wash your face. I bet our Nessie will be sent down for me later.'

'I don't think I can face Ginny yet. She's—'

'Got a flaming letter from *him*, I know. She told me. Can't the stupid little madam get it into her thick head that he doesn't love her and won't ever marry her?'

'I was awful to her, but I was so upset! I called her a fool.'

'I wonder what he's written to her about?' Elizabeth's mind strayed momentarily from their predicament.

'He'll want something, that you can be sure of,' Tessa said bitterly. She had never hated her brother so much as she did now.

'Should I ask her?'

'Oh, if you want to.'

'I don't want to, I just feel we should have some warning of what he intends to do or what he wants.'

They both went into the kitchen where Ginny was sitting by the fire, the letter in her lap.

'I'm sorry, Ginny. I shouldn't have yelled at you, but there's been a terrible row at home and everyone's upset.'

'That's all right,' Ginny replied, still with a note of injured pride in her voice.

Tessa went into the scullery to wash her face.

'What does he say or is that private?'

Ginny smiled and Elizabeth sighed.

'Some of it's private, but he's coming home on leave, just after Christmas. Oh, I'm so excited!'

'Well, that's good news for you, isn't it? But does he say anything about going abroad?'

'No, but he's bound to be sent somewhere soon. Do you think that's why he's coming home?'

'I don't really know.' Elizabeth wasn't in the least bit interested in what Colin O'Leary was doing. She hoped the Army would send him to the other end of the world and keep him there. He was trouble and that was something they had enough of right now.

It was late when Jack Harrison himself called at the O'Learys'. May had just come in and been informed of the situation. Her eyes had darkened with anger. Delia Harrison had gone too far this time and she'd tell her so when she saw her. Just because her bloody sister had had the nous to marry a successful businessman who had conveniently died two years later, leaving her enough to send money regularly, didn't give Delia the right to look down on her neighbours who were also her bloody customers, for God's sake.

'I've come to take Elizabeth home,' Jack stated.

'Then I hope you've made your wife see sense, Jack,' snapped May. 'She's no right at all to carry on like that. She lives in a slum like we do. If she wants to carry on with her airs and graces, then let her do it in Walton or Aintree, but then of course she'd have to rely on their bloody Margaret who, if my memory serves me right, worked in a factory herself before she up and went off to America. She wouldn't like that and neither would you, Jack, being dependent on your sister-in-law to keep you all.'

Jack nodded firmly. May's appraisal of the situation was very similar to the argument he had used with Delia.

'Get your coat on, Elizabeth.'

'If she carries on about Tessa any more, Da, I meant what I said, I'll move in here – as long as they'll have me.'

'I think we've heard enough on this subject, Elizabeth. Get your coat on. You're coming home. Your mother will say no more about it and Tessa will be welcome in *my* house at any time. There's enough fighting going on in the world without having to contend with it at home too. Get your coat and say goodnight to Tessa and Richie and May.'

Elizabeth knew her mam would give her the cold shoulder treatment from now on but she didn't care. She'd got her own way again.

Chapter Twenty-Two

Elizabeth had only been working in the munitions factory at Kirkby for a week before she began to wonder if all the trouble she'd caused was really worth it. The atmosphere at home was terrible, far worse than after she'd left school. Her mam hardly spoke to her. Most of her questions were greeted with a silent nod or shake of Mam's head. And she couldn't bear to tell Delia about Mike. Her father was also annoyed with her for being so awkward, even though for once he had actually supported her. But Jack's backing her had created a rift with Delia and it upset Elizabeth to know she was the cause. Nessie's silence also added to the burden. Nessie was different now, Elizabeth thought. Her sister's silence wasn't due to the fact that they'd quarrelled, they'd always done that, but it was the silence of disapproval, disappointment and a certain amount of sadness, which made Elizabeth feel strange and uncomfortable. Nessie too was upset by the all-too-noticeable coldness between her parents and sister.

Tessa hadn't been near the shop despite what Jack had said about it being *his* house. She was still very upset and no matter what Elizabeth said or how much she tried to put it to the back of her mind, Delia's cruel words kept coming back to her.

Elizabeth had accompanied Tessa that Monday morning and she'd found Kirkby to be a small, pretty village. There was the church with its big square tower, some cottages, a few shops and a pub called The Railway, which was very apt, it being situated almost beside the station. It was a pity that such a place should have its peace shattered by the huge single-storeyed munitions factories and the clanking of railway wagons that transported the ammunition.

'OK, luv, you go to the office, they'll sort you out,' the man on the gate had told her.

'I'll walk part of the way with you, but I can't be late,' Tessa had offered.

Tessa had left her at the office where she was given her official papers to sign, her identity pass, her hours of work and the Rules and Regulations. She'd also had a medical, of sorts. The doctor had rattled off a list of illnesses and conditions from a printed card

223

and she'd answered 'No' to everything. He sounded her chest, looked down her throat, her ears and into her eyes and that was it. Then she'd been issued with her working clothes, which consisted of a navy blue boiler suit, a white turban and flat shoes. Everything was strange to her and that's when the first niggling doubts beset her.

'It's all so . . . sort of "military",' she said hesitantly to Tessa at the end of their twelve-hour shift when they boarded the special bus that would take them back into the city.

'Of course it is. What did you expect? We're making ammunition, for God's sake.'

Elizabeth shrugged.

'You haven't changed your mind, have you? Not after going all through that carry-on? It must be awful at home.'

'It is, but no, I haven't changed my mind. I just thought it would be different,' she'd replied, and as the week went on she found it indeed very different from anything she'd ever done in her life before.

She worked with three other girls in a room graded number eight. Every job was graded from one to ten. Group One was the most dangerous, the girls who worked there fitted detonators. She filled anti-tank mines with TNT which had a strong, obnoxious smell and needed stirring to stop it clouding. Her nose and mouth were protected by a mask, her hands with white gloves. She also filled 3.8 shells which then went to Group One where there seemed to be an accident nearly every day and she, like Tessa, cringed at the awful screams of injured girls and women.

'It's all the palaver we have to go through,' she complained to Tessa at the end of the week. They were both very tired. Elizabeth had never worked so hard in her life.

'I know, but I suppose it's necessary.'

'All that "Dirty Room" and "Clean Room" nonsense.'

They both fell silent thinking about the tedious but necessary procedure. First they were ushered like sheep into the 'Dirty Room' where shoes, clothes, hair clips and jewellery were removed and placed into lockers. Wedding rings were taped over. 'It only needs one spark and you won't live to see another day and neither will anyone else in your room,' they'd been told seriously. Then in the 'Clean Room' they were issued with the boiler suits, turbans and shoes rather like plimsolls. The buildings were set out with two rows of small rooms running down each side, with a wide blast-proof corridor between them.

'I don't mind the money though,' Elizabeth added with a grin.

She was irrepressible, Tessa thought. She'd never known anyone like her before.

'I thought you'd like that bit. What are the other girls like?'

'Not bad. At first they were a bit wary of me. They'd all worked in factories before and maybe I sounded a bit posh, my accent's not as broad as theirs. But once I said I'd been training to be a hairdresser things improved and news is spreading. I've even been asked to go to Emily's house to give her mam a home perm, but I don't know how to use them. I hadn't got as far as perming and dyeing and bleaching and doing roots. She said she'd pay me but I still don't want to run the risk of ruining her hair. I said I'd cut and set it and show them both how to pin wave it and brush it out.'

'Have you never thought of charging for advice?'

Elizabeth looked thoughtful. 'No. I really haven't learned much at all.'

'But you are quick to learn. Look how you cut Ginny's hair and mine and transformed Alice Collins—'

'Until the episode of the peroxide,' Elizabeth interrupted. 'No, I don't think I could charge.'

'Why not? You could build up a little business. Travel around and set people's hair or show them how to do it.'

Elizabeth looked aghast. 'How on earth will I get time for that?'

'Christmas isn't that far off, people always want to look their best for the parties and dances.'

'Do you really think there'll *be* parties and dances?'

'There was last year.'

'I know, but it's sort of different this year, more serious.'

'It'll be Mike and Johnny's last Christmas at home for God knows how long,' Tessa reminded Elizabeth.

They sat in silence for the rest of the journey, their thoughts turning to the buildings that had already been bombed and lay in ruins. The Customs House, Wallasey Town Hall, Central Station and even the huge but as yet unfinished cathedral had been damaged.

Elizabeth knew for certain that the affection she'd always had for Mike Flynn had turned to love. She wasn't a kid now and neither was he. Whenever they went out together they had to be certain no one saw them until they got into town and inside the cinema. Mike didn't need an explanation for the 'cloak and dagger' stuff, as he called it. Delia would have had a fit.

'Why is Mam so awful to people like Tessa and you and your family?' she'd asked the night after the huge row. They'd gone to the pictures; they always did but they seldom watched the film. The Pathe News and Forthcoming Attractions was as far as they got.

'She's always had some funny ways of going on.'

'She thinks because of the shop and the money from America that we're all better than everyone else and we're not.'

Mike had sighed and put his arms around her, drawing her close and kissing her and that had been the end of the discussion. Soon he'd be going away to face not only the perils of the sea, but the dangers that lurked beneath it in the form of the U-boat packs that lay in wait just beyond the safety of the Western Approaches. She would write to him, of course, but she knew all his replies would have to be sent via his mam. But Eileen Flynn wasn't known for her ability to keep a secret; they'd have to go to Tessa's house, she decided. May wasn't quite as bad as Eileen and Ginny, poor deluded Ginny, was too wrapped up in dreams of Colin even to notice.

Tessa's thoughts were running on similar lines. After Christmas things were going to be miserable with Johnny away and *him* at home being fussed over by Ginny who was getting so excited that she was unbearable. Tessa was thankful they worked on different shifts and so didn't really see each other for long periods of time. She had her own little piece of news which she hadn't told anyone about yet – not even Elizabeth. Johnny had asked her if she'd get engaged after his first trip or first leave from Chatham whichever was the soonest. She'd thrown her arms around his neck and had clung to him; she'd felt like laughing and crying at the same time and she'd only been able to nod her acceptance. She knew no one would object, except perhaps Johnny's da. But she was a good worker and she'd make a good housewife, so she couldn't really see what his da could object to. They were going to announce it formally on Christmas Day. She had no ring but then how many women in this area did?

They alighted at their stop and had begun to walk down Scotland Road when the now familiar wail of the siren sounded its warning.

'Oh God! Come on, Tessa, we'll have to make a dash for the shelter!'

'No! I hate that place. It's cold, damp, dirty and we're all squashed like sardines,' Tessa protested as she ran.

226

'Then where are we going to go?'

'Home. Under our stairs.'

'Under the *stairs*? Have you gone mad?'

'No, all the Flynns did it during the last raid and Mr Flynn said it was as good a place as any. Didn't Mike tell you? Public shelters have taken direct hits too.'

The droning in the sky could be clearly heard now and the searchlights swept the dark heavens with wide silvery beams.

People were running past them, mainly in the opposite direction, and when they fell into the lobby of number twelve Tessa screamed for Jimmy, her da and May.

'Tessa, for God's sake why haven't you gone to the shelter?' Richie yelled. He was wearing his tin hat and his warden's coat. Already they could hear the explosions as bombs and incendiaries found their targets.

'I'm not going there!'

All three of them froze in terror as they heard the unmistakable whistling of a bomb growing louder and louder.

Richie got a grip on himself and shoved them all towards the space under the stairs.

'Da, where are you going?' Tessa cried.

'To see what I can do. It's my duty, remember.'

'Oh, sweet Jesus have mercy on us all,' May cried, blessing herself but thanking God she hadn't left for work otherwise she'd have been caught out there. She was thankful too that Ginny was on nights.

For three hours they sat, cramped, frightened and cold, listening to the droning and shrill whistling of falling bombs. Intermittently they heard the furious clanging of fire engines and ambulances and the dull, earth-trembling rumble as buildings collapsed. They also heard the sound of the anti-aircraft guns that were sending thousands of rounds of tracer upwards at the raiders caught in the dazzle of the searchlights.

'It's never gone on for as long as this.' Tessa tried not to let the fear show in her voice. They were all close to hysteria.

'I just hope to God Richie is safe.'

Elizabeth thought fearfully of her da. He too would be out there, somewhere in that hell of flames, explosions and tottering buildings, heedless of his own safety.

At ten o'clock, when the 'All Clear' sounded, Elizabeth crawled on her hands and knees from under the stairs. She was still trembling with fear but she had to go and see if her mam and Nessie and Da were safe. What would greet her when she opened the front door?

'Do you want me to come with you, luv?' May offered.

'No, no thanks, I . . . I'll be fine.'

'Well, if you're sure . . . If anything's . . . wrong you just come back down here.'

A dark sky broken with patches of red and orange shooting flames greeted her. Broken water mains flooded the street and gas from fractured pipes could clearly be smelled. The stench from broken sewage pipes was terrible and all around her were piles of rubble that until three hours ago had been homes and businesses. The docks had been hit again and the noise of fire engines and ambulances was constant.

She stumbled into the shop, her feet crunching on the glass-strewn floor. A blast had blown the window in despite the tape Delia had criss-crossed it with after the night the Customs House had been bombed.

'Mam! Nessie!' she yelled. Had they gone to the shelter? She knew her mam hated it almost as much as Tessa did.

Nessie, her cheeks streaked with tears, appeared from beneath the stairwell.

'Oh, where've you been? We've been worried sick.'

'I've been at Tessa's. We'd just got off the bus when the siren went. Where's Da?'

'Out with the others, I can't see him being home until morning,' Delia answered as she emerged white-faced and shaken. 'Why didn't you go to the shelter?'

'Mam, you know how awful it is and besides, there wasn't time. I thought . . . I thought it was never going to end. Nearly all the houses in Paul Street have been flattened.'

Delia shook her head. God help them, most of them didn't have much to start with, now they had nothing.

'Mam, the shop window's in. There's glass all over the floor.'

Delia had expected far worse. 'We'll have a cup of tea and then we'll clean up. We'll save what we can for tomorrow, it'll be business as usual.'

'The water mains, the gas pipes and the sewage pipes are all broken. The tram lines and electricity lines are down.'

'Then we'll just have to make do until they get them fixed. Was there any damage in this street? A few of them sounded very close. Once or twice I'm certain this place moved.'

'Not that I could see, but the docks have been hit. There's fires everywhere.'

Nessie began to cry.

'It's all right, Nessie, honestly it is.' Elizabeth for the first time in her life comforted her sister. She was very shaken herself.

'Nessie, pull yourself together. We've got everything intact: the shop, the stock, the roof over our heads, and unless we hear different, you'll go to school as usual in the morning. It's important that we all carry on as best we can. That's the main thing now.'

They worked on late into the night and it was the first time since she'd had the row with her mother that there was some semblance of normality between them. Delia had sent Nessie to bed at midnight and she and Elizabeth wiped the dust and dirt from tins and packets that thankfully hadn't been too damaged. Food was too precious now to be discarded if the tin were dented or the packet torn.

It was four o'clock in the morning when Jack, his face covered in grime, his eyes red-rimmed, walked into the kitchen. Elizabeth and Delia were sitting at the table in the candlelight and firelight with cups of tea in their hands.

'Oh, thank God you're all right, Jack! I've been worried to death about you, luv.' Delia threw her arms around him and kissed him, despite the fact that his clothes were filthy.

'At least we've got the fire in the range and there was some water in the kettle.' Elizabeth got to her feet to make her father a drink.

'Was it very bad?' Delia asked

Jack nodded. 'It was the worst so far. There's fires burning all over the city. All the telegraph and phone wires are down, so are the tram wires. The water mains and gas mains are fractured, but you know that. They've already started to clear away the rubble and people are searching for relatives or whatever they can salvage from the debris. I saw an old lady, bent double with age and arthritis, poking with a long piece of wood at what was left of her home and calling for her cat! It was heartbreaking. Someone eventually came and led her away. I think it was a granddaughter.' He passed his hand over his stinging eyes, eyes that had seen so many horrific sights that night.

'None of us went to the shelter,' said Delia as she fussed over him. 'You're safer under the stairs, I reckon. Those shelters are disgusting. There's nowhere to sit, wash, make a drink or even go to the toilet. They stink. I'm sure the Sanitary Inspector would close them.'

'Delia, luv, these days the Sanitary Inspectors won't be bothered

229

about that. They've got their work cut out with the broken sewage pipes and the threat of disease. Thank God it's not summer, it would be unbearable.'

'I sent Nessie to bed, she can go to school later, and we've cleaned up the mess in there as best we can. It'll be business as usual.'

Jack nodded. He was worn out but they'd open at seven just the same and Elizabeth would report for work at seven o'clock too.

Tessa was still up, peering from the window at the glowing sky and wondering if it was worth even going to bed as she'd have to start out for work even earlier than usual, what with the bomb craters and the unsafe and still burning buildings *en route*. Ginny would find her journey home a long and hazardous one. Suddenly she caught sight of someone wandering aimlessly up the street. The streetlights were out and all the blackout curtains were drawn but in the eerie orange light from the blazing warehouses by the docks she saw it was Johnny Doyle. Dragging on a coat she went out into the street.

'Johnny! Johnny? What's the matter? Where are you going?' She caught his sleeve.

He turned to her, his eyes filled with shock and grief. 'It's . . . it's . . . Mam.'

'What happened? Where is she?'

Johnny fought to control himself. 'She'd been to church – don't ask me why, Tessa. She was coming home along Scottie Road . . .'

A feeling of dread crept over Tessa. 'Didn't she go to the shelter?'

He shook his head.

'Then . . .?'

'A building collapsed on her. Oh, Tessa! Tessa! She's . . . dead! My da went to look for her after the "All Clear" and someone had pulled her out. He . . . Da could only recognise her by that little cross and chain he'd bought her.'

Tessa reached up and drew him closer. 'Oh, I'm so sorry, Johnny, I'm so sorry. I know what it's like to have your mam die.'

He looked down at her, his eyes filled with tears. 'You do. I'd almost forgotten. You *really* know.'

'Yes, I do, but at least it would have been . . . quick. All over with in a couple of seconds, not like my mam dragging herself around in agony for months.' She took his face in her hands and kissed away the tears. Her heart was aching for him. 'Go home now, you've got work later on. We can't give up, it's just what they want us to do. Think of your mam and go to work.'

Johnny held her tightly for a few minutes before he drew away. She was right. He'd go to work, thinking of Mam, and soon he'd be able to join up and do something really worthwhile. That's surely what his mother would have wanted.

When Eileen Flynn emerged with her brood from under the stairs she'd sent young Harold out to see what the damage was like and if anyone's house had been hit. Mike had wanted to go and see if Elizabeth was all right but Eileen told him firmly that her need was greater. Harold returned with his face and hands filthy and with his father, in the same condition, right behind him.

'I've brought 'im home. I caught 'im climbin' over a pile of rubble. 'Ave yer no sense, woman, lettin' 'im out? He could 'ave been killed.' Frank's nerves were shattered too although he'd never admit to it.

'I didn't send 'im out ter go climbin' and messin' about. Come 'ere, yer little get! 'Aven't I got enough ter worry about?'

'Well, no one's been bombed out in this street, thank God, but I'll 'ave ter get back, there's people buried under bricks and mortar in Paul Street. The whole flaming lot 'as gone over there. God 'ave mercy on their souls. They'll need a fleet of bloody ambulances. 'Ave yer time ter make us a quick brew, girl? I'm spittin feathers, it's all the soot and dust.'

'It'll be half cold. It'll take all flaming night for the kettle to boil on that fire. Maureen, go an see if Tessa's gorrany water.'

'Ah, Mam, it's freezin' out there!'

'I know and so does yer poor da! Now shift yerself before I give yer a goalong, yer selfish little madam!' Eileen took a swipe at her daughter. 'That's lovely, isn't it? A nice way to treat yer father, there's none of yer any good, what with meladdo there only interested in Elizabeth Harrison, that young hooligan out "*playing*" while the whole place is burnin' around him and now you!'

Maureen fled and before she returned the door was opened and Brenda appeared.

'Brenda! Luv! What's up with yer, comin' all the way down 'ere!'

Brenda burst into tears. 'Oh, Mam, I *had* to come. I was worried sick about you. All of you. I knew Da was out there, just like Thomas was, but I couldn't settle, I could see the fires and hear the bombs . . . I just wanted to see . . .'

'Come here to me, girl, and stop upsetting yerself, it's bad for yer and the baby. We're all fine, yer can see that for yerself. Our Maureen's gone to see if Tessa's gorrany water, then we can all 'ave a cup of tea before yer da 'as ter go out again.'

Brenda eased herself down on to the sofa. She'd had to walk all the way because the tram lines were just twisted spirals of metal; she'd passed three trams all of which had been abandoned and were badly damaged. One of them lay on its side like a beached whale.

'Oh, Mam, I've got terrible pains in my back! I walked all the way.'

Eileen threw up her hands in horror. 'Oh, Jesus, Mary and Joseph! Get your feet up on that sofa. Frank, make yerself useful an' find something to roll up as a cushion for her back. I hope ter God she's not started. What a time ter 'ave a baby.'

Eileen was seriously worried. If the baby came now it could stand no chance at all of surviving: it would be little more than a miscarriage. She called the Luftwaffe all the names she could think of and cursed them to hell and back, not knowing that this was only the beginning of Liverpool's ordeal by fire. It would be an ordeal that, before it was over, would bring them all to their knees.

Chapter Twenty-Three

Brenda didn't lose her baby. Eileen had insisted she stay in Naylor Street and she'd sent Mike along to the house in Breck Road to inform Thomas Kinsella that his wife would remain where she was until her mother felt she was well enough to go home.

'I'm prayin' ter St Anne, every day, that she'll not have a miscarriage. What possessed her ter walk all the way 'ere I don't know! Well, she's on the sofa and she's stoppin' there so I can keep me eye on 'er. Our Maureen an' 'Arold can just do more to 'elp,' she'd informed Delia in the shop later that week. Then she launched forth to the other customers about the state of affairs in Paul Street, which had taken not two but three direct hits. Twenty people had been killed or died from their injuries. There was nothing left but piles of rubble and a few gaps where the bricks had been carted away. 'It's shockin' 'ow they treated them women, so I 'eard. They sent them trailing to offices all over the city ter get new ration books and identity cards and food and clothing vouchers. Lots of them 'ad kids with them and they'd lost everything and with their 'usbands and sons away, too. It's just shockin'.'

'Shockin'!' Maisie Keegan echoed.

'Well, it certainly got my idle, useless feller off his backside. He's never worked so hard in his life. Got a bad back now or so he says. Bad back my flaming foot! It's "idleitis" he's got,' Katie Collins said cuttingly.

'A nice Christmas this is going ter be. Do yer think you'll 'ave trouble gettin' stuff, like?' Eileen asked Delia.

'It shouldn't be too hard, and I've got some "emergency" supplies if it gets really bad.'

'She would have,' Katie Collins said *sotto voce* to Maisie Keegan.

'Our Mike's goin' off to the Navy, the proper Navy, after Christmas, so maybe when 'e gets 'ome 'e'll 'ave got some stuff. It could be dead useful that, 'im bein' on convoy duty. They 'ave all kinds of fancy stuff over there in America.'

'Well, if it's "fancy stuff" you want, maybe you should go to Cooper's,' Delia said acidly.

'Don't go gettin' all airyated with me, girl,' retorted Eileen. All

I said was they 'ad fancy stuff over there. 'E's got ter get there and back in one piece and 'e might not be on convoy duty. I'm only guessin'.'

Katie Collins shook her head. 'I don't envy them if they are. We're losing too many ships an' some of them cargo boats are so old they were sailing up the Mersey when Noah built 'is Ark!'

'Yer can always be relied on, Katie, for a bit of cheerfulness,' Eileen remarked sarcastically. 'Do yer think Eddie Doyle 'as got over the shock of Dora's death yet? Our Frank says 'e's even more miserable now than he was before.'

'Well, he would be, wouldn't he? Poor Dora getting caught like that in a raid,' Delia stated.

'Why was she going to church anyway? There's no special novenas on,' Maisie asked.

'God knows,' Eileen replied.

'Well, I think *He's* just the one who would know,' Delia answered. 'Now, is anyone going to give me something for the Christmas Club?'

The Christmas Club was a fund Delia started immediately after Christmas each year and everyone paid a set amount each week, although sometimes they had to miss a week or two when things were bad moneywise. That way it ensured that there was some money for groceries for the festive season. Some of the women belonged to 'Tontines', which were run along the same lines.

'Well, this'll be the last until we start again after Christmas,' Maisie Keegan said, handing a sixpence to Delia. 'How much 'ave I got?'

Delia bent and picked up an exercise book from the shelf under the counter and flicked through the pages. 'You've got three pounds, four shillings and ten pence.'

'God, I've never 'ad that much before.'

'It's the war. The fellers have to do some work for a change, and there's all the "ovies" they've worked. How much have I got, Delia, luv?' Eileen asked.

Delia turned a page. 'You've done well this year, Eileen. Five pounds and fourpence.'

'Jesus, Mary and Joseph! Me dream's out! It must be with not havin' our Brenda at home and our Mike and Frank's wages an' our Maureen's few bob. It's more than I've ever had in me life and now there's hardly anythin' ter spend it on!' Eileen complained. For once everyone in the shop agreed with her, including Delia.

* * *

'We've got to do something *special* this Christmas,' Mike said to Johnny as they stood on the platform of the crowded tram.

'Too right we have.' Johnny was thinking of his mam and of Tessa. He'd bought a silver cross and chain from Cooke's pawnshop to be a Christmas and engagement present. He'd really wanted to ask his da for his mam's gold one but he wasn't sure what Eddie's reaction would be to the request. After all, Mam had only been dead three weeks.

The shock had affected them all in different ways. Most of the time all he felt was anger. Anger at the Luftwaffe. Anger at his da for letting her go out, for treating her like a doormat, and anger at God for allowing her to be caught in a raid. His da had become even more silent and morose and now went to mass every day. His younger brothers seemed lost and he often heard them crying at night.

The funeral had been terrible. Everyone had been great, they always rallied at such times, but without Tessa's support and comfort and the knowledge that she too had stood crying at the graveside of her mam it would have been unbearable.

'We'll treat the girls to a show,' Mike suggested.

'Where?'

'The Empire. I'll see if I can get tickets for the twenty-first. It'll be a proper treat. We all deserve one, I reckon.'

The nearer Christmas got the more excited Tessa became until she just couldn't keep her secret any more.

They were walking down the road after alighting from the bus when Tessa caught Elizabeth's arm and turned to her, her eyes shining. 'I've *got* to tell you! I just *can't* keep it to myself any longer.'

'What? You look as though you've won the Football Pools!'

'On Christmas Day Johnny is going to tell everyone that . . .' She suddenly felt shy.

'Tell everyone *what*? Oh, come on, Tessa, tell me, I'll burst with curiosity in a minute!'

'We're getting engaged.'

Elizabeth let out a shriek that could have competed with an air-raid siren and flung her arms around her friend. 'When? When did he ask you?'

'Last month.'

'Last *month*! Tessa O'Leary, you . . . you . . . spoilsport!'

'I couldn't tell you! I promised. Don't you dare tell anyone – and I mean *anyone* – else. It was to be a surprise—'

'Oh, it's that all right!' Elizabeth interrupted, laughing. 'Have you got a ring?'

'No. I'm not having one, not yet anyway. Maybe after he's been in the Navy for a month or so, when he's got enough money.'

'Did . . . did his mam know?'

Tessa's expression changed. 'No, that's the awful part of it. She never knew and I really did like her.'

'I wouldn't fancy old misery-guts as a father-in-law.'

'He's got a reason to be miserable these days.'

'I suppose he has but he never treated her very well, did he? She was terrified to look sideways at him. You'd have been great company for her, Tessa. So, when is the big day going to be then?'

'I don't know for certain yet, but we were talking about May. Next May.'

'Isn't there some daft superstition about it being bad luck to get married in May?'

Tessa shrugged. 'I haven't heard of that one, and anyway it is a *daft* superstition.'

'You're right. It was probably dreamed up by the clergy so they could go on holiday or something,' Elizabeth replied with her usual lack of respect for priests and nuns when she was out of earshot of her mother. She was beginning to have what Sister Francis would have called a 'crisis of faith'. She'd looked around her on the night of the last raid and wondered if there was a God at all.

Tessa looked at her askance. 'You say some terrible things, Elizabeth Harrison. I'm sure that's counted as blasphemy.'

'Oh, shut up, don't we get enough of that at home and at mass, Mrs Doyle-to-be!'

Tessa grinned. It sounded very odd to hear herself described as Mrs Doyle. Odd – but very nice.

Mike and Johnny had managed to get four tickets for the Empire's Christmas Revue in the four and sixpenny seats.

'That's sheer extravagance!' Elizabeth remonstrated. 'Especially as you're—' Just in time she remembered that she'd been sworn to secrecy.

'It's not a waste. We're both off to Chatham soon.'

'And it's Christmas,' Johnny added, winking at Tessa who smiled back. She'd be miserable when he went away but she tried not to think of that.

'You two sound like a double act,' Elizabeth laughed. She delved into her bag, bringing out a white paper bag. 'I've pinched some barley sugar twists. Mam's been hoarding them, but she won't mind.' In fact she would mind and Elizabeth knew it but she was determined to make this the best Christmas yet for Tessa.

'Don't tell everyone in the queue, we'll be mobbed!' Johnny joked as the people ahead of them began to move forward.

They were very good seats, Elizabeth had to admit: the front stalls, but not right at the front where you'd get a crick in your neck from having to look upwards all night.

The theatre was full and there was an atmosphere of excited anticipation. They all settled back into their seats as the lights dimmed.

The conductor, resplendent in evening dress, raised his baton and there was a slightly discordant fanfare from the orchestra pit. Then above it, drowning out the instruments, rose the banshee-like wail of the siren.

Elizabeth grabbed Mike's arm but Tessa just froze in her seat.

'Oh, go to hell, Fritz! Gizza break, don't yer know it's bloody Christmas!' someone bawled from the back. Everyone cheered.

Both girls managed a weak smile, but inside they were quaking with fear. Mike and Johnny looked grim as they tried to concentrate on the show. The music could hardly be heard at times, the spotlights flickered and the huge chandeliers suspended from the ceiling swayed dangerously, but no one moved. The defiant audience cheered and clapped every song performed by the artists, who themselves were afraid.

Elizabeth, clinging tightly to Mike's arm, half rose from her seat at the sound of every explosion. 'How long is it going to go on for?' she begged of him.

He squeezed her hand. 'I don't know, but hold on to me,' he answered with a confidence he didn't really feel.

They had no idea of the time but it seemed the raid was lasting for an eternity, when a massive explosion rocked the building. Plaster flaked from the ceiling, the stage lights dimmed and silence descended. Then the rumour ran quickly through the theatre that St George's Hall, on the opposite side of Lime Street, had been hit and was on fire.

There was no panic as everyone filed out and huddled under the canopy that ran across the front of the building.

'Oh, Mary Mother of God!' Elizabeth cried, crossing herself. Tessa's face drained of all colour and she began to shake. Mike and Johnny gazed upward with impotent fury. The beams of the searchlights picked out the sinister outlines of the enemy bombers still overhead. They looked like giant bats and just as evil.

'They're so bloody near you could almost reach up and snatch them out of the sky!' Mike said.

'And I know what I'd do if I caught one!' Johnny replied.

Everyone was stunned. As far down as William Brown Street the sky was bright as daylight and the heat was intense. The museum, the art gallery and the library had all been hit.

'There's nothing short of a bloody miracle that can save the Hall now,' someone close by said with a catch in their throat.

Flames were rushing and roaring from the long roof of the beautiful colonnaded building. The two huge bronze lions that stood guard over the plateau where the Punch and Judy show took place every Sunday appeared to be glaring their defiance. The flickering flames made their faces almost animate.

Many of the crowd were in tears, including Tessa and Elizabeth, as they watched Liverpool's greatest architectural treasure burn before their horrified gaze. The Assize Courts were burning out of control and thousands of legal documents fuelled the flames. The noise was so tremendous that the yells of rescue workers and the frantic clanging of fire engines that were converging on the whole area could barely be heard.

'I've come ter see the show, I've paid me money an' 'Itler an' 'is bloody firework display ain't goin' ter ruin me night!' came the shout from the back of the crowd.

'Good on yer, lad, I've paid an' all!' someone else shouted and to both girls' astonishment, everyone began to move back inside.

'Shouldn't we . . .' Tessa said tentatively.

Johnny put his arm firmly around her shoulders. 'No, Tess, we're all going to stick together.'

They stayed in the theatre, their community singing, led by the conductor of the orchestra, sometimes being drowned out by the droning of the planes overhead and the ferocity of the anti-aircraft batteries as they tried to shoot down the raiders. It was three-thirty a.m. before the 'All Clear' sounded and everyone cheered with what little voice and strength they had left. For all of them it had been a nerve-racking experience and they were exhausted. It was like something out of a nightmare, Elizabeth thought, having to sit there for hours, never knowing if you'd live to see tomorrow.

'It's going to take us ages to walk home and we've still got to get up early for work,' Tessa complained.

The two boys exchanged fearful glances. Would their homes still be standing? It looked as though the whole city was on fire. As a harassed, grim-faced policeman remarked, 'What a fine bloody Christmas present!'

It was after half past four when, after an horrendous journey, they finally reached Naylor Street. Both girls were trembling as the boys guided them around huge craters, buildings that were in danger of collapsing and others where firemen were fighting a losing battle. There were no streetlights and they had to pick their way over fire hoses, electricity and phone wires, broken gas and water pipes and tram lines that glowed red hot in some places and rose up in weird, unnatural shapes.

Tessa found Jimmy sitting with the Flynns on their doorstep. Not a window in any of the houses had escaped and the pavement and cobbles were covered with a carpet of crushed glass.

'Mam, are you all right?' Mike asked.

Eileen shook her head dazedly.

'Where's Da?' Tessa begged.

'He and Frank are out . . . out . . . there.' Eileen pointed a trembling finger towards the dock estate.

'Are my da and Mr Harrison out too?' Johnny asked.

Eileen could only nod. Her nerves were strung out like piano wires. She, like so many in the city, had been certain that she was not going to survive the night.

They learned next morning that St George's Hall had survived but the Gaiety Theatre, St Anthony's School, Crescent Church and St Alphonsus's Church hadn't, nor had many of the streets that bordered the dock estate.

After a brief doze, the girls set off for work again. Buildings were still smouldering and the emergency services continued digging in the piles of rubble. WVS women were handing out cups of tea and rounds of toast from a canteen lorry. Engineers from the gas, electricity, phone and sanitation companies were working frantically and shopkeepers were clearing up. They passed many signs bearing the words 'Business As Usual' and one that read 'Closed for Refurbishment and Decoration'. It brought a hint of a smile to both their faces. They weren't beaten yet.

At work there were familiar faces missing. The faces of those there were lined with worry and lack of sleep; their eyes were filled with mute misery and shock. Then, as they got back to a shattered city, after another exhausting day, the siren wailed and the raiders came again.

This time they all did run for the shelter, although Eileen took some persuading.

'If me name's on it then I want ter go in me own 'ome.'

'For God's sake, Mam, yer not stayin' 'ere and yer name won't be on any bloody bomb!' Maureen had yelled, which had snapped her mother out of her stubborn mood sufficiently to make a swipe at her for swearing.

Again, it went on for hours. They were cramped, cold, hungry and thirsty and unable even to sit down, while outside and above them the sky was bright with the flames of burning buildings which acted as beacons for the enemy planes. More than once the whole shelter shook, its concrete base cracking. There were very few able-bodied men inside, they were all out doing whatever they could to help. No one cried aloud, except for the young children and babies, although every girl and woman was verging on hysteria. Delia decided at one stage that if things didn't get better they'd all start screaming and wouldn't be able to stop, so she suggested that they either sing or pray or both and she started them all off with 'Eternal Father Strong to Save'. Their voices were weak to start with, and quivered noticeably whenever there was an explosion, but they kept on. Catholic and Protestant alike, differences forgotten, they were all in it together.

When the 'All Clear' sounded Eileen Flynn looked at her daughter with annoyance. 'Didn't I tell yer ter take that pan offen the cooker before we come 'ere? The bloody bottom will be burned out!'

'Jesus, Eileen, is that all you've got to think about?' Maisie said.

At that their composure broke; they all fell about laughing, but it was laughter with more than a hint of hysteria in it.

Chapter Twenty-Four

'It'll be a "make do and mend" Christmas,' Eileen said to Delia with a look of resignation in her eyes. It was a feeling that every woman in the city had now. For the first time they'd experienced just what heavy and continuous bombing could do and they were all appalled, afraid and some of them were grieving too.

'I'll agree with you on that, Eileen. Thank God they packed it in after those two terrible nights,' Delia replied. It was Christmas Eve and she was giving out the Christmas Club money. It had all been checked against the book, counted out and put into brown envelopes marked with the recipient's name.

'I'll never forget that night as long as I live, an' if they start up again that won't be long. I'm tellin' yer, Delia. I've 'ad shockin' palpitations ever since.'

'Haven't we all. We're all damned lucky we've still got roofs over our heads.'

'Our Rita 'asn't, not any more,' Maisie said grimly. 'I tell yer, I'm wore out with 'er. 'Er nerves is destroyed and them flamin' kids of 'ers, I'll swing for the lot of them before long! I know me own aren't angels, not by a long chalk, but *that* lot! Runnin' wild they are. Up an' down the flamin' stairs by the minutes, yellin' and screamin' and fightin'. Some days I've gorra 'ead like Birkenhead what with the row out of them.'

'Well, what do yer expect, Maisie? They was never allowed ter do anything in their 'ouse. Not with 'er feller acting like a tinpot soldier,' Eileen said, silently thanking God that her own sister, who had eight kids, had not been bombed out.

There was no stopping Maisie now. 'An' that's another thing, Delia. I'll have him 'ome soon and when 'e lands on me doorstep I'm goin' ter tell 'im that if he doesn't like the way I keep *my* 'ouse, then 'e can take the lot of them somewhere else! There'll be no crusts cut offen the bloody bread in our 'ouse!'

'That's not a very charitable thing to say, Maisie, especially at Christmas,' Delia said, still sorting out the envelopes.

'*You* don't have ter put up with them all. I'm tellin' yer, they'd drive the Archangel Gabriel mad!'

'Didn't she manage to save anything?' Eileen asked Maisie.

Doubling, even trebling up was not infrequent now, so many families had been bombed out.

'Just some clothes an' blankets that were in an old seaman's trunk. They built those things ter last, I'll tell yer. Black as the hobs of hell on the outside, inside just a few scorched edges and the stink of smoke.'

'That's something we're all living with. It gets everywhere and nothing seems to shift it. I've got two of them Airwick bottles on the mantelshelf but you can still smell it,' Delia informed them.

'Do you mind if I have my Club money now, Delia? I'm sorry if I'm jumping the queue,' May asked.

'What's the rush?' Maisie queried.

'Same as usual, work. We're still cleaning up from the other night and I've been asked to get something a bit special for Christmas – just what I don't know.'

'Who asked for that?' Maisie demanded.

'Tessa, and our Ginny backed her up.'

'Just what are those two up to?' Delia asked, handing May her envelope.

'Well, our Ginny's getting so excited about *that* feller coming home she'll make herself sick. He's not home until after the holiday, thank God, so it can't be that.'

'Tessa's been courting Johnny Doyle for ages now, do yer think they might be planning something, what with him going away an' all?' Eileen asked.

'Well, she has been more cheerful of late, if any of us could be called "cheerful".'

'I'm sure our Elizabeth would know if there was an announcement in the offing,' Delia said speculatively.

'Aye, she would. They're like Siamese twins those two. When you see one, the other's not far behind.'

'So, what "special" something do you want, May?'

Maisie and Eileen looked on, very interested, while young Bertie Collins, who had been sent down on a message, started to trace his name in the dry soil from the potato bin. He'd be hours at this rate, he thought. Why did they always have to take so long with their shopping?

'How much boiled ham can I have, Delia, and have you got any tins of fruit?'

'No fruit, May. Jelly and a tin of evap. Pass me your ration book.'

May looked thoughtful. Everyone bought their fowl and vegetables in the market last thing on Christmas Eve, you got good bargains then. 'I wonder, should I get some flour and eggs and make a cake?'

Maisie and Eileen exchanged glances. May Greely baking! May Greely making a cake! It was unheard of.

'Not that I'm turning away trade, May, but you might be better seeing what Skillicorn's or Lunt's have on offer. When do you get time for cake-making?' Delia suggested diplomatically.

'I think you're right, Delia. I won't get much of a break, we're open on Christmas Day and Bernie Daley will only give me an hour off! Talk about "goodwill to all men", that feller's never heard of it. Our Ginny and Tessa will have to cook the dinner.'

It was on Eileen's lips to say wasn't that what they always did so Christmas Day would be no different, until she caught a warning look from Delia.

'Will you put them to one side for me? One of the girls will pick them up later.'

Delia took the money May handed her and nodded. She certainly played on those two girls, she thought.

'I wonder what Tessa's up to?' Eileen speculated when May had gone.

'Well, no doubt we'll all find out soon enough.' Delia answered. She hoped it had nothing to do with Elizabeth and she hadn't been too pleased about May's remarks about Tessa. Although her relationship with Elizabeth was now less fraught, she hadn't forgiven Tessa for, as she saw it, enticing Elizabeth to the munitions factory. Siamese twins, indeed!

It made the street look like something from the front of a Christmas card, Elizabeth thought. As well as being Christmas Day, today was the day Tessa was going to announce her engagement. She wrapped her warm red dressing gown around her and stood looking out of the window at the fairytale scene of the snow glistening in the pale winter sunlight, covering the craters and disguising the bomb sites. It was going to be a perfect day for Tessa and it would help to relieve the strain and sorrow for Johnny. It would be the first Christmas without his mam. Without anyone to have decorated the house, done the shopping and cooked the traditional meal. Eddie and his two younger sons were going to his brother's house for dinner. Johnny was having his with Tessa and the rest of her family.

After mass they all wished each other the Season's Greetings which Father Walsh thought more apt than Happy Christmas or a

Peaceful Christmas. There was not much for anyone to be happy about and definitely no peace. Tessa asked Eddie Doyle and his two young sons to come back with herself and the rest of the family just for an hour.

'Well, our Billy is expecting us and we don't want to be late and ruin the dinner.'

'You won't be late, Da, I promise,' Johnny urged.

'Don't look at me, Eddie, it's a mystery to us as well,' Richie added.

So they all agreed and began to walk home, hanging on to each other to prevent themselves from slipping and falling, as it was still freezing hard.

'It's dead good! We'll get the oven shelf after dinner and go out and slide down the street on it!' Jimmy said to Vincent Doyle, the youngest of Johnny's brothers, and Harold Flynn who was tagging on behind.

Eileen had overheard him. 'Oh no yer won't, meladdo! Them streets are dangerous enough without youse lot making them worse.'

'Ah, Mam, it's Christmas!' Harold protested but his protest was ignored by his mother, which he took to be a good sign. He'd be all right, his da always went to the pub and Mam always fell asleep after dinner and he never took any notice of their Maureen. She'd got a gift box from Woolies that had perfume and stuff in it and had been made up with it. Their Brenda was coming over though, and with *him* too. He bet Thomas Kinsella had never made a slide in the street or used the oven shelf or a tray as a sledge, he was too miserable. And he was still afraid of his mam. Mind you, even if Mam did forbid him the oven shelf, he'd got a football for Christmas and you couldn't have everything. The casey would give them all hours of fun, long after the snow and ice had gone. In fact, some of his pleasure in making slides and snowmen and snowball fights dimmed as he realised he wouldn't be able to play footie until the snow cleared.

When they reached the shop Elizabeth turned to her mother. 'Mam, will it be all right for me to go to Tessa's for half an hour?'

'What for? You've only just left her and I'll need help with the dinner, you know that.'

'Yes, but . . . but, well, today is special.'

'It is, it's Christ's birthday,' Delia answered.

'And mustn't He be pleased at the way the world is celebrating it? By killing and maiming each other and blasting innocent women and kids to kingdom come!' Jack answered grimly.

'Mam, please?' Elizabeth begged.

Delia pursed her lips.

'What's so special?' Jack asked. The last thing he wanted today was another row between his wife and daughter.

Elizabeth became impatient. 'Oh, if you must know, she and Johnny are going to announce their engagement.'

Delia looked taken aback. 'When was all this planned?'

'Weeks ago, but I was sworn to secrecy. His poor mam didn't even know about it before she was killed.'

'Go on then, just half an hour. Your mam hasn't slaved away to have the dinner ruined,' Jack said but he was smiling, unlike Delia.

'Well, that's a turn-up for the book, but I've got to say they are suited and he's away next week.'

'I just hope Elizabeth doesn't take it into her head to do anything stupid.'

Jack shook his head, glancing at Nessie, and Delia said no more.

It was all a bit of a squeeze, Tessa thought, but they managed it, and when everyone had perched themselves on something, she looked up at Johnny, her eyes shining, her heart full of love.

Johnny cleared his throat nervously. 'Da, Mr and Mrs O'Leary, we . . . we've got something to tell you.'

'Well, get on with it, lad, we're all waiting for that goose that's in the oven,' Richie urged.

'Tessa and . . . well, we have decided to get engaged. I know we're both under the age of consent and we really need your permission, but I'll be away soon and I reckon if I'm old enough to fight, then I'm old enough to get engaged.'

May clapped her hands to her cheeks, she'd thought it was something like this. 'Oh, isn't that great, Richie! Tessa, come here to me while I hug you, and you too, Johnny!'

'Will you . . . will you have a ring?' Ginny was utterly devastated but then remembered that Colin was due home soon.

'Not yet, but . . . here, Tessa, this is to make it sort of official.'

Tessa took the little box and unwrapped the paper, then she cried with delight and threw her arms around her new fiancé. It was the signal for Richie to shake Eddie's hand vigorously and May, Ginny and Elizabeth to dissolve into floods of tears while Johnny fastened the chain around Tessa's neck.

'I'll never take it off! Never. Not as long as I live!' Tessa said, quietly.

'Your mam would have been pleased. She liked Tessa a lot. She's a good girl, son,' Eddie said with a tinge of regret and sadness in his voice. He missed Dora far more than he thought he ever would. He'd never noticed or even mentioned how hard she'd worked to keep a good home, and now that home had started to look neglected and shabby. They all missed her.

'When . . . when will you get married?' Ginny asked.

'In May, and before anyone starts on the bad luck thing, we don't care!' Tessa said.

'It's just a load of superstitious nonsense anyway,' Elizabeth added. She was so happy for Tessa and she knew Mike was too, but it set her own thoughts on the same question. The announcement of her engagement certainly wouldn't be met with such joy and enthusiasm. It would mean yet another huge row and probably the permanent alienation of all her family, although she would be welcomed by Eileen and Frank.

After lunch Elizabeth and Nessie washed and dried the dishes while her mam and da dozed before the fire. It was still bitterly cold and reminded Elizabeth of the first Christmas Tessa had spent in Naylor Street. Everything had been so different then. Who would have thought that they would be in the middle of a war now? That May and not Mary would be Mrs O'Leary? They had all certainly grown up: even Nessie wasn't so bad these days.

'What are you thinking about?' Nessie asked as she wiped her hands on the roller towel Delia kept in the scullery.

'Oh, how things have changed. You, me, Tessa . . .'

'And Mike Flynn?' Nessie queried.

'Yes, and Mike too.'

'Do you think you'll end up marrying him?'

Elizabeth shrugged. 'I don't know. Anything could happen in the future, especially . . . especially when he's away.'

Nessie looked at her solemnly. 'But you do *hope* you will?'

'Oh, God, Nessie, please don't start with the Grand Inquisition, I thought you'd changed.'

Nessie looked hurt. 'I wasn't going to say anything to Mam.'

'Then don't even mention it, please? I do . . . like Mike, but . . .' She shrugged.

Nessie nodded and went through to the kitchen, leaving her sister thoughtful and uneasy.

* * *

Saturday January 4 1941 had arrived and still the snow lay heavily on the ground and each night the temperature dropped, making the roads and streets hazardous. Jack said to Frank Flynn that he'd never known so many horses that had had to be put down because they'd fallen on the icy cobbles. It was a pitiful sight to see them thrashing about, screaming with the agony of broken legs. It was pitiful too to see the carters, with tears in their eyes, take the guns they all carried and put them out of their misery. Their horses were like old friends, some of the carters thought more of their horses than they did of their wives, Jack had said, and Frank had nodded his agreement, thinking that a loyal, dumb animal would be preferable to Eileen at times. A horse would wait patiently outside a pub, quite happy with a nosebag of oats, and wouldn't rant and rave about 'wasting time and money'. Everyone now threw the ashes from their fires on to the pavements and roads to help give a better grip for both people and animals.

Both Elizabeth and Tessa had been granted a half-day's leave to see Mike and Johnny off from Lime Street station.

They looked so different now, Elizabeth thought. The uniforms made them look older than eighteen. They were boys no longer, she mused sadly, they were young men and they were going off to war. She squeezed Mike's hand and he looked down at her and smiled into eyes that were unnaturally bright.

'Elizabeth, you promised, no waterworks!'

'I know I did, but . . . but look around, everyone is crying.'

The station was filled with couples embracing; mothers and sweethearts and wives clinging tearfully to their menfolk. Fathers were shaking the men's hands or were slapping them on the back.

'You will write to me?' she begged.

'I've promised a hundred times. They'll go to Tessa's address.'

'Oh, I wish we didn't have to be so . . . so secretive about it.'

'So do I, but for the time being it's best to say nothing of our plans.'

She nodded, her heart beating in on odd jerky fashion, her throat dry. On Christmas Night they'd gone for a walk, despite the bitter cold, and it had been then that he'd asked her to wait for him. To marry him when the war was over. She'd clung to him, pure joy flowing like wine through her veins. And when he'd kissed her she hadn't wanted him to stop – ever.

'I'll get you something, Elizabeth, something as a token.'

247

'Not a cross and chain, Mam will be certain to start asking questions.'

'What then?'

She'd thought for a minute. 'A brooch.'

He'd looked amused. 'What kind of brooch?'

'I don't know. Something . . . something unusual.'

'I've never been much of a one for looking at women's jewellery,' he'd laughed, 'but I saw a brooch once – well, it was more like a badge. An officer, a naval officer, was wearing it. It was made up of two gold fishes – strange fishes they were too, with long sort of snouts. The noses, or whatever they were, were holding up a silver anchor and above it was a gold crown with bits of it painted in red. It was so unusual, that's why I can remember it so clearly. Would you like something like that?'

Elizabeth deliberated. It did sound unusual. 'Yes, I think I would. I'd wear it all the time and no one could object to that. If Mam asks I'll say it's a military badge – well, a naval badge.'

'I wonder what it represents, or *who* it represents,' Mike pondered.

'Maybe Da will know. But I won't ask him until you give it to me,' she'd added hastily.

'I wish now I'd asked him what it represented and where I could get one, but I'll find out and when I'm home next, you'll have your brooch.'

The Tannoy system crackled into life and a disembodied voice informed everyone – not very clearly – that all naval personnel were to board the special trains immediately.

Tessa flung her arms around Johnny's neck. 'Oh, take care! Please take care of yourself, I love you so much!'

He held her closely. 'Don't worry, Tessa, I'll be back. It'll soon be May. We've got that to look forward to.'

Eileen and Brenda and Maureen were in tears. Frank was keeping a wary eye on young Harold who had a fascination with steam engines, and who was all too likely to take this rare opportunity of a closer look and get lost in this crowd – and then Eileen would be livid and blame him.

'Goodbye, Mam, Da, and you two, don't go misbehaving yourselves. Brenda, you see you take care of my niece or nephew and yourself too.' Mike embraced his family in turn and then caught Elizabeth to him.

'I love you, Mike. I'll always love you. Come back for me. I'll wait for ever for you!'

'Oh, Elizabeth! Elizabeth!' He hid his face in her hair so none of them could see the tears in his eyes. He was scared; they all were. God alone knew what faced them. 'I love you, Elizabeth. Take care of yourself.'

He finally disentangled himself from her embrace and with Johnny and four other lads from Naylor and Oriel Streets walked through the barrier that separated them from their loved ones. For some it was to be the last sight they'd ever have of those dear, familiar faces.

Chapter Twenty-Five

On a freezing cold night almost a month to the day later, it was Ginny's turn to stand on Lime Street Station, under the clock, waiting for Colin's train to arrive. She'd been counting the hours and the minutes but she hadn't told Tessa or her Mam because she knew they would ridicule her.

She could hardly contain herself, she was so excited. She hadn't slept properly for the past two nights either. She'd spent hours in front of the mirror examining her face for spots that might suddenly appear and fiddling with her hair until she'd made such a mess of it that Elizabeth had been called in.

'I just can't do *anything* with it! And I don't know what to wear,' Ginny had wailed.

Tessa, who was writing to Johnny via the Naval Dockyard at Chatham, raised her eyes to the ceiling. She certainly didn't view her brother's homecoming as anything to be overjoyed about. In fact Ginny was the only one who showed any enthusiasm at all and she was really taking it too far. Her da hadn't even mentioned it. All May had said was, 'Another mouth to feed,' and Jimmy was disappointed to learn that his elder brother hadn't actually done any fighting yet. Two of the lads in his class had fathers who had been rescued from the beach at Dunkirk when all the ships – even the Mersey ferries – had sailed to France to evacuate the French and British soldiers caught between the sea and the German Army. Now *that* had been exciting. Something to boast about. All Colin had done was train at Aldershot.

'What in God's name have you been doing to it? Have you been cutting it? It's all lengths,' Elizabeth said disparagingly.

'Just my fringe. I only cut the tiniest bit off!' Ginny wriggled on the chair and looked apprehensive.

'Obviously your idea of "tiny" and mine is different. You look as if you've taken a pair of garden shears to it. I'll have to even it all off now and once I've set it I don't want any more fiddling with it, so stop fidgeting. What are you going to wear? It's as cold as the North Pole out there.'

'My best blouse, navy skirt and my good coat.'

'You'll freeze in that blouse, it's only got short sleeves,' Tessa remarked.

Ginny didn't reply. She'd put up with the cold.

'Presumably you'll be wearing a hat?' Elizabeth asked as she snipped away.

'The one I bought last year – I've got some new ribbon to put around it. There's nothing in the shops now. Nothing decent.'

'Well, there is a war on. I'll wave your hair – that'll look better under a hat and it won't be all flattened when you take it off.'

'Oh, I'm so thrilled!'

'You won't be if you don't sit still and my scissors slip and cut your ear!' And you're the only one who seems to be delighted at the return of the Prodigal. Even your Jimmy isn't over the moon,' Elizabeth answered.

'Oh, he's just a kid. All he wants is something to boast about to his mates. Even the Christmas raids didn't stop them all hankering after a hero to worship.'

The train was late. Ginny and every other woman on the station concourse kept checking the time by the big clock whose fingers seemed to move with infinite slowness. Ginny stamped her feet, turned up the collar of her coat and thrust her hands deeper into her pockets. Trains these days were always late.

There was an indistinct announcement over the Tannoy and everyone surged forward towards the barrier as, with a shrill whistle and a grinding of iron wheels on the track, the train pulled in, wreathed in clouds of steam.

There was total chaos as the soldiers, airmen and civilian passengers started to reach the barrier and it wasn't until a policeman and a railway official cleared the immediate area around the barrier that some semblance of order was restored.

In the crush Ginny's hat had been knocked sideways but she didn't care. In seconds he'd be here with her.

Colin saw her before she caught sight of him. His searching gaze had swept the faces of the crowd, to find that she was the only one of them who'd come. He was hurt and angry – everyone else seemed to have huge numbers of relatives fussing and crying over them. He was certain that had she been alive Mam would have been here. It was probably May's fault that his da and Jimmy hadn't come, and probably Tessa too. Then he remembered that Tessa wouldn't have come even if he'd been abroad and was coming home covered in medals. But he'd expected his da to be there, at least, and maybe Jimmy.

Ginny flung herself into his arms with such force that he almost overbalanced.

'Hey! Hang on a minute, Ginny, or you'll have us both over! I've heard of "fond greetings" but this is a bit over the top!' He laughed, making no attempt to kiss her except on the cheek. He'd grown up a lot since he'd been away and she looked even more of a kid than ever. A silly, soppy, doe-eyed kid. He was used to women now. Proper women, and not all of them had wanted paying for their favours.

'Oh, I'm so glad to see you! I've missed you so much! It's been awful. Why didn't you write more often? I sent you hundreds of letters!' Ginny babbled.

He disentangled himself. 'Because I've not had much time, Ginny. I've been training, remember? There's a war on.'

'Oh, everyone is saying that all the time now,' she replied petulantly.

'Well, it's true. Right, hang on to me while I get us through this crowd.'

With shining eyes she clung to his arm while he, with his kit bag over his other shoulder, pushed his way forcefully towards the exit and on out to Lime Street.

'Will we go . . . somewhere first, like?' she asked shyly. She wanted time alone with him before they got home to their crowded kitchen.

'Where?'

'Well, I don't know. A pub?'

Colin looked at her with irritation. 'Ginny, you don't even look seventeen, let alone twenty-one, and I'm not being told to leave because you're under age, not in front of all the customers.'

'I'm nearly eighteen,' she protested.

She'd managed to change her shift so she'd be home in the evenings, like Tessa and Elizabeth, and could spend time with him while he was on leave. She was very tired when she got in, they all were, but that wouldn't matter. She could catch up on her sleep when he'd gone back. Although she didn't want to think about that.

'So, you're back then. How's it going?' Richie greeted his son from over the top of the newspaper he was reading. He hoped the Army would have knocked Colin into shape. He certainly looked well in his uniform, so maybe things were getting better.

'Bloody hard work, it is.'

'Hard work never killed anyone,' May said.

'We've had air raids, in case it's escaped your notice,' Tessa remarked.

'I did notice. London was pretty battered-looking.'

'And so are we,' May cut in with an edge of impatience in her voice.

'Well, this is a nice homecoming I must say! I don't know why I bothered, I've not had a civil word from anyone except Ginny.'

Ginny gazed at him adoringly. 'I'll get you something to eat and make a whole pot of tea, just how you like it.'

Colin smiled. 'That's my girl.'

He was sorry he'd come home now. You could cut the atmosphere with a knife. They were all obviously still annoyed about that bank raid. He'd been fool enough to turn down the chance to stay with one of his new mates in London for this.

'Just you remember, Ginny, that that tea has got to last,' May called to her daughter, who totally ignored her and put three heaped teaspoons in the pot.

'I suppose Ginny wrote and told you that Johnny and I are engaged?' Tessa asked.

'I suppose she did but I don't remember. That's a bit quick off the mark, isn't it?'

'It is not. We've been courting for ages.'

'I mean he's only a bit of a kid.'

'He's man enough for the Navy and so is Mike Flynn,' May shot back at him.

'I didn't mean it like that. I just meant he's a bit . . . well . . . young.'

'Oh, would you just listen to Old Father Time there! All of nineteen, he is,' May remarked sarcastically.

'I don't think it's young. Well, not in wartime,' Ginny said, bringing the teapot and mugs in, plus two rounds of bread spread with Marmite.

'Young or not, we're getting married in May, but I expect you'll be away.' Tessa hadn't expected him to be enthusiastic. After what had happened on the *Ascania*, Colin must hate Johnny. The feeling was mutual.

'I will be. Where will you live, at the pub?'

'Most probably. We really didn't have much time to discuss it.'

'They'll have you for a skivvy, what with Mrs Doyle getting killed.'

Tessa glared at him. Obviously some of the things in Ginny's letters he read and remembered.

'They won't,' she snapped.

'I bet his da is all for it, though. I don't suppose any of them know one end of a brush from the other or how to boil an egg. She waited on them hand and foot and she got no thanks for it, and neither will you.'

May's patience snapped. 'If you haven't got anything better to say than that, the sooner you get back to your flaming Regiment the better!'

Colin got to his feet, took the pot, a mug and the plate from a dumbfounded Ginny and left the room.

'Well, you can't say he didn't ask for it, Ginny,' May said firmly. 'Not a "Congratulations" or "Good Luck", nothing but snide remarks.'

'Oh, Mam, that's a nice way to welcome anyone home! He's only got a week and then he'll be going abroad to fight and I . . . I . . .' Ginny broke down in tears and fled to the semi-privacy of the room she shared with Tessa.

'Ginny! Come back!' May called, but Ginny ignored her. 'For God's sake, what am I going to do with her, Richie? Did you see the look on her face when he said "That's my girl"? He can still twist her around his little finger I get so worried about her.'

'She'll be all right, he's only home for five days. He'll be travelling back for his last day and after that, well, she said herself he'll be going abroad. And about time too.'

May sighed. 'Let's just hope he behaves himself for the next five days because I know I can't do a single thing with her.'

Tessa nodded her agreement and returned to her letter.

The following day Colin slept late. After he'd washed, shaved and dressed he decided to go for a bit of a walk to think about how he could keep Ginny quiet and content with the minimum of time and effort. She was a real pain in the neck, but she had his money so he couldn't upset her. He knew though that he'd made the right choice in giving the money to her to mind. He knew that wild horses wouldn't have dragged the knowledge or hiding place from her. Not after he'd trusted her completely, not after all she'd been through when she lied to the police.

He caught a bus and went down to the Pier Head.

It was viciously cold and a few snowflakes were borne on the east wind. There were other men in uniform just walking, like himself, taking in the familiar sights and sounds, or waiting to board trams and buses. He walked down the floating roadway and on to the George's Landing Stage where, leaning against a wooden post, he looked out over the grey waters of the Mersey. Today was the first of his five days and nights, and he certainly didn't intend to spend them all in *that* house with *them* and Ginny mooning around, hanging on to his every word. It would drive him mad. But she had the money. He could have a bloody good time on that much money but he wanted to save most of it. Still, he could ask her for a few pounds. He had no idea where she kept it and turning the rooms inside out looking for it would certainly make someone ask why. Oh, when this war was over he was going to America or Australia and he wouldn't be sorry to leave any of them. Especially not Ginny.

His attention was caught by four warships moving slowly up river against the ebbing tide, the vanguard of a convoy. He wondered just how many ships had set out and how many had managed to make it back. The speed of the naval vessels was dead slow, about ten knots probably. They were useless for protection. What was needed were big, fast ships that could home in on the U-boats, release their depth charges and make a kill. By the time the naval escorts got to a ship in danger it was too late, the U-boat had done its job and was away. He knew that having lost the battle for the air, the Germans were engaged in another: a battle for the Atlantic and the safety of the shipping lanes. He shook his head as four battered, rusting merchant ships came into view. They and two more on the horizon were all damaged in some way. Rigging and funnels gone, holes above the waterline. They looked like tired, grey old warhorses; six of them in total. Just six. How many had set out? How many men had been drowned or been killed? It was vital that the port be kept working otherwise Hitler could starve them into submission. He'd gathered as much from a conversation he'd overheard on the train – and *that* hadn't been wise. There were posters everywhere warning 'Careless Talk Costs Lives'.

'Well, I never expected to see you again, Colin O'Leary.'

He turned at the familiar voice. 'Vera!' She looked very smart, he thought, and wondered where she'd got the money for the cherry-red military-styled suit she was wearing under a thick black coat, the collar and cuffs of which were trimmed with black fur.

'You look . . . great! Have you got yourself a rich feller?'

Vera arched her neck and cast him a seductive glance from beneath her lashes.

'What if I have?'

Colin shrugged. 'It doesn't matter to me.'

'My feller *is* rich but he's old as well and he's away a lot so I'm on my own, if you know what I mean.'

Colin smiled at her. He certainly did know what she meant.

'What are you doing down here? I'd have thought you'd be working in munitions like everyone else.'

'I do, you can't get away with not bloody working there, but I've got some time off. I've come to meet him.' She indicated with her head the first of the cargo ships which was now almost alongside.

'He's in the Merchant Navy?'

'Yes, he's a Chief Sparks. He'd have been retired if there hadn't been this bloody war. I've got a dead nice house now. Two bedrooms, kitchen, scullery and a proper parlour. The third bedroom he's had made into a bathroom, would you believe? A bath and an inside flush toilet. Mam and our Nelly are dead jealous, that's when they bother to think of me. His wife died ages ago and they had no kids.'

'That's great, Vera, you certainly landed on your feet there.' Privately, Colin wondered how someone with Vera's reputation and humble background could have caught herself a Chief Electrical Officer.

'After tonight, he won't want to go out again. We go for a drink and something to eat and he's worn out by midnight. He goes into a deep sleep. He says they never sleep properly when they're at sea. Always waiting for the alarm to go.'

Colin smiled again. 'So, does he let you out on your own at all while he's on leave?'

'Of course. He doesn't keep me on a collar and lead. He knows I've got me mates from work, and if he thinks I'm off with a feller he doesn't say so. He doesn't get all narked like some fellers do. He just likes someone to meet him when he comes home and then a bit of company. I try not to go out very much when he's home, but for some fellers . . .' She shrugged.

'So, would you like to go out with me, say tomorrow night?'

Vera arched her plucked and pencilled eyebrows. 'Well, that's a bit too soon.'

'What about the night after?'

He was like an eager drooling puppy, she thought. The Army had certainly done wonders for him, though. He looked smart and far more confident. He'd always been good-looking.

'OK. Where will you take me?' She wasn't going out to be stuck in some poky dirty pub. She'd had enough of that. She was used to better things now.

'The State on Lime Street.'

'Great.'

'I'll meet you at the tram stop at the top of Freemasons Row at half past seven.'

Vera smiled. 'Fine. I'd better go. See you then.'

The gangway was down and the crew of the cargo ship were starting to come ashore so Colin turned away. Things were looking up, but he'd need some cash if he was going to squire Vera around all week. She certainly wouldn't be content sitting in a park and he'd have to buy her little gifts. He'd have to ask Ginny for the money.

'Ginny, can I have a bit of a word, in private, like?' he asked, almost as soon as she'd set foot in the door.

Her eyes lit up and the weariness fell away. What was he going to say?

'Is Tessa in yet?'

'No.'

'Then come into the front room.'

'What is it?' she asked as she closed the door behind them.

'You've still got *our* money, haven't you?'

'Of course I have.' Oh, this was it! He was going to ask for some to spend on her, she *knew* it!

'Well, I'll need a bit for . . . certain things.' He could see by her expression that she was hoping it was to buy her something. Well, hell would freeze over before he bought her anything expensive.

'How much? How much will you need?'

Colin looked thoughtful. Too much and she would suspect it wasn't for a ring, too little and he'd never be able to keep Vera happy.

'About ten pounds. If there's anything left over I'll give it you back. I've got my Army pay.'

'I'll get it for you now.'

She opened a drawer of her clothes chest under the window. Delving in, she fumbled beneath the garments, took out two white five-pound notes and handed them to him.

'That's great, Ginny.'

She automatically assumed he'd be taking her out. 'Where are we going tonight?'

'We're not going anywhere. I'm still tired out. Later in the week.'

She nodded, trying to understand.

'Much later, I mean. I've made arrangements to meet some of my Army mates for a few bevvies on Saturday.'

Ginny's heart dropped like a stone. 'Saturday! But everyone goes out on a Saturday! Oh, Colin, can't you put them off?' she begged.

'No. We all made a sort of pact,' he lied. 'Every time we're all home together, and it won't be often, we'll meet up and have a drink. Don't look so upset, Ginny, luv, I've . . . we've got plenty of time. I don't leave until next Tuesday.' He had to keep her happy.

Ginny smiled. He'd actually called her 'luv' and last night he'd said, 'That's my girl'. She *was* his girl and she was being selfish. Who knew what Colin and all his mates faced? Maybe they wouldn't have a chance to get together again for years.

'Yes, we've got the rest of your week. I was just being selfish and stupid.'

He bent and kissed her cheek. 'No, you're not. You're being really thoughtful and understanding.' The lies tripped easily off his tongue and Ginny was pacified.

On Saturday night she watched him get spruced up with something akin to adoration. He was so handsome, especially in his uniform now it had been pressed and all the buttons and badges burnished so they shone.

'You're taking your time getting dressed up, who are you meeting tonight?' Tessa asked.

'He's going for a drink with some of his mates from the Regiment,' Ginny answered.

Colin smiled at her through the mirror.

'Really? The time he's spent polishing those buttons and cap badge, I'd have thought he was going out on a date.'

Colin glared at his sister. Why the hell couldn't she just mind her own business? He saw the look on Ginny's face change. 'Well, I'm not. We always have to do this "spit and polish" bit. We can't let the Regiment down,' he snapped.

Tessa shrugged but she could see Ginny was perturbed about something.

He kissed Ginny on the cheek again and went out, whistling.

'Why are you always so nasty to him?' Ginny demanded of Tessa.

'Because he's always so nasty to me . . . us. Have you forgotten that he's brought nothing but trouble to us? He even got you to lie for him, and if you think he's going off to meet his mates then you're more of a fool than I thought.'

'What do you mean by that?' Ginny demanded angrily.

'He's not going to see the blokes he sees every day, for God's sake! He's going to meet someone. A girl. Oh, Ginny, for heaven's sake, can't you see him for what he is? And why did he need all that money? I saw him put two five-pound notes in his wallet when he thought I wasn't looking. I know him. That money was to pay for a night out, obviously a very expensive one, and maybe a present of some sort. He must get well paid!'

Ginny leaped to her feet. 'No! No, I won't listen to you, Tessa! You hate him, you've always hated him. He's not like that. I believe him. I love him and he loves me.'

'Oh, I give up!' Tessa cried. 'I'm going to Elizabeth's.' But before she could move Ginny had grabbed her coat, shrugged it on and pushed past a startled Richie who had come in through the scullery.

'Where's she going? What's up with her?' he demanded.

'My dear brother is obviously taking some girl out tonight but he's told her he's meeting some mates. When I told her not to be such a fool as to believe him she up and stormed off.'

'He's not home five minutes before he's causing trouble,' Richie said angrily.

'Well, I'm going to Elizabeth's. I don't want to be here when she comes back, nor do I want to be the one who has to say "I told you so".'

'Neither do I. I'm going up to the pub.'

Chapter Twenty-Six

Ginny didn't know where she was running to. She'd just *had* to get out of that house. They'd all back Tessa up, and she couldn't stand it. It was as if they all actually hated him. How could Tessa be so nasty and malicious when he was her brother? Poor Colin had only just got home and everyone was treating him like a criminal, an outcast. He *had* gone out to meet his mates. He *had*! Why didn't Tessa believe him? He'd kissed her, wasn't that proof enough?

She didn't feel the freezing cold. Most of the streets had been cleared of snow but it was still icy and she almost fell a couple of times. By the time she reached Scotland Road she was out of breath and trembling. She clung to a lamppost; it was so dark the only light came from the moon, around which there was a milky-white rim which foretold another heavy frost. It was the worst winter she could ever remember. Well, she wasn't going to let them carry on being so awful to him. She'd catch him up and tell him what Tessa had said; he'd reassure her and tell her that Tessa was lying; then she'd kiss him and send him on his way to enjoy himself.

She crossed the road with care, seeing in the distance the small crosses of light that came from the hooded headlights of a tram and the white flash of paint on its bumper. He'd be at the stop at the top of Freemasons Row but she'd have to hurry. She tried to run but it was too dangerous. She slipped a few times, only just recovering her balance. If she fell and hurt herself she'd miss him. She clutched at anything that would give her support. Lampposts, bollards, shop windowsills, and all the time the tram was getting nearer and nearer.

Finally she was within earshot of the stop and she could see a couple of figures standing waiting. She wasn't too late.

She took a few steps forward and then stopped. She just managed to stop herself from calling out to him. He definitely wasn't alone. Before her horrified gaze Vera Morley, dressed to the nines, linked her arm through Colin's and reached up and kissed him on the cheek. She continued to watch, frozen like a rabbit caught in the glare of headlights. She was unable to run away, paralysed by what she was seeing: Colin, laughing, then bending down to kiss Vera and say something that made her throw her head back and laugh too.

Ginny felt sick. She leaned back against the window of a shop and closed her eyes. No! *No!* She refused to believe it. She *wouldn't* think about it. She had imagined it. It was a dream; she'd wake up soon. But she didn't. She opened her eyes; it wasn't an apparition. You couldn't miss Vera with her bleached hair. She watched wide-eyed with disbelief as Colin took Vera's arm and helped her on to the platform as though she were a delicate piece of china. They disappeared from view, the conductor rang the bell and the tram trundled away, the noise growing fainter and fainter until there was nothing but silence and emptiness. Emptiness that filled her and turned her heart to ice. She couldn't move. She just stood there, looking in the direction the tram had gone, taking Vera Morley and . . . him into town to enjoy themselves.

Her feet and hands were numb, but she still wasn't aware of the cold.

'Are you all right, luv? Are you lost?'

She looked up to see a policeman, clad in his thick heavy cape, the hands in which he held his torch encased in cream woollen gloves.

'No. No . . . I'm not lost.'

'You're frozen, girl. Where do you live and what's the matter?'

Ginny tried to pull herself out of the trance that gripped her. 'There's . . . nothing the matter. I'm . . . I'm just off home now.' She pointed along the road. 'I live along there. In . . . in Naylor Street.'

'Do you want me to walk with you?'

She shook her head. 'No, no thanks. I'm . . . fine. Thank you, thanks.' She began to walk in the direction of Naylor Street and he shrugged and turned away. She was obviously upset, but then so were an awful lot of girls these days.

Ginny didn't turn into Naylor Street.

She wandered around the Dock Road and its adjoining side streets for hours. She ignored the shouts, cat calls and openly coarse remarks that were yelled at her from the doors of the pubs she passed. A couple of times she'd been forced out of her reverie by the presence of seamen and dockers who'd blocked her path. They'd turned away and left her alone after taking in the wax-like skin and wide, staring eyes, thinking she was a wandering lunatic.

Tessa had been right. They'd all been right. She was the one who was stupid. She was the only fool who'd believed him. He didn't love her at all. He only wanted . . . Vera Morley. How could she have believed in him so implicitly? She adored him, he knew that. He'd always known she loved him and wouldn't even look at another lad. Tremors of shock ran through her. Vera Morley: that painted, over-dressed tart! He preferred *her*. He'd looked proud to be seen with her hanging on to his arm. He'd treated *her* like a princess. Surely Vera Morley had tricked him into taking her out? But her heart told her that this time putting the blame on someone else wouldn't work. She'd seen him with her own eyes; she'd listened to his lies with her own ears. It was over. He didn't want her.

When she at last returned home May was sitting beside the range, waiting.

'Oh, Ginny, luv. I was so worried about you. Richie said you'd had a row with Tessa over Colin and had just run off.'

'Mam . . . Mam . . . I don't want to talk about it. Not now, please?'

May got to her feet. Her heart bled for her daughter but at long last she looked as if she might just be coming to her senses over him. She wouldn't press her.

'You're frozen. Let me make you a drink and then I'll wrap the oven shelf in a bit of towel and you can take that to bed with you. Tessa's already asleep so try not to wake her. You've both got work in the morning and so have I.'

'Mam, I don't want a drink or anything. I just want to sit here . . . get warm . . . think . . .'

May nodded; she thought she understood. Somehow Ginny must have found out the truth about Colin. That was the only thing which could have affected her so deeply. All they could do now was support her, give her time and comfort. And not even mention it, never mind torment her with the words 'I told you so'. May just wished *he* didn't have a few more days at home. She'd have a word with Richie about it. Maybe he could think of some way of getting that cheating, conniving little sod to go back before his leave was up.

The house was so silent, Ginny thought as she huddled in the chair by the fire, still with her coat on. Only the ticking of the clock on the mantel broke it and seemed to get louder and louder until it filled her aching head. She sat gazing into the flames and suddenly snatches of conversation and fragmented images began to come back to her. Images of Colin with Vera Morley in his arms

262

once before. Only this time they were in the park and it wasn't cold or frosty. He had his arm around her and was kissing her. She clenched the arms of the chair so hard that her knuckles became white. *No! No!*

She didn't want to remember, but she couldn't stop the images. They were so vivid and real that she could smell the scents of that warm summer evening. The roses and the flowering beds were a riot of glorious colour. She saw Vera's mocking smile, heard her call her an ugly, stupid kid. Then Colin's face loomed up at her and he was saying the same thing and telling her to go away and leave him alone. He'd called her a bloody nuisance and told her to go home, and he'd called her mam a floosie. She remembered running away, her eyes full of tears, then the screech of brakes and the sound of a frightened horse. She clapped her hands to her cheeks. There was no escaping the memories now. When she'd come to and found him beside her looking pale and concerned she'd believed his explanation, but he hadn't been worried about her at all. He'd only been worried for himself if she'd been killed or injured. And now . . . now he was out with *her* again. Holding her, kissing her, and . . . other things. And he'd taken the money to spend on Vera Morley. The money! Oh, God! She'd lied for him. Barefaced lies that blackened her soul. Just to keep him out of prison. She'd believed him then too. She'd believed he was innocent. That he'd been set up. Oh, they'd all known he was guilty – except her. How could she have been so stupid? She'd suffered hours of torment at the hands of the CID and for what? He'd stolen that money! He'd had no intention of sending for her once he reached America. He was running as far away from her and everyone else as he could get!

She heard the scullery door open and then she watched him come into the kitchen. The only light came from the fire and the flames made his shadow loom large on the wall. She couldn't see his face properly so she stood up.

'Ginny! What are you doing still up?'

'I . . . I saw you, with . . . her.'

'Jesus! You've been up to your old tricks, following me. I can't even have a bloody minute to myself without you being there, all the time.'

She gripped the edge of the table to steady herself. His words brought back the memories again and she felt faint. 'You lied to me. You've always lied to me. Lied about everything. The money, America, wanting money to go out tonight. I . . . I've been sitting here and I've finally remembered everything. The park where I found you with *her*. What she said to me. What you said to me. What you called my mam. The way I lied to keep you out of jail. I *believed* you!'

Colin panicked. 'Ginny! Ginny, you've got to listen to me.'

'No! I've listened to your lies for long enough.'

He caught her wrist. If she started to yell she'd have the whole house up and she'd tell everyone about everything. He would be arrested by the police – or would it be the Military Police? Either way, he couldn't let that happen. He had to talk her round. He'd done it before; he could do it again.

'Ginny, let me explain. I love you, you know that—'

Inside she was screaming: Lies! Lies! Lies! She hated him! She hated *herself*! She couldn't stand him touching her now and she tried to pull away from his grip.

'Stop struggling! Ginny, for God's sake, listen to me.'

She couldn't stand it any longer. Words and pictures flooded her head until she felt it would burst. Her fingers closed around the handle of the bread knife and she snatched it up and thrust it into him. She saw the horror and disbelief in his eyes, watched the colour drain from his face, and then he slid slowly to the floor, sprawling at her feet.

She was shaking all over. She couldn't think clearly. The pictures just wouldn't go away. Why was he lying there? She couldn't see his face. She looked at the bloody knife and the blood on her hands. Oh, God! What had she done! No! No!

She hadn't meant to hurt him. She hadn't meant to . . . kill him. He wasn't moving. She *had* killed him. She hadn't meant to, the pictures had driven her to strike out at him, to punish him for the hurt she was feeling. She bent down and shook him.

'Colin! Colin, wake up! I didn't mean it! Oh, God, I didn't mean it!'

He didn't move, not a single muscle.

She was frantic. He was dead. They'd come for her soon. They'd take her away and then . . . She began to fight for her breath, it was as if the noose was already around her neck. Oh, God, this is what it must feel like! she thought in panic. She couldn't let that happen. She couldn't fight and gasp out her life at the end of a rope. Without really knowing or understanding she turned the knife around, gazed at it blindly then plunged it into her chest.

★ ★ ★

It was Tessa who found them both. She'd been restless all night. Ginny had been in such a state that May had said she'd wait up for her. In the darkness she felt around the bed but Ginny wasn't there. She shook her head, trying to dispel the drowsiness. It must be the middle of the night, so where was Ginny?

She got up and wrapped the quilt around her. The bedroom was freezing. She made her way into the kitchen. The fire was almost out so she reached up and lit the gas jet, then she froze in horror before she began to scream hysterically.

May was the first to run into the kitchen and when she saw both Colin and Ginny on the floor, and that floor covered in blood, she clutched the back of the sofa as a wave of dizziness and nausea washed over her.

'Oh, Christ Almighty!' Richie cried, pulling Tessa towards him.

'Da! Da! Is she . . .?' Tessa sobbed.

'I don't know, luv. Here, May, luv, keep hold of her.'

Tessa and May clung to each other for support, both on the brink of hysteria.

Richie bent down and gently turned Ginny on her side but he could see that she was dead. He closed her wide-staring eyes and then turned to his son. Colin was dead too. Rigor mortis hadn't yet set in. Both Ginny and Colin's skins were still faintly warm to the touch. He got to his feet, very shaken.

'I'll have to go for the police.'

'Oh, Mary Mother of God!' May reached out for his arm. 'How . . .? Is she— Is he—?'

'They're both dead, luv. I think maybe she killed . . . him and then . . . herself. She's still got the knife . . .' He choked. He couldn't go on.

'Oh, it's my fault!' Tessa sobbed. 'If I hadn't gone on about him going out to meet someone, she wouldn't have—'

'Stop that, Tessa!' Richie said sharply.

'She . . . she'd seen him with someone, I'm . . . sure of it. She was frozen and dazed and she'd been crying. I should have stayed with her! If I'd stayed up or made sure she went to bed then this . . .' May's knees began to buckle.

'Da! Da! She's going to faint!' Tessa cried and Richie caught his wife before she fell.

'Go and make sure Jimmy isn't up or awake, Tessa, I'll see to May.'

Tessa fled from the room. It was a nightmare! A terrible nightmare and Johnny wasn't here to hold her and comfort her.

Her brother was still asleep and she came back downstairs and stood at the door of the kitchen, clinging to the doorframe.

'Da, can I go for Elizabeth?' she begged.

Richie was so shocked and confused that he nodded. 'Get . . . ask Jack if he'll come too? I don't know what to . . . do.'

Jack, Elizabeth and Delia came back with Tessa. They were all white-faced and shocked. Elizabeth was comforting her friend, unable to believe what had happened.

'What a bloody mess, Richie!' Jack said seriously. Delia had gone into the front room to look for something to cover Ginny and Colin.

'I just don't know what to do. I can't believe it!' Richie shook his head.

'Well, it's real enough, Richie.'

Delia came in with a blanket which she draped over the two prostrate forms. 'Elizabeth, luv, put the kettle on. Everyone's in shock. Oh, May, come here, my heart bleeds for you!' Delia took a sobbing May in her arms and held her close, wondering how she would feel if it were Elizabeth lying there instead of Ginny. Jack had made Richie sit down and now turned to his daughter.

'Elizabeth, do you think you could wake young Jimmy and take him next door? The police will be in and out all night.'

'Jack! Eileen will have the entire street up, you know what she's like!' Delia protested vehemently.

'It'll be up anyway. We can't keep something like . . . this . . . quiet and the lad shouldn't have to see . . . them.'

Delia nodded. 'You're right. Elizabeth, go and get him.'

Tessa got to her feet. 'No, I'll go. He'll be terrified.'

'Are you sure, Tessa?' Elizabeth asked with concern. Tessa looked terrible.

Tessa nodded.

'Take him out the front way,' Delia advised, filling the kettle to make a pot of very strong tea. It was going to be a long night and she suspected that the worst part of it lay ahead, if anything could be worse than the scene in this kitchen.

Delia need not have worried about Eileen. This was too serious a matter for just idle gossiping. Eileen had wept for May, thinking of her own two girls. Yet the news still swept through the whole street like wildfire as first the police and then a doctor came. Finally an ambulance arrived and both Colin and Ginny were placed on stretchers, their faces covered by blankets, and put inside to be taken to the City Mortuary. Statements had been taken from everyone and the CID inspector had informed Richie that as far as they could see it was a murder and a suicide. There would be an inquest but that would be much later. The man was as tactful as he could be, feeling sorry for the devastated family.

'Oh, dear Lord! Why? Why? Suicide! My poor Ginny won't even be buried in consecrated ground! You know as well as I do, Delia, suicide's a mortal sin!'

And a crime – as was murder, Delia thought silently. Her heart went out to May. For Ginny there would be no requiem mass, no church service of any kind. She would be buried heaven knows where, while Colin would have a mass, and a grave. It didn't seem fair.

Mick Collins had seen Vera Morley with Colin and when he'd heard about the tragedy at number twelve he'd gone straight round to the police station at Rose Hill. Vera had been questioned, and everyone reckoned that May was right, Ginny must have seen the two of them together.

Tessa was still in a terrible state but Elizabeth had persuaded her to return to work on Monday. 'It will take your mind off . . . things, I promise you.'

'I don't think *anything* can take my mind off it!' Tessa exclaimed. I should have kept quiet! If I hadn't said all those things she'd be alive now.'

'Stop it! *Stop* it! You can't blame yourself. How were you to know what would happen? You aren't a mindreader or some sort of clairvoyant. It's *not* your fault! The police, Dr Duncan and Father Walsh have all told you that and it's true!'

'Oh, Elizabeth, I wish Johnny were home!'

'So do I, but they've only just gone and neither Johnny or Mike is related so they can't get compassionate leave.' Elizabeth wished with all her heart that Mike could come home. She needed him so much, just as Tessa needed Johnny. 'Tessa, I know it's terrible, really terrible, but there's still a war on. Our lads need weapons and ammunition and it *will* distract you. I'll write to Mike if you don't feel you can write to Johnny. Mike will tell him.'

'I . . . I . . . couldn't write it all down, Elizabeth.'

'I know. Leave it to me.'

'How . . . how can I get married . . . now?'

'Stop that! Life has to go on. The best possible thing for everyone will be your wedding. Ginny would have hated it if you'd cancelled everything because of her. You know she would.'

'Yes. You know, it's a terrible, terrible thing to say, but I

267

don't really care much about . . . him.'

'It's not that terrible, Tessa. No one liked him at all and the way he treated poor Ginny, well, in my view he got what he deserved. Leading Ginny on, getting her to lie for him about that money – because no one will ever make me believe he didn't rob that bank. What are we going to do about the money?'

They'd found the wad of folded notes when they'd been going through Ginny's clothes.

'I don't know. We'll leave that for Da and May to sort out. I just don't want to hear anything more about it.'

Elizabeth nodded. She could understand.

Tessa suddenly looked stricken. 'What will I tell them at work?'

'The truth. Ginny was on the opposite shift to us until lately so they don't know her well and no one knew him at all.

Eventually Tessa had agreed and gone back to work.

A few of the neighbours turned up for Colin's requiem mass, mainly out of respect for Richie and Tessa and Jimmy, who had been told as little as possible and was utterly confused by all the conflicting stories. His mates' version of what had happened and his da and sister's were so completely different. Vincent Keegan had said that according to the *Echo* Ginny had murdered their Colin and had then killed herself. He didn't know what or who to believe.

However, they all turned out for Ginny's journey to her final resting place, a small plot of land on the opposite side of the wall that bounded Ford Cemetery. Even Father Walsh was perturbed by the situation. Ginny had committed two crimes, two heinous sins, but surely she'd been driven to them. They certainly weren't premeditated. He'd known her all her life. She'd always been quiet, dutiful, devout. The girl must have been completely out of her mind, for there wasn't ever the smallest bit of violence in her character. He'd heard all about Vera Morley too. But his hands were tied. He was the parish priest and the Church had decreed things like this were absolutely beyond the pale. His young curate had different ideas though, so he'd agreed to let Father Sharpe follow the procession but without his clerical garb. 'As a private mourner, Father, and as long as the Archbishop doesn't hear of it,' he had said.

May was inconsolable as she followed the coffin, supported by Richie, Tessa and Jimmy.

'Ah, God luv 'er. Me heart bleeds for her. It's bad enough 'er being dead at seventeen, but to 'ave no service, no . . . nothing,' Eileen sniffed to Maisie Keegan as they gathered at the graveside.

'She must have been, what's them words they say, Eileen? Official-soundin' like?'

' "While the balance of the mind was disturbed",' Delia answered.

'Aye, that's it. She must 'ave been demented and while it's wrong to speak ill of the dead, God forgive me,' Maisie crossed herself, ' 'e must have driven her to do it, the swine! Poor little Ginny Greely, all she ever did wrong was to love that flamin' no-mark who's no loss to anyone. Thank God Mary isn't here to see all this.'

'What do they do at things like . . . this?' Eileen asked.

'Jack's going to say a few words – Richie is so upset he can't do it. And our Elizabeth is going to read a bit out of the Missal and then we'll all say the Our Father, Hail Mary and Gloria. We . . . we thought that would be best. We don't know how . . . anything like this is done.'

'We never 'ad to know. But God will understand and he'll forgive, so Father Sharpe said. He's gorra lovely way with 'im for such a young priest,' Eileen finished, dabbing her eyes.

It was awful, Elizabeth thought as the ceremony commenced. Worse than anything she'd ever experienced. But she'd sworn she'd get Tessa through this poor little excuse of a funeral, and that's what she'd do.

When her father finished speaking she took a step forward, keeping her eyes fixed on her prayer book and not the yawning mouth of the freshly dug grave where Ginny's coffin, covered with flowers, had been lowered. She was determined to keep her composure.

She glanced quickly at her mother who nodded her encouragement and then, with slightly shaking fingers, turned to the page she'd marked, cleared her throat and began. 'Enter not into judgement with Thy Servant, O Lord, for in Thy sight no man may be justified, unless through Thee. Remission of all her sins be granted unto her. Let not, therefore, we beseech Thee, the sentence of Thy judgement weigh heavily upon her whom the true supplication of Christian Faith doth commend unto Thee: but, by the succour of Thy grace may she be found worthy to escape the judgement of vengeance who, while she lived, was sealed with the seal of the Holy Trinity. Who livest and reignest, world without end. Amen.'

'Amen,' the little group added as she stepped back and grasped Tessa's hand. 'It's all over now, Tessa,' she whispered, 'and I'm sure she's happy. I don't believe God is so awful as to abandon her.'

Tessa nodded her agreement, but was too choked to reply.

'It won't be long until May now, and Johnny'll be home,' Elizabeth consoled her.

'I . . . I . . . want him now.'

'I know you do, but he'll be home soon, they'll both be home. We'll never forget her, poor little Ginny. Come on, Tessa, let's go home.'

Chapter Twenty-Seven

The snow and ice gradually gave way to the cold blustery winds of March: the branches of the trees in the parks swayed and bent before them as daffodils began to push their way upwards in the ground beneath them. They were in full bloom in April when much warmer weather moved across the country.

None of them had really got over the shock of Ginny's death or the terrible circumstances in which she and Colin had died. The whole street was still stunned; there wasn't a single house where, when Ginny's name was mentioned, someone didn't break down and cry.

For weeks Tessa, May and Richie went through the everyday tasks as if they were in a half-trance. At work, at home, in the shop, it was as if Ginny were still there. They just couldn't fully accept it.

The inquest that had taken place in March had only dredged up memories and opened wounds that were just beginning to heal. As expected the verdict on Ginny was 'Suicide' and on Colin 'Murder'.

During those long and terrible months both Tessa and Elizabeth took comfort from the letters they received from Johnny and Mike, but Elizabeth did not have the joy of being able to read them over and over as Tessa did. Her letters remained with Tessa and she had to make special visits to be able to read them. But now on the very last day of the month the waiting was over. The boys were due back home and both Tessa and Elizabeth had begged time off work to go and meet them. Not at Lime Street Station, but down at the Pier Head where the frigate *Hercules* – Johnny's ship – would tie up and the cruiser *Juno* – Mike's ship – would come alongside too.

It was a glorious day, mild and sunny. The breeze coming from the river smelled of salt but it was also balmy. The buildings of the waterfront were bathed in bright light; even the river itself wasn't the usual turgid grey but reflected the blue of the sky, and sunlight turned the crests of the waves to gold.

'Oh, it's such a beautiful day – don't the ships look sort of out of place?' Tessa said as they walked down to the Landing Stage.

'Yes. Those dull and rusted grey hulls look morbid,' Elizabeth replied.

It seemed to take for ever to get the ropes ashore and secured to the bollards, then the gangways finally manoeuvred into place.

'Where will I meet you?' Tessa asked. They would have to separate.

'By the main door of the Liver Building,' Elizabeth called as she pushed her way towards where *Juno* was berthed.

She shielded her eyes with her hand to try to pick out Mike, and when she saw him she started to wave and shout. Her heart was beating so fast that she felt breathless.

Mike pushed his way through the crowd of relatives and friends waiting for their nearest and dearest. Elizabeth flung her arms around him. 'Oh, I've missed you! I've missed you so much!'

'I've missed you too, Elizabeth. It wasn't so bad in the day, they kept us busy, but it was the nights. I'd lie in my hammock and just think about you and what you had gone through . . . I just couldn't believe it when your letter arrived. Johnny wanted to come home – we both did, but we couldn't get leave on compassionate grounds.'

'It was terrible. It still is. No one can help remembering . . . her . . . and Tessa's blaming herself still.'

'Well, let's try and put all that behind us now,' he urged. She'd had a bad time of it, but Tessa had had the worst time of them all.

'How long are you home for?'

'Until May the eighth, only we're not supposed to tell anyone.'

She smiled up at him. 'Don't you know, "Careless Talk Costs Lives",' she quoted.

She held his hand tightly as they walked towards the Liver Building.

Suddenly he stopped.

'What's the matter?'

'Nothing. I got you your brooch.' He delved into his pocket and brought out a small box, which he handed to her.

She opened it. 'Oh, it's beautiful! It *is* a badge but it's so pretty it looks like a brooch.'

'And now do we consider ourselves to be engaged?'

'Oh, yes! You're mine now – for always.'

He bent down and kissed her, ignoring the amused and wistful looks cast at them. These days it wasn't such an unusual sight.

Tessa and Johnny had got there before them.

Elizabeth hugged Johnny and Mike hugged Tessa.

'You don't know how happy we are now.' Tessa's eyes were

shining and Elizabeth looked at her friend with relief.

'We do. It's good to be home. It's dirty, scruffy and a bit battered but it's home and it always will be,' Mike said.

'Coming up river and seeing the buildings at the Pier Head gave me a lump in my throat. I can understand now why so many sailors say it's the most wonderful sight in the world. A couple of the lads had tears in their eyes but wouldn't admit it.'

'Will we go and have something to eat?' Elizabeth suggested.

'Why not? Let's celebrate. I think we all need a bit of cheering up,' Johnny agreed.

They walked to Castle Street where there was a small Lyons Teashop on the corner of Castle Street and Cook Street.

Mike ordered tea and homemade teacakes, limited to one per person.

Elizabeth took the brooch out of the box. 'Look. It's not just a brooch, it's a bit like your cross and chain.'

Tessa reached across the table and took her hand. 'So you've made it "official", ' she smiled.

'But only between us. I . . . I can't tell Mam or anyone else. Oh, I hate it, not being able to tell people. She doesn't know I'm here and not at work. I couldn't even wear my best things and I really wanted to. I look a mess.'

'You never look a mess,' Mike told her.

'I know you can't bear to start another argument with your mam, but the right moment will come. I know it will,' Tessa tried to cheer her up.

Elizabeth pinned the badge to the lapel of her coat and smiled at Mike.

'So, what's it like being in the Navy?' Tessa asked. She didn't want to talk about Ginny. That would come later when she and Johnny were alone.

'It's not bad. The food's nothing to write home about but then Mam's cooking was always a bit hit and miss too,' Mike answered.

'It takes a bit of time to get used to sleeping in a hammock, but they're comfortable and they're necessary. You wouldn't believe just how cramped everything is. There's pipes and cables all over the place and you keep banging your head on the bulkheads if you forget to duck climbing from section to section. And the ladders are vertical, you slide down just using your hands.'

'Aye, I've nearly knocked myself unconscious many a time,' Mike laughed. He was over six foot and had had great difficulty in remembering.

Both the girls were staying on in town. Elizabeth couldn't go home until much much later as her parents thought she was at work, and even then she'd have to say she'd been feeling ill. She'd blame it on the smell from the TNT. Tessa was going to make the most of her time off to look for something for her wedding.

'You'll have to remember to take that brooch off before you get in,' she said as they walked towards Lord Street and the boys had both boarded a tram at the bottom of Castle Street. Elizabeth had been loath to let Mike out of her sight. She wasn't as lucky as Tessa. She couldn't take Mike into the shop and say, 'We're engaged.' She couldn't even steal a kiss or hold his hand or look up at him and believe he was *really* home. At least now that he was away, she didn't need to tell so many lies as to where she was going and with whom. She did however keep thinking of what she'd said. 'Now we belong to each other.' She knew that was true and the thought cheered her up.

They stopped and looked in the window of Frisby Dyke's.

'That's quite nice.' Elizabeth pointed to a pale blue linen costume, the jacket of which was fastened with very pretty blue and gold buttons.

'I'd get a lot of wear out of it too. More than I would a proper wedding dress.' Tessa had decided that it wouldn't be very fitting to have the dress, veil and all the trimmings because it was so soon after Ginny's death.

'What colour would you wear with it?'

'White or cream. I think I'd settle for cream myself. Or perhaps navy blue.'

'I think I'd prefer navy. It's more serviceable and things are getting harder to buy now. I wonder how many coupons I'll need. I mean, I'll have to buy a blouse and a hat and shoes and bag.'

'You can have mine. I told you that ages ago.'

The suit looked very smart, especially with the navy rayon blouse the assistant had brought.

'Now doesn't that just finish it off,' the woman said, tying the folds of material at the neck into a loose bow.

'It's not going to look fussy? I mean, with the hat and all.'

'Oh, no, madam,' the woman protested then disappeared to find a hat.

'What do you think, really? They'd tell you anything just to get a sale.'

'No, she's right. It's great and for once in your life you *should* dress up, it's a really special day,' Elizabeth said wistfully.

The hat, shoes and bag completed the ensemble and Elizabeth clapped her hands with pleasure. 'Oh, Tessa, you look . . . wonderful. Elegant but not too overdressed.'

'Are you sure?'

'Of course I'm sure,' both Elizabeth and the sales assistant said together and they all started to laugh.

She'd gone down to Eileen's later that night to welcome Mike home 'officially'. 'They'll both be going away again soon,' she'd replied to her mother's question as to where she was going at this time of night.

'Aye, and God knows when they'll be back,' Jack added, much to Elizabeth's relief.

She returned with the news that Johnny was in fine form and that Mike was also happy to be home and had brought her a little 'keepsake' – the brooch.

'See what he got for me. Isn't it pretty?' She opened the box and held it out for her mother to see.

Delia looked at it closely. 'Well, it's unusual. 'I've never seen fish like that before—'

'It *is* unusual and they're called dolphins. I've seen one before,' Jack interrupted, examining it.

'Where?' Elizabeth asked, as her father pinned it once more to her lapel.

'Old Len Williams, you know, from the market, his son's been in the Navy for years. He had one. It's a naval badge.'

'What kind of naval badge?' Elizabeth asked, genuinely interested and thankful her mother hadn't asked just why Mike Flynn had bought her anything at all.

'Submarines. It's the official badge of all submariners.'

Elizabeth's heart sank. Her da's words were ominous. Mike had bought her the badge of a branch of the Navy whose job it was to lurk beneath the sea and sink surface vessels, just as the U-boats were doing so successfully now. She hoped it *wasn't* an omen.

She hadn't arranged to see Mike that night. It wasn't fair, she'd told him. His mam was always worrying about him and, besides, her mam would get suspicious. They'd go out tomorrow. Tessa was seeing Johnny of course. She was cooking him a meal.

Everyone had welcomed Johnny home with hugs and smiles and words of welcome although Johnny sensed the sorrow in the air. Tessa had told him that if housing hadn't been so scarce they'd have moved. Every time she went into the kitchen she said she could see them both lying on the floor. She'd only just stopped having nightmares about it.

'You've got a fair bit of leave,' Richie said while Tessa and May were setting the table and cooking the bit of liver May had managed to get.

'Well, I won't be getting much from now on, I suppose.'

'Oh, hell and damnation!' May cried as the now familiar sound of the siren started.

'Leave it, luv, we'll have it later,' Richie said, pulling on his coat and taking his tin helmet from the hook where it was always kept.

'I'll come with you,' Johnny offered as May covered the frying pan with a lid and took it off the fire in the range, then shoved Jimmy and Tessa towards the lobby and the stairs.

'No, you stay here, lad. It's your first night at home, don't let the buggers ruin it. If I need help I'll come for you.'

'How often does it happen now? I know London's been hit pretty badly,' Johnny asked Tessa as they all sat squashed in the space beneath the stairs.

'We've had a couple of raids, but nothing as bad as before Christmas,' she replied.

He put his arm around her and felt her trembling. 'Don't get upset, Tessa.'

'I'm trying not to,' she answered. 'At least you're here with me.'

The raid was a light one and as they crawled out then went back into the kitchen May put the half-cooked meat back on the range. 'Well, it's not totally ruined,' she remarked with grim satisfaction.

The following evening Elizabeth had to cancel her date with Mike for as soon as she and Tessa got off the tram, just after seven o'clock, the siren sounded and they'd both run as fast as they could along Scotland Road and down Naylor Street.

'I'll have to go home!' Elizabeth cried as Tessa reached number twelve and Johnny opened the door to her.

'Go on, Mike won't mind,' Johnny yelled at her. Already they could hear the droning in the sky getting closer and louder.

Elizabeth ran through the shop and into the kitchen. There was no panic now. Delia was organised. She'd managed to get an Anderson shelter put up in the back yard because theirs was much bigger than those of the neighbouring houses. And she'd sworn never to go to a public shelter ever again. She picked up the items that were always to hand in the scullery: blankets, matches, candles, a biscuit tin with whatever was available, usually only plain Marie biscuits, and a Thermos flask.

In the shelter there were two bunk-type beds which they sat or lay on. She'd covered the floor with rush matting and had a small paraffin stove that was used to boil water and give some warmth.

'I hope everyone else will be all right,' Elizabeth said worriedly, thinking of Mike. He was so near and yet so far; she'd feel far better, far safer, if she were with him.

'Don't go saying things like that. It's not good for anyone's morale,' Delia chided.

They played 'I Spy', Ludo and tiddlywinks, and Delia had her knitting. Elizabeth was supposed to be learning how to knit too, as was Nessie, but as the hours dragged on nerves were beginning to get frayed. Elizabeth threw down the needles and the ball of wool. 'Oh, how much longer? How much longer, Mam? Why don't they just go back and leave us alone?'

'Elizabeth, stop that this very minute! Pull yourself together.' Delia herself was worried sick about Jack for all around them they could hear the whistling and then the explosions. The area was taking a heavy battering tonight and he was out there. But she had to appear in control of herself for the sake of her daughters.

'Pass me that Thermos, we'll have a cup of tea.'

Elizabeth reached over for the flask and it began to shake in her hand although she knew her hands were steady. The shrill whistling increased until its piercing stridency forced them to press their hands over their ears. Naked terror was in all their eyes.

The whole shelter vibrated. The ground under their feet moved and cracks appeared in the concrete base. The blast threw Elizabeth to the floor and sent Nessie sprawling across the bunk, the candle falling on her arm. She screamed in pain and terror.

Delia was the first to recover, scrabbling on the floor for the matches, it was so much worse being in the dark. She relit the candle.

'Oh my God, that was close!'

Elizabeth pulled at her arm. 'Mam! Da's out there and it sounds like *everywhere* is being hit!'

'Well, you're not going looking for him and neither am I. He'd have ten fits if he thought we were out there too. All we can do is wait and pray.'

'What time is it, Mam?' Nessie whispered, terrified. Would this moment be her last?

Delia looked at the wristwatch Jack had bought her for their twentieth wedding anniversary. 'It's just after nine o'clock. Calm down, Nessie, luv, it'll be over soon.'

But it wasn't. At midnight, with no sign of an end to the bombs, Jack appeared like an apparition in the doorway. He was covered from head to foot in dust.

'I can't stop! I just came to see that you're all right.'

'Jack, stay and have a cup of tea, please?' Delia begged him, filled with relief and reaching for the flask.

'Just a few seconds then, luv. It's bad out there.'

'How bad?' Elizabeth asked, praying that Mike and Tessa and Johnny were safe.

'There're fires everywhere. They've hit the docks heavily again. Maisie's house is just rubble and so is Katie's. They've gone to the public shelter but I don't envy them when they come out!'

'Oh, Holy Mother of God! What will poor Maisie do now? She already had their Rita and her kids staying with them.'

'Da, what about next door – Mrs Flynn?'

'Thank God her house is still standing, so far, but all the windows are in again and I think the front door has been blown into the street with the force of the blast of the one that hit the Keegans'.' Jack gulped back the tea. 'They'll all have to find somewhere else, God help them,' he added grimly before kissing his wife and daughters and going out once more into the night.

An hour later when they too emerged from the shelter they were shocked into silence at the sight that greeted them. Fires raged everywhere, silhouetting half-demolished buildings. Debris was strewn across the road and further down four houses were now just piles of rubble.

People were beginning to return to their homes, picking their way through the bricks, broken glass and ruptured pipes. When Delia caught sight of Maisie she quickly went across to her while Elizabeth hammered on the Flynns' door.

'It's me, Mrs Flynn! It's Elizabeth!'

Eileen emerged from the lobby with Mike behind her and Elizabeth flung herself at him, laughing and crying.

'Oh, Elizabeth, 'e's 'ad me demented over yer!' Eileen sniffed, wiping the dust from her face with her apron.

'Thank God you're safe!' he exclaimed. 'It was only because Mam was screaming at me that I didn't come and see you.'

'Oh, Mike, it's terrible out there. Far worse than anything we've had before and it went on for so long.'

278

'I know. Look, I'm going to find my da, they'll need all the help they can get.'

'If you see Da tell him we're all safe.'

Delia had her arm around a weeping Maisie. The devastation was terrible.

'Oh, God, me 'ouse! Me lovely little 'ouse!' Maisie sobbed.

Delia thought about the 'lovely little house'. It should have been pulled down years ago, but she could understand Maisie's feelings at the loss of every stick of furniture she'd struggled to accumulate over the years.

'Come on into the shop, all of you. We'll have a cup of tea to calm our nerves and then see what we can do to help. Come on, Katie. Eileen, that means you too.'

They followed her through the shop and crammed into her kitchen. There was broken glass everywhere and the furniture had been blown across the room and was piled in a heap against the far wall. Elizabeth helped Nessie to tidy up a bit so everyone could sit down.

Katie Collins turned on her daughter Alice who was loudly bemoaning the loss of her jewellery.

'Oh, shurrup, Alice, fer God's sake! We 'aven't even gorra clean pair of drawers an' all yer can think about is that tatty stuff yer used ter drape yerself in. Yer'd think they was the Crown Jewels! Gorrup like a flamin' Christmas tree sometimes, she was. I told 'er it was dead common ter wear all that stuff at once.'

'Eh, Mam, that cost thousands!' Alice retorted, exaggerating as usual.

'Cost thousands! Yer gorrit all from Woolies an' yer looked like a tart sometimes! I'm glad it's all flaming well gone! Maybe I'll gerra bit o' peace from yer now.'

'Here, Katie, have this tea,' Delia intervened. 'I think I can make the Marie biscuits stretch out. We'll just have to wait for the men to come in and tell us how bad things are, then we can get going and see what we can rescue from this terrible mess.'

Chapter Twenty-Eight

Johnny and Mike made their way down to the docks early next day to see if their ships had been damaged. The sights that met their eyes were appalling and stunned them both into silence.

As they walked – half of the tram lines in the area being broken and twisted – they often stopped to help people salvage their belongings or tear with their bare hands at rubble underneath which people were trapped. Relatives were standing in groups or sitting on the kerbside with whatever they'd managed to collect, numb with shock or weeping. Men too were unashamedly in tears as they searched for their wives, children or parents.

'God Almighty! I hope the bastards that did this will be in the same state themselves one day!' Johnny cursed as the broken little body of a child, still clutching a rag doll, was lifted gently by a fireman and passed to her distraught father.

'What goes around comes around. They'll pay – in the end,' Mike answered grimly.

It took them all morning and part of the afternoon to reach the docks where firemen and dockers and stevedores were still working to keep the fires under control and pull out what cargoes could be salvaged. Their ships, thankfully, were miraculously untouched, but a corvette and another cruiser had been badly damaged; the corvette was lying on her side. Obviously the amount of water that had been pumped into her to extinguish the fires had made her list and then roll over.

'Sometimes the water does more harm than the bloody fire.'

'I know, but they had to douse the fires: she was still carrying depth charges and ammunition for her guns which could have gone off. Anyway, those things are like toy boats, they're so flimsy,' Mike answered.

They split up to report to their Commanding Officers. Because the loss of men and ships had been so heavy, when he'd completed his training, Mike had been promoted to an Engine Room Artificer and Johnny to Petty Officer. These days it didn't take very long to rise through the ranks. It was only because he wasn't twenty-one that he'd not been made a C.P.O.

There was plenty of work for them to do. All the debris that had been hurled across the dock from the other stricken ships and the dock sheds had to be cleared and the dockside itself brushed. Cargo had to be restacked and sorted through. Decks had to be scrubbed – just because there'd been an air-raid it didn't mean sloppiness was the order of the day. Soot and dust had to be wiped off superstructures, gun emplacements, ventilators and funnels – in fact everywhere it had settled.

When the May sunlight began to fade and the evening sky turned to duck-egg blue shot through with bursts of rosy light, Mike suddenly realised he'd had nothing to eat since his breakfast.

'Any chance of a spello, sir?' he asked his superior, a dour Scotsman named Macintosh.

'The cook's no here. What do ye think this is, laddie, a bloody restaurant?'

'No, sir. It's just that I haven't had even a cup of tea since this morning. You remember me telling you how come we were so late getting down here.'

'Aye, I do. Go over to yon woman an' see if she's anything t'gie ye.'

Mike proffered his thanks and went ashore, over to the mobile canteen manned by ladies of the WVS. He was exhausted, they'd had hardly any sleep last night. Even it they'd been able to sleep through the noise of the bombing, their terror and his mam's screaming every time there was an explosion ensured no one got a wink. While he could understand her reaction, it had still grated on his nerves.

'You look done in,' Johnny greeted him cheerfully.

'So they let you off too.'

'Aye. The Chief said seeing as I was officially on leave I could come over here then go home for a bit. I've worked my fingers to the bloody bone.'

'Home! You lucky bugger. I'll be here until after I drop or Mac drops or we both do. Will you get Tessa to tell Elizabeth where I am? We were supposed to be going out tonight. Fat chance of that now.'

'She'll still be at work. They both will.'

'Well, when she gets home.'

'She'll probably be home by the time I get back, if it takes me as long to get back as it did to get here,' Johnny said morosely.

'God, but where do you start out there? There's buildings still smouldering.'

'I know. I'd best get going. See you later.'

'Just how much later I don't bloody know!'

'Why did he have to stay?' Elizabeth demanded of Johnny when she went up to Tessa's after her tea.

'I don't know. His Chief's a bit of a stickler. Been a Navy man all his life and doesn't think any of us lot are up to the mark. He'll have that ship looking brand new before he's satisfied.'

'But Mike's on leave. We were going out.' She was very disappointed. It would have been the first few hours they'd spent alone together.

'All I know is that he'll get home as soon as he can. It's a mess out there. It'll take a week to clear the worst of it and get services running again.'

'Do you think they'll come back?' Tessa asked fearfully.

'No. They'll have got fed up by now. We've never had raids for longer than two nights in succession, but if Mike's not back by ten I'll go and see why. I promise.'

Elizabeth managed a smile. They'd had a terrible day themselves. Of course the further into the suburbs you got the less damage there was, but there had been enough around Kirkdale and Everton for her to think herself lucky she still had a home to come back to.

By ten there was still no sign of Mike and so Johnny set out again for the docks. He thought Mike's Chief was taking things too far. After all, they *were* on leave and they had worked damned hard! It didn't take him quite as long this time as some of the tram lines had been cleared and buses were running, skirting craters in the road and being directed away from buildings that were unsafe. He was amazed at just how quickly demolition was being carried out and telephone engineers, gas and electricity workers had been able to restore some of the most necessary services.

It was turned eleven though, he thought, glancing up at the clock tower of the Liver Building. You could just see the fingers of the clock by the light of the moon. He cursed the moonlight. It was perfect flying weather.

Two minutes later the siren sounded and, cursing, he began to run. The bloody thing hadn't given them much warning, he thought, you could already hear and see the planes and then the first incendiaries found their target, sending a shower of sparks into the air. He increased his pace, oblivious to the explosions around him. He had to get to the precious cargoes on the dockside.

It had cost hundreds of men their lives and God knows how many ships had been lost to bring them in and now they were in danger of being destroyed.

He reached number two, Husskisson Dock barely able to speak. He stopped and leaned against the wall of a shed to catch his breath. Already fires were raging and fire engines were hurtling in from all directions.

The bastards! The bastards! he cursed to himself. Women, children and old people were back there, totally defenceless except for the anti-aircraft batteries. Ahead of him, outlined by the glare, was the S.S. *Malakand*. Men working frantically at the pumps were successfully dousing the flames over her No. 1 hatch. He jerked into action. 'Jesus Christ!' he cried aloud. The *Malakand* was loaded with one thousand tons of high-explosive bombs!

He ran the remaining distance and up the gangway as a shower of incendiaries burst around them. Explosions rocked the entire dock and soon the cargo sheds were alight as well as the ship. The fire engines continued to arrive, disgorging firemen to ply their hoses on the sheds on the east and south sides, dim shapes that became lost in the dense smoke. As he raced along the deck he could feel the heat through the soles of his boots. Sweat poured down his face from the searing heat, but he set to work with the crew.

The blaze had reached the contents of the cargo shed on the south side and the building erupted into a solid wall of flames.

'It's no use! It's spreading!' someone yelled.

He turned. The flames from the dock had reached the *Malakand*.

'She'll go up! Get the hell out of it,' the officer in charge yelled.

The fire was a blazing beacon and the raiders homed in on it. The heat and smoke were suffocating as more incendiaries fell and the bombers flew lower, so low at times that their black shapes seemed only a few feet above them.

Johnny began to cough and his eyes were smarting and streaming. The deck was red-hot. Above the cacophony he heard Captain Kinley give the order to 'Abandon ship' and he followed the others down the gangway and to a point where the shed was least affected by the fire. The *Malakand* was ablaze from bow to stern.

The Fire Officer in charge, Mr Lapin, shouted for them to help his men and Johnny grappled with a hose alongside two firemen, his arms and shoulders aching with the renewed effort. The enemy aircraft droned overhead, unheeded. It was useless, the blazing wall of cargo sheds made it impossible to get near enough to try to train the hoses on the ship. Even worse, he could see the roof of the nearest shed was about to collapse.

Across his line of vision he saw a blurred figure running alongside the shed, trying to reach the line of firefighters. Whoever it was was taking a terrible risk, he was too close to the shed and the blazing ship. He rubbed his eyes with the back of his hand. In this hell of heat, smoke and flames it was impossible to recognise any individual, but as the figure ran towards them there was something about it that was familiar. A face flashed into his mind. Mike! He heard the others curse him as he began to run. The roaring and rushing of the flames drowned out his warning cries. He looked up and then launched himself bodily across the few feet that separated them. They collided, falling on the wet cobbles, rolling over and over with the momentum of the impact. There was a groaning, splintering sound as the roof of the shed collapsed just feet behind them.

They were both soaking wet, the cold water drenching them as a fire hose was played on them, extinguishing their burning uniforms.

Johnny dragged himself to his knees. Mike was lying sprawled on the floor.

'Get up! For God's sake, Mike, get up!' he yelled, dragging Mike to his feet.

Mike shook the water from his eyes. 'Johnny!'

'For Christ's sake, run! Come on, run! Run for your bloody life!'

Mike raced along beside him, his breath laboured, his legs moving like pistons until a blinding flash of white light and a roaring in his ears, so loud that he thought his brain would burst, sent him sprawling again. The *Malakand* had exploded.

The raid went on but Mike was so frantic that he refused to go to the nearest shelter, so they both half ran, diving for any sort of cover when the bombs exploded near them, and half walked until an hour later they reached Naylor Street.

'Oh, God Almighty, would you look at it! Would you just look at the state of it!' Johnny cried in impotent fury as Mike dragged him towards number ten. There was no need for lamplight, it was as bright as day. The whole city was on fire. 'At this rate there won't be a bloody building left standing!'

'Get in to Mam, they'll be under the stairs!' Mike urged his friend but Johnny refused.

'No, I'll go and see if Tessa's all right, then go down to see Da.'

Tessa, May and Jimmy had been huddled together for hours under the stairs and they were all sobbing. It seemed as though the end of the world had come. Many explosions had come close enough to rock the house; plaster had flaked all over them, and the dust filled their lungs. May had managed to tack up a blanket as some protection from flying splinters of glass.

'Oh, sweet Jesus! We'll never come through this, Tessa!' May had screamed once. Tessa had bitten her lip hard and held Jimmy even tighter. He'd wanted to go out on his bike, they'd need messengers, he'd pleaded in vain.

When they heard Johnny's voice, Tessa burst into tears, she'd been terrified that he'd been killed.

'Oh, thank God! Thank God! I . . . I . . .'

'Are you all all right?' he rasped, his throat dry from the smoke and the dust.

'Yes. Oh, how much longer will it go on?' May sobbed.

'I don't know and that's the truth. Is your da out there?'

Tessa nodded, tears streaming down her cheeks. 'And Jimmy wanted to go too. On his bike.'

Johnny looked at the lad. He was scared stiff but he was trying not to show it. 'Do you think you can do it, Jimmy? I won't tell you any lies, it's like . . . like hell out there but they will need messenger boys.'

'No! No!' Tessa cried, clutching the boy to her.

'Tessa, luv, you don't understand. I can't stay here with you. I've got to go and see if Da and the boys are unhurt, then I'll have to go out and help – they need every pair of hands. Go on, Jimmy, get your coat, your tin hat and your bike and call for Harold Flynn too.'

'Is Mike—?' Tessa queried, half afraid of the answer.

'Mike's fine. I'll call and see Elizabeth. They've got their own shelter, haven't they?'

Tessa nodded.

Johnny bent and kissed her and then he was gone, gently pushing young Jimmy before him.

'Oh, God help us! God help us all!' May sobbed in fervent prayer.

As Johnny went into the shop that had neither door nor window he saw Jimmy and young Harold start to cycle along the pavement. Their faces were white with fear but they pedalled furiously. They knew where to go for their instructions.

Above him the raiders still droned like a swarm of angry bees, there must be at least three hundred of them, he thought with fury. He found Delia with her arms around her daughters. Nessie was crying hysterically.

'Johnny! What . . . what are you doing here?' Delia cried. She'd been praying hard for hours now and there was still no end in sight.

'I've just come to tell you that Tessa and May are fine.'

'Thank God!' Delia said with genuine relief. These days there was more to worry about than silly snobbery.

'Young Jimmy and Harold Flynn have gone up to the air-raid post and I'm on my way to see if everything is all right at the pub.'

'Mike? What about Mike?' Elizabeth cried.

'Don't worry. He's OK too. He's with his mam now but he'll be back out with me for the rest of the night.'

'How much longer? Oh, Blessed Virgin, why don't they leave us alone! Haven't we suffered enough for one night!' Delia was just holding on to her sanity.

'It can't be for much longer, they must have run out of bombs by now!'

'Did you see Jack or Richie or Frank?'

'No, but I'm sure I will before the night's over. I'll tell them everyone's OK and that we've still got roofs over our heads – for now,' he muttered.

A terrific explosion shook the whole shelter and both Elizabeth and Nessie screamed, Nessie holding her hands over her ears.

'Hush! Hush! It's all right. It's the *Malakand*. She's full of bombs and she's on fire. There'll be more explosions until she's blown sky high, then she'll probably take the whole dock with her. Hang on for just a while longer!'

When he got to the pub, to his horror he found it was on fire. Catching the arm of the nearest fireman he yelled at him, 'Was there anyone inside? My da runs it. Are my two brothers inside?'

'Not as far as we know. A woman further up said Eddie Doyle was out with the ARP and the two lads were with her. Is that your family?'

Johnny nodded thankfully. The kids were safe and so, as far as he knew, was his da, but everything he had owned, even down to a change of clothes, had gone up in the inferno that had been his home. For once he was glad his mam wasn't alive. He satisfied himself that his brothers were indeed with a kindly neighbour, then he turned and began to run back towards Scotland Road. Nearly every house and business had been hit. There'd be plenty to do before the night was over.

The bravery of the men and boys that night became legendary. As Liverpool burned they fought back with everything they had. The young messenger lads, trembling with horror at the sights they saw, kept going; communication was imperative between the police, the fire service, ambulances and the ARP volunteers. Firemen battled for hours with bombs and land mines exploding all around them. Volunteers helped lead people to safety, ambulance crews drove at top speed trying to save time lost by having to skirt fires and falling buildings. And still there was no let-up.

Johnny finally caught up with Mike in Banastre Street where, until earlier that night, an ARP post had stood. Now it was nothing more than rubble. He was clambering over a pile of bricks and dodging half a dozen stampeding terrified horses, some with their manes and tails on fire.

'Get something, Johnny! Anything that we can use as a lever!' Mike yelled. Sweat was pouring down his blackened face. His scorched uniform was covered in soot and dust and his hands were cut and bleeding.

'Will this do?' Johnny yanked at a long spar that had once been part of a doorframe.

'That warden over there said a wall collapsed and he's sure there are people underneath it. Did you find your da?'

'No, he's out, but the lads are with Mrs Weston. The pub's gone – well, it was burning like hell when I left. Tessa's OK and so is Elizabeth. They're all bloody terrified but who can blame them?'

'Push down on that end, I think I can prise one of these blocks up. Jesus! They made these buildings to last. These blocks weigh a ton!'

Johnny pushed down with his entire weight as Mike, the veins in his temples standing out with the effort, prised the corner of a square slab up. Johnny hung on to the lever and two other men scrambled across to give him a hand.

With a crack and a shower of dust the slab moved upwards sufficiently for Mike to see two bodies.

'Can you shine a torch down here?' he yelled up as he eased himself down into the space.

Johnny clambered down to give him a hand.

'Is that bloody slab safely out of the way?' Mike asked.

'Yes. Those two have moved it aside. Come on with the bloody light!' he called.

Bright torchlight swept the darkness, falling first on a split and jagged roof beam which had to a small degree protected the blackened, bloody faces of two men, and Mike felt himself sway. One was his father, the other Jack Harrison.

Chapter Twenty-Nine

He couldn't speak. He just stared in disbelief at the two half-buried bodies, arms flung above their heads as if they'd known and had tried to protect themselves. But there had been no protection, not even their tin hats, that could withstand the weight of the slabs of stone and the tons of bricks that had come crashing down. Johnny had to help Mike out of the crevice and he sat on the concrete slab, put his head in his hands and cried.

Johnny sat down beside him. He couldn't believe the ill luck that had led Mike to the very spot where his father had died. Suddenly he remembered how he'd felt the night his mam had been killed. It all came flooding back. The shock, the disbelief, the sorrow. He looked around him. How many more? he thought. How many more would die tonight? There was nothing anyone could do. He felt so helpless. He was surrounded by fiercely blazing buildings and still the planes droned overhead, clearly visible in the light from the buildings that incendiaries had set on fire. They couldn't take much more of this. The city and its people couldn't stand much more of this continuous bombardment.

He helped Mike gently to his feet. Together they would lift Frank and Jack over to a place of level ground, close their eyes, fold their hands across their chests and wait for an ambulance to take them to a church or church hall until they could be buried.

They did everything together, careless of their own safety, ignoring the inferno that surrounded them. Like a pair of mechanical figures they went through the motions, Mike barely aware of what he was doing. They sat on the kerb, bone-weary, eyes smarting, the slight burns on their hands beginning to sting.

'What . . . what am I going to tell Mam?' Mike asked brokenly of the lad who only hours earlier had saved his life.

'The truth. I . . . I only hope it was quick, and even if it wasn't, tell . . . tell her it was.'

Mike felt as though he himself had been crushed. 'And Elizabeth? Elizabeth . . .?'

'Oh, God!' Johnny realised the burden was doubly heavy for Mike. His father and Elizabeth's father too.

'I'll go to Elizabeth first. She'll have her mam and Nessie, and

Delia's always been . . . stronger than my mam. Oh, God Almighty! Mam was in a terrible state when I left, how she's going to take . . . this, I don't know.'

'She'll cope, Mike, they all will. We're not beaten! We'll never be beaten!'

Mike looked at him. 'What about your da?'

Johnny shook his head. 'I can only hope and pray. Come on, get up, there's an ambulance coming now.

'Where will you take them to?' Johnny asked the driver, who looked as if he'd had no sleep for a week.

'The Royal. Mill Road's taken a direct hit, Walton's had a near miss, the Nurses' Home took the brunt of it, so has Broadgreen. They can't take any more casualties at Stanley Hospital and neither can the Northern. I wish to Christ I could get my hands on just one of those bastards! Pregnant women and babies! Bloody babies at Mill Road!'

Mike just nodded as he lifted the limp form of his father inside. A proper funeral would come later, if anyone survived to bury the dead.

It was with leaden feet and heavy hearts that both lads walked down Naylor Street, still ignoring every danger that surrounded them. They'd seen the worst.

'Do you want me to come too?'

Mike shook his head. He felt a bit more in control of himself now.

'You go and see Tessa. Tell her—'

'I will,' Johnny cut in firmly. Nevertheless he escorted Mike past his own house, still standing but soon to be wreathed in sorrow, up to the Harrisons' shop, through the kitchen, the floor of which was covered with broken glass and wrecked furniture and crockery, and to the door of the shelter in the yard. Then he just gripped Mike's shoulder in a gesture of support and turned away.

Mike stood there for a few seconds. There was no easy way to put this when he was feeling so broken himself.

As soon as she saw him Elizabeth tore herself from her mother's arms. 'Mike! Mike! Oh, thank God you're safe.'

For a second he held her close and then shook his head.

Delia gazed at him in bewilderment, and her heart began to beat faster. There was something wrong. She knew it.

Slowly Mike disentangled Elizabeth's arms and held her away from him.

'Elizabeth . . . Mrs Harrison . . . I've just come from Banastre Street.'

Delia was on her feet, pushing young Nessie aside. 'No! Oh, please God, no!'

Elizabeth's eyes were wide and full of fear.

'It's . . . it's Mr Harrison and . . . and my da. They're dead,' he choked.

'Da! My da . . . and . . . and yours . . . dead?' Elizabeth couldn't take it in.

'Yes. A building fell. It would have been . . . quick!' He couldn't hold back the tears. Reaching out for Elizabeth, he drew her to him and broke down.

Delia sat as though carved from stone, holding a sobbing Nessie. Mike felt similar racking sobs tear through Elizabeth as he clung to her. Well, their love was in the open now but he didn't care. Death was a great leveller.

Gradually Elizabeth's sobs diminished and he released her, gently propelling her to her mother who reached out and took her hand.

'I'll have to go now, Mrs Harrison. Mam doesn't know . . . yet.'

'Oh, Lord have pity on us tonight, we . . . we've all lost so . . . so much.' Delia managed to keep her voice steady. Inside she was screaming for Jack but she had to try and stay calm for the sake of her children.

Mike stumbled back out into the street, knowing that the hardest part was yet to come.

When dawn came the raiders finally turned for home, the anti-aircraft batteries fell silent and the first rays of the sun pierced the cloud of smoke that hung over a city in ruins. In the middle of what was left of Derby Square the solitary statue of Queen Victoria stood untouched surveying the destruction.

For a radius of three-quarters of a mile surrounding her there was hardly a building left standing. Along the waterfront and in the docks ships had been damaged and sunk; sheds, warehouses and their contents destroyed; dock communications interrupted; gates, basins and quaysides struck; cranes left as mangled twisted lumps of metal – and still the *Malakand* burned.

The Head Post Office, the Central and Bank Exchange, the Mersey Dock buildings, Oceanic Buildings, India Buildings, George's Dock buildings and the Central Library had been badly hit. St Luke's Church at the top of a devastated Bold Street and the parish church of St Nicholas at the Pier Head were only two of dozens of churches that lay in ruins.

Never had the city suffered so much. And it was destined to go on suffering until that week was over and the last of the raiders dipped its wings over the waters of the Mersey on May 8. They never returned.

Eileen had taken it very badly. Neither Brenda, whose baby was nearly due, nor Maureen, now a quieter, more serious Maureen, could console her. She sobbed for hours on end until Brenda, at her wits' end, went to Delia for help. It seemed insensitive to worry Delia, but there was no one else. The rest of the neighbours, bombed out and homeless, were scattered all over the city.

'I'm so sorry to bother you at a time like this, Mrs Harrison, but you *know* what it's like. I don't. I . . . I . . . loved my da, we all did. Oh, he had his faults and there were always rows, but we loved him. But Mam . . . Mam's going to make herself really ill if she carries on like this. She'll lose her mind.'

Delia nodded. She'd spent long hours in tears herself as the raids had continued night after night. She couldn't believe that Jack had gone for ever. Oh, people thought she was strong but that strength had come from Jack. From his love for her and the two girls, from his guidance in business matters, from the security of his always being there, caring for them all in his quiet, unassuming way. Theirs had been a good marriage, but from now on she'd have to cope alone with . . . everything. She prayed that God would give her the strength.

Both men had been buried in St Anthony's churchyard, surrounded by the smouldering ruins that had cost them their lives. It had been a terrible day for them all. Mike, his own heart breaking, had supported Eileen's sagging figure throughout the mass. She was in such a state that Dr Duncan had been called and had given her a mild sedative.

'Just enough to get her through the day,' he'd said to Brenda as she had shown him out.

Delia had held both her daughters' hands, but Elizabeth, unable to stop the tears, looked frequently at Mike, trying to draw comfort from him.

Nessie and Maureen Flynn found it barely comprehensible. They were already in a state of constant terror because of the bombing; now they were heart-broken too. For Maureen it was worse. Her mother wasn't as strong as Delia appeared to be.

Father Walsh was worn out. He and Father Sharpe had had virtually no sleep for days. They did what they could to console their parishioners and had spent hours during the air raids helping the rescuers, giving Extreme Unction to the victims who were Catholic and praying just as earnestly over those who were not. And, witnessing so much suffering, Father Walsh had had a few doubts about the God he'd always believed in so fervently.

Remembering the old priest's strength, Delia knew she had to help her neighbour. 'I'll come up to her, Brenda. You should go home, luv, all this isn't good for you, not now. Your da wouldn't have wanted anything to happen to the baby.'

'How can I leave her like this, especially as our Mike's leave is nearly over?'

'You'll have to, Brenda. She'll come round eventually. It might be the best thing for her. There's still your Maureen to keep an eye on her.'

'That one hasn't got the sense of a two-year-old!' Brenda had declared vehemently.

Delia steeled herself for the visit. She might not be much of a housewife, but Eileen had always been a kind, caring mother and a loyal, loving wife, despite the frequent rows with Frank. Well, there'd be no more rows between them in this house, she thought wearily as she pushed open the front door.

Eileen was sitting in a chair by the range, her head in her hands, still sobbing.

Delia went over and took her hands. 'Eileen, luv, this has got to stop.'

'I . . . I . . . can't 'elp it.'

Delia reached out and held her. 'I know what you're going through, Eileen. God help me, I *know*. But for the sake of Brenda and the baby, for Maureen and young Harold, who's been so brave, you've *got* to pull yourself together. I've had to. Grieve alone, that's what I do. When the girls are in bed or when Elizabeth's at work and Nessie is at school.'

Eileen looked at her mystified. 'Work? School?'

'Yes. Everyone's even more determined now to keep things going. The troops still need ammunition and Elizabeth says each shell she fills, each anti-tank mine makes her feel she is doing something her da would be proud of. They got a bomb in the gardens of the Convent but Mother Superior said it will take more than that for her to close her doors. They all say a special prayer every day that soon the Anti-Christ, as she calls Hitler, will be defeated. Eileen, luv, would Frank want to see you like this? Would he want you to just give up? Be beaten down and defeated?'

Eileen shook her head.

'No and neither would . . . Jack.' It was so painful just to say his name aloud. 'You've got to think of Brenda now. She's due in a couple of weeks.'

'It's a mercy she 'asn't gone into labour already, what with . . . with . . . everything.' Eileen wiped her eyes and sniffed.

'Come on, I'll put the kettle on, there's something I want to talk to you about.'

For the first time since Frank's death there was a glimmer of interest in Eileen's red, puffy eyes. 'What?'

'Your Mike and our Elizabeth.'

'What . . . what about them?'

'I think they've been holding out on us.'

Eileen was very confused. ''Olding out?'

'Yes. I'd say they were more than just good friends.'

''As she said anything?'

'No, the little madam hasn't.' Delia managed a smile. 'But I'm going to get the truth out of her before he sails.'

Fresh tears sprang to Eileen's eyes. 'I don't want 'im to go. I couldn't stand to lose 'im too! Oh, 'e'll 'ave to stay at home. I can't manage.'

Delia sighed. 'He'll *have* to go. No one wants them to go, but it's their duty and they won't shirk it. They're all good lads. Now, why don't you start by tidying up a bit? Make a fuss of Brenda, Maureen and young Harold. Those young lads have really gone up in my estimation. Out in the thick of it, cycling all over the city with urgent messages. They all deserve medals.'

'Aye, but who'll give medals to the likes of us, Delia?'

'No one, so we'll just have to give ourselves a pat on the back, keep the home fires burning, like the song says, and make do with that.' Delia didn't notice the irony in her referring to the old World War One song when many of her neighbour's homes were now little more than ashes.

When Elizabeth returned from work Delia had made a huge effort and was cooking the evening meal on the fire in the range. Her gas cooker was useless, of course, as the gas supply was cut off.

'Right, I want some straight answers from you, miss.'

Elizabeth sat down. She was so weary now, but she wasn't alone in her troubles. Nearly everyone at work had suffered in some way. Mary Clarke who worked in her room had lost her father and grandfather and her home as well, but her mam had made her come to work. 'Fill as many of those shells as you can, girl,' Mrs Clarke had said.

'What kind of answers, Mam?'

'How long have you been seeing Mike?'

Elizabeth looked up at her mother and was surprised to see she wasn't annoyed. 'Seeing?'

'Courting, then?'

Elizabeth was too tired and heartsore for any more lies. 'Over a year. I . . . I love him, Mam. I won't give him up.'

Delia sat down at the table facing her. 'Did I say anything about giving him up?'

Elizabeth's eyes widened. 'You don't mind? You're not upset?'

'No. A couple of weeks ago I would have been very annoyed. I'd have been livid. But not any more. Losing your da has changed . . . everything. Who knows what tomorrow will bring? I don't, not any longer.' Delia couldn't stop her tears and Elizabeth got up and put her arms around her mother, incipient tears sparkling on her own lashes.

'Oh, Mam! Mam! Why did it have to be Da and Mr Flynn? Why couldn't they have bombed the flaming prison? Da was so good and kind and—'

'Elizabeth, don't go on! I can't stand it.'

'I'm sorry, Mam, truly I am. And . . . and Mike's due to leave in two days' time.'

'I know that too. I sat with Eileen this afternoon. Go and bring him down here.'

'Now?'

'Yes, now. I want to give you both my blessing and . . . this.' Delia slowly pulled off the small ruby and diamond ring from the third finger of her left hand. It was her own engagement ring. 'Hold out your hand.'

'Oh, Mam!'

'Go and get him, Elizabeth.'

Elizabeth smiled through the tears which had begun to flow in earnest. This was something she'd never expected, but after these last few days so many things seemed to have changed, her mother amongst them.

There was something that Tessa wanted to change too. The date of her wedding.

'How can I go ahead now?' she said to May.

'I know how you feel, luv, but, well, everything was planned, you've got your outfit and he'll be sailing very soon, I'm certain. They won't be left to kick their heels around here, not after the nights we've had.'

'But Elizabeth and Mike, it's terrible! I can't ask them to come to my wedding when they've both only just buried their fathers. I just can't. Mrs Flynn's in a terrible state and so is Elizabeth's mam.'

'Delia's always been able to cope and Eileen's a lot better. She's made their Brenda go home.'

'But it's all too soon, far too soon. I can't do it.'

'Tessa, do you want to marry Johnny?'

'Of course!'

'Then, for God's sake, marry him before he sails, like you planned. You've seen what can happen, without warning . . . People have had to face disaster. I know no one will mind, but if you're worried I'll go myself and ask Delia and Eileen. It was always going to be a very quiet "do".'

So Tessa had agreed. Both Delia and Eileen had admitted that it was the best thing to do. Even they would welcome the chance to put aside their grief and the harrowing sights for a couple of hours.

'At least you've got a church to be married in,' Elizabeth said when Tessa told her of their decision.

'I'm . . . I'm going to put my flowers on your da's grave. He was always good to me.'

Elizabeth nodded slowly, her heart heavy.

'I never thought your mam would have agreed to you and Mike getting engaged, let alone giving you her ring!'

'No, neither did I, but she's changed. We've all changed.'

'It would be a miracle if we hadn't, with what we've gone through. When do you think you'll get married?'

'I don't know. We haven't really talked about it. We both felt it was too soon.'

'But you'll still be my bridesmaid and Mike will be best man?'

'Yes, if you don't mind your bridesmaid wearing black.'

'Of course not. I wouldn't have expected otherwise. Johnny's had to buy a suit. When the pub went up he lost everything. There's still some confusion over his uniform, getting a new one, I mean, to replace the one he lost. The one he was wearing is scorched and filthy dirty.'

'There's confusion everywhere you turn, but we'll get through it. If we broke down now we'd be letting everyone like . . . Da down. That's what Mam keeps telling us. I don't know how she keeps going. I hear her crying in bed at night and it's terrible. I cry myself and so does our Nessie, but poor Mam's been left to do everything.'

'Elizabeth, it's only natural,' Tessa consoled her friend. She'd long ago forgiven Delia her harsh words during the big row.

The church looked bare and cheerless. There were no flowers, except the few blooms Tessa carried and the flower in Johnny's buttonhole. Elizabeth was dressed in black, as were Delia, Eileen, Maureen and Nessie. Young Harold wore a black armband on the sleeve of his jacket, as did Eddie Doyle and his two young sons. Mike wore his uniform, the one he hadn't been wearing the night the *Malakand* had exploded. There was only immediate family present.

Father Walsh smiled tiredly at the young couple standing before him. A wedding was a nice change, even though there was sorrow and suffering on the faces of the wedding party. Tessa and Johnny, both of whom he'd baptised, looked tired too.

Tessa looked shyly up at Johnny. If only Mr Flynn and Mr Harrison were alive – and Ginny. But this was not a time for 'if only'. She concentrated on the priest's prayers and on the promises she was making to Johnny. She wished her mother could have been with her today.

It was over so suddenly, Elizabeth thought, as she took Mike's arm and followed the new Mrs Doyle and her husband down the aisle and out into the sunlight, trying to ignore the blackened wreckage that seemed to be everywhere they turned. She and Mike had consoled each other. Each knew what the other was going through. When they were alone together, after Delia and Nessie had gone to bed, they'd talked and cried and clung to each other. Mike had proved to be a comfort to Delia too. She especially appreciated that he'd been the person who had found Jack and had treated the older man's body with dignity and respect, which obviously Jack had been unaware of, but was important to Delia.

Tessa and Johnny had no honeymoon, just one night, Johnny's last before sailing, spent at Tessa's house. May and Richie had given them their bedroom. The joy they discovered in each other that night would have to console them through the long separation to come.

The following day Tessa, Elizabeth, Delia, Eileen and Eddie Doyle had gone to see the boys off. Eileen was happier than she'd been for a long time. Brenda now had a baby son and was going to call him Francis Joseph after his two grandfathers, now both deceased.

'We won't ever forget Da now, Mam, not when we've got little Frank.' Brenda had smiled through her tears as she placed the tiny bundle in her mother's arms.

At the dockside Tessa clung to her new husband. 'Promise me you'll take care! Don't go doing anything stupid. I don't want a dead hero.'

'I'll do my duty, Tess, but I promise I won't do anything daft. I'll be back before you know it.' He tried to sound cheerful. God knew *when* they would get back.

Mike had hugged and kissed his mother and sister and then turned to Elizabeth. 'You take care of yourself.'

She clung to him. 'Oh, Mike, I don't want you to go! What if they come again?'

'You'll come through it. You're a born survivor, Elizabeth Harrison. And when I get back I'm going to remedy that.'

'What?'

'Your name. Harrison. There's going to be a new Mrs Flynn before the summer's over. If your mam will give her permission.'

'Nothing would please me more,' Delia said, overhearing him.

The loud *whoop-whoop* sound, the signal for every man to get aboard, startled them all. It was a sound made only by naval vessels, merchant ships still held to the three long blasts on their steam whistles.

With a last kiss on Tessa's cheek Johnny followed Mike down to the Landing Stage and they both turned to wave before separating to board their respective ships. Soon the naval escort would depart to meet up with the convoy assembling somewhere beyond the Mersey Bar.

Elizabeth linked her arm through Tessa's. Her emotions were in turmoil. This was her happiest moment since her da had been killed, for Mike had publicly declared his intention of marrying her, but of course it was tinged with sadness. She knew she'd never stop praying for either of them. Her da's soul and Mike's safety.

The further behind they left the boys the more their spirits plummeted. They all felt dispirited as they walked from the tram stop and around the corner into Naylor Street, where one of the neighbours was keeping an eye on the shop.

'What's that?' Nessie cried, pointing to a big black shiny car.

'It's a car,' Maureen Flynn answered.

'I know that, silly, but it's outside the shop, Mam! No one's ever seen a car like that around here before. Oh, I hope it's not more bad news.'

'We'd better find out who it belongs to, then,' Delia answered, quickening her steps. But as she drew nearer to the shop a figure emerged from inside and she stopped dead.

'Mam! Mam, what's the matter?' Elizabeth cried, tugging at her mother's sleeve.

'I don't believe it! I don't believe it!'

They all looked mystified and then Delia ran forward and into the arms of the plump, smiling, well-dressed woman.

'It's yer Aunty Margaret. It *is*!' Eileen cried. 'She's hardly changed at all!'

The two women were laughing and crying at the same time until Eileen interrupted them.

'I never ferget a face. It's little Maggie Sullivan as was.'

'Eileen Flynn!' Margaret cried, still with a faint trace of her Liverpudlian accent. 'I'd have known you anywhere.' She kissed Eileen on the cheek and hugged her. Eileen wrinkled her nose appreciatively at the smell of expensive perfume that wafted around the other woman.

'Oh, this really does call for a bit of a celebration. I think I can manage some biscuits and tea,' Delia cried, still unable to take in the fact that her sister, who had gone to America twenty years ago, was now standing beside her.

'Delia, keep them. I've got cookies – sorry, biscuits, cakes, candies and the Lord alone knows what else in my luggage. I thought you'd need them.'

Elizabeth and Nessie were struck dumb. They'd never expected to see 'Aunty Margaret' in the flesh, never mind here in their street and now in their home.

Everyone stared at her as she seated herself in the chair by the range, taking in her expensive clothes and hair-do, the make-up, the manicured nails and the two rings she wore, both of which sparkled brightly. She wore nylons too, Elizabeth noted, and she had a big leather handbag that she called a 'purse'.

Delia kept touching her as if to reassure herself that this

wasn't an apparition, it really *was* her sister.

'How in the name of God did you get here?' she demanded when everyone was settled with a cup of tea.

'By ship,' Margaret answered, taking a sip of tea. It seemed to have a sort of 'smoky' taste to it, but she'd been away for so long she couldn't really remember what 'the great British cuppa' was like.

'I thought no one was carrying passengers now.'

'Oh, they will for a consideration, but they won't take any responsibility for your safety. "There'll be no compensation for the family," they told me, quite firmly. "What family?" I told them back.'

Delia was astounded. 'You came over with a convoy?'

'Sure did. It was pretty scary at times, too. They were a grand bunch of guys though. They nicknamed me "the unsinkable Molly Brown".' Margaret laughed.

'Why?' Elizabeth asked.

'Oh, after that American woman who was on board the *Titanic*. She made it. She was quite a character, so I hear tell.'

'But why did you come? I don't mean I'm not overjoyed to see you.'

Margaret's expression changed and she took another sip of tea. 'Well, I read in the papers and saw on the newsreels what's been going on over here and I thought, Maggie Van Holste, this is not the place to be right now. Your place is over there with what family you've got. But, Holy Mary, was I ever surprised . . . No, that's not what I mean: *shocked* at what they've done to the place.'

Delia nodded. She wished Margaret had let her know of her imminent arrival in some way. 'It's been . . . unimaginable. You must have missed Elizabeth's letter. Jack and Eileen's Frank are . . . dead. They were out there during the bombing and a wall . . . fell on them.' Delia fought to control herself and she heard Eileen sniff.

'Oh, no! If I'd only known, Delia!' Although very shocked Margaret pulled herself together. There'd be time later to talk about Jack and she could see Eileen was upset.

'We've just come back from seeing Eileen's lad Mike, our Elizabeth's fiancé, and Johnny Doyle from the Globe go to sea, to pick up another convoy.'

'So, congratulations are in order, Elizabeth.'

Elizabeth smiled at her aunt. 'It's been a very bad time.'

'I can see that for myself. It looked like something from an

H. G. Wells novel as we came up river. I just couldn't believe it.' Margaret put the thoughts from her mind – for now. Later she would tell Delia how unprepared she'd been for the reality and what she intended to do about it.

She addressed herself to young Harold. 'Now, young man, go out to the car and tell the driver to bring in my trunks and we'll have a real treat of a tea. Do you still call it tea? I've gotten used to calling it dinner.'

'We have that in the middle of the day,' Harold ventured. He'd never met anyone like this woman who spoke with a strange accent and had sailed across the Atlantic on a cargo ship and who seemed to have plenty of money and food.

'I remember now. Dinner is at lunchtime and tea is at dinnertime. I've forgotten how long I've been away.'

'How long do you intend to stay?' Delia asked, thinking her sister was well named by the crew of that ship. This 'Molly' was pretty unsinkable too.

Margaret settled back in the chair. 'For ever if needs be. I've put the house up for rent. I can sell it if I need to and get a good deal.'

'You mean you've left that beautiful house and all those luxuries to come to . . . this?' Delia was astounded.

'I told you, family comes first, and by the look of things you need all the help you can get.'

Delia broke down and her sister went to comfort her. Margaret had been right. She was needed here, and so was her money.

Chapter Thirty

There were no more raids and people started to pick up the threads of their lives again. Margaret van Holste made such a difference. She had a way of cutting through red tape and demolishing the petty officials who crossed her path. She had brought with her food and clothing, all of which was swooped upon with cries of delight by both her sister's family and the Flynns, for she had taken pity on them and now included Eileen, Maureen and Harold as extensions of her own family. They were still all 'getting by' though, as she put it. There were things that even she couldn't put right or obtain.

She'd had a serious talk with her niece and had been surprised that Elizabeth was so mature for her age.

'I suppose it's the war,' Elizabeth said.

'I always thought that girls back home were precocious, but half of them would think themselves hard done by if they couldn't have a bath or shower, never mind having to resort to gravy browning and the like instead of nylons, and being allowed only four inches of water in the tub and having to go into the yard to go to the bathroom as they call it. What's wrong with lavatory I don't know.'

'But they haven't gone through what we have.'

'I know, child. But one day it will be over and what will you do then?'

'I don't know. I haven't thought about it. We take each day, each week as it comes.'

'Of course you'll marry Mike, and in the best wedding gown that money can buy, but what then?'

'I . . . I . . . suppose I'll go back to hairdressing, if there're any salons still open.'

'You do well at it, I've watched you.'

'I never finished my apprenticeship.'

'Does that matter so much?'

'I don't suppose so now.'

'Well then, start thinking about having your own salon.'

'Me! I'm not even trained!' Elizabeth had cried.

'You can employ someone who is and learn from them.'

301

Elizabeth had shaken her head. She couldn't seem to get her aunt to understand that things were different here; she just couldn't snap her fingers and get everything taken care of. They were fighting for their very lives. America wasn't at war with anyone, although they supplied money and arms. And what would Mike think about her having her own business? What kind of a job would he get when it was over? He'd had no chance to start evening classes before they were suspended for the duration. She'd told her aunt she would think about it.

Margaret then turned her attention to her sister and younger niece.

'Will you keep the shop going?' she asked.

'What else can I do? We had a bit put by for emergencies, but I . . . I used it for Jack's funeral. I've no other source of income, apart from what Elizabeth earns in that factory.'

'What about Nessie?'

'What about her?'

'What does she intend to do when she leaves the Convent? She's a bright girl.'

Delia smiled. 'She's had a very expensive education, thanks to you.'

'When all this is finally over – and please God we'll all live to see the day – would you both consider coming back home with me? Nessie could finish her training there and teach.'

'And what would I do?'

Margaret stared at her with mild surprise. 'Why, live with me. There's plenty to keep you occupied. I'm on the committees of several societies and charities. You'd enjoy it, Delia.'

'I couldn't live off you.'

'Holy smoke, Delia, why not? You're my sister and Lars left me a lot of money. And I don't have anyone to share things with, simple things like taking tea and reminiscing. I miss the company of my own family. Will you think about it? We'd have a good life.'

'What about Elizabeth?'

'I've already spoken to her. She won't leave and neither will Mike, not when Eileen's on her own without a man to sort things out for her. So I'll buy her a hairdressing salon.'

'Margaret, you just seem to be able to . . .'

'To what?'

'To wave a magic wand and make things right. But it's not as easy as that. Liverpool, battered though it is, will always be home. I don't know if Nessie or me could settle anywhere else.'

'Well, we'll see. Will I put it to Nessie?'

'No, let me do it. It'll be the best way.'

Nessie, to everyone's surprise, thought it the best idea she'd ever heard of. America! America, where everything was so new and modern and up to date, like you saw in the pictures. Maybe she'd qualify for one of their colleges and all the social events that she heard went with it. Girls and boys went to the same schools over there and mixed freely and there were marvellous clothes and no war! Oh, yes, she'd love to go, even if Elizabeth and her mam didn't.

'It will be to live, Nessie, not just for a holiday.'

'I know that, Mam, but I think it'll be the best thing for both of us. Apart from Elizabeth, what is there to stay here for?'

For your da's grave and all the memories, Delia thought. But it was so early yet. This war could still go on for years and years.

Mike was on watch. He stood with Macintosh on the bridge, scanning the horizon and the sea with binoculars. The weather was bad for the time of the year, but then the great Western Ocean was always unpredictable, which made it the most dangerous of them all. A cold drizzle was falling. The sea was heavy, breaking over *Juno*'s bows, and the wind from the south-south-west was threatening to develop into a full gale. They were well into the danger zone, some sixty miles north of the coast of Ireland. Ahead of them, strung out, was the convoy. They must be close to where the *Empress of Britain* had gone down and a shiver ran through him, but he dismissed it as superstition. Macintosh had already informed him as they'd sailed into Liverpool Bay where the wreck of the *Ellan Vannin* – the Isle of Man mail ship – lay, a watery tomb, for all on board had perished. He'd also said he would point out where the *Titanic* had sunk.

'Christ, Chief! I'll be taking to the boats and rowing back!' he'd retorted and Macintosh had grinned sardonically.

'We're in for a wild night, laddie,' the older man said ominously. He delighted in trying to upset the enlisted men. The ship was indeed beginning to plunge and strain as the strength of the wind increased.

'Any sign of the convoy? Darkness will be on us soon.'

'Faintly, sir.'

'Bloody fool merchantmen! Can they no' follow instructions! They'll be scattered by dawn in this weather and have nae protection at all.'

A huge wave broke over *Juno*'s plunging bows.

'Look! Look, far over to port!' Mike yelled, pointing to where a huge column of water rose in the air, followed by a terrific explosion.

'God ha' mercy on them! It's a tanker, she'll go down by her bow, she isnae full. She's top heavy.'

Mike watched in silence, peering through the binoculars and the curtain of drizzle. It was the first time he'd ever seen a ship sink. There had been no warning. Not a sight nor a glimpse of the U-boat.

'Is there anything we can do, sir? Anything?'

'No. They'll no' survive for long in this water and those that do, well, maybe the U-boat will pick them up. Some of the time they do. I'll gie their Navy their due, they're no' as evil as their Army.'

'Or Air Force,' Mike added. Nothing was now visible except a few bits of wreckage. It sobered him considerably.

The weather got worse as what passed for daylight began to fade until, scanning the sea, Mike yelled and cast the binoculars aside. 'It's *Hercules*! *Hercules* has been hit, sir!'

'Gie me those things!' Macintosh demanded and Mike passed him the binoculars. His heart was pounding. Johnny! Johnny was on that ship!

'Can't we turn back, sir? For God's sake can't we turn and do something? I've a mate, more like a brother he is, that's on *Hercules*.'

'There's nae turning back, lad, ye know that. Only the old man can gie that order and he willnae give it.'

Mike grabbed the binoculars and began to peer at the frigate. Smoke and flames were coming from her stern and she was listing badly to port. His cry was like that of a wounded and maddened animal as he watched another torpedo find its mark and *Hercules* sank further down by the bow. She was almost vertical now and he could just about see figures jumping into the sea from her disappearing Boat Deck. It must have been impossible to lower any boats. Those that weren't on fire were plunging down with her – as was Johnny! Johnny who had saved his life the night the *Malakand* had been hit. His best mate, and there wasn't a single thing he could do about it. He was fighting for his self-control, knowing the senior man would put him on a charge if he broke down.

There was a dull thud, but he took no notice, his gaze fixed on the foundering *Hercules*. Then *Juno* shuddered and another huge column of water erupted high into the air. The cruiser listed to starboard, sending him and Macintosh sprawling.

'Torpedo! We've been hit!' Macintosh yelled.

Everyone looked tired, Elizabeth thought when she went into the kitchen. Mam was out in the shop, trying to tidy things in the darkness. Nessie was diligently poring over her books and her aunt was writing a letter.

'Sit down at the table and I'll give you your tea. It's in the oven.' Margaret got up and bent over the cooker.

'I can't see why Mam has to try and keep that place tidy, there's not much in it and it's dark, she can't see what she's doing.'

'I've told her the same myself, Elizabeth, but I think keeping busy takes her mind off . . . things.'

Elizabeth nodded and looked without enthusiasm at the meal of Woolton pie and a meagre portion of mashed potato. The pie took its name from the Minister of Food; it was made entirely from vegetables and tasted terrible. But food was so scarce now that no one ever complained. As she ate she thought of Mike. She really shouldn't complain, everything they had was brought in by convoy and he was out there somewhere, risking his life to make sure the food and arms and fuel *did* get through.

After tea she helped to wash up and then sat, worn out, on the sofa as Margaret switched on the wireless set she'd bought. Sat on the top of the food press, it cheered up the long evenings.

'Oh, good, *ITMA*. Delia, come in and listen, luv. I love this. It cheers me up no end,' Margaret said, fiddling with the knobs. Both Delia and Elizabeth nodded and Nessie closed her books. The programme brought smiles to their faces and for a short time they forgot their troubles, until it finished and the cynical, upper-class voice of William Joyce, known as Lord Haw Haw, came clearly over the airwaves.

'Germany calling! Germany calling!'

'Oh, I hate that man!' Delia said with venom.

'Everybody does, he's a traitor. Sitting somewhere in Germany and broadcasting lies and German propaganda!' Margaret replied. 'I wonder what it'll be tonight? More cities flattened? The people of London all waving white flags! The man's a fool as well as a traitor.'

Elizabeth wasn't taking much notice, she always tried to ignore it.

'Soon you will be getting telegrams. Telegrams from the

Admiralty. You all know the type I mean. "The Admiralty regrets . . ." ' The voice was full of malice and contempt but they couldn't help beginning to pay more attention to him. Elizabeth looked worriedly at her mother.

'Take no notice, the man's a liar.' Margaret tried to calm her sister and her niece.

'Unfortunately for you poor deluded fools, the Admiralty *does* regret to announce the loss of three of your ships from one of your pathetic little convoys. The *City of Glasgow*, a cargo ship, and two of the escorting warships: the *Hercules* and the *Juno*. So be prepared. You have been warned. Why don't you all give in or capitulate . . .' The rest of the sneering abuse was cut short as Margaret got up and switched the wireless off. Elizabeth was staring at the set with horror.

'No! No!' she cried. She jumped up, tore her coat from the hook and, after a struggle, pulled off the brooch and threw it into the fire. 'It *was* an omen! It *was* unlucky!' she cried before she ran out.

She found Tessa in tears, being comforted by May and Richie.

'Tessa! Oh, Tessa, have you heard? Did you listen to *that* man? Both . . . both of them . . . gone!' She burst into tears and both May and Tessa put their arms around her; all three of them clung together in shock and desolation.

'Don't believe the daylights out of that bloody traitor!' Richie tried to console them.

'But he always knows the names of the ships, Richie,' May said shakily.

'I'll give you that, luv, but they could be just picked at random.'

'But they *were* on convoy duty and he must get the information from somewhere. From their U-boats, probably,' May replied.

'All we can do is to wait. We'll know one way or another when the telegrams do arrive,' was all Richie could say.

When Elizabeth went home, red-eyed and exhausted, Delia got up and put her arms around her.

'Elizabeth, luv, don't give up hope!'

'Oh, Mam! First Da and now . . .'

'I know. I know,' Delia soothed her. 'But you mustn't believe everything you hear.'

'Mr O'Leary said that, but most of the time it's . . . true.'

Margaret shook her head at her sister. The time she had spent here had given her an inkling of what they'd all been through and this latest blow make her more determined than ever to take Delia and Nessie – and now it looked like Elizabeth too – back to New Jersey. And she'd go soon. It would be dangerous, but she'd done it before and she'd do it again, just to get them out of this terrible predicament they were in, where grief and suffering was always present.

'Get to your boat station, Flynn, we're going down!' Macintosh had shouted but without any panic in his voice.

Every light had been extinguished and from the angle of the deck Mike had realised they were beginning to settle by the stern. Bloody U-boats! Just how many of them were there? He had fished in his pocket for his electric torch. Other small flickers of light could now be seen in the darkness. He knew the drill, but he'd hoped he'd never have to go through it.

Four boats had been lowered, the others had been smashed by the column of water. In pitch darkness they had managed to unhook the huge blocks. He heard someone yell, 'Mind the blocks!' and then they were plunging downwards, frighteningly close to the dark shape of the sinking cruiser. They hit the head of a breaker then plunged down into the trough, taking in water. They all knew the danger they faced and strained to pull away, otherwise they'd be dragged into the maelstrom as *Juno* went down.

He saw glimpses of the lights from the other boats but the great combers roaring down from windward were too steep to enable them to stay together. The only thought in all their minds was survival.

The only officer in the boat was Macintosh and as the wind rose to gale force and the spray flew over them in sheets, he decided the only thing they could do was ride to a sea anchor and hope for a break in the weather.

The heavy seas filled the boat and they had to bale continuously. Everyone was cold and saturated, many of them were sea-sick, but there was no time to feel terror at the sight of the mountainous walls of water that bore down on them. Unless they continued to bale they would be swamped.

'Mr Macintosh, sir, the sea anchor's gone!' someone yelled.

'Lash three oars together, laddie, they'll have tae do!' Macintosh yelled back.

To Mike it seemed as though there were hours and hours of baling. Time had no meaning and there was no sense of place either. His brain was sending only one message to his leaden limbs: Bale! Bale! Bale! It was with a feeling of detached surprise that he realised that the light he had thought he had seen in the distance was the breaking of a wan dawn, struggling through the tattered clouds.

The wind and the sea had abated a little and he slumped back against the boat's gunwale. The indomitable instinct to stay alive had brought him through so far. They were up to their knees in water. The faces of the men were grey and haggard. Four of the crew were dead from their injuries and exposure and Mr Macintosh recited the Burial Service then committed their bodies to the sea.

'There's nae use trying to sail, we'll ride tae that improvised sea anchor and hope. The best advice I can gie ye is to pray!'

Mike dropped his head and tried to remember the formal decades of the Rosary but couldn't. All he could remember of the Lord's Prayer, learned when he was four years old, were the words: 'Our Father which art in heaven.'

These he repeated over and over to himself until he heard the faint cry and looked up.

'There's something out there, sir,' a young rating shouted.

'Where? I canna see anythin'.'

'Just to starboard, sir.'

'It's wreckage, just a spar of wood.'

Mike stared hard at the object. 'No, sir, it's not! There's someone clinging to it.'

'All right then, pull toward it. Come on wi' ye, lads, pull together!' Macintosh shouted.

It was heavy going. The boat hardly seemed to be moving, Mike thought as he strained at the oars, but eventually the jagged piece of wood was clearly visible and so was the face of the man clinging to it, eyes closed, skin waxy and lips blue. He didn't seem to be alive. Frantically Mike lunged out as far as he could and caught the splintered keel and pulled it towards them. They might not survive – any of them – but at least they'd go together. For, against all the odds, the man he heaved into their own boat was Johnny Doyle.

Neither Tessa nor Elizabeth slept that night and in the morning they got up, weary, grief-stricken and sick with worry.

'I won't believe it until I get a telegram, I just *won't*,' Tessa said firmly as they made their way home after their twelve-hour shift.

'Then neither will I. But . . . but at least the telegram will come to you, I'll have to go to Mrs Flynn's.'

'How is she taking it?'

'The same as we are. Mam went in last night to tell her and she just broke down again. Like we did. Like we've been fighting all day to keep from breaking down.'

'Did anyone else at work, the other three in your room, know any more?'

Elizabeth shook her head. 'No. I asked but no one has any relatives on either ship. Oh, Tessa, I don't know what I'll do if . . .'

'I don't either,' said Tessa quietly. 'But it's worse for you, you've already lost your da. And Johnny and I did at least spend one night together.'

Tears sprang into Elizabeth's eyes. Yes, Tessa had had one wonderful night; by comparison, she'd had nothing.

They agreed to inform each other immediately there was any news and both went into their respective homes bowed down with worry.

Elizabeth ate the meal put in front of her, and answered all questions briefly; her mother and aunt looked at each other with concern. They were both helpless. Everyone was. All they could do was wait and that was the hardest part of all. Not knowing.

They had all decided to go to bed early.

'We're all worn out, we might as well go to bed and try and snatch a few hours' sleep, especially you, Elizabeth,' Margaret urged.

'I'll stay down here for a bit longer, if you don't mind?'

'Of course we don't mind, but I think you'd be better coming up, you have to get up so early.'

'Oh, please, Mam? Just a bit longer?' Elizabeth begged.

Delia nodded. She couldn't force Elizabeth to do anything.

When they'd all gone Elizabeth just sat, staring into the fire. If *Juno* had really been sunk, it didn't necessarily mean he had . . . drowned. And the same went for Johnny. She wondered if Tessa had thought of that. They had lifeboats; they drilled for such eventualities.

Then that moment of hope had gone. Suppose he had not been able to get into a boat? How long could he survive in the waters of the North Atlantic? They were bitterly cold at any time of year. Even if they had launched the lifeboats, what if no one spotted them? She pushed the thought from her mind. She *had* to hope. She *couldn't* give up on him.

She'd fallen into a light doze when the sound of the doorknocker woke her with a start. It took her a few minutes to gather her wits.

Who in God's name was it? It was almost eleven o'clock.

Tessa was standing on the step. Over her nightdress she clutched a shawl and in her hand was the dreaded telegram.

'Oh, Tessa! Tessa! No!'

Tessa smiled. 'It's all right, Elizabeth. They're both safe. I called next door to see if Mrs Flynn had heard anything.'

'They're safe! Both of them?'

Tessa nodded. 'It was true, both ships were sunk, but they got away somehow and were picked up by an American cargo ship. Look.' She shoved the telegram into Elizabeth's hand.

Elizabeth switched on the light, scanned the few lines. She leaned against the doorframe, suddenly feeling weak, and then they clung to each other. They were weeping again, but this time it was for joy.

Epilogue

1944

Tessa and Elizabeth sat on the step of number twelve, Naylor Street. They'd both continued to suffer agonies of worry when Mike and Johnny were away, but it seemed that Captain Johnny Walker with his 'hunter-killer' warships was winning his battle with the U-boats. Things were still hard. Everything was on ration but they'd all got used to that and to the blackout, although there had been no further raids on Liverpool.

Elizabeth and Mike had been married when Mike had eventually got home. It had been a much grander wedding than Tessa's. Margaret had paid for everything and they were all astounded when she managed to procure food and drink that hadn't been seen for years. She'd also paid for the two-day honeymoon in Llandudno's most exclusive hotel.

Now they all knew that something was going on, something big. It was rumoured that a huge invasion force was being assembled, ready to cross the Channel to liberate France. Bombing raids on Germany itself had increased and now many of their towns and cities were in ruins. America had finally come into the war when the Japanese had bombed the naval base at Pearl Harbor, totally unprovoked and without any warning. Now, at last, in May of 1944, after nearly five years of war, the end seemed to be in sight. At least they prayed it was.

Tessa and Elizabeth were making the most of the long light evenings. They both loved these minutes at the end of the day. In the warmth of late spring they could relax after the long hours they still worked.

'Who would ever have thought things could have changed so much from the day you moved in here?' Elizabeth mused.

'I know. It's so difficult to believe. It all seems to belong to another age.'

'It was. Thank God we didn't know what was in store for us. Do you ever think of him? Your Colin?'

'Occasionally. Usually when I think of Mam.'

311

'Sometimes, when I catch a glimpse of someone who looks like Ginny, I have to stop myself calling after her. Yet it's so long ago now.'

'I know May still thinks about her and grieves. I suppose she always will. Sometimes she takes flowers to that little bit of land.'

'I wouldn't have wanted her to have gone through everything we've faced. She was so quiet and timid,' said Elizabeth.

They both fell silent for a few minutes, memories of Ginny filling their minds.

'So, when are your Mam and Nessie going then?'

'Next month. Mam's given notice to the landlord. I can hardly believe I'll be on any own then!'

'Do you think you've really made the right decision?'

'Yes. One day Mike will come home for good. He'll probably get a decent job, being an officer now.'

'I hope Johnny will too and I hope we'll be able to find somewhere to rent, even if it is just one room to start with. I . . . I . . . wouldn't feel easy here. You know how thin the walls are.'

Elizabeth smiled. She knew what Tessa meant.

Suddenly Tessa looked stricken.

'What's the matter?'

'Mam. I promised her I'd make something better of myself. Be a stewardess.'

'You can keep part of your promise. You could get an office job.'

'Me!'

'Yes, you. It's not *that* hard. Sometimes it can be really boring. It would help if you learned to type.'

'Where in the name of God would I do that?'

'There's that Commercial School in Slater Street. Machin and Harper's. I know you have to pay but you could save up. Then you're bound to get a job. It's their policy – if I remember rightly – to find you one. One of the customers told me when I worked at Hill's.'

'Will you go back there?'

'No. Bold Street's in ruins, especially at the top end by St Luke's. I'm to have my own salon, so Aunty Margaret says. She'll leave me the money.'

'You'll miss them terribly.'

'I know I will, but maybe one day we could go over and visit them. It will be better for Mam. She can leave behind all the bad memories. And our Nessie can't wait to go.'

'And talking of Nessie . . .' Tessa pointed down the road.

When she reached them, Nessie grinned. 'You can't sit on that bloody wall now, it's gone. Along with the tannery. So the two of you sit on the step instead.' Tessa and Elizabeth both laughed.

'I've always envied you – I never had a best friend. And now my life's going to be so different.'

'You're still going, though?' Tessa asked.

'Yes.'

'Well then, you'll make lots of friends.'

'Maybe I will when I get to New Jersey.'

Elizabeth gazed past her sister and into the far distance as if trying to remember everything.

'Tessa and I have always been close. We've come through poverty, hardship, death and destruction, terror, despair and relief and happiness. War has made no difference to us.'

Tessa smiled and took Elizabeth's hand. 'No, the ties will never be severed.'